The Piaras Legacy

Scott Gamboe

Medallion Press, Inc.
Printed in USA

DEDICATION:

Dedicated to all the men and women of the military, who are serving or have served their country. The sacrifices of these brave people keep our nation free and strong.

Published 2008 by Medallion Press, Inc.

The MEDALLION PRESS LOGO
is a registered tradmark of Medallion Press, Inc.

Typeset in Baskerville
Printed in the United States of America

ISBN# 978-193383625-6

10 9 8 7 6 5 4 3 2 1
First Edition

ACKNOWLEDGEMENTS:

First, I would like to thank my wife, Jill, for her continued support, and for reading my books even though she has never been a fan of science fiction or fantasy. I would also like to thank Helen, for taking a chance on an unpublished writer and making all this possible. Finally, I would like to acknowledge the support I have received from family and friends, including Darrell, whose high school nickname provided a basis for one of the races in this series.

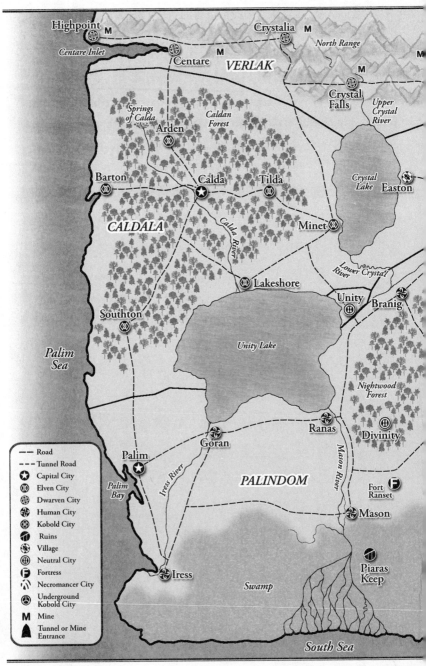

1 inch = 20 leagues

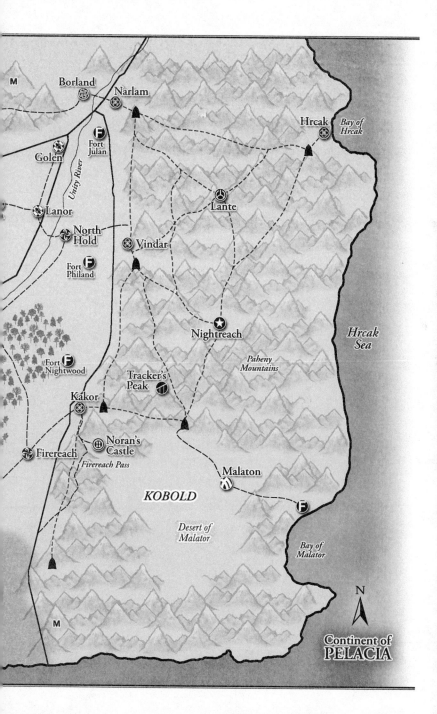

Prologue

I f there was one thing Silvayn had learned after four hundred years of teaching, it was that students listened more closely when the topic was macabre. The lecture he was about to deliver promised rapt attention from his pupils.

"In the year 951, Piaras Keep was built to guard the southern reaches of the Human kingdom of Palindom. A thousand Human troops occupied the Keep at all times. They were commanded by a council consisting of seven knights headed by a noble named Sir Draygen.

"In the year 1390, undead forces began raiding outlying Human settlements. After one particularly bloody raid in which three villages were razed, the seven knights at Piaras Keep vowed vengeance and made a blood oath that before they died, the Necromancers would be destroyed."

"Then in 1393, the Elven ship *Nature's Way* was attacked and sunk near Barton by a ship flying the Dwarven banner. The same day, the Dwarven ship *Dream of Sarlot* was sunk by an Elven ship in the Centare Inlet.

"After nine years of war, the two sides learned Necromancer naval forces flying false banners conducted both attacks so all three nations declared war on the Necromancers. But the enemy attacked first with a four-pronged invasion, taking Crystal Falls and Tracker's Peak from the Dwarves, and razing the Elven cities of Lakeland and Minet. The Necromancers held everything north and west of Crystal Lake.

"Their largest division attacked in the South, striking the Humans. The Death Knights commanding the undead forces knew taking Piaras Keep would prove costly, so they contented themselves with a siege, preventing the army inside the Keep from entering the war.

"In 1408, the Necromancers launched a massive assault on Ranas. However, the Humans reinforced the city with infantry and archers while staging their cavalry units farther west. With no help forthcoming, the Humans decided to cut off enemy reinforcements by retaking Firereach Pass on their own.

"They sent an army by sea from Palim, disembarking south of Piaras Keep. Heavy and light infantry, backed by archers, pressed the undead forces, destroying them where they stood. When the undead lines were forced inward nearer to the Keep, the gates were flung open and those inside sallied forth. By sunset of the sixth day, the Keep was liberated and the entire undead army was destroyed.

"The seven knights were poised to fulfill their oath. To help them, several Priests and mages gathered, and they cast great enchantments on certain items belonging to the knights. Abandoning the Keep, they sent their entire army against Firereach Pass. They completely annihilated the undead defenders.

"The Dwarven army threw itself at Crystal Falls, overwhelming the weakened undead contingent there in only two days. They pushed east and south, driving the Necromancers before them. The Elves also swept the undead from their lands.

"The army of the Humans marched out of Ranas, and sent the undead armies into a full retreat. With the Dwarves attacking southward along the western foothills of the Paheny Mountains, the Necromancers were cut off from the safety of those peaks. Each of these armies entered Firereach Pass one by one, were stopped by the defenders, and set upon from behind by the attacking Humans. Within a week, the three undead armies had been destroyed.

"Unfortunately for the seven knights from Piaras Keep, the battles had sufficiently weakened their forces to prevent them from mounting an assault on Malaton, the home of the Necromancers and their leader, Volnor. In retaliation, Volnor placed a curse upon Piaras Keep. The Mason River's current slowed at its delta with the South Sea, resulting in the creation of what came to be known as the Mason Marsh. The marsh continued to expand, eventually swallowing the ground around the Keep. In 1450, the Keep was abandoned.

"The seven knights, having failed in their blood oath, committed suicide. Their ghosts still haunt the ruins of Piaras Keep, and will continue to do so until the Necromancers are finally defeated."

Chapter 1

Blac's horse splashed noisily through the ford, crossed the Unity River, and dashed off once again toward the perceived safety of the land of the Elves. His wiry frame did little to slow his charger, and it ran with long, smooth strides. He wore a tight-fitting cap over his short-cropped brown hair, and was dressed in plain gray merchants' robes. The long grasses of the Northern Plains whipped at his horse's legs as he raced across the rolling landscape.

The problem was, the Kobolds were gaining on him. He sneaked a quick glance behind, and caught a glimpse of their standard waving defiantly, a black and white banner bearing crossed swords. The brazen soldiers drove deeper into the Kingdom of Palindom, land of the Humans, following him with implacable determination. With the Kobolds so blatant, they would have no qualms about a border violation with the Elven nation of Caldala, which meant his only hope was for a random Elven patrol to cross his path. The normally peace-loving Elves would attack the Kobolds on sight.

He found the Golen Road, and his spirits soared while he pounded his way down the unpaved lane to the nearby village. Clouds of dust rose into the air behind him, drifting ponderously higher on the gentle spring breeze. Elac turned and looked back at the Kobolds behind him, and his heart dropped to his toes. The patrol chasing him had closed the gap considerably, and several of the lead riders were plainly visible, less than a mile behind him. Their fur-covered, muzzled visages appeared grotesquely Human from a distance.

After another league, his horse lost speed. The faltering beast had given everything it had. Minutes later, the horse stumbled and went down, throwing its rider onto the dusty road and thrashing about in agony. Elac rolled to his feet, cut his equipment loose from the exhausted animal, shouldered his longbow and quiver, and continued on foot, a hopeless race against time.

Elac decided he had gone as far as he could, and knew it was time to make a stand. The Kobolds trotted closer, less than a hundred yards away. He nocked an arrow, watching while the Kobolds formed a circle around him, still fifty yards out. The ring slowly contracted around him, his hunters howling with anticipation. Elac drew his arrow, took aim, and fired. The shot went wide, narrowly missing its target. The circle of Kobolds collapsed upon him.

An arrow hissed past Elac to sink into the throat of a Kobold, who fell, gurgling, from his saddle. Then there was another arrow, and another, and within moments, a half dozen of the Kobolds lay dying in the road, while the rest roared in helpless rage, trying to find the source of the barrage. For the moment, Elac was forgotten, and he took the opportunity to dash off the roadway into the concealing grass.

A new figure appeared in the fray. He arose without a sound from his concealed vantage point, his sword sliding from its sheath with a steely hiss. His round shield was embossed in black and overlaid with a golden eagle in flight. He wore loose-fitting brown and green clothes with his hood thrown back, his short brown hair untouched by the breeze. The Elf faced his opponents with a proud bearing that exuded confidence, fixing the Kobolds with a deliberate stare. He stepped into the open and prepared to meet the raiders.

Two Kobolds broke off from the group and charged, bearing down on the lone figure in the roadway. The Elf stood his ground, bringing his shield and sword into a defensive posture. The first Kobold gave a quick swing at the Elf's head. He easily deflected the blow with his shield, and a retaliating slash of his sword nearly cut completely through the Kobold's leg. The Kobold tumbled from his horse, blood gushing from his thigh. The other Kobold reined in, circling cautiously and waiting for the remaining four Kobolds to join him. One, presumably the leader, dismounted and approached the lone Elf. The other Kobolds also warily dismounted, and Elac emerged from hiding to stand beside his would-be rescuer.

"Stand aside!" the first Kobold ordered in his growling, harshly accented tongue. "We have business to finish, and you would be wise not to interfere."

"You have invaded the country of Caldala," the Elf replied with aplomb, once more assuming a combat stance. "In the absence of Elven troops, I find I must act in their stead. Leave, or die."

"You are one, against five. You have no chance."

"It used to be one against twelve," the stranger reminded his antagonist with a shrug. "Five more dead Kobolds won't make much difference to me."

Elac wasn't sure what had the greater chilling effect on the Kobolds: the Elf's threatening words, which he was probably capable of backing up with action, or the absolute dead calm with which one Elf faced down an entire squad of Kobolds. A terrible silence hung in the air, and even the wind stopped blowing, the long prairie grasses no longer undulating. It was as if all of nature was holding its breath, awaiting the outcome of the confrontation.

The wait didn't last long. One Kobold, who had lounged indolently off to one side, abruptly lunged, a sword stroke already falling toward the Elf's unprotected back. Suddenly, the Elf was a blur, countering the stroke and launching a furious counterattack, disemboweling his foe even as the other Kobolds closed in. Elac raised his bow and fired at the leader, and this time his aim was better. The Kobold fell hard to his knees, numbly staring in shock at the arrow protruding from his chest. Elac nocked another arrow, but he could only watch in stunned disbelief while the Elf systematically destroyed the Kobold patrol. When the one remaining Kobold turned and fled for his mount, the Elf drew a dagger from his belt and threw, all in one fluid motion. The dagger flashed through the air, striking the Kobold's back with a solid *thunk*. The final attacker staggered into his horse, then fell limply to the ground.

With the threat finally vanquished, a wave of reality washed over Elac. His bow dropped from his suddenly nerveless fingers and he crashed to his knees, shaking violently, the realization of how close he had come to dying washing over him in a wave. If it hadn't been for the timely intervention of a lone Elf, Elac would surely have been killed, like the others in his party. He caught his breath while his rescuer calmly rounded up the remaining Kobold horses. Elac rose unsteadily to his feet and approached the other Elf.

"I'm Elac," he began, his voice shaking. "I want to thank you for saving me."

"Rilen," the stranger replied shortly. "Where did these Kobolds come from?"

Elac shook his head. "I'm not sure." He briefly recounted the day's earlier events.

"I'd say you were lucky. I was out this way hunting and happened to see all the dust they were kicking up chasing you on the Golen Road." Rilen's eyes narrowed. "What did you do to make them chase you this far? Kobolds never chase someone into Caldala."

"Nothing! We were taking a shipment of goods to Fort Julan when they attacked."

Rilen shook his head. "Something is wrong about this. Kobolds are terrified of the Elven army. They wouldn't follow you this far without good reason."

Rilen examined the bodies of the fallen Kobolds. Each wore a black pendant with the emblem of a coiled snake, and he planned to collect them all. When Rilen reached the first Kobold he had fought, Elac could see the Kobold still lived. He had lost a lot of blood from Rilen's sword stroke, and his injured leg was twisted grotesquely to one side. Elac edged tentatively forward, a morbid curiosity overcoming caution, and he took a closer look at someone who, mere minutes earlier, had been trying to kill him. Though his face was contorted in excruciating agony from his wounds, the Kobold still managed to glare defiantly at the two Elves. He even made a weak attempt to push Rilen away, but Rilen slapped the Kobold's hands down and removed another of the black pendants, then firmly grasped the bloodied front of the Kobold's tunic.

"What's your name?" Rilen demanded harshly.

After a moment's consideration, he responded, "Lecarse."

"Why did your patrol attack this man and his friends?"

Lecarse shrugged, grimacing in pain. "Wrong place, wrong time. The Kobold High Command is afraid to move against the West. We aren't."

"So your group was a band of entrepreneurs looking to make a profit?"

"We will restore the glory of the Kobold Empire."

Rilen rose to his feet. "We'll see." He drew his sword, placing the tip against Lecarse's throat.

"Wait!" Elac interrupted, leaping forward to grab Rilen's sword arm. "You can't simply kill him in cold blood!"

Rilen looked at him menacingly, and his expression chilled Elac to the bone. "He would have shown you no mercy. Besides, he referred to his group in the present tense. That means there are more of them, maybe even close by. Do you want him telling them where to find us?"

Elac met his gaze for as long as he could, then looked away. "I would rather you didn't."

Rilen shook his head in disgust. "Suit yourself. Take one of their horses and follow me. I'll see you to safety. We can try to find your horse later, when we have my militia to help us."

They continued along the road to Golen, following the hard-packed lane, which meandered through the rolling countryside. They were close enough to the village to have reached the extensive farmlands in the surrounding area, fertile ground where patient farmers worked the land in an endless cycle of seasonal toiling. The spring crops had already emerged, pushing green shoots toward the sapphire blue sky. Here and there, Elac saw an Elf working the fields, most of them clearing away weeds they knew would stubbornly come back within a matter of days. Each plot of land was divided from its neighbors by a low row of stones, decorated with flowers and an occasional tree.

They finally entered the village, an orderly place Elac found to be slightly larger than the term "village" implied. Their horses' hooves clattering hollowly on the cobblestone streets, Rilen led the way purposefully through the hamlet. They passed through the central square, where merchants shouted out a cacophonous din, trying to draw attention to their wares. While most of the villagers were Elves, there were a significant number of Dwarves and even a few Humans. As with any Elven settlement, however, there were no Kobolds to be found.

Finally, Rilen guided his mount off the road and into a barn, which was attached to an average-sized log cabin home. Three disinterested-looking grooms emerged from the barn's dark recesses to take the reins of their horses after they dismounted. Rilen gave several brief orders concerning the disposition of the horses taken from the Kobolds, then motioned for Elac to follow him into the cabin. Elac obliged without a word, walking tiredly through the small courtyard and into the cabin. When he retired for the evening, his dreams were troubled . . .

✤ ❀ ★ ✿ ❁

The sun was high overhead, and the fine spring morning carried the promise of another beautiful day. The caravan rolled along noisily, the wooden wheels of the wagons bouncing off the holes and snags in the uneven thoroughfare. Elac was surprised at the road's state of disrepair, and made a mental note to bring it up to the commissioner of public works.

The Paheny Mountains were clearly visible in the distance, but the terrain they traveled was fairly flat. They were near Fort Julan, where an area anomaly had developed a series of jagged rock formations. The towering stone projections were a dazzling array of colors, each in its own layer. When he could stand it no more, he told the caravan master he was going to ride out for a closer look, and would catch up shortly. The gruff old Dwarf leading the caravan merely shrugged and grunted, and Elac galloped across the grassy plateau.

Elac reined in his horse and dismounted. He ran his hands along the smooth sides of the colossal stone formations. They seemed to be made of some sort of sandstone, and grains of the rock slid away at his touch.

He heard a rumble like distant thunder. Puzzled, he checked the sky, but there was not a cloud to be seen. He returned his attention to the stone, but the sound repeated, rolling on and on as if it would never end. He was able to ignore the clamor until he heard the screams. His heart pounded in his chest like a sledgehammer, and fear caught him in its icy grip.

The thunderous racket grew louder, and Elac poked his head around the corner of the rocks. A Kobold cavalry ran alongside his caravan, which was rolling away as fast as the wagons allowed. They were no match for the Kobolds, who easily overtook them. The Kobolds drew their swords and systematically slaughtered the caravan guards. The poorly trained fighters tried to gather into a defensive knot, but they all fell beneath the Kobolds' blades.

The Kobolds didn't stop with the defenders. Although the merchants from the caravan fell to their knees and begged for mercy, the Kobolds rode up and down the line, swords hacking. Some women were dragged kicking and screaming into nearby wagons, while everyone else was slaughtered where they stood.

Elac dashed to his horse, leapt into his saddle, and was off at a gallop. He heard shouts and cries from the caravan, and a dozen Kobolds broke off their attack to take up the pursuit. His wits slowly returned, and he cursed himself for not staying hidden. There was nothing he could have done to help the caravan, but he would have still been safe. Now, he needed to find a place to hide . . .

Chapter 2

Blac rose early the next morning, ate a quick breakfast consisting mainly of cold chicken, and donned his gear for the trip to Lanor. Rilen was waiting in the courtyard with a dozen saddled mounts, their saddlebags filled with enough supplies for two or three days. When Elac looked questioningly at the bags, Rilen quietly explained how he liked to be prepared for any eventuality. Elac shrugged and moved to the horse he was to ride. Not for the last time, he fidgeted with the sword Rilen had given him, then tried to hide his unease with the weapon by checking the straps on his saddle. Ten more Elves dressed in woodland clothing soon joined them, six men and four women. At a signal from Rilen, the other Elves closed in for their briefing.

Rilen introduced Elac to the members of his militia. There was Caros, a lean, wiry Elf with a shaved head, who served as a scout. Lurae brought her medical skills to the group, while Sanara, an attractive young woman with blond hair, served as Rilen's second in command. Serot and Nedlig, two burly farmers who lived at the east end of the village, stood off to one side. Judging by the looks exchanged between the bulky Rance and the attractive, raven-haired Shof, he surmised the two were very close. Kedow stood listening intently to Rilen, her hair pulled back tightly and her bow slung across one shoulder. Turin and Triff, Rilen announced, were expert archers.

Rilen briefly recapped his instructions, and the patrol hastily mounted and was underway. They rode out of the village at an easy canter, and Elac was on the road to Lanor. There were five Elves in front of him, four to his rear, and one riding alongside. Rilen ranged far to the fore, scouting for signs of danger.

A few hours later, they crested a hill to find Rilen waiting for them. Sanara, leading the squad in Rilen's absence, started to rein in her mount until Rilen motioned the group forward. Sanara picked up the pace, and the squad trotted to Rilen's side.

"Something is wrong," Rilen stated in a calm voice. "It's already mid-morning, and we still haven't seen anyone coming from Lanor. I've also seen signs of a large force moving around out here. They're trying to conceal their numbers, but I'd judge their size at fifty or more. It could be the Lanor Militia on maneuvers, but let's be careful. I'm going to stay on the point. Caros, I want you to ride on ahead. Stay clear of the road, but find out if there is anything between here and Lanor we need to know about. If all is well, grab as many men as you can from the Lanor garrison and come out to meet us. Let's move."

Caros drove his heels into his horse, and was immediately galloping off to the west, leaving the road behind him. Elac assumed they would move faster, but if anything, the group moved along even more slowly than before. He mentioned it to his new escort, Kedow, and she nodded in agreement.

"We've actually slowed down some. If we were to ride faster, not only might the noise give us away, but our dust cloud could be seen for miles. Besides, this way, we avoid riding head-long into an ambush."

Elac nodded in understanding, noting absently that Kedow tended to talk a bit more than Triff. He found the easy-going conversation helped to pass the time. Taking advantage of the moment, he decided to try to push her for more information about Rilen.

"You'll never see his better with the longbow, that's for sure," Kedow told him in answer to his question. "Or any other weapon, for that matter. He's been training to fight since he was a child, mainly under his father, who was a master swordsman. He obviously learned his lessons well. Only the most skilled fighters are asked to be the Prime Minister's personal body-guard. I've served with him for two years, and I can't think of anyone I'd rather have watching my back. He also attended the War College at Fort Julan, something few Elves have done. His knowledge of tactics is astounding. He's a good man to have on our side."

They stopped for a brief lunch, moving well off the road and into a nearby grove of willow trees. The long, stooping branches created a curtain about them, rendering them invis-ible to all who might pass by. Soon, Sanara announced it was time to move out, and within moments the group was again rid-ing southwest to Lanor.

Elac was dosing in his saddle, having gone light on sleep the night before, when a commotion at the front of their formation snapped him out of his revelry. Sanara halted the group and dismounted, studying an innocuous-looking pile of stones at the side of the road. She crouched, seeming to orient herself with the surrounding countryside, then stood and called for everyone to move in closer.

"We've got trouble," she told them plainly. "Rilen has spotted several patrols of Kobolds in the area. They seem to be looking for someone, and they're taking it pretty seriously."

"How can you tell?" Elac asked, interrupting before he thought better of speaking out.

She frowned, thinking. "Rilen left this formation of stones to warn us. He developed this . . . let's call it a code. Basically, the rock pile tells us there are several small patrols in the area, and he suggests we move off the road a mile or so and shadow it the rest of the way to Lanor." Sanara remounted and led the group due west, swinging wide of the road before again turning southwest in the direction of their destination. Elac was alert, all traces of his earlier bout with exhaustion gone. They angled slightly west, and Elac figured Sanara was likely guiding them to a distant wooded area plainly visible in that direction, which would provide the group with cover. When they neared the trees, Rilen rode out to meet them, his longbow in his left hand. Elac could tell something was wrong; with his pulse quickening, he awaited the news.

"There is a sizeable force of Kobolds coming in from the West," Rilen told them when they had gathered around him. "They've been thoroughly searching each group of trees they come across, so there's little chance of hiding from them. We can't risk going back, because if we were to be found and engaged by one of the smaller groups, the larger group could join in and slaughter us. We're going to have to fight them, but it'll be in a time and place of our choosing. Follow me."

They rode a bit more quickly, dismounted when they entered the shaded coolness of the woods, and formed a single file line. For the next ten minutes, Rilen led the group along a trail left by small forest animals, until they reached the western edge of the trees. Rilen signaled a halt, and positioned his militia a short distance back from the undulating grasslands. Elac, too, was assigned a spot, and was told to do what he could. He propped his quiver in front of him and lay in wait. The hunters were about to become the hunted.

For the first thirty minutes, they saw nothing, and Elac was beginning to think perhaps Rilen was mistaken. Then, without warning, a lone Kobold rode into view, searching the terrain for signs of his quarry. Elac silently nocked an arrow, waiting for a signal from his Elven escorts. To his surprise, Rilen allowed the scout to pass unmolested. The unsuspecting Kobold rode south, keeping his eyes on the thick grove of trees, then wheeled about and headed back over the hills to the west. Elac, puzzled by Rilen's decision to allow the enemy to escape, edged closer to the Elf positioned on Elac's right.

"Kill the scout," Rilen announced in answer to the unvoiced question, eyes still on the surrounding landscape, "and you announce your location. The scout will ride back and tell the other Kobolds there's nothing to be seen here, and they'll come in unprepared. Watch, and learn." He lapsed back into silence, turning to face the plain once more.

From out on the grasslands, a movement caught his eye.

Appearing to rise out of the ground, a large patrol of Kobolds came over the hill at a rolling trot. Elac's hands were trembling, and he was perspiring freely while the Kobolds drew nearer. He glanced over at Rilen, but the Elf was as outwardly calm as ever, seemingly unperturbed by the approaching force that was probably four times their size.

The Kobolds were close, and they appeared to be expecting no trouble. Not only was there not a single Kobold with a drawn weapon, but those who carried bows had them unstrung and attached to their saddles. They slowed when they were about fifty paces from the woods, stopped at about twenty paces, and gathered around the leader, who was issuing orders. At that point, only the leader was still on his horse, the others having dismounted in preparation to search the trees for their quarry. Rilen slowly rose to one knee and drew back his bow. When Elac saw it, he too selected a Kobold and took aim.

Rilen's bow snapped, and the Kobold leader tumbled from his saddle, an arrow protruding from his chest. The other Elves fired as well, and Kobolds dropped at a surprising rate. Elac fired as rapidly as he could manage, but Rilen was getting off two shots for every one shot Elac took. The Kobolds were in a state of panicked confusion, rushing about uncertainly and howling in frustration. A few tried to run, but were cut down by the archers Rilen had placed on his flanks.

The besieged Kobolds finally managed a reckless charge on the Elves' positions; upon their approach, the Elves fired one last volley before charging out to meet them. Rilen shouted a warning to Elac to stay where he was before drawing his short sword and entering the melee. Rilen's Elves were all skilled fighters, and the Kobolds gave way before them, but none compared to Rilen. As he had the day before when he stood alone against an entire squad of Kobolds, Rilen danced through the enemy ranks, a living weapon leaving a trail of carnage.

Two Kobolds charged Rilen in unison, intent on eliminating what they perceived as their greatest threat. One arrived a half second before the other, and the difference proved fatal for both of them. The first Kobold swung his sword at Rilen's head. Rilen easily deflected the blow with his shield, then lashed out with his sword, severing the Kobold's arm below the elbow. Without slowing, Rilen reversed his stroke, changing it to a thrust at the last moment and ramming the sword home in the second Kobold's chest. He kicked the Kobold off his bloody blade, then turned and finished off his other assailant. All around the meadow, there was the ring of steel on steel, and cries of pain when a weapon hit home.

Elac was so engrossed with the violence of the encounter, he failed to see the lone Kobold who slipped free of the battle and rushed his position. At the last moment, Elac realized he was in trouble and cried out, ducking under the hasty sword stroke that would have decapitated him. The sword whistled menacingly overhead, and Elac rolled free, drawing his sword and backing away from the encounter. The Kobold swore an oath and closed with him again, growling menacingly, spittle dripping from his bared fangs.

Elac silently cursed himself for not running, but by then it was too late to do anything except defend himself. He held his sword in front of him, weaving it back and forth as he had seen others do. The Kobold grinned in anticipation, perhaps realizing Elac was an inexperienced swordsman. With a sudden flurry of strokes, the Kobold forced him backward, each stroke coming perilously closer to finding flesh. He was close enough to the others to smell the coppery reek of freshly spilled blood and hear the groans of the dying. He continued his slow retreat, hoping one of the others would notice and come to his aid.

His foot came down on something soft, and a glance downward told him he was standing on the hand of a fallen Elf. He hastily raised his foot in revulsion, throwing himself off-balance, and he fell to his back. The Kobold rushed forward eagerly, setting his sword point under Elac's chin. The Kobold gave a roar of rage, raising his sword for the downward strike that would end Elac's life—

And fell forward, his weapon dropping from his dead fingers, Kedow's short sword protruding from his chest. Before Elac could thank her, Kedow had dashed back to the fight, where the remaining four Kobolds had backed into a tight circle, the Elves closing on them. With a sudden steely clash, the Elves charged, cutting down the remaining Kobolds.

"Is anyone hurt?" Rilen asked anxiously. He wiped his blade on the cloak of a fallen Kobold, and glanced angrily at the body of Nedlig, a member of Rilen's militia. He motioned to Rance and Serot, and both Elves immediately dashed off to the woods to retrieve the party's horses.

"I am," Shof replied, staggering to her knees, injuries finally overcoming her. Triff, a number of small wounds on his arms and shoulders caked with dirt and blood, rushed to her aid. Shof appeared to be the only surviving Elf with a major injury, a slash to her side which would need immediate attention. When

Rance and Serot returned with the horses, Lurae retrieved her medical supplies from her packs and immediately set to work on Shof's wounds. The other Elves simply dressed their own minor injuries and prepared to move out. Rilen gingerly picked up Nedlig's body, securing it to the fallen Elf's horse.

"Let's get ready to ride," Rilen told them calmly. "Caros has been gone long enough that he should be on his way back with reinforcements, if all went well, so I'll be swinging back toward the Golen Road from time to time to check for help.

"Watch for my signal and stay alert. Between the fight and our slower pace, we won't make it to Lanor tonight, so I'll be watching for a defensible spot to spend the night."

With that, Rilen wheeled his horse and rode off to the southwest. The clouds were building in the west, bringing with them the promise of a late afternoon thunderstorm. The heat of the day was fading, and the cooler air rushing out in front of the approaching storm blew across the plains. A small herd of deer, made more skittish by the weather, darted in front of them, running to the relative safety of the woods. The sweet smell of flowers on the afternoon breeze was soon replaced by the damp, dusty odor of approaching rain.

Elac rode slightly off to one side of the group, eyes searching the ground. He had some knowledge of healing herbs, and was hoping to find something to help ease Shof's pain. From behind them, the rumble of thunder drew closer, the rushing wind stronger. Elac noticed Rilen riding back to the group, turning west and motioning for them to follow him. Kedow moved around the column, and handed out cloaks as protection against the rain. Elac rode over to help Rance wrap a cloak around Shof while the party continued at a trot. The first rain-drops fell, and Elac pulled his own cloak tighter in an effort to stay dry.

Within minutes, the rain turned to a heavy downpour. The group caught up with Rilen, who led them to the top of a ravine. Water was rushing freely down the center, and would probably rise with the storm, but by staying to the sides and stretching tents overhead, their camp would be able to stay out of the worst of the weather. The wind shrieked insanely, and the full force of the storm hit, setting the tents to vibrating rhythmically as nature put on a display of sheer power.

By nightfall, the heavy downpour slowed to a steady shower. The pattering sound of the rain on the shelter was soothing, and even Rance and Shof, with the worst of the party's injuries, were able to sleep. Rilen ordered a watch be set with two people awake at all times, then donned his heavy cloak and ventured back into the rain. When Elac wondered aloud where he might be going, Sanara answered that Rilen was checking the area for enemy camps. Rilen, a seasoned combat veteran, would leave nothing to chance.

The next morning, Elac arose early and left the shelter in search of the healing herbs his escort needed so badly. He found several healthy plants a short distance away, and in a few min-utes, had mixed up a liquid poultice. Rance limped up behind Elac, shouldered his equipment, and looked curiously at the pot of water. "Breakfast?" he asked shortly.

Elac shook his head, dipping several bandages into the murky liquid. "The medicine I told you about last night. Let's have a look at Shof before we go." He hefted the heavy metal pot and carried it to where Shof lay in agony. He carefully lifted her blanket, becoming slightly nauseated when he saw the extent of the wounds her body had sustained. Elac had seen people injured before, but her laceration was his first experience with the kind of damage a sword could cause. His stomach churning, he cut away the bandages and remnants of her smock before cleansing the wound. He applied his medicine-soaked bandages to the gash in her side, binding it up with a clean strip of cloth. After a few moments, some of the mute agony seemed to leave her eyes, and she nodded in appreciation, still too weak to speak. Elac repeated the procedure with Rance and the other injured Elves.

They rode cautiously while the morning progressed. The mostly flat plains farther east had given way to rolling prairies, which offered opportunities for ambushes. It was about mid-morning when Rilen returned to them at a gallop, a wide-eyed Caros close behind him. Rilen slid out of his saddle before his horse had even stopped, and anxiously waved the others over to him. Removing his helmet, he ran one hand through his sweaty hair, and knelt down in the center of their little party.

"We have a major problem," he told them in no uncertain terms. "I rode ahead to determine whether the garrison out of Lanor had marched to our relief. I met Caros about a league outside of Lanor. Caros, go ahead and tell them what you saw."

Caros, still visibly shaken, stared at the ground, unmoving.

He was silent for a few more moments, swallowing hard before he was able to speak. "The entire village has been destroyed. The Kobolds burned it to the ground and massacred everyone inside." There were audible gasps from the little group, and Elac felt his head spinning. "I approached town from the west when the sun was setting. I'd been seeing smoke for over an hour, so I knew there was trouble. When I got there, the entire village was burning. Kobolds were everywhere, and the only villagers I could see had been impaled in the village square."

"What about their militia?" Turen protested, hands on his hips.

Caros shook his head. "They must've been caught by surprise. All their equipment was being loaded into wagons, but none of the villagers were wearing militia uniforms. Then the rainstorm came through, and doused the flames."

"As you can see," Rilen said quietly, "there is no point in going on to Lanor. Here's my plan. We're going to split up into three groups. Elac will remain with me, and we'll make for Unity. Turen and Caros, you're with me, too. Triff, Kedow, I want you to return to Golen. You have to warn them to put the militia on full alert until the Elven army can mobilize. The rest of you will escort Shof to Easton. You'll take Nedlig's body with you."

He stood and brushed the dirt from his hands, the pride plainly evident in his weathered features. "We've come this far together. We lost Nedlig, but let's not allow his sacrifice to be in vain. Sanara, once you have Shof on a ship, I want you to hustle back to Golen."

❁ ◉ ✪ ✿ ◈

Elac and his escort rode in silence, each lost in his own thoughts. The sun continued its stately trek across the sky, and the temperature was rising. He wondered how the other Elves were faring in their armor, but he couldn't see any signs of discomfort in either Turen or Rilen. At noon, they stopped in another of the seemingly endless groves of trees to rest their horses and eat a sparse lunch. Elac marveled at Rilen's foresight in bringing extra rations on a journey that should have taken less than a day. He was only halfway through his meal when Rilen arose, brushed away the crumbs on his cloak, and moved to the edge of the trees.

"Trouble?" Turen asked, reaching for his sword.

"No," Rilen replied calmly. "I just want to have a quick look around. Keep the horses hidden and stay out of sight," he told them before slipping out of the trees and back into the oppressive sunlight. Elac's nervousness must have been obvious, because after a few moments Turen came up to stand beside him, placing a calming hand on Elac's shoulder.

"Are you wondering what prompted Rilen to scout ahead?"

Elac simply nodded wordlessly.

Turen smiled. "If there's one thing I've learned after five years of serving under Rilen, it's we should trust his instincts. If you knew about half of the encounters he has survived, you'd understand."

Elac was about to respond when Rilen returned, slipping soundlessly through the trees and giving Elac a start. The big Elf smiled his apologies at having frightened his charge, then took the reins of his horse from Turen. With smooth, fluid grace, he swung up into the saddle.

"I haven't been able to find fresh signs of the Kobolds, and that puzzles me. They have definitely been here, but not in the last twelve hours. I still have an uneasy feeling, though, and I learned long ago to listen to my inner voice. I think we should wait here until nightfall and start moving only under cover of darkness. I spoke with Caros, and he'll be joining us shortly."

Since it was still a few hours before sunset, they took turns trying to sleep. During Elac's watch, the burning yellow sun gradually shifted to a hazy red hue, and the light slowly fled from the sky. A sudden crunching of twigs snapped him out of his daydream, bringing him around to face deeper into the woods, his heart pounding. He peered into the gathering gloom, unable to see who or what had made the noise. Painstakingly, he edged toward the supine form of Rilen, intent on waking his protector. He nudged him with his foot, keeping his eyes on the surrounding trees.

"What—" Rilen started to speak but brought himself up short, catching the look of mingled fear and anticipation on Elac's face. Silent as smoke, he gathered up his sword and unsheathed it, reaching out with his short scabbard to gently prod Turen and Caros awake. The four of them waited side-by-side, weapons drawn, eyes intent.

"Perhaps I was mistaken," Elac whispered quietly.

Rilen nodded slowly. "And perhaps not," he replied.

For several more minutes, the four of them maintained their tense vigil. Elac stared until the silence became so overwhelming he wanted to shout, just to fill the air with sound once more. Even the insects and birds were quiet, creating an eerie feeling and adding to Elac's unease.

A putrid odor washed over him in a wave, assailing his sense of smell.

"What is that stench?" he hissed between clenched teeth.

"Carrion," Rilen replied tersely. "There's something dead out there."

"Something that's been dead for a while," Turen added quietly.

Caros and Turen spread out in a defensive posture, swords held ready, leaving Elac and Rilen in the middle. Elac wished belatedly for his longbow, since he was far from proficient with a sword. Nonetheless, he tightened his grip on the hilt of his weapon and prepared to meet whatever was coming for them.

To their immediate front, a scant twenty yards away, a shambling figure staggered into view. The flesh seemed to be rotting off its frame, and the bones underneath were plainly visible in several places. Its clothing was soiled and torn, and it wore nothing on its feet. The jaw hung slackly open, and a low moaning issued from its throat. A sudden, irrational fear came over Elac, and he would have run if he could but order his muscles to move. Around him, his three companions were similarly frozen, standing as immobile as statues while the apparition drew closer. Rilen was the first to recover his wits, and he stepped forward, sword coming up. The others drew courage from him, slowly shaking themselves free of their paralyzing fear.

"Who are you, and what do you want?" Rilen demanded harshly. The creature did not respond, but continued shuffling closer. Rilen raised his sword, and the two Elves under his command followed suit, moving closer to their antagonist's flanks.

"Stop where you are!" Rilen commanded, his lip curled in anger. "I won't warn you again!"

With a speed that belied the sluggishness it had previously displayed, the creature rushed at Rilen, a short dagger held in its hand. Rilen parried the first thrust, and a quick swing of his short sword easily severed the creature's wrist. Without pause, it stooped and grabbed the dagger with its remaining hand, menacing Rilen once more. Rilen's next strike severed the arm at the shoulder, and his team moved in for the kill.

Elac's near-incapacitating fear grew stronger when he realized that, despite the two grievous wounds, their foe wasn't bleeding. It hardly even seemed fazed by its injuries, charging closer and swinging a blow at Rilen's head with the stump of its remaining arm. A stroke from Caros, aimed at a knee, knocked the creature to the ground. Turen rushed in, plunging his sword into its chest. When it struggled to rise once more, Rilen severed its head, and the body fell limply to the forest floor, struggling no longer.

Elac, still trembling with fear, stumbled forward for a better view. "What . . . what was that thing?" he gasped.

Rilen chewed on his lip, staring in disbelief at the form lying at their feet. "I need to consult with an old friend when we get to Unity." He wiped his blade on a pile of leaves, removing the putrid slime. "I think it was undead," he said shortly.

"Wait," Caros protested. "A thrall? Outside Nightwood Forest? That's impossible!"

"As I said, I must consult with my friend when we reach our destination. I believe this was a thrall, but only Silvayn can tell me for sure. I—"

He broke off, spinning around to peer out at the trees surrounding them. If the odor was putrid moments before, its sudden intensity could only be described as overpowering. Rilen placed a solitary finger to his lips, then pointed to the horses with his still-drawn sword. They all padded softly, drawing steadily closer to their waiting mounts, eyes on the surrounding trees.

With a sudden crashing of branches, a dozen more of the creatures lurched out of hiding, shambling after the Elves with various weapons in hand. Elac's fear rose to new heights, and he again found himself frozen with terror. Rilen shouted his battle cry, pushing Elac closer to the horses while slashing at their closest pursuers. Elac shook off his sudden paralysis and made a desperate lunge for his horse. He pulled himself into the saddle with one smooth motion, seized his bow, and tried to calm his shaking hands while he nocked an arrow.

His companions were hard-pressed, and it was obvious they were fighting a delaying action at best. He chose a target near the back of the group of creatures and fired. His first shot went wide, but the second found its mark, striking the lumbering foe with a solid *thunk*. The creature scarcely seemed to notice.

"Go for their heads!" Rilen shouted. So saying, he drove several wild swings at his closest foe's abdomen, then suddenly reversed his swing, splitting the creature's head down the middle. With a sigh, it collapsed slowly into a crumpled heap.

But Elac's elation was short-lived. He spun sharply to his left at Caros's sudden cry of mingled pain and terror. Caros dropped to his knees, a rusty short sword protruding hideously between his shoulder blades. When he fell, three of the creatures closed on him and began to rend the flesh from his bones, ignoring his weakening cries. Turen leaped to his defense, ignoring the sharp warning from Rilen. Elac fired two ineffective arrows at the forms hovering over the bloody mess, which had previously been an Elven soldier.

Rilen backed away, calling for Turen to join him and for Elac to ride to safety. "Go!" he shouted. "We'll catch up! Get out of here and ride east!" Elac hesitated briefly, then turned his mount and kicked his heels into its sides. He held on tightly and the horse leapt forward, almost seeming as eager to escape as he was.

He burst clear of the trees with a bound and reined in, slowing to a brisk trot and looking behind him. Nothing else cleared the trees, which he found to be a mixed blessing. He was no longer being pursued by those creatures, but he had lost his escort. The light was failing, making it more difficult for him to see, even with his keen Elven eyesight.

Elac rode east for several hours, finally reaching the Lower Crystal River shortly after midnight. He decided it would be a good place to rest, but then thought better of it and searched for a place to ford the river. The Elf dismounted and led his horse southward, pushing through thorn bushes and tall patches of reeds, following the meandering course of the river. He listened intently for fresh sounds of pursuit, but he could hear nothing other than the night songs of frogs mixing dissonantly with the chirping of the insects of the night.

Finally, exhaustion overcame his battered body. In his fatigue, he stumbled over unseen vines and furrows, going to his knees more than once. At last, he resolved to go no farther, and stopped to survey his surroundings. He toyed with the idea of confusing any pursuit by turning the horse loose and swimming across the river alone, but immediately discarded the idea, knowing he was too exhausted to swim any distance at all.

Elac selected a thick stand of tall, narrow reeds, and pushed his way into the middle while being careful not to crush the reeds nearest the edge. He carefully coaxed his mount in with him, then rather meticulously concealed their entrance point. Fortunately, the reeds there were exceptionally high, and they were able to conceal his horse, even when it stood at its full height. After securing the reins to a fallen log next to the river's edge, he pulled a bag of oats from his pack. While his horse ate hungrily, he rubbed the big animal's muscles, knowing if he was chased again, his safety depended on his mount's continued health and stamina. After taking a few bites of food for himself, he fell asleep while the sun crept up over the horizon.

It was well past midday when he awoke. He crawled to the river's edge, splashing water on his face to wash the fog of sleep from his mind. The water was cool and refreshing, and Elac found renewed strength to face the day's challenges. He would hide there for a few more hours, then strike out south once more along the river's edge.

When his mind finally came into focus and he was fully awake, he noticed a second horse in his hiding place. He spun around in a panic, suddenly realizing he wasn't alone. Rilen sat across from him, reclining against his packs, his face streaked with dried sweat and blood. His woodland cloak was torn, and the scratches on his Elven armor gave mute testimony to the ferocious battle that had raged in the grove of trees after Elac fled to safety. He looked around the small clearing, directing an unvoiced questioning to Rilen. The image of silent fury in Rilen's narrowed eyes told him that both Caros and Turen were dead.

Chapter 3

The blazing sun had nearly completed its daily trek through the sky. The two Elves saddled their horses and rode south. Rilen agreed with Elac's assessment about their danger being significantly reduced if they managed to cross the channel. By his estimation, if they rode south at an easy pace, they could reach the Temel Ferry by dawn, cross the river, and follow the banks south to Unity.

The trees and undergrowth were thicker by the river, but despite the conditions they still located a small but well-worn path to follow, and were able to keep up a decent pace without too much effort. There were clouds of flying insects at first, but after a time they thinned out and gave the two travelers a reprieve.

They reached the ferry sooner than they had expected, and Elac guessed dawn was still about an hour away. Due to the early hour, he was not surprised to find the ferry unattended. Despite the frequent usage it saw in daylight hours, the ferry was not in very good condition. The railing was falling apart, and several sections were missing. The rings holding the rope in place seemed fairly secure, however, and Rilen wasted no time in boarding the low-beamed barge.

"Cast off those lines," Rilen whispered once the horses were aboard. "We're going across."

Elac looked at him incredulously. "But, the ferrymaster—"

"Our need for this ferry right now is much greater than any sense of moral guilt I might have over a free boat ride. If we go wake the ferrymaster, he'll bring the boat right back over to this side, making it available to our pursuers, if they're still on our track. This way, it'll be sometime before anyone on this side can come after us." He gave Elac a direct look. "Cast off."

It took the two of them the better part of a half hour to pull the barge across the rapid waters of the Lower Crystal River. They disembarked, and Elac was surprised when Rilen handed him the reins of both horses. While Elac watched with disapproval, Rilen went to rather extreme means to secure the boat to the bank, then turned and casually cut the line running from their side of the river back to where they had come.

Rilen bounded into his saddle, and he spoke before Elac could pose the obvious question. "If someone is tracking us, they'll know we crossed here. It'd be a simple matter for them to send someone over on the rope and retrieve the ferry. Now it'll take them a bit of work, and it won't be easy for them to get the boat loose once they get here." He turned his horse and started moving at an easy canter, guiding his mount away from the river.

"Actually," Rilen continued, "I considered stealing the ferry and floating it down the Lower Crystal River to Unity, but there's no way to steer it. If it makes you feel any better, at least I didn't set the boat adrift or sink it. The ferrymaster will eventually get his boat back."

They rode in silence for a time, and Elac stared abstractly at the surrounding landscape while considering what Rilen had told him. The sun was peeking above the horizon, splashing its ruddy hue on the fading night sky. The birds came alive, and the air was filed with the sounds of their singing.

At length, Elac's curiosity forced him to voice his concerns over their last encounter. "Those creatures who attacked us back there," he said haltingly. "Do . . . do you really believe they were thralls? I was always under the impression that the undead, if they ever actually existed, were mostly destroyed in the Second Necromancer War, with the few remaining creatures confined to Nightwood Forest."

Rilen shifted slightly in his saddle, directing a slightly sympathetic gaze toward Elac. "Your viewpoint is typical of people who live in the cities. You believe in magic, because you see it used from time to time. But since you've never seen a thrall or a skeleton, you assume they are either mythical or conveniently confined to a small area you'll never visit. Do you know much about the Necromancers and the undead?"

Elac leaned forward slightly and reached for his waterskin. "I've heard the tales. I always assumed there was a more rational explanation."

"I've been hearing reports of strange creatures roaming the Northern Plains, and I can only assume these are the creatures people have spoken about. When we reach Unity, my friend Silvayn can clear the affair up for us." He squinted into the distance. "What do you know of the Necromancer Wars?"

Elac chewed distantly on his lip for a few moments. The change in Rilen was strange; he had never been so talkative. "In the schools I attended, they taught us that the Necromancers were a band consisting of mostly Humans, with some Dwarves and Elves among their numbers. They sought to overthrow the nations of Caldala, Verlak, and Palindom, first through subterfuge, then through open warfare. At the time, people believed undead legions filled the ranks of their armies. According to current opinion, they merely had armies of berserkers." Elac trailed off, realizing the dichotomy of his professed skepticism. One moment, he believed these undead creatures to be confined to the dark reaches of Nightwood Forest, and in the next, he considered them to be the figments of very active imaginations. He wondered why he had never seen the inconsistency before.

Rilen shook his head. "Popular belief, I'm sure." He squinted into the bright sunlight, rubbing the stubble on his chin. "I'll give you the true history of the Necromancer Wars.

"For now, the Second Necromancer War is more critical, since this conflict led us to where we are today. About nineteen hundred years ago, in the year 3220, the war between the Humans and Dwarves had just ended. The Necromancers managed to infiltrate a force of skeletons and thralls into Nightwood Forest, and the creatures frequently waylaid travelers.

"In 3618, Volnor's forces struck. An army made up primarily of mercenaries drove hard into Firereach Pass, forcing the badly depleted Human soldiers from their defensive positions. Simultaneously, undead units struck at Tracker's Peak, annihilating the Elves who were garrisoned there. The Humans sent a reactionary force with the intent to retake Firereach Pass, then joined the other races in an attempt to marshal their reserve units.

"When the Humans engaged the mercenaries holding Firereach Pass, they were ambushed by hidden undead forces and slaughtered. Disenchanted by their defeat, the Humans abandoned all holdings east of the Mason River. The absence of Human defenders left the Elves and Dwarves open to invasion, but the slow pace of the fighting withdrawal had done its job. The Elves had pulled back into the Caldala Forest, reinforcing their cities there, while the Dwarves retreated to a position at Crystal Falls, where they fortified their lines in the narrow passes of the frigid North Range.

"After months of studying and planning, a battle plan was created. A fleet of Human ships set out from the port city of Iress. They sailed through the South Sea, west of the haunted ruins of Piaras Keep, where they disembarked a large force comprised of Human heavy cavalry and heavy infantry, Elven longbowmen, and Dwarven axemen. The ground forces conducted a forced march and retook Firereach Pass. While the infantry dug in, the cavalry units ranged across the Ranset Plains to the west and the Malaton Desert to the east, acting as scouts, harassing the enemy, and eliminating the Necromancers' patrols.

"Fifty legions from the armies of the combined races flanked Nightwood Forest to the north and entered the Paheny Mountains, falling upon Tracker's Peak. A brutal five-day battle ensued, and the undead forces were defeated. The surviving thirty legions solidified their position at Tracker's Peak. They were reinforced by ten legions, bringing with them the Temira."

Elac chuckled. "The Temira? Isn't that supposed to be a

magical artifact with special powers against the undead?"

Rilen frowned slightly. "You can decide later if you want to believe me or not. Right now, it's important to know the history. They hoped the presence of the Temira would enable the army to destroy Volnor, the leader of the Necromancers. Volnor emerged from his desert fortress with a massive undead army, which attacked Tracker's Peak, throwing everything they had into the fray. The armies of the three races repulsed assault after assault during three days of the most intense fighting of the war.

"Finally, with most of his undead forces destroyed and his mercenaries routing, Volnor played his trump card. A large party of Necromancers and Liches rode forth, with Volnor trailing behind carrying the Orb of Malator. The Necromancers and Liches cast a great spell, which Volnor channeled using the Orb. The spell would have collapsed the Pass, destroying Tracker's Peak and killing all within. However, the Elven mages had sensed the spell and were prepared. Using the Temira, they redirected the spell's energy into the Plane of Mist."

Elac, against his better judgment, interrupted once more. "The Plane of Mist? I don't . . . What is this 'Plane of Mist' like?"

"No one knows for certain, since no one has been there. There are numerous suppositions, but none of them are important, since no one will probably ever see it.

"There were dire consequences on both sides. As Volnor probably expected, his Necromancers and Liches were destroyed, because they had used up all their chala, the mystical energy used in the casting of Death Magics. But the backlash on the Elves and their allies was completely unexpected. There was a terrible explosion, shaking the pass from one end to the other. When the dust cleared, the castle of Tracker's Peak, as well as all the armies and mages inside, were gone. All that was left was a massive crater, surrounded by a dense, impenetrable fog. Some mages who were far enough away survived the explosion, and they're the only reason we have any account of the battle.

"The few remnants of the undead army retreated to Malaton, and there were not enough soldiers left on our side to mount a pursuit. Instead, the survivors of the combined army regressed into its component parts, with each race scouring their own lands to cleanse them of stray undead units. The exception to this was Nightwood Forest."

Elac rode in silence, mulling over what he had been told while he guided his horse around a fallen tree. "Obviously," he said, "you believe what you told me. The gods know I want to believe. This is something I've never told anyone. I've always wanted to be more than a merchant, something more heroic, I guess. I used to dream the legendary creatures were real, and I would somehow be the hero in a great battle against them. Now, look at me. My friends are dead, my village was destroyed, I've been attacked by Kobolds and the gods only know what else, and all I've done is run."

Rilen regarded him shrewdly. "You've shown great strength in getting as far as you have. Remember the pinch you were in when I found you? Many people would have begged for their life at that point, but you showed defiance by fighting."

"I shot an arrow and missed."

"You gave them pause," Rilen told him directly. "Had you not done that, they might have finished you before I could help."

Rilen stared contemplatively at the rolling grasslands around them. "Let's stop and eat, and while the horses get some rest, I can start your training."

"Training?"

"Yes, training. Archery, swordplay . . . Something tells me you may need it."

❁ ⊗ ★ ⊕ ⊛

The sun was sinking low in the western sky when the two weary travelers approached the gates of Unity. Rilen swung down off his horse when they neared the sentries. Elac, sensing this was something of a protocol, did likewise. His muscles protested, but he lowered himself to the ground, the pain a legacy of days in the saddle and an extended bout of physical exertion with Rilen that afternoon. Elac followed his guide, who strode purposefully toward the city, but they were stopped by two sentries who stepped forward, barring the way with crossed pikes.

"What is this?" Rilen demanded incredulously, hands on his hips.

"New orders," one of the guards replied. "No one may enter or exit the city from just before sunset until the sun is above the rim of the east wall. Trouble with brigands and such. The gates will be closing momentarily."

Rilen threw back his cloak, revealing an intricately carved pendant bearing the likeness of an eagle, with wings flared and talons extended. The guards stared in wide-eyed amazement, then hastily stepped aside.

"A thousand apologies, sir," one guard said with a shaky

voice. "Had we recognized—"

Rilen dismissed the apology with an imperialistic wave of his hand and, with a quick jerk of his head, motioned for Elac to follow him into the city. They led their horses past the contingent of soldiers guarding the main gates, and all stood aside when Rilen strolled past.

"I used to be a member of the Elven Royal Bodyguard," Rilen said by way of explanation. "Sometimes it comes in handy." He looked around, seeming to get his bearings. "Come on. My friend, Silvayn, may be able to get us in to see the Unity Council a bit quicker than if we go through normal channels."

Elac studied the gates as they passed through. They were designed primarily to defend the entrance to the walled city, and as such the architecture was primarily military in origin. Windows were high and narrow, which allowed archers to shoot at approaching enemies while providing them with maximum cover. The walls of the buildings were thick and made of stone, designed to withstand the impact of siege weapons.

They moved deeper into the sprawling metropolis, and Rilen guided them to one of the countless residential sections. They rode past small but neat wooden houses, many with meticulous landscaping and well-manicured lawns. Elac sighed; when he had gone into business, one of his goals had been to own a house just like any one of these.

Rilen turned onto the long drive of an opulent mansion, and the two weary travelers were met in a spacious courtyard by a group of enthusiastic servants. They handed over the reins of their horses, and an aged Elf in a plain white robe sauntered up, smiling broadly. His hair was white and cut to shoulder length. He carried a staff in his left hand, but Elac was fairly certain he didn't need it for aid in walking.

Rilen took the Elf's hand and shook it warmly, turning to Elac. "This is Silvayn," he said, motioning for Elac to join them. "Silvayn, this is Elac."

Silvayn greeted Elac, and then returned his attention to Rilen, a wry grin on his face. "What brings you here this time? Whenever you show up unannounced, it's never good news."

Rilen glanced around uneasily, then murmured, "Can we talk in private?"

Silvayn pursed his lips, nodding his head slowly. "Come with me." He spun on his heel and led the way into his house, with Elac and Rilen close behind. They passed through several rooms, all ornately decorated in an oak finish, and entered a well-furnished study. Row upon row of books lined one wall, and there were several large, highly polished tables set against the opposite wall. At one such table sat a young woman, her long, dark, curly hair flowing over her shoulders and down her back. She wore a simple brown tunic, caught at the waist by a black leather belt. She glanced up when the group entered, then turned back to her studies.

Elac sat gratefully while Silvayn sent a servant to bring refreshments. Rilen plopped down heavily beside him, leaning wearily against the back of his seat and propping his head against the wall. "Silvayn and I have been friends for years," he explained suddenly. "He used to teach at the Aleria School of Magic, but now he's been sent here to serve as a liaison between Aleria and the fools on the Unity Council."

Silvayn pulled up a chair, seated himself, and shook his

head, laughing. "I told you leaving here would get you in trouble, Rilen. What've you done now?"

"I'm not entirely sure," Rilen replied cautiously. "I was hoping you could shed some light on the subject." He glanced past Silvayn, his gaze falling on the young woman. "Is that Adalyn?"

"Rilen?" She looked up enthusiastically, quickly coming to her feet and rushing to Rilen's side. She gave him a fierce embrace, then stepped back, laughing. "I haven't seen you in almost five years!"

"Has it been that long? I wouldn't have guessed more than four." After introducing Elac to Adalyn, Rilen motioned to the remaining empty chair, and Adalyn seated herself. Adalyn was a mage undergoing her field studies under Silvayn, Rilen explained.

"So, Elac," she said, "how long have you known Rilen?"

"Only a few days," he explained. Elac then related the hectic events of the last week, starting with the ambush of his caravan, and describing the multiple assaults he and Rilen had survived. The calm demeanor displayed by Silvayn changed when Rilen described the creatures that had set upon them just east of the Lower Crystal River. At Silvayn's prodding, Elac and Rilen both gave all the details they could recall, even going so far as to describe the irrational feelings of fear and apprehension stirred up by the creatures' presence.

"And this was how far north of the Unity River?" Silvayn asked.

Rilen frowned, thinking. "I would make it about ten leagues."

Adalyn looked sharply at Silvayn, a worried frown creasing her features. "Thralls?" she asked. "So far from Nightwood Forest?"

"That's my conclusion, based on what we know," Silvayn

said cautiously.

"Then it's true? The thralls are real?" Elac wondered, his heart racing.

"Yes," Adalyn replied, looking at him curiously. She brushed her hair back from her face, revealing the fact that like most mages, she was an Elf, not a Human. "You don't believe in them?"

"I didn't know what to believe," Elac admitted, his face flushing in embarrassment. "I grew up in the city, so undead creatures have been more of a legend to me than reality."

Silvayn nodded knowingly. "I shall see to it you receive the proper education on the matter of these creatures, but now is not the time. What's more important is the pursuit by the Kobolds. They've been attacking caravans for some time, but your situation is unusual. Under normal conditions, if someone escapes one of their ambushes, the Kobolds might pursue them, but not for days on end. There may have been more to the attack than a simple ambush. In fact, you may have been the target, specifically."

"Me?" Elac gasped, his heart pounding in his chest. "Why would the Kobolds want to kill me? I've never done anything that would—"

"It may not be what you've done," Silvayn interrupted, "but rather what you may be capable of doing. I can't be certain without casting a scrying spell, but I believe I can find the purpose behind the assault. May I?"

Curious, Elac nodded. He watched with interest while Silvayn muttered words in the language of magic, accenting his words with brief but sharp gestures. The old wizard closed his eyes in concentration, and Elac held his breath, waiting nervously for the outcome. Strangely, his mind began to wander, and his memories played out before him like an obscure dream.

Finally, Silvayn opened his eyes, a look of shocked disbelief showing on his weathered features. He looked in turn at the others seated near him, then pursed his lips, his face set. "Adalyn, make sure no one is watching."

"What is Silvayn talking about?" Elac whispered. "Why did the Kobolds do this?"

"I have no idea," Rilen replied, swirling the wine in his glass.

Finally, Silvayn seemed to find what he was looking for, and he returned to his chair, receiving a reassuring nod from Adalyn. "There is a mystery shrouding your destiny, Elac, an enigma I cannot decipher. Somehow, the curse of Piaras Keep has touched you."

Silvayn gave Elac a direct look. "One other thing. Although I could not determine the reason, I believe the Kobolds were looking for you specifically, and they hunt you still."

Chapter 4

W hat do you want me to do?" Elac asked nervously.

"For the moment, nothing," Silvayn said, nodding reassuringly. For some reason, there was a soothing quality about the old Elf's voice that Elac found relaxing. "I'll speak with my contact on the Unity Council. He can arrange an audience for me before the Council. We'll bring up the raid on your caravan, the destruction of the village of Lanor, and the pursuit by the Kobolds. Let's see where the Council will lead us."

"The Council?" scoffed Rilen. "Lead? That, I would like to see."

"You haven't changed," Adalyn noted.

"In the meantime," Silvayn continued, "enjoy the hospitality of my home. I'll see to it you are provided with food, a hot bath, and a bed. I recommend you get some sleep, if you can. Tonight may hold some surprises for you."

A firm hand shook Elac awake, and he opened his eyes to find Rilen standing over him. The Elf was dressed in a formal blue cloak, his eagle pendant prominently displayed on his chest. His chain mail had been polished until it glowed, and his black boots were nothing short of glossy. He indicated a neatly folded stack of formal clothing, which, presumably, had been left for Elac.

He dressed and found Rilen and Adalyn waiting patiently in the hallway, chatting quietly. "Silvayn is outside," Adalyn told him. "We're being granted an executive session with the Unity Council. Are you up to a little public speaking?"

Elac nodded confidently, some of the tension running out of his body. "I might be incompetent with a sword or a bow, but I can handle myself in politics." Elac followed Rilen and Adalyn through Silvayn's sprawling house, his shoulders held a little straighter.

It took them about fifteen minutes to reach the Unity Council's chambers, a ride spent comfortably in one of Silvayn's well-padded carriages. The guards at the main entrance snapped smartly to attention when Silvayn stepped to the paved walkway. They passed along a wide, carpeted hallway into a circular waiting room filled with priceless paintings and sculptures. At regular intervals, ornate benches had been placed, thickly padded for the comfort of waiting politicians and heads of state. Silvayn motioned for them to sit, and Elac sank slowly onto a nearby divan, running through his speech in the silent vaults of his mind.

An hour later, the doors to the council chamber opened, and the four were escorted into the Great Hall. The Council was seated behind curved wooden tables arranged in the shape of a horseshoe. The air had a slightly musty smell, although the room appeared to be kept meticulously clean. An aged but distinguished-looking Dwarf sat in her high-backed chair at the center of the tables, flanked on either side by Dwarven men. All three wore dark brown surcoats bearing the emblem of the Dwarven nation of Verlak, a pickaxe set against a background of mountainous terrain. To the Dwarves' left sat three Elves, two women and one man, wearing long forest-green cloaks and light brown half-boots. While the Dwarves bore stern looks on their faces, the Elves seemed to be more relaxed. On the other side of the Dwarves sat three Humans, and they were a study in contrasts. Two of the Humans were older men wearing chain mail, but the third was middle-aged and wore a blue and silver robe. The older two rolled their eyes in boredom, but the third sat leaning forward in his seat, eyes and ears alert.

Silvayn stepped forward, taking his position on a raised platform surrounded on three sides by a wooden railing. "My thanks, great Councilors, for seeing me on such short notice. I believe you know me well enough to realize I would not ask such a favor lightly. The information I have for you this evening may have dire consequences in the weeks to come.

"You'll notice I've brought others with me: a warrior, a mage, and a merchant." Elac started slightly, and he was ashamed to realize he'd almost taken offense at being called a merchant. "Two of these, the warrior and the merchant, have come through great peril to stand before you and deliver this most urgent information. Without further delay, I call upon Elac to speak before you."

Silvayn turned and gestured to Elac, who came forward hesitantly, like a schoolboy about to receive his punishment for a misdeed. The room was lit by three large fireplaces scattered around the perimeter, casting deep shadows into the corners. In one of those corners, Elac could barely discern the silhouette of a cloaked and hooded figure flanked on either side by Dwarven soldiers.

"My name is Dralana. What brings you before us?" the Dwarf at the head of the table asked. "What is so important that Silvayn believes we must interrupt our normal proceedings and hear you out?"

"An attack on my people, your Grace," Elac responded, trying to quell the shaking in his voice. "Less than a week ago, I was traveling with a caravan from Lanor en route to the Human army outpost at Fort Julan. We were still some distance from the fortress when the caravan was set upon by a Kobold raiding party. The caravan was taken, and everyone else was killed. The Kobolds pursued me for many leagues, and only the timely intervention of the Elf, Rilen, saved my life." Elac went on to describe the perilous journey from Golen, including Caros's description of the destruction of the village of Lanor.

Todos, the Dwarf to the left of Dralana, interrupted. "Elac, we hear your tale, but we've seen no evidence. This Council deals in hard facts. Do you have any bodies from either your caravan or the Kobold raiders? Did anyone here this evening even see the village? I would like to hear from this Caros, who claims to have seen the strike on the village."

"Caros was killed before we made it to safety," Elac countered. "Everything we know about the village of Lanor, we heard from him. Rilen felt it would have been dangerous to go anywhere near the village, since the Kobolds may have been patrolling the area."

"If the village was burned to the ground, as you say, then surely you would've seen the smoke?" Tanne, the oldest of the three Humans, asked with a quiet voice.

Elac shook his head. "A rainstorm came through and put out the flames before we were close enough."

"So." It was Roktal, the Dwarf seated to the right of Dralana, who spoke. "You cannot prove the village was even attacked, let alone attacked by Kobolds. In fact, we have only your word to back the assertion your caravan was attacked by Kobolds. For all we know, it could've been common highwaymen."

Rilen strode forward angrily, drawing a large leather pouch out from under his cloak. "To the Council at Unity, I offer this as my proof, if the word of a former member of the Elven Royal Bodyguard isn't enough." He opened the pouch and approached the Dwarf, Dralana, at the head of the Council. Reaching inside, he grabbed a handful of black pendants, which Elac recognized as the ones Rilen had taken from the first Kobold patrol. "These pendants belong to the Drablok clan, a group of renegade Kobolds known to operate in the plains to the west of the Paheny Mountains. I took them off the bodies of the Kobolds I killed when I first met Elac."

There were some surprised whispers while Rilen distributed the pendants for the Council to see. A disturbance from the corner of the chamber drew Elac's attention, and he was surprised to see the shadowy figure he had noticed earlier approach the Council. The figure threw back its hood, and Elac's eyes flew open wide when he realized the figure was a Kobold.

"Good merchant, I am Rodok, a diplomat of the Kobold nation. It pains me to hear these wild tales of misdeeds by Kobolds. I believe they are wild rumors, and nothing more."

Elac, bewildered and more than a little intimidated, could not find his voice, and he stood silently, heart racing, while Rodok approached. Rilen, however, had no such problems. "I have shown you the pendants from the Drablok tribe. They wouldn't yield those pendants while they yet lived. Do you deny this?"

"Not at all," Rodok replied smoothly, clasping his hands in front of his chest. "In fact, I am willing to concede that a group of Kobolds has been slaughtered. However, I must question this tale on many fronts. First, the people of the Drablok tribe are not associated with my nation. They are renegades, acting on their own, so my government bears no responsibility for their actions. Second, they are fearsome warriors. I find it highly unlikely you could have killed twelve of them without assistance."

Rilen's eyes went flat, and he reached for his dagger. "You doubt my word?"

"You are out of order, Rilen," Dralana said. "This is a formal hearing, and he is permitted this challenge. You will stand down immediately or leave."

"Rodok's point is well taken," Oaklyn said. She was seated closest to the Dwarves, and Elac assumed proximity to the head of the table was an indication of authority. "Despite the veiled hostility between our people and the Kobolds, I still find this tale hard to believe. You bring little to us in the way of proof. You have pendants, which we will concede came from dead renegade Kobolds. But none of you present, indeed no one living from your party, saw the assault on the village of Lanor. How can we be certain it was, in truth, Kobolds?"

"Hold," Silvayn commanded, striding forward quickly. "I vouch for these Elves. I firmly believe their tale to be true." He turned to the youngest of the Humans, seated to the far end of his two countrymen. "Falstoff," Silvayn said, "you appear troubled. Surely you believe?"

Falstoff glanced down at the table, then looked up nervously, his eyes darting around the room. "I fear for the village. I have long said these raids by renegade Kobolds were worsening, and we needed to stop them. However, the Council can't agree on a course of action."

"Ralore," Dralana said, "would you like to extend a motion to the Council?"

"Certainly. I move for the Council to establish a committee to look into this incident."

"I agree," Cordos replied, pushing a lock of hair over his Elven ears. "Before we can make any determination about what has happened, we need more facts."

"What of my people?" Rodok asked. "We are being accused of an atrocity here, which could have disastrous implications. Even if you were to decide this actually was perpetrated by renegade Kobolds, there would still be repercussions on the relationship between our peoples."

Elac could hardly believe what he was hearing. His friends, indeed his entire village, had been slaughtered, marauding bands of Kobolds were ranging the countryside, and the Council was thinking of appointing a committee? He leaned closer to

Silvayn, who was standing beside Elac's pedestal, and looked at him questioningly. He mouthed the word "thrall," but Silvayn shook his head darkly. After reflecting on that, Elac had to agree. If the Council believed he was lying about Kobolds, they would assume he was insane bringing up thralls.

Roktal rose to her feet. "I would like to amend Ralore's motion. The commission should consist of eight members, two from each race, including the Kobolds. Rodok, would your personal retinue be able to spare two members to join this commission?"

"Certainly."

"I will second the motion," Oaklyn announced.

Dralana pounded a large, multicolored orb on the table. "The motion is now before the Council. All in favor?" The only opposing vote came from Falstoff, of the Humans.

"Then this motion passes, and the session is adjourned. Ralore and Oaklyn, who presented the measure, will be responsible for setting up this commission. The Council will meet again in an executive session upon the committee's return, to discuss their findings. Elac, Rilen, as material witnesses, we'll need you to be present. This meeting is adjourned."

They gathered again in Silvayn's study, having eaten dinner in stunned silence. Finally, Elac could bear it no longer. "A committee? Hundreds of people have been murdered, and the Council is going to wait until the committee comes back before they even talk about it?"

"As I said before," Rilen told him coldly, "the Unity Council is a bunch of impotent fools. The Elves on the Council are the only Elves I've ever known who could stand to be in the same room as a Kobold without wanting to kill him. They're so interested in their money and power, they forget who they are and where they came from. Nothing else matters, including loyalty to their own people."

"The Council has always been slow to action," Silvayn said. "We have other options available to us."

"Yes we do," Rilen said pointedly. "Like returning home. I am washing my hands of this entire mess. I still have a village to protect. I'll be leaving in the morning."

"That's it?" Elac protested angrily. "I'm not the only one who lost friends this past week, you know. You lost at least three of your soldiers, maybe more, and you're just going to let the Kobolds get away with it?"

Rilen whirled to face him, his eyes as cold as ice, and jabbed a finger at Elac. "Do not seek to rise above yourself. I need no one to remind me of what I've lost. But I can do nothing about it while I sit here waiting for action that will never come. When I return to my militia, I'll hunt down the renegade Kobolds, and I will make them pay!"

"I have further need of your services," Silvayn said simply, cutting off Rilen's tirade. "If you'll indulge me by accompanying me yet one more time, I believe we can find the answers."

"I don't want answers! I want blood!"

"And you shall have it!" Adalyn responded angrily. "By the time this is finished, even you shall have your fill of blood. But for now, let's hear what Silvayn has to say."

"My plan is simple. First, Rilen, I agree with you. We cannot sit idly by and watch events unfold. But Elac being directly targeted by the Kobolds has me worried. We need someone who can commune with the spirits, someone who can find what is hidden and give us some guidance. We need the Diviners."

Elac had no idea what Silvayn was talking about, but he was definitely alarmed by the responses Rilen and Adalyn had to the suggestion.

"The Diviners?" Rilen asked incredulously. "You want us to go to Divinity? I think you need to go back to your crystal ball."

"Crystal balls are the tools of charlatans," Silvayn said thunderously. "You are a good man, Rilen, and I need you. I know you're upset about recent events. I promise you, if we learn nothing at Divinity, I'll ask nothing further of you."

Adalyn smiled at Elac, seeing the puzzled look on his face. "Divinity is the home of the Diviners. They're able to speak with the spirits of the dead, and Silvayn believes they can help us here. Unfortunately, the answers tend to come in riddles, leaving them open to interpretation."

"That's not the only problem," Rilen offered.

"True," Silvayn admitted, sighing. "Divinity is located in the heart of Nightwood Forest. The stories of the undead roaming the forest are true. Fortunately, through some type of enchantments we don't quite understand, the undead won't enter Divinity."

"I'll go," Elac said quietly. "I don't know what else to do. I'm not a warrior, so I can't fight. I'm not a mage or a Priest, so I can't use magic to protect myself."

"Okay," Rilen said grudgingly. "I owe you a number of favors, Silvayn, so I'll go with you. But I intend to go no further with this business. I've already stayed away from my duties at home for far too long."

"And I'll go, as well," Adalyn announced suddenly. "You may have need of my magic, and I can certainly hold my own in a fight."

"Okay," Silvayn said, nodding, "then it's settled. We leave at dawn. I'll have my servants pack our horses with the supplies we'll need. Let's get some sleep."

Elac slipped into bed, wondering what he would do once and if they returned from Divinity. If they learned nothing, the answer was obvious: he would try to pick up his life where he left off. But what if there was something so important it required Elac to do more? It was one thing to fantasize about doing some heroic deed, but Elac had to face the realities of life. He was inept with a sword, and he knew nothing of magic. There was nothing he could do to help on any quest. *Unless the quest involved buying supplies for the army.* He exhaled sharply, bitterness rising in his chest.

Elac squinted into the early morning sun as they crossed the Unity Bridge and entered the Human kingdom of Palindom. Silvayn's plan called for them to stay on the highway until they reached the bridge to Ranas, at which point they would turn east and enter Nightwood Forest.

Elac rode in silence until his curiosity got the better of him. He nudged his horse closer to Adalyn, his presence bringing her out of her half-bemused revelry.

"I can see you have a question for me," she noted with a smile.

"Indeed. Silvayn was able to use magic to determine general circumstances, but he seemed unable to determine any specifics surrounding the incidents of these past few days."

"It's a common misconception about the way magic works," Adalyn explained patiently with a disarming smile. "Determining generalities is easier, because you carry your fate with you. It trails you like a miasma. But to determine specific outside factors involved in a series of events is beyond the power of any living mage.

"When a person uses magic, Life Magic, it drains the mage's Kata, or life-force. Kata is in all living things, and life requires it. It is found in sunlight, which is why the creatures of the night tend to shun the daytime. Kata can be found in the waters of the Springs of Calda, which may explain the healing properties of those mystical waters. When a mage casts a spell, it drains the mage's Kata at a rate proportional to the power of the spell. The more powerful the spell, the more Kata will be required."

Elac's brow furrowed in concentration. "Then what happens if the mage uses too much?"

"The effects of Kata loss can be serious, including fever, headaches, hallucination, unconsciousness, or even death. It may be days or even weeks before the mage can cast spells again, and during the recovery phase the spellcaster will age at an accelerated rate.

"As a mage practices and gains experience, the amount of Kata the mage can use will also increase, just as a long-distance runner gains endurance through extensive running. The more spells a person casts, the greater their Kata potential. This is why Elves tend to make the best mages: they live longer, so they develop a higher Kata potential.

"But this brings us to the most important rule: No mage can use Life Magic to harm or kill another living thing. Our magic can counter spells cast by Necromancers, see that which is hidden, protect the caster, and so on. But Life Magic cannot be used as a weapon against other people."

"What happens if a mage hurts someone accidentally?"

"We're not sure, although everyone agrees it's not an area for experimentation. I can tell you, though, the same restriction doesn't apply to the Necromancers. They operate under a completely different set of rules. If anyone uses Life Magic in violation of this prohibition, they suffer a horribly painful death, followed by damnation of their soul."

"I didn't know any of this," Elac admitted.

"Few people do," Adalyn told him grimly, her brown eyes serious. "It is important for you to know, due to the nature of our quest, but it is equally important for you to understand other limits Silvayn and I will be under. Any use of magic sets up a sort of resonance that pinpoints our location to other users of magic who may be in the area. The range at which the resonance can be detected depends upon the strength of the spell, the skills of the mage casting, and the abilities of the mage or Necromancer who may be listening."

Elac nodded, mulling over what she had told him. They continued riding south, sticking to the heavily traveled road for both anonymity and ease of travel. The avenue was broad and straight, having been paved decades earlier. The trees had been cleared to make a grassy swath of ground about a hundred yards wide, allowing the travelers to see for some distance. The cloudless sky was a deep crystal blue, and the scent of fresh wildflowers was in the air. They stopped for lunch and chatted amicably while they ate, other than Rilen, who maintained his stoic silence.

❁ ⍟ ★ ✚ ❂

Rilen woke the others shortly before dawn the next morning. The sun was just beginning to stain the eastern horizon when Elac arose from his makeshift bed. Rilen pressed a single finger to his lips for silence, and the group gathered their gear, keeping the noise to a minimum. In just a few short minutes, they were leading their horses eastward, away from the road and closer to their destination in the Nightwood Forest. They had traveled at least a mile before Rilen indicated it was safe for them to mount up and ride.

"What was that all about?" Elac asked him quietly.

"Just being cautious," Rilen replied. "Most of those people were merchants, and merchants tend to talk a lot. Seeing a group of travelers leave the road and head directly for Nightwood is likely to be a topic of conversation, and would be a good way for the wrong people to find out about our mission. You never know where spies might be hiding."

"Speaking of the 'wrong people,'" Adalyn noted, "the entire Unity Council knows the four of us are together. Do you suppose they figured out where this little side trip of ours is going?"

"Doubtful," Silvayn answered, scratching his short, white beard. "They know Elac is under my protection, but we told no one we were leaving."

"Wait a minute," Elac told them. The last exchange was too much for him, and another of the cornerstones of his world was crumbling. "Do you mean to tell me the Unity Council is not only weak, but it's corrupt, too?"

Rilen tried to answer but was unable. He broke into hysterics, doubling over in his saddle and shaking with laughter. Adalyn gave him a withering look, then turned sympathetically to Elac. "You have lived a sheltered life, my friend. You were taught by your family, your friends, and your teachers to believe the Council is the best solution to maintaining peace and security for the nations. In truth, the members of the Council are more interested in furthering their own wealth and power than they are in continuing the Council's true mission."

"They are not to be trusted," Rilen snapped suddenly, shoving the cork back into his waterskin with more force than was necessary. "When Kobold raiders burned two of the villages under my protection and slaughtered most of the people who lived there, I appealed to the Council to allow me to track and destroy the band of Kobolds responsible for the atrocities. The Council forbade me from crossing any national boundaries. Even the Elven Prime Minister wouldn't help me with this issue." He spat angrily. "They should dissolve that worthless body and let the nations take care of themselves."

Elac nodded in realization, a new understanding coming to him in a flash of insight. "That's why you left the Elven Royal Guard, isn't it? You wanted to avenge the attack, and they wouldn't let you."

Rilen stared darkly ahead without moving for several long moments, then he nodded curtly. Adalyn moved smoothly to change the subject. "The Council seemed to be almost unanimously opposed to any kind of response."

"Then why were they pushing for a committee?" Elac wondered.

"Don't let them fool you." Silvayn said. "Whenever the Council is faced with a situation where it is difficult for them not to act, they appoint a committee. By the time the committee is formed and completes its task, people will no longer care what happened to your friends. The committee is a delaying tactic."

"So we have no friends on the Council?"

Silvayn raised a solitary finger to his pursed lips, seeming to consider something. "I wouldn't quite say that. Falstoff may be different. He's new to the Council, and he seemed to be more sympathetic to our cause."

Adalyn looked at him curiously. "Falstoff? How can you be sure? He's not even a full-fledged member of the Council. He's actually the mayor of Palim, and for now is simply standing in for the King's nephew, who is ill."

"True," Silvayn conceded. "But I made some inquiries last night. He is a born politician, but he cannot be selected to serve full-time on the Council, because the Humans only allow relatives of the King to serve in that capacity. Rumor has it, he's trying to convince King Aldaris to appoint him ambassadorial status."

Elac cocked his head to the side, a grin playing at the corners of his mouth. "If we make something of this trip, and

Falstoff backs us, it might give him the boost he needs to become an ambassador. That alone should make him more willing to help us."

"Very good," Adalyn said approvingly.

"I may be a terrible shot with a bow," Elac laughed, "but I know politics."

They continued riding in a generally easterly direction, crossing through a rolling prairie. Elac found comfort in knowing there were still places to hide if necessary, since the ground was folded like an unmade bed, with many draws and hills.

They kept their pace an unhurried one, saving their mounts' energy in case it would be needed later. The horses strolled leisurely through the knee-high wildflowers, tails swishing almost of their own volition as flies swarmed the travelers. On the distant horizon, the dreaded Nightwood Forest slipped grudgingly into view. Even from their vantage point, at least a league from the feared woods, there were no other travelers to be seen.

Rilen called a halt when they reached the trees, dismounted, and motioned for the others to stay put. He drew his short sword and crept cautiously into the woods, disappearing from sight. Adalyn swore in frustration, drew her own sword, and swung down from her horse. She peered into the trees, but she made no attempt to enter, apparently unhappy with Rilen's orders but willing to obey them. Elac sat astride his horse, and once again the familiar helpless feeling overcame him. He drew the short sword that had been a gift from Silvayn, and took his place beside Adalyn. She nodded in approval but said nothing.

Rilen reappeared moments later, sword sheathed, moving casually back to their side. "The way is clear," he told them. "I checked for several hundred yards, and I can't find any trace of undead anywhere."

"One moment," Silvayn said. From atop his horse, he spoke in the tongue of magic, emphasizing his words with sweeping gestures. He pointed toward Rilen, then suddenly stopped moving and sat motionless, head bowed in concentration. Finally, he looked up and nodded. "Rilen is now spiritually connected to Divinity. He'll be able to find the path for us."

Without another word, Rilen led the band into the trees, taking them on a path leading northeast. That part of the ancient forest was made up mainly of oak trees, their thick boughs allowing only an occasional gleam of sunlight to peek through. In time, Elac's eyes adjusted to the darkness, and he was able to see clearly. Overhead, he could hear the chattering of families of squirrels, and he watched them scamper to and fro on the wide branches of the enormous trees. He also caught a glimpse of an occasional deer, although they tended to flee when the group drew near.

Rilen suddenly stopped his horse and, motioning for the others to halt, he vaulted from the saddle. Elac's heart raced wildly while he watched Rilen slip to the rear of the party, where he took cover behind a conveniently located oak tree. He stood immobile for several long minutes, watching the trees around them, but nothing appeared. Finally, he shook his head in frustration and returned to his horse.

"I thought I heard something behind us," he explained quietly. "It may have been my imagination, or just an animal of some kind."

"Perhaps," Adalyn conceded, "or perhaps not. I'll drop

back a short distance and listen for any signs of pursuit."

They rode even more cautiously after that, all four of the weary travelers keeping a watchful eye on the surrounding trees. Rilen stopped frequently, listening to the sounds of the forest with the others waiting in hushed anticipation. Elac's hands cramped, and he realized he was gripping the reins on his horse so tightly that his knuckles were turning white.

A hiss of warning came from behind him, and he snapped around to see Adalyn had dismounted and was staring into the distance behind them. The others also stopped, waiting curiously for Adalyn to tell them what had caught her attention. She waited for some time, then finally shrugged her shoulders and returned to her horse, her eyes distant and bewildered.

Elac was about to suggest a stop for lunch when a small, thatched-hut village came into view. He looked sharply over at Silvayn, who nodded in obvious relief. They had found Divinity.

Chapter 5

They entered the village, and Elac noticed the primitive lifestyle the residents of Divinity had adopted. The streets were little more than dirt paths, worn bare by the continued passage of people and animals. The huts were all elevated about a foot off the ground, most likely in an effort to keep the inside of the huts dry during a rainstorm. There seemed to be no specific plan to the layout of the village, with huts springing up seemingly at the whim of the builders.

The exception to this pattern was the large structure in the center of the village. Its obvious location of prominence spoke volumes about the structure's stature, but just as obvious was the construction itself. While the other buildings were mainly assembled from thatch, the massive edifice before them was made from logs. It stood half again as tall as any other structure in the village, and seemed to cover enough ground to house four or five of the huts so common in the rest of the settlement. His voice barely a whisper, Silvayn told them the place before them was the Temple of Divinity. They rode directly to the main doors and dismounted.

A robed and hooded Elf opened the door at their approach, bowing respectfully. "Greetings, Silvayn, mage of the Elves." He greeted each of them in turn. "Adalyn, pupil of mighty Silvayn. Rilen, master warrior." He finally faced Elac, no emotions registering on his face despite the obvious hesitation in his greeting. "And this can only be Elac, merchant by trade, who is hunted by enemies he has never met. My name is Hemet. The monks will see to your mounts." He swept into the temple, robes billowing behind him. The travelers relinquished their reins to the robed men who seemed to have appeared from nowhere, and followed Hemet inside the massive log building.

The interior of the temple was well lit, with candles placed at regular intervals on plain metal candelabra and fires burning in stone-lined fire pits. The walls were plain, decorated only with crudely carved holy symbols representing each of the gods worshiped by the different peoples. Even the unholy symbol of Malator, god of the Necromancers, was present, to Elac's great discomfort. The flaming white skull, set against a black background, definitely made him jittery. The polished wooden floor, while uncovered by rugs or carpets, was nonetheless kept conspicuously clean by the monks who tended the temple. They were taken into a large hall outfitted with long wooden benches, where Hemet motioned for them to sit.

After a few moments, the doors at the rear of the hall opened, and a line of robed monks filed through the open portal. Wordlessly, the mysterious figures formed two lines, one on either side of Elac and the others. Hemet approached the central fire pit, where he stood motionless for the span of several heartbeats before chanting in a strange tongue. His voice rose to a fevered pitch, and he raised his hands imploringly over his head.

He reached into his robe and retrieved a leather pouch, dumping the contents into the fire. The flames flared up brightly, and the air was filled with a pungent odor that caused Elac's eyes to water. Puffs of smoke of varying hues wafted from the flames to chase each other around the room, many of them coming close to Elac and his friends, circling them tightly for several seconds before returning to their exploration of the enormous temple chamber. The occasional touch of these ephemeral globes filled Elac with the chilling kiss of death.

The strange ritual continued for an hour, and culminated in a group chant by the monks surrounding Elac's party. Their mantra built into a crescendo, and the great fire pit in the center of the room suddenly flared up, the flames licking the ceiling hungrily. In an instant, the flames receded, and the entire room fell silent. The monks bowed their heads in wordless meditation.

"Honored Silvayn," Hemet intoned in a deep, monotone voice. "The spirits of the dead have shown me much. I will tell you what I have learned. The hunted one is in grave danger. The faces of the enemy are many, and while they are not in harmony, they all seek his demise."

"Elac was in a caravan that was attacked by renegade Kobolds," Silvayn said. "This attack was directed at him specifically?"

Hemet closed his eyes, appearing to consider what he had learned. "There is a powerful force guiding the Kobolds, much greater than you suspect." He paused, again seeming to reflect on information known only to him. "I see two paths."

"For me?" Elac asked.

"Yes. One choice is for you to do nothing. You can continue your life as if none of this happened. But whether you pick up your life as a businessman or hide behind walls of stone protected by brave soldiers, the result I see is the same: Death. Destruction. Despair across the land."

Elac chewed nervously on his lip, his stomach churning. "And my other path?"

"I see darkness there, as well. There is treachery and danger at every turn."

"What must he do?" Silvayn asked softly.

Hemet looked at each of them in turn, his scrutinizing gaze seeming to assess their strength. "There is a long journey ahead, one that will take him to many lands. I see a number of companions who must be there to help along the way. The three who have come this far must stay with the hunted one."

"Impossible," Rilen cut in. "I have other responsibilities. I won't be tied up in some obscure quest. I've done enough already."

"Then he will die."

The words hung in the air between them. Rilen shook his head in disgust, leaning back on the bench and folding his arms across his chest while he awaited the rest of what Hemet would tell them. Hemet remained silent for a few long moments. "I do not know the names of your other companions. I can only describe how to find them, and it will fall to Silvayn to determine who shall accompany you.

"I see two hawks living in the mountains. Their auras and

their fates are bound together. I see a burning axe to hammer your foes into submission. In the same land, there is a shimmering crystal. You must recover it 'ere the first part of your journey is complete.

"Deep in a vast forest, I see a woman, a shadow, adrift in the world. She will join your cause, albeit reluctantly. Seek out the dark blade. In the same land, you shall need to gather the water that heals.

"In the land of oceans, there is a man who seeks a circle of jewels. Seek out the blue knight. You must also seize the bejeweled knife.

"After you have completed these initial tasks, you must seek out the dead in their hallowed halls. You will have gathered the three keys to their domain. You must enter the labyrinthine lair beneath their ancient fortress and defeat the wards left behind to guard their sleep. Should you succeed, the seven spirits will speak with you, and all will be made clear." He hesitated, closing his eyes for several long moments. "I can see no further. The future is in turmoil, and our sight is limited. I can tell you no more."

With that, Hemet and the other monks filed slowly out of the hall, leaving Elac and the others alone. Silvayn glided wordlessly to the central fire pit, Adalyn at his side. Both chanted in the language of magic, moving their hands in slow circles over the dying embers. Finally, Adalyn stepped back, looking expectantly at Silvayn, who stood motionlessly near the fire pit. He raised his face to the ceiling, eyes closed, and breathed deeply. He shuddered violently and staggered, almost falling to his knees before easing himself onto a nearby bench to face the others.

"I managed to get a glimpse at the Diviners' vision before it faded. I believe I can now more readily recognize our compatriots when we see them. I won't know them by sight, but hopefully I can recognize their auras. Let's return to Unity and decide what to do next."

"I'll tell you what we do next," Rilen told him plainly. "It's still early enough to leave the forest without spending the night here. I'm returning to my militia and mount a punitive expedition against those Kobolds. Elac can go back to his career, and you two can go back to your studies." He marched out of the hall.

They met no one on their way out of the temple, and they found their horses tied up near the entrance. They mounted wordlessly and rode back through the village, retracing their steps in order to follow the shortest tract out of the forest. The village was strangely deserted, as though no one had lived there in years.

Elac reluctantly concluded that his previous life was over. Silvayn and Adalyn obviously put a tremendous amount of faith in the Diviners, so he did not feel he could dismiss their vision as easily as Rilen seemed to. He didn't know what to think about the strange Elven warrior. One minute, he seemed anxious to get to the bottom of the events swirling around them, and the next, he wanted nothing to do with the entire situation.

Elac was startled by a sharp, pungent odor arising thickly from the trees, west of the village. The others noticed it, too, and Silvayn softly whistled for Rilen to stop. After a brief whispered conference, Rilen turned his horse to the right and led the way at a brisk trot. Elac was quick to follow, and he soon found himself on the northern edge of Divinity. Rilen paused, scanning the trees ahead. Satisfied with what he found, he led the group into the forest.

For the first league, they moved relatively swiftly. There was no sign of any pursuit, and they could see nothing ahead of them. Once clear of the village, the group angled more to the northwest to reach the edge of the forest as expeditiously as possible. However, the trees were denser there, and the undergrowth more pronounced, limiting their field of vision. Rilen slowed their pace noticeably, sacrificing speed for safety. Elac did not choose to draw his sword, but he did loosen it in its scabbard, and he kept a nervous eye on the trees around them.

They came to an area of heavy deadfall, an impassable barrier barring their way forward. Rilen turned his horse eastward to navigate around the obstruction. Since the danger they had likely left behind them at Divinity would be to the west of them, Elac found it to be a sound decision. His sense of security slowly dissolved, however, when Rilen unobtrusively tightened the straps holding the small shield to his left arm.

The attack came without warning. One moment the four travelers rode in silence, and the next, a group of twelve cloaked figures leaped from behind a mound of fallen branches. They efficiently surrounded Elac's party, bearing a variety of swords, their weapons splotched with rust. As Elac drew his own sword in defense, he heard a strange grinding sound coming from their foes, sounding eerily like tree branches grinding together.

Rilen leaped to the attack, sliding from his horse, giving up the advantage of being mounted for the mobility of being on foot. He charged two of their foes, swinging his sword in a short, deadly arc. He deflected a blow from the nearest cloaked attacker, and his sword slid into his opponent's chest. To Rilen's obvious surprise, the sword met no resistance, and his attacker didn't slow. He pulled his sword back for another blow, and the cloaked soldiers threw back their hoods.

Elac felt the all too familiar terror return, and his heart pounded in his chest. The men before them were not men. They were not even alive. Skulls fixed in hideous grins leered at him, and the fleshless bodies closed on Elac's group once more.

"Skeleton warriors!" Rilen shouted in warning. He had to give ground, apparently trying to reassess his strategy while he fought. The slow enemy advance continued, and the skeletons tightened their circle. The eerie silence was broken only by Elac's labored breathing and the occasional grunt when Rilen swiped at a skeleton that had come to close. Adalyn dropped to the ground, motioned for Elac to stay where he was, and edged over to stand with Rilen, sword drawn defiantly.

Silvayn chanted, and a few seconds later, he gestured and sent a blast of blue-white energy from his fingertips. The bolt caught three of the skeletons, and they detonated with an ear-splitting explosion. The others paused momentarily, realizing where their biggest threat was, and Rilen took advantage of their hesitation. Using broad strokes instead of the short, deadly thrust he had tried earlier, he drove into the closest skeleton. With three rapid blows, he smashed the undead creature's rib cage, and it collapsed in a great clatter of bones.

Adalyn noticed his change in tactic and followed suit, shattering the closest skeleton. Elac heard another energy blast, and two more skeletons shattered, sending bone fragments flitting into the trees. Rilen and Adalyn moved in on the remaining skeletons together, fighting side-by-side. The skeletons were systematically destroyed, the last falling under a furious barrage of blows from Rilen.

"Everyone all right?" Silvayn asked. Seeing three nods, he said, "Let's get out of here. This was obviously a trap, and there may be more."

Rilen and Adalyn remounted, and they hastily trotted around the barrier of fallen trees. Gone was the easy pace Rilen had set earlier. He was not exactly riding at a gallop, but he was definitely riding harder than prudence would have suggested in a wooded setting. The trees seemed somehow closer, and the darkness beneath the trees deeper. Every sound made Elac jump, believing some other unimaginable horror was emerging from concealment to rip out his life.

The race dragged on. He had come to consider their flight from the forest to be a contest, a competition against the death threatening to consume them. They splashed noisily across a small, shallow brook, and scampered up the other side.

At last, with the sun dipping dangerously close to the horizon, they broke free of the stifling forest. The four bedraggled travelers picked up the pace when Silvayn told them the undead creatures were likely to await the setting of the sun before they emerged from the shelter of the trees. They rode hard until they reached the road to Unity, where they slowed to a brisk trot. They passed other groups of travelers who were also headed steadily northward, some of them unarmed, others accompanied by parties of well-armed bodyguards. Drizzle turned to light rain, and soon Elac was soaked and chilled to the bone. He pulled his cloak tighter and rode on, shivering with the cold.

It was nearing midnight when the bridge to Unity came into view. Through the rain and heavy mist, Elac could see the sentinels standing watch at the bridge, preventing all from passing until morning. Silvayn led the party to an open area, where they set up camp for the remainder of the night. After they had all settled in, Elac found he couldn't sleep, and he eventually rolled over to face Rilen, who had taken the first watch.

"Can I ask you something?" Elac whispered. Seeing Rilen nod, he continued. "When you and I came to Unity, the guards were barring entry at night, just as they are now, but you got us inside right away. Why didn't we do that tonight?"

"Silvayn and I discussed this earlier. Since our trip was unofficial, we decided against attracting unwanted attention to ourselves. We'll be safe enough here, hidden in this crowd of people waiting to enter Unity and protected by the unit of soldiers guarding the gates."

Elac's breath came in small puffs of steam, and he wrapped himself deeper in his blankets. "I guess I'm still upset about what happened after we left Divinity. Ever since we were attacked by the thralls on the Northern Plains, I've been trying to convince myself they were just men, and somehow my eyes had fooled me. The attack in Nightwood Forest has changed everything. There's no way to deny those were undead skeletons attacking us."

Rilen nodded in understanding, and his hardened features softened somewhat in sympathy. "We all come up with ways to safeguard ourselves from the harsh realities of life, and when those barriers are broken, it can be painful. My advice would be for you to get some rest. Silvayn will continue to guide you, regardless of what I decide to do."

Elac felt his pulse quicken a bit at the possibility Rilen might stay with him for a bit longer. And with Adalyn and Silvayn, as well . . . Silvayn. What was it Silvayn had done to those skeletons during the skirmish?

Rilen laughed when Elac voiced the question. "Silvayn is full of surprises."

Elac raised himself up on one elbow. "Could you cast a spell like that?"

"No," Rilen said, shaking his head with a hint of a grin on his face. "I don't even know if Adalyn could do it, and certainly not with the amount of power Silvayn used. It takes many years of study to cast a spell of that magnitude. I could cool their beer for them, or find out which way is north, if they were lost."

"Where did you learn your magic?"

"Adalyn used to teach me bits and pieces. Of course, we haven't seen each other for some time. And Silvayn frowns on her tutoring me. He believes everyone who wants to learn magic should go to the School of Magic at Aleria."

"I don't think I'm ready to learn even the simplest of magic. I'm having enough trouble learning about using a sword and a bow without confusing the issue."

❁ ❀ ★ ✿ ✪

Dawn came quickly, and Elac found himself in the center of a crush of humanity trying to enter Unity. It took some patience, but by mid-morning Elac's little group rode casually along the broad avenues leading to Silvayn's residence. By the time Elac had devoured his second helping of eggs and ham, bathed, and changed clothes, the others were gathered in Silvayn's study. When Elac entered, the others were engaged in idle chatter and sharing a barrel of ale. A servant brought Elac a brimming tankard, and he seated himself comfortably on a small divan.

There was a light knock at the door, and Councilor Falstoff entered. He bowed in greeting before handing his cloak to a waiting servant. "Good morning, Silvayn. I came as soon as I received your message."

Silvayn rose and crossed to the interim Councilor, shaking his hand warmly. "Thank you for coming so quickly. I'll try to be brief." He motioned the newcomer to a chair before seating himself. "Has the Council received any new information regarding the business we brought before them?"

Falstoff shook his head sadly. "They have yet to hear from the advance party they sent to investigate the allegations regarding the atrocities committed at Lanor. They won't even consider a course of action before then."

"It is as I anticipated," Silvayn replied. "In the absence of action by the Council, I found it necessary to take steps of my own. What I am about to tell you needs to be kept in the utmost secrecy. Obviously, the Council and your King need to know this, but no one else can be told." Falstoff hesitated briefly, then nodded in agreement. "We traveled to Divinity and spoke with the seers there."

"Are you serious? Despite the risks involved? Did you take along an escort?"

"No. We felt secrecy was more important. We made it to Divinity unmolested, although we can't say the same about our return trip. We were set upon by undead forces as we attempted to leave the forest."

Falstoff's eyes narrowed in disbelief. "If this is a joke, I am not amused."

"It's no joke, I assure you," Rilen told him pointedly.

"Falstoff," Silvayn continued, "we must have the Council's cooperation in this matter. If we are to complete our task, we'll be crossing national borders, and it'll be easier with Council sanction. The seers have tasked us with gathering certain people and items from all three nations. There may be more to the quest, but we'll worry about it at a later time."

Falstoff stared incredulously at Silvayn for several long moments, eyebrows raised. "What do you need me to do?"

"We'll present our case to the Unity Council this very evening. We would like you to sponsor the sanctioning of our quest. If we can return something momentous, it would reflect very highly on you as an interim member of the Council. It might even allow you to rise above your current political limitations."

Falstoff slowly rubbed his hands together. "Something for everyone." He rose to his feet, extending his hand to Silvayn. "All right, I'll help you in this. Let's hope it doesn't come back to haunt us." His eyes darted around the room. "No pun intended."

Falstoff spun on his heel and strode from the room, closing the door softly behind him. Adalyn flashed a brilliant smile to Elac, giving him a hearty pat on the back. "You read him like a book, Elac. He wants to move up, and he knows he has to assume some risks to do it."

"I'll believe it when I see it," Rilen noted skeptically with a disapproving scowl.

"We only have a few short hours before tonight's Council meeting," Silvayn said. "We need to prepare."

❀ ⊗ ★ ⊞ ⊛

Elac nervously entered the Unity Council chambers, noting with concern that Rodok, the Kobold ambassador, was standing at the right hand of Dralana, the Dwarf who was presiding over the Council. Vainly, Elac tried to quell the trembling in his hands while he and his three companions approached the podium at the center of the room. Dralana called the Council to order, banging her orb on the table.

"Greetings, Silvayn. You come before us once again. We have news for you regarding the incident you brought before us. Our scouts have returned, and they have found, as you said, the village of Lanor has been destroyed. With the help of the Kobolds who accompanied our commission, we were able to determine it was, indeed, a band of renegade Kobolds who were responsible."

"On behalf of Overlord Hamedon and the Kobold people, I wish to offer condolences to the Elven nation of Caldala," Rodok announced. "This heinous act has shamed Kobolds everywhere, and it should not go unpunished. In light of this incident, I would like to offer the services of the Kobold army in chasing down and destroying the renegades. I believe it would be an enormous step toward permanent peace between our peoples."

Ralore rose to his feet. "On behalf of the Human people, I would like to offer my endorsement of this. Perhaps by allowing the Kobolds to help defend our territory, we can ease some of the distrust our people, and possibly even the Elven people, have for Kobolds."

The representatives of the Elves conferred among themselves briefly before Oaklyn stood to speak. "We see wisdom in this course of action. Our own forces have proven woefully inadequate for the task."

Rilen took an angry step forward and, ignoring protocol, spoke up, his arms folded across his chest. "Inadequate? You tie the hands of the Elven soldiers, yet you criticize us when we fail. Give us the tools we need, and we can defeat these raiders without allowing our nation to be overrun by enemy troops."

Oaklyn gave him an amused look. "We? As I recall, Rilen, you left the service of Prime Minister Lornell years ago."

"I left because of the policies enacted by this body. If I'd been allowed to cross national borders, I would have destroyed the renegades long ago."

Todos, a white-haired Dwarf, rose swiftly to his feet, a sneer on his weather-beaten face. "We are not here to discuss your past problems, sir. We are here to resolve the issue of a raid by renegade Kobolds, which resulted in the destruction of a village and the loss of life. Ambassador Rodok has offered assistance, and I believe we should take it. I call for a vote on the issue."

Nasontas, a younger Elf with long, pale-blond hair, nodded her head in agreement. "I second the motion."

Dralana lifted her highly polished ceremonial orb and slammed it to the table with three measured strokes. "A vote has been called. The matter before us is the assistance offered by the Kobold nation. All in favor?"

The entire Council stood, unanimously passing the measure. Rilen stalked to the rear of the room, his hands on his hips. Silvayn shook his head darkly, but said nothing. There was a brief recess while a scribe was summoned to write up the proclamation, and the entire Council signed it before Dralana placed the Council's seal on the parchment. The scribe bowed respectfully and left. Rodok, the Kobold ambassador, followed him out to receive his copy.

Silvayn stepped boldly to Elac's side and addressed the assemblage. "We have another issue to present before the Council. The situation is even more desperate than previously believed. There are other forces besides the Kobolds that need to be dealt with. Undead creatures from Nightwood Forest have crossed the Unity River, and even now they seek out unwary travelers."

"Undead? On the Northern Plains?" Roktal scoffed, stroking the long, braided beard all Dwarves seemed to wear. "You dare waste this Council's time with such stories? I should—"

"Hear me!" Silvayn shouted, seeming somehow to grow in stature. The room fell into silence, and Roktal froze, his mouth agape. "We didn't mention this before, because I knew the Council would be skeptical. But we no longer have the liberty of hiding our heads in the sand. Most of you have no trouble believing the undead exist, yet you refuse to admit these fiends might leave Nightwood Forest?"

"They have no power outside the haunted realm," Roktal countered, his face turning red with anger. "No undead creature has left the forest since the Second Necromancer War."

"I tell you now, Rilen and Elac were set upon by thralls in the Northern Plains, barely escaping with their lives. They weren't entirely certain of what they had faced, of course. They were as reluctant as you to believe it. But this all changed in the last few nights. While we awaited the Council's determination on our other matter, we traveled to Nightwood Forest and visited the seers at Divinity. When we tried to return here, we were attacked by a force of skeleton warriors who lay in ambush."

"You entered Nightwood without Council sanction?" Cordos asked, his Elven eyebrows creased with an arrogant scowl. "We could have you imprisoned for that."

"I gave them permission." All heads turned to see Falstoff standing, an uneasy smile on his face helping complete his deception. "They informed me about the purpose of their visit, and I gave them special dispensation to penetrate Nightwood Forest and reach Divinity."

"And what 'special purpose' was that?" Dralana asked.

"I was able to divine something unique about Elac, and the seers confirmed it," Silvayn told them. "The renegade Kobolds were specifically seeking Elac's death in their attack. The burning of the village was purely diversionary. There is something unique in Elac's past, or his future, and whoever is the driving force behind these Kobolds seeks to destroy him."

The curious stares greeting Elac at this announcement were intimidating, and he found it difficult to meet their gazes. Silvayn allowed the initial shock to settle in for several long moments. "The seers told us he must travel the three nations, gathering certain artifacts and companions along the way, then commune with the spirits of those who have gone before us.

The culmination of his quest will then be made clear."

Oaklyn frowned in confusion. "Why come to us? If you wish to run this fool's errand, you don't need our blessing. We have other matters to deal with. Do you realize seven citizens of Unity have gone missing in the last week?"

"While we could do this on our own, it will certainly make our trip easier if we have Council sanction to make the journey."

Once again, Falstoff came to the rescue. "How about a compromise? We grant them the sanction they seek, under the condition that once they finish with this business, they return here to brief us on what they have learned."

The Council chambers erupted into a heated discussion, with members shouting to be heard over the din. Eventually, Dralana was able to restore order, and another voice vote was taken. The measure passed by a narrow margin, and while the scribe approached once again to write up the proclamation, Silvayn motioned for Elac and the others to exit the hall. They waited in a small antechamber until a servant arrived with their copy of the Council's order. Without any further delay, Silvayn led the way back to his home.

Chapter 6

The decanter clinked with a crystalline shimmer as one of Silvayn's servants poured Elac another glass of wine. Rilen had left the house over an hour earlier, saying he was going to speak with the Elven ambassador before returning to Golen and his duties there. Elac was sharply disappointed that Rilen would not be coming along, but the decision had been made.

Adalyn leaned closer to the map and pointed to the Caldan Forest, more than twenty leagues northwest of Unity. "Why not head through Caldala first?" she wondered aloud. "We could make our way to the Elven capital at Calda, then take the road through Arden straight north to Verlak and the Dwarven capital at Centare. Once we finish with the Dwarves, we could take ship from the port at Centare or Highpoint, and sail south to Palim."

"It would be the easiest way," Silvayn agreed, "but we need to do this in a specific order. The seers at Divinity deliberately mentioned the mountains first, meaning the Dwarves. Quite possibly, if we were to go through Caldala before Verlak, we might miss one or more of the companions we're supposed to pick up."

"What about Rilen?" Elac asked. He sighed, slumping his shoulders in defeat. "We were told we needed him, as well, and he's not going."

"It troubles me, Elac, but there isn't much we can do," Silvayn told him gently. "He must choose his own path. Perhaps we'll meet him yet again."

"So, what now?" Adalyn asked, still studying the maps. "Do we sail up Crystal Lake, or do we take the roads?"

"I would rather stay as far from the Northern Plains as I can, so we need to stay west of Crystal Lake. With Kobolds still trying to find Elac, we would be well advised to keep a low profile. I'm certain they have an extensive spy network among the people of all three nations."

"Then you agree with Rilen?" Adalyn asked. "You assume the so-called renegade Kobolds are actually still tied to the Kobold leadership?"

"I know them well, and I'm certain of it. They are a fanatical race, and I can't imagine any of them defying their Overlord." He gazed out the window of his study. "The placement of Kobold forces within our borders worries me. With their increased military presence, they could easily launch a full-scale invasion of the West."

He paused, fondly running the tips of his fingers along the length of his mage's staff. "Actually, to an extent, this could work to our advantage. The Kobolds might end up solving one of our problems for us. If their forces are patrolling the Northern

Plains, they're bound to encounter bands of thralls. Since un-dead creatures will attack the living on sight, the Kobolds might end up reducing the number of thralls out there."

Suddenly there was a commotion in the hallway beyond the closed door of Silvayn's study. "Out of my way!" someone shouted, followed by a great clatter of falling glass. Adalyn was on her feet in an instant, sword in hand, and the door to the study burst open. Rilen stood before them, seething anger in his eyes. Without another word, he stormed into the room, and slammed the door behind him.

"Rilen," Adalyn gasped, slowly lowering her sword, "what—"

"It seems the Unity Council is not content to simply meddle in international affairs," he announced coldly, kicking a foot-stool out of his way. "After our first session before the Council, one or more of the Council members used their influence to have me replaced as the head of the militia. In fact, I was re-moved from the militia—permanently." He dropped heavily into a cushioned, high-backed chair, pouring himself a glass of wine and putting his feet up on the nearby table. "I guess I'm coming with you."

"Destiny," Adalyn told him. "Fate had to give you a nudge, that's all."

Rilen glared at her unhappily, drained his glass in one long drink, and moved to an ale barrel in the corner, where he filled a great flagon. "Fate or not," Elac told him, "I'm happy you're coming."

Rilen grunted noncommittally, flopping back into his chair once more. "Okay, Silvayn. Where are we going first?"

Following Rilen's lead, Elac guided his horse off the road and into a copse of elm trees. It was a pleasant, sunny spring day, and the cooler temperatures in the shaded woods were very inviting. They had been riding since daybreak, and with Rilen setting an easy pace they made their way northward toward Verlak, the land of the Dwarves.

Elac enjoyed a meal of dried beef and cheese, an ale skin close at hand. He finally decided to ask a question that had been bothering him. "Silvayn, what exactly were you able to decipher out of the instructions the seers gave us?"

Silvayn offered him a quick smile. "Fortunately, this time they were unusually direct in their dissertation. They spoke of finding two men in the mountains. While I'll grant you it doesn't necessarily mean the Dwarves, the other major mountain range on this continent is home to the Kobolds. I doubt we want them joining us on our quest. Besides, they spoke of a stone. In Dwarven history, there is an artifact called the Orion Stone, which may be the stone the seers referred to.

"If we assume the first reference was to the Dwarves, then it follows that the next part of their prophecy referred to the Elves. We'll find an Elf and convince her to join us, although the seers did say she would resist coming along. Also, they mentioned the healing water, which likely refers to the Springs of Calda. We'll just need to convince Prime Minister Lornell to allow us to take some. She can be very . . . difficult where the Springs are concerned.

"From there, we go to the Kingdom of Palindom. The

'Land of Oceans' most likely refers to the Humans, with their love of sailing and the sea. Seeking out a man who desires the crown will not be easy, though, since many in their government have such a tendency. And the 'bejeweled knife' is likely to be the Dagger of Rennex."

Silvayn stood, brushing away the crumbs from his lunch. "All that remains is the last part of the riddle. Hemet spoke of seven spirits and an ancient keep. He can only mean we need to visit the haunted ruins of Piaras Keep and speak with the ghosts of the seven knights who committed suicide there."

They remounted and rode north once more, and by night-fall they had reached the Minet Road. At daybreak, Rilen surprised Elac by leading the group off the road, riding toward the Caldan Forest. As Silvayn explained, they were bypassing the town of Minet in an effort to avoid attracting attention.

They reached the woodland in about an hour, and followed the tree line north for the remainder of the day. Other than when they were in sight of the road to Tilda, they saw few other people. The skies were a heavy gray color, and by late afternoon a relentless rain was falling. It was not a thunderstorm, but rather the steady, soaking rain that can last for hours. By the time they stopped for the night, their clothes were thoroughly drenched.

Dawn came grudgingly, the sky slowly turning from a deep black to the familiar gray. The rain slackened off to a mist while they ate breakfast, and had stopped by the time they broke camp. Elac groaned inwardly at the thought of another day on horseback. He rode in silence, chewing absently on dried beef. He sighed remorsefully, another of his life's illusions shattered. In all the heroic stories he had read, in all of his fantasies where he was the hero, the part where the great warriors suffered through wet clothes, short rations, and sore backsides seemed to have been left out.

About an hour before sunset, their horses clattered onto the road, and Elac sighed in relief. He had hoped reaching such a natural guidepost would mean they were stopping for the night, but Rilen led them northward with a single-mindedness that grated on Elac's nerves. He knew Rilen was upset, but the veteran Elf hadn't said two words since they left Unity. His instructions from Silvayn were answered with noncommittal grunts, and any attempts at conversation were met with baleful glares.

After the last of the day's light had faded, Rilen guided them off the road and into a copse of fir trees. Although it hadn't rained since morning, the skies still carried a threat of inclement weather, so they prudently set up their shelters before beginning their evening meal.

"Silvayn, do you know much about the undead?" Elac asked.

Silvayn chuckled, taking a drink from his wineskin. "Some."

"Do they require a Necromancer to be nearby, or can they operate on their own?"

"Actually, they are fairly autonomous. They're imbued with a hatred of the living, and they exist only to kill."

"So, there wasn't necessarily a Necromancer around when the undead attacked us?"

"Probably not." Silvayn added another branch to the dying embers.

The fire popped, causing Elac to jump involuntarily. "Are Necromancers more powerful than mages?"

"Not necessarily. That's actually a difficult question to answer, because we don't really have comparable abilities."

"But what if a Necromancer and you were to do battle right now? You told me before that users of Life Magic can't use their power to harm another living being."

"The most powerful Necromancers are not, technically, living creatures." He turned to Adalyn with a smile. "Let's see how well my star pupil is learning her lessons."

"Most Necromancers are Humans who are frustrated by their lack of progress with Life Magic," she said. "Their first step is to pray to Malator, the god of death, whom all Necromancers worship. To begin, the novitiate has to kidnap his greatest enemy and his closest loved one, bring both with him to the fortress at Malaton, and sacrifice them to Malator.

"If the means of death wasn't cruel and lingering enough, or if the Gatekeeper divines that the sacrifices are not the most hated and the most loved, the novice fails the test."

Elac sat with his mouth gaping in horror at the tale. "And?"

"His soul is condemned to eternal punishment by Malator. But if he passes, he is accepted as a student of the black arts. A Necromancer, having tasted power, may seek to be transformed into a Lich by sacrificing himself with a ceremonial dagger. If Malator wills it, the dead Necromancer will be raised as a Lich."

"Quiet," Rilen said suddenly, rising to his feet. "Someone is approaching."

In the sudden silence that followed, Elac found he could hear his heartbeat pounding in his ears. He listened intently, and his sharp Elven hearing picked up the sound of many booted feet skulking through the woods. Following Rilen's lead, Elac slowly drew his sword, minimizing the sound of the steely blade clearing its protective sheath. He tried to peer into the surrounding darkness, but he found his night vision hampered by the fire.

"Everyone look directly into the flames," Silvayn whispered, bringing his staff onto his lap. "Pretend nothing is amiss." Elac obeyed the terse order, and he could hear Silvayn muttering under his breath in the language of magic. Elac mimicked the others by hiding his sword in his cloak, his back to the surrounding trees.

There was a sudden rush from behind them, met almost simultaneously by a few shouted words from Silvayn. The darkness vanished in a brilliant, pulsating light. Elac whirled to face his opponents, and he heard their shouts of rage and dismay. They were stopped in their tracks, hands covering their eyes, some dropping to their knees in agony. Rilen was the first to react, leaping into the fray, his short sword swinging. The closest man tried to bring his shield around, squinting into the light, but he was too slow. A quick slash from Rilen's blade left him shrieking in pain and holding the gaping wound in his side. Adalyn joined Rilen, and they methodically cut their way through the attackers.

While their enemy outnumbered them better than three-to-one, the advantage Silvayn's light spell had provided proved to be overwhelming. One wounded man, a bloody, wicked-looking dagger still gripped in his hand, staggered away from the fight. Squinting in the intense magical light, he spotted Elac and Silvayn, and charged them with a howl. Elac brought his sword up as Rilen had taught him, moving forward to meet the rush. The man took a swipe with his blade, and Elac managed a clumsy parry. The two weapons came together with a crash, and Elac responded with a downward stroke. His foe, already weak from his injuries, couldn't stop the attack. Elac felt the sword cut through cloak, leather armor, and flesh as he completed the blow. He watched the life drain from the man's eyes, feeling sickened as the blade dragged on bone when he withdrew his sword. The man toppled lifeless at Elac's feet, his blood spilling across the pine needles carpeting the forest. He stared in uncomprehending astonishment for a long moment, and then he fell to his knees and retched uncontrollably.

Elac was only dimly aware of the cessation of the sounds of battle around him. He scarcely paid attention to the hurried conference of his companions, who were trying to determine the purpose for the attack. He sat back, staring at his upraised sword, which was still stained with his enemy's lifeblood. Then Rilen was beside him, helping him to his feet. Adalyn took the weapon from his hands, and he watched dumbly while she cleaned and sheathed the sword for him and led him to his horse. He wondered briefly when his friends had managed to saddle the horses and pack their gear. Rilen boosted him into his saddle, and the group rode north, following the road.

He had killed a man. Certainly, it had been in self-defense, and no one could fault him for what he did. No one, that is, but himself. He felt the nausea rising again, but with effort, he managed to maintain control of himself. He stared at his hands, stained a dark crimson color from the blood he had spilled. Once again, in his mind's eye, he saw the still form lying on the ground at his feet, the chest bared to the sky by Elac's sword, the tattoo on the man's neck showing a dagger thrust through a manacle seared into Elac's memory. He heard a horse plodding along next to his, and he looked up to see Rilen next to him, concern mirrored in his eyes.

"Do you want to talk about it?" Rilen asked him.

Elac was silent for a time, staring uncomprehendingly ahead. He finally faced Rilen, a look of undisguised horror on his face. "I . . . I can still feel the blade sliding through him. I can feel his pulse down the length of my sword, just as surely as I can feel my own. He—"

"He was going to kill you," Rilen said sternly. "Above all else, you must remember that. And he would have felt no remorse. He has killed before, and he would kill again without a second thought." They rode on in silence for a few minutes.

"That day on the Golen Road, you killed a Kobold," Rilen continued, reaching out to place a comforting hand on Elac's shoulder. "That was completely different, though. Kobolds are not so similar to Humans, Elves, and Dwarves. When you shot the Kobold chief, to your subconscious mind it was no different than hunting deer in the forest. But you must realize, Elac, killing another person is not a natural act. In time, however, you get . . . numb, I guess. I don't know whether that's a good thing or not."

They rode hard that day, concerned their attackers may have had accomplices, and anxious to avoid another skirmish. By midday, they were climbing the steep, winding road that meandered into the mountains of the North Range. By nightfall, they reached Crystalia.

They approached the city gates and dismounted, waiting in a line of travelers who were seeking entry. Dwarf axemen lined the walls, looking gruffly out over the throng below, their faces unreadable behind their thick beards. The gate guards carefully scrutinized all who passed through the opening in the city walls. Elac wondered if the entire city was so edgy. At length, their turn came, and they were approached by the Sergeant-at-Arms.

"State your name and your business in Crystalia," he said with a gravelly voice.

Silvayn stepped forward, limping and wheezing, and it seemed old age would claim his life at any minute. "My name is Nagel," he lied glibly. "This is Serana," he said, indicating Adalyn, "my granddaughter. This is her husband, Jolhan," he announced, gripping Rilen's shoulder. "And this is Jolhan's friend, Straum. We are seeking shelter for the night."

"I see." The armored Dwarf scrutinized the travelers shrewdly. "The best inns are to be found in the southwestern quarter of the city. Anyone in the area can point you in the right direction."

"Thank you, kind sir," Silvayn replied, gasping for breath.

When they were several blocks away, Elac finally felt he could restrain himself no longer. "Why did you lie to the guards?"

"Until I find out who was responsible for the attack last night, I'm not taking any chances by announcing our presence. It may have been a random band of brigands, out for profit, but then again it might have been something more. The Unity Consulate is this way."

The streets of Crystalia were narrow, and the buildings low, clearly designed for the primary denizens rather than the occasional visiting Human or Elf. The buildings were made mostly of stone, which came as no surprise to Elac since the Dwarves were so proficient at mining and stoneworking. He glanced off to his right, and gave a sudden gasp of surprise when a group of a half-dozen Kobolds emerged from a merchant's market.

Rilen heard Elac's startled exclamation, and he followed Elac's gaze. His eyes narrowed with hatred, and he took in the situation at a glance. He casually edged closer to Adalyn and muttered something to her, then approached Silvayn. Elac tried watching the Kobolds out of the corner of his eye for some hint of hostility, but the group seemed to be paying them no attention.

Silvayn stopped suddenly, pretending to tighten a strap on his horse's saddle. The others drew nearer, and he whispered, "Keep walking, but keep your horse between you and the Kobolds. I don't think they're here for us, but let's not take any risks." Despite Silvayn's fears, the Kobolds entered a battered carriage, and were lost from sight. Silvayn led them confidently through the busy, dark streets, eventually bringing them to the Consulate.

Rilen pulled his strange medallion out of the folds of his cloak where it could hang in plain view, and they entered the building. The stone floor of the Consulate was well polished, and the walls were hung with paintings of the different Dwarf ambassadors who had served there. Unlike most of the other buildings in Crystalia, the ceilings in this structure were high enough to allow the visitors to stand unimpeded, and Elac assumed the variance was for the benefit of visiting dignitaries. From down the well-lit hallway, the sound of an argument reached their ears.

"It's embarrassing to the family, and especially to your uncle," someone said in a deep, booming voice.

"You make too much of it," said another, his words coming out somewhat more quietly.

"Too much of it? She was the daughter of the Elven ambassador! When he finds out what happened—"

"Nothing will come of it. You worry too much, big brother. I . . . oh! Sounds like we have guests!"

Elac followed his friends into an office, where bookshelves and filing cabinets lined the walls and an oak desk filled the center of the room. There were two Dwarves, both dressed in formal cloaks. One was standing, his red hair carefully braided behind his head, his neatly combed beard reaching nearly to the middle of his chest. The other Dwarf was sprawled in a large, leather chair, a tankard of ale close at hand. The tunic beneath his robe was rumpled and unlaced, and his hair and beard looked as if he had just gotten out of bed. His eyes were puffy and bloodshot. The first Dwarf eyed the newcomers carefully for a moment, and then his eyes fell on Rilen's pendant.

"Rilen?" he asked in a powerful voice.

"Yes. Have we met?"

"Once, years ago, at the King's court in Centare. You were a part of the Elven Prime Minister's entourage." He paused, pursing his lips behind his great beard. "We were told you would be coming."

Silvayn cocked his head. "You were told? How did the information get here before we did? I hadn't thought the bureaucracy could act so swiftly."

The Dwarf gestured to a pile of papers on the desk before him. "One of the Council members sent us a sheaf of dispatches by fast messengers. They use a relay system of fresh horses to get messages delivered quickly. But I'm forgetting my manners. My name is Gillen, and this is my brother, Hadwyn. Our father is Halles, the Crown Prince of Verlak."

Rilen made the introductions for his party and shook hands with Hadwyn. "A Council member actually sent news about us? They weren't very happy about the whole idea in the first place, as I recall."

"Actually, he wasn't a full-time member of the Unity Council. I guess he's just keeping the seat warm for someone. His name is Falstoff."

Silvayn chuckled. "He was about the only one on the Council who really wanted this mission. Did he send any other news?"

"Let's see . . . there was something about some attacks by renegade Kobolds out east and the patrols the regular Kobold army is sending after them, a few assorted unimportant proclamations, and a list of promotions within the bureaucracy." Gillen leaned over his desk, digging through a pile of parchments. "There was also something about some disappearances in Unity. Here it is." He held up one of the dispatches, scanning the contents. "There have been several people who have disappeared in and around Unity over the past few weeks. No bodies have been found, but the people are still missing. Yesterday, the Duke of Branig was in Unity, and he disappeared on his way to a meeting. They're still looking for him."

Hadwyn gestured wildly with his tankard, spilling some on the floor. "So what exactly brings you to Crystalia? Besides the wonderful scenery, of course."

Rilen managed a smile, which to Elac seemed out of place given the Elf's foul temperament he'd had since they left Unity. "We need to speak to the King about obtaining a religious artifact. Your assistance there might expedite things for us."

"Actually, you're in luck," Hadwyn said, rising unsteadily from his chair. "My uncle, the King, is here in Crystalia, meeting with local leaders about a new mining project. We could take you to see him right now."

Gillen shook his head, rolling his eyes. "Hadwyn, you are not going to embarrass me by taking important people to the King, looking the way you do. Go clean up, and I will see to some refreshments."

While Hadwyn made himself presentable, Gillen made arrangements for transportation and took care of their horses. They loaded into a hay-lined cart drawn by a pair of sturdy mules. After a brief ride, the cart bumped to a stop in front of a rather plain, gray stone building, and the Dwarves led the way inside. Like the Consulate building, the structure had high ceilings, and the stone walls were accented by a floor of polished marble. Dwarf guards, dressed in brightly burnished breastplates and holding ceremonial spears, flanked a doorway. They snapped smartly to attention when the two Dwarf princes approached. One guard struck the butt of his spear on the ground in five even, measured strokes, and the doors swung cumbersomely inward.

The only word Elac could think of to describe the audience hall was "functional." The hall was wide, dotted here and there by stone columns. The floor was made of a smooth black stone, contrasting with the gray stone walls. Banners of the various kings who had ruled over Verlak lined the walls, and the current King's standard, a brown hawk perched upon a branch and set against a sky-blue background, hung over the throne. Ervik, King of the Dwarves, was consulting in quiet tones with a pair of Elves. He was a short man, even for a Dwarf, with graying hair and beard. At the group's approach, the Elves bowed and took their leave, one of them scowling darkly in Hadwyn's direction.

The King leaned back, slapping the arms of his marble seat. "My nephews!" he shouted in a deep voice. "What brings you here at this hour? You especially, Hadwyn. I figured you'd still be entertaining Ambassador Darlen's daughter."

Hadwyn coughed uncomfortably and looked away, but Gillen stepped forward with a fluid bow. "My Lord King, I bring honored guests. This is Silvayn, one of the mightiest mages of our time. He brings his apprentice, Adalyn, who is becoming a powerful mage in her own right. And this is Rilen, formerly the Elven Prime Minister's personal bodyguard, and Elac, a merchant by trade, from the Elf village of Lanor." The group bowed deeply, and the King surveyed his visitors.

"So these are the travelers the messengers told us about. Welcome to my kingdom!"

Silvayn stepped forward, leaning on his staff. "My Lord, gladly would I stand here and exchange pleasantries with you, but we are pressed for time. Our mission is of the utmost importance."

The King leaned forward, resting his elbows on his knees. "To what do I owe the pleasure of this visit?"

"I'm leading young Elac here on a pilgrimage across the continent of Pelacia. We are under orders from the Unity Council to retrieve certain artifacts and return them to the Council."

"What is it you need?"

"In your kingdom, we seek the Orion Stone."

King Ervik's jaw dropped in surprise, and his face flushed red. "The Orion Stone? What on earth would possess you to drag that accursed rock back into the light?"

"It is needed for a greater purpose, my Lord."

Ervik stroked his beard for several moments , considering the possibilities. Suddenly, his eyes narrowed shrewdly. It was only a momentary gesture, but Elac believed there was some surreptitious planning going through the King's mind.

"All right. The Orion Stone is yours, if you can manage to retrieve it. The problem is, the Stone is deep in an abandoned mine several leagues east of town. My Priests can supply you with a map." He glanced briefly at Hadwyn, and then quickly looked back to Silvayn. "You must be careful, however. The Priests who hid the stone conjured a guardian. I know not what form this guardian takes, but many treasure hunters have been reported missing in the mine."

"We appreciate any assistance you can offer in this business, your Majesty."

"Perhaps I can help you yet one more time. I will send my two nephews with you. Both are good men to have with you in a fight. Gillen is a Priest of Zantar, which could prove useful. Maybe Hadwyn can find a function for his war hammer besides cracking open ale barrels."

"War hammer?" Silvayn asked suddenly, whirling to face the two Dwarf Princes.

"Yes," Gillen said, looking at the ceiling, his mouth slightly agape, shaking his head slowly. "Almost every Dwarf in the army uses an axe, but he has to be different. The hammer he carries is hideous."

Silvayn raised one hand, palm out, and he closed his eyes and lowered his head in concentration. He chanted softly in the language of magic for several moments, then slowly raised his head.

"Your Majesty, we were told of certain people along the way who would join our quest, and we were warned that without them, we would fail. Your nephews are two of these people. I would like them to accompany us for the duration of our quest."

"How long is your quest likely to take?" Gillen asked, his brows furrowed in concern. "We have responsibilities here—"

"Nonsense!" the King roared, rising from his chair. Elac shrank back from this sudden onslaught, afraid of what the aging King would do next. "The Unity Council has spoken. You two are hereby relieved of all duties until the completion of the journey."

"As your Majesty commands," Hadwyn said in a voice dripping with sarcasm. He bowed deeply, spun on his heel, and strode purposely from the room. The King scowled darkly while the party took their leave, but he said nothing.

Hadwyn was already in the cart when the others emerged from the building, and he sat seething in stony silence for the duration of the ride back to the Unity Consulate. He leapt from the cart before it had rolled to a stop, his hands balled into fists. He stomped his way to the door, kicked the wooden portal aside, and stormed through the opening. Gillen held up a restraining hand to the others, motioning them to silence and urging them to wait outside. The door slammed shut behind Hadwyn, and was immediately followed by a loud crash.

Gillen shook his head darkly. "My brother has a violent temper sometimes. I could see this one coming the moment my uncle ordered us to accompany you. Give him a few minutes and we'll go in."

Elac stood in uncomfortable silence, listening to the sounds of Hadwyn's rage playing out in all its unrestrained fury. Finally, after several minutes, the door slid slowly open, and Hadwyn sheepishly poked his head outside. "It's safe now," he said with a rueful smile.

Elac followed the others inside, and he was amazed by the damage one Dwarf had done in such a short time. Furniture lay smashed into ruins, pictures were torn from the walls, their frames crushed, and gaping holes marred the walls. A servant was already dutifully cleaning the mess, the faintly detached look on his face giving Elac the impression this was a common occurrence.

Hadwyn had carefully avoided damaging the ale barrel, and he immediately resumed a drinking binge he had obviously started earlier. "How can he do this?" he raged. "The Kobolds will own this country before we return!" He drained his tankard in a few long gulps, and the ale was dripping from his beard. Without stopping, he reached to fill his tankard once more.

Silvayn looked at him sharply, his arms crossed. "The

Kobolds? What are they doing?"

Hadwyn was already deep into another tankard, so Gillen answered for him. "Our uncle has been allowing the Kobolds greater and greater freedoms in our country. It started with sweeping trade reforms, vastly increasing the commerce between our nations. This seemingly harmless decision led to an exchange of mining technology. The next thing we knew, our uncle had agreed to let the Kobold engineers explore our mines to compare our digging methods to their own. Now, the Kobolds have extensive maps of our entire mining complex, while we know practically nothing about theirs.

"The final straw came in the last week or so. There have been reports of strange creatures near our eastern borders, and they've been attacking travelers. The King decided to accept an offer of military assistance from the Kobolds, and their armies roam freely through the entire eastern half of Verlak."

Hadwyn slammed his empty tankard on the remains of a table. "We fought against this each step of the way, but my uncle just won't see it. He is no warrior. He has never even held a weapon in his hands. He has no idea what kind of tactical advantage he has handed them."

"This is indeed disturbing," Silvayn said. He sketched in the events at the Unity Council, whereby the Kobolds had gained passage to Human and Elven lands under the guise of hunting down the rogue Kobolds who had razed the village of Lanor.

Hadwyn growled something unintelligible. "Word of that reached us here, as well. In fact, according to the latest dispatches, there have been a few battles. It seems the Kobold army has succeeded in wiping out three separate patrols of the

Drablok clan. Two of those battles were witnessed by elements of the Elven army."

Elac chewed on his lip shrewdly. "So by sending you away, King Ervik hopes to eliminate the dissent from his affairs with the Kobolds."

"Indeed," Gillen answered. "Silvayn, I know you wouldn't ask for our help unless it was absolutely necessary, but if there was any way for you to find someone else to help you . . ."

He left his question hanging there, but Silvayn was already shaking his head, even before Adalyn answered for him. "Your participation was predetermined."

"If it helps any," Silvayn added, "by aiding us, in the long run, you will be doing Verlak a lot more good than by staying here, arguing with the King, and destroying the Unity Consulate."

Hadwyn gave a hearty laugh, drawing himself yet another tankard and raising it high. "Well spoken, my new friend. Here's to being a thorn in my uncle's side."

Chapter 7

T he party rode out of town early the next morning, much to Hadwyn's obvious discomfort. His hair was unkempt once again, and he winced looking into the rising sun. He wore a suit of splint mail armor over a dark brown tunic. A fierce helmet hung from the saddlebow of his small horse, with a long nosepiece and an exquisite carving of a bird of prey in flight mounted on top. The family crest bearing the familiar hawk was emblazoned on his burnished silver shield. Gillen was similarly outfitted, but Elac noticed one difference between the two warriors immediately. While Gillen had a standard battle-axe strapped to his back, Hadwyn bore a massive war hammer that Elac could only describe as intimidating. One side of the head of the hammer was a huge mallet, while on the opposite side was what Hadwyn affectionately referred to as the "crow's beak," a protruding cone of solid metal resembling the beak of some great bird of prey. The curving rod narrowed to a sharp point, and with the weight of that hammer behind it, Elac had to imagine it would penetrate almost any armor.

The road they followed wound through the rugged terrain, following the path of least resistance by staying away from the higher peaks. They were still below the tree line, and great copses of fir trees crowded in on both sides. By the time they stopped for their midday meal, snow was falling, great, feathery flakes drifting peacefully to the ground. An hour later, the snowfall had increased to the point where they could barely see fifty yards in front of them. Ice had formed in the exposed beards of the Dwarves, but they didn't appear to notice.

The sun was setting by the time Gillen called the group to a halt. In a hushed conference, he told them the entrance to the mine where they would find the Orion Stone lay just ahead. They could take the horses inside a short distance to get them out of the weather, then proceed on foot. Gillen turned his horse from the road and led the way cautiously into the surrounding trees. Elac wasn't sure what to expect, although the Dwarf's obviously warlike precautions led him to believe there was trouble of some kind ahead.

In the distance, a pair of stone figures slowly materialized through the blinding snow, taking shape before Elac's eyes as if they were emerging from a dream. They were statues of great Dwarf warriors, armored in ring mail and bearing massive battle-axes. The two giant guardians flanked a gaping darkness in the side of the mountain. Gillen dismounted, lit a pair of torches, and he and his brother led the party inside. Elac grabbed his bow and quiver, and his short sword was already secured about his waist. Silvayn muttered an incantation, accented with a sharp clap of his hands, and a ball of light appeared in front of him, floating higher to illuminate the cavern. The two Dwarves looked at each other, shrugged, and doused the torches.

They moved deeper into the tunnel, the Dwarves in the lead with Rilen close behind, and Elac in the middle with Silvayn. Adalyn trailed behind, acting as a rear guard. Silvayn's globe of light provided enough illumination for Elac to see some distance ahead. The tunnel, while roughhewn, was solidly buttressed at regular intervals by thick wooden beams.

Rilen snapped his fingers once, then placed a solitary finger to his lips. Gillen looked back, brows furrowed in confusion. Rilen pointed to his ears, then motioned to their front. Elac carefully fitted an arrow to his bowstring, nervously fingering the fletching. Hadwyn hefted his terrifying hammer, and Rilen drew his short sword without a sound. The three warriors crept forward, the others close behind.

It was then Elac noticed something was wrong. To their immediate front was an area of absolute darkness, which even Silvayn's magic wasn't penetrating. "Hold," Silvayn told them in a normal tone of voice. "Let's see what lies ahead."

The Dwarves stopped, weapons held at the ready, while Silvayn cast another spell. He gestured toward the wall of darkness with his staff as if he held a lance. With a sudden detonation that set Elac's ears to ringing, the shadow ruptured into shards, accented by a sharp cry of pain from somewhere ahead. Six Dwarves stood revealed in the passage, each bearing maces and cloaked in robes of the purest white. Chain mail was in evidence beneath the robes, although none had shields or helmets. An Elf was behind them, also cloaked in white, but he was down on one knee gasping for breath. He had long white hair tied in a ponytail, and his thin white beard was neatly trimmed. The tallest of the Dwarves glanced back at the Elf.

"State your business," he growled.

"Our business is our own," Gillen answered, bringing up his shield to reveal the family crest. "You would be wise not to interfere."

"I'm sorry, your Highness," the Elf said, regaining his feet. "But none shall be allowed to pass, even were the King himself here. The danger is too great."

Hadwyn stepped forward, his hammer held high. "So you would kill us to protect us?"

"Your body is not what is endangered, but rather your soul. It has been foretold that should the Orion Stone be allowed to surface again, the Evil One would use it to unlock the Gates of the Dead. He would unleash a darkness such as this world has never known."

"We will have the Stone," Silvayn told him calmly. "I suggest you stand aside."

"We cannot."

With a roar of rage, Hadwyn rushed forward, his deadly hammer already falling in a killing stroke. A white-robed Dwarf hastily raised his mace to deflect the blow, but the hammer barely slowed, blasting through the Dwarf's defense and crashing with lethal force against his head. Another Dwarf raised his mace to strike a blow from Hadwyn's side, but Gillen's axe caught him in the side, cutting through the chain mail and spilling his entrails on the cavern floor. Rilen's bow snapped twice in rapid succession, and two Dwarves collapsed to the ground, arrows protruding from their unprotected throats. While the remaining two Dwarves rushed the party, the Elf behind them chanted, his voice echoing harshly over the din of combat.

"I want one alive!" Silvayn shouted.

Rilen grunted, cast his bow aside, and charged ahead with his short sword held ready. Hadwyn swung his hammer, taking a Dwarf in the side and sending him sprawling into the cavern wall. Rilen parried a strike from a mace, and his return blow severed the Dwarf's arm. The mace fell with a hollow clatter, and the Dwarf staggered back with a sharp cry of pain. Adalyn moved forward swiftly, setting the tip of her sword against his throat.

"Don't move," she told him.

Suddenly, the Elf's chanting rose to a hoarse shout, and he pointed to the fighters with both hands extended, palms outward. Silvayn shouted an oath and rushed forward, cloak billowing behind him, his staff raised urgently. Twin flashes of lightning shot forth from the Elf's hands, streaking across the cave with a thunderclap that drove Elac to his knees. Silvayn extended his staff, caught one of the bolts, and tumbled to the ground. The other bolt struck the Dwarf Adalyn had captured. With a horrifying scream of anguish, the Dwarf writhed in pain, flashes of blue-white energy rippling across his body. Adalyn jumped clear, whirling to face the Elf, sword held up in defense.

The Elf before them moaned in sudden agony, and he held his hands up before his face in disbelief. "No!" he shrieked, his body contorting with pain. Great creases appeared on his exposed skin, and he fell forward onto his side, clutching his stomach. A howling wind tore through the mine, increasing in intensity and moaning with the voices of a thousand tortured souls. A new darkness formed over the supine form of the enemy mage, swirling in a vortex, moving faster as it grew. The white-robed body rose from the ground, arms flung wide, and he appeared to have aged a hundred years in a matter of moments. The horrible screams of the dying man grew more desperate, and his body spun with the maelstrom about him. There was a final flash of light, and with a deafening *snap*, the vast swirling darkness was gone, taking the figure of the Elf mage with it.

Elac couldn't find words to voice a question, but instead stood in place, mouth agape, staring at the blackened spot on the floor. Silvayn was still down, gasping for breath, and Adalyn went immediately to his side. Rilen was the first to shake off his surprise, sheathing his sword and examining the Dwarf knocked senseless by Hadwyn's war hammer.

"What happened?" Elac said finally.

"He was a user of Life Magic," Adalyn said, without looking up from Silvayn. "For some reason, he attempted to harm us with magic, which isn't allowed. His physical form was destroyed, and his soul is now damned for all eternity to the vile punishments of Malator."

"What in the name of all that is good and holy would possess a mage of his power and experience to do such a thing?" Gillen asked. "He had to know the consequences."

The Dwarf whom Rilen was examining stirred. "We will do anything to protect the Stone," he gasped. He convulsed in a fit of coughing, and a fountain of blood erupted from his mouth. Another fit of coughing took him, racking his body in spasmodic waves. With one last gasp, he finally lay still, his unseeing eyes staring at the tunnel's ceiling. Rilen placed a hand on the side of his neck, feeling for a pulse. After a short pause, he shrugged and shook his head, wiping his bloody hand on the Dwarf's stained robes. Gillen whirled angrily to face his brother, an accusation already forming on his lips.

"Hey, I tried," a smiling Hadwyn protested. "At least I didn't use the pointed end."

While the two brothers argued, Silvayn staggered to his feet. Adalyn handed him a waterskin, and he drank deeply. Elac peered more closely, shocked at the mage's disheveled look. His eyes had dark rings beneath them as if he hadn't slept for days, and his cheeks looked drawn and cadaverous. Adalyn helped him over to an outcropping of rock, and Silvayn slowly settled onto his stone seat with a grateful nod, his breathing coming in great gasps.

"I need a moment to catch my breath," he told them finally. "I sensed what the Elf was doing, but it caught me off guard. I didn't realize how desperate he was to stop us. I didn't have time to work a counterspell, so I had to absorb the spell's energy. He was actually quite powerful, and that spell was almost the end of me."

Silvayn stared at the scarred floor where the Elf had fallen, his eyes appearing unfocused as if his mind were elsewhere. "I believe it would be best if you went on without me." He held up a trembling hand to stop the protest from Adalyn. "Adalyn, I'd like you to stay here with me. The rest of you can safely get the Stone. It should be in a large cave, probably on some type of altar. Be careful . . . it may be protected by traps, or even by magical wards."

"As a Priest of Zantar, I believe I can avoid any mystical traps,"

Gillen volunteered. "I'm more concerned about this 'guardian' my uncle mentioned." He turned to his brother with an accusing glare, but his brother simply shrugged his indifference.

"Next time we want one alive, you hit him."

Elac noticed it had grown considerably darker in the cave, as if Silvayn's power was waning. Adalyn apparently realized this, as well, so she cast her own light spell, and Silvayn allowed his to fade away. Rilen, too, produced a magical globe of light, somewhat dimmer than those Adalyn and Silvayn had produced, but still bright enough to see by. Elac looked back to Silvayn, and he saw the dark look on the Elf's face when Rilen spoke the words of magic.

After a short distance, the passage opened into a vast cave, with the roof lost in the gloom above them. The walls were much more jagged than what the tunnels had been, and Elac assumed it was a natural cave. The floor was the only place where the Dwarves appeared to have made modifications; it was too smooth to have been formed naturally. A strange, fungus-like growth covered much of the walls, giving off an eerie, yellow glow. Directly across from Elac and his companions was a statue of a creature Elac had never seen before. It had the massively muscled body of a Dwarf, but the head of a serpent. Standing ten feet tall, its hands were clasped together in front of the enormous chest. A closer look told Elac there was something in its hands, as though the statue was protecting it, and he could only assume it was the Orion Stone. Rilen allowed his light globe to dissipate.

Hadwyn edged forward, but his brother caught his shoulder and held him back. Gillen bowed his head in silent concentration, his eyes closed. Finally, he opened his eyes and gazed out across the room. Under his careful scrutiny, several areas on the floor began to glow, dimly at first but growing brighter in intensity, most of them roughly in the shape of squares about four feet across. The soft red light from the enchanted spots contrasted sharply with the light from the fungus-encrusted walls. Strangely, the floor around the statue was free of the glow from Gillen's spell, as if something about the statue was keeping his magic at bay.

"Avoid the spots that are glowing," Hadwyn advised them tersely. "They mark the traps guarding the Stone."

"Wait," Rilen said, looking rapidly around the room. "There has to be more to this. As fanatical as those Dwarves were about protecting the Stone, I don't think they would've only protected the area with a few easily found traps."

Hadwyn hefted his mighty war hammer. "Wait here."

"Watch for trouble," Rilen warned him.

While Hadwyn edged forward, Elac scanned the room, and he realized the tunnel they had followed was the only way into or out of the grotto. The statue itself was set against the far wall, so there couldn't be any foes hiding behind it.

Hammer in hand, the Dwarf reached the statue. However, instead of immediately seizing the Orion Stone from the statue's hands, he meticulously inspected the area, checking for signs of any traps his brother's spell might have missed. Finally satisfied, he returned to the front of the stone figure, took a deep breath, and reached carefully forward. He grasped the fist-sized Stone and slowly lifted it free.

Hadwyn stood immobile for the span of several heartbeats,

eyes everywhere. Finally, he set down his hammer and placed the Stone into a pouch at his waist. Retrieving his hammer, he turned to retrace his steps. He only went a few feet before he noticed a problem: at his approach, the areas that had been glowing, dimmed, then faded out completely.

Gillen chewed his lip shrewdly. "It might be the Orion Stone canceling out my magic."

Hadwyn nodded, untied the pouch containing the object of their quest, and gave it a heave. The pouch sailed across the room to where Gillen stood waiting. The glowing squares around Hadwyn immediately brightened, and he stepped forward once more. But Elac noticed something the others hadn't. With the removal of the Orion Stone, the hands of the enormous statue were glowing just as brightly as the areas of the floor. It was another trap, hidden by the presence of the Stone itself.

"Hadwyn! Behind you!" he shouted.

Hadwyn spun on his heel, his veteran instincts warning him as much as Elac's cry. The eyes of the statue opened, lit from within as if by a wicked yellow flame. It straightened, towering above Hadwyn, and lumbered forward. One stone fist swung downward, missing the Dwarf by inches and slamming into the ground, sending shards of the stone floor flying. Elac drew his bow and fired, but the arrow bounced off the creature's stone skin.

Hadwyn swung his hammer, taking the statue in the side. A low hiss escaped its reptilian lips, and it raised its hand for another strike. "*Give . . . me . . . the . . . Stone . . .*"

Gillen struck from behind, his axe drawing a shower of sparks when he hewed at a great stone leg. With a sweep of its arm, the statue sent Hadwyn flying. Miraculously, his tumbling body missed the traps dotting the ground, but when he stopped rolling, he lay still. Rilen darted in with his short sword, slashing the creature in the back and moving out of its reach before it could retaliate. It made a futile swipe at Gillen before turning its attention to Rilen.

"Keep it busy!" Gillen shouted, retreating a few steps to open his pack. From off to the side, Elac heard a weak groan come from Hadwyn. Elac allowed himself a glance to check on his comrade, and he saw the Dwarf shaking his head and struggling to stand. Hadwyn managed to rise up onto his hands and knees, but his trembling limbs would lift him no farther.

Then Gillen was back in the fight. From somewhere in his pack, he had produced a great flail. The handle was two feet long and wrapped in leather. A chain, at least six feet in length, connected the handle to a spiked ball of steel. Gillen swung the flail over his head, and the chain whistled ominously through the musty air. He planted his feet firmly and delivered a crushing blow to the side of the statue's head, sending great chunks of shattered stone flying and leaving a gaping hole in the side of the serpent-like skull. With astonishing agility for so bulky a creature, it spun to engage Gillen with a hiss of rage. He wielded the flail in its deadly arc once more, readying himself for the statue's approach.

But the blow never came. When the stone nightmare took two steps toward Gillen, its huge bulk dropped into a suddenly open hole in the ground. One hand reached out abruptly, caught the edge of the trap, and temporarily halted the descent. In a display of raw tenacity, Hadwyn struggled to his feet and rushed to the edge of the trap, his hammer already descending. The blow took the statue on the hand holding the pit's edge, shattering the fingers. It dropped into the pit with a great clatter of stone, and disappeared from their view.

"Why did it step into its own trap?" Elac asked, panting heavily even though he himself had not gone hand-to-hand with the creature.

"The Orion Stone," Hadwyn answered simply. "The Stone cancels magic within a few feet of it, so the statue couldn't sense where the traps were. I looked for the trap closest to it before I moved up and attacked."

They carefully backed out of the room and retraced their steps, finding Silvayn looking much better than he had when they left. Although Adalyn wanted more time for Silvayn and Hadwyn to recover before they resumed their trek, Rilen found the proposal to be unwise, fearing another attack by an as-yet-unseen guardian of the Stone. They led their horses from the mine, and Gillen handed the pouch containing the Orion Stone to Elac.

"This quest is ultimately for you," Gillen told him solemnly. "As such, I believe this artifact is yours."

Elac pulled the Orion Stone from the pouch. From his earlier glimpse of the Stone, he had expected something in the nature of a perfectly round orb, but it was actually flatter, almost like a disk. It was four inches thick in the center, maybe half that at the edges, and five inches across. A rainbow spectrum of colors swirled sluggishly across the face, eddying rapidly where his fingers touched the smooth surface. He stared in wonder at the beauty of the Stone, then tucked it safely back inside the pouch.

They returned to the highway and turned west toward the Dwarf's capital at Centare. They only stayed in the saddle for about an hour before Rilen led them away from the road once more. They slipped off the thoroughfare about a hundred yards into the trees, and set up camp. While Adalyn and Gillen checked on the injured members of their party, Rilen returned to the roadway and erased all traces of their passage.

They reached the city of Centare by noon, and the two Dwarf princes gained immediate entry for the travelers. They found an inn near the harbor, and while the others took care of their accommodations, Elac and Rilen went to the harbor master to see about booking passage to the Elven port at Barton. They arranged the transport under false names, in a further attempt at deception. Elac didn't see the necessity for the skullduggery, but he knew better than to question Silvayn's judgment.

❦ ❀ ✪ ❀ ❀

Two days later, they led their horses down the gangplank and into the city of Barton. Unlike the Human port cities Elac had seen, Barton appeared to be a very clean and orderly place. The usual smell of dead fish hung in the air, an odor that seemed to be unavoidable around so many ships, but the Humans' casual disregard for cleanliness was not in evidence here. Even the tar protecting the wooden buildings from the elements had been painted pleasing colors. The dock workers, mostly Elves, bustled about the wharfs, moving freight from ships to warehouses.

Rilen led them into the heart of the town, and stopped in front of a brown stone building. He told them to stay with the horses, and he strolled purposefully to the main doors, where two Elves were standing in idle conversation. He spoke with them briefly, then motioned the others forward. They left their horses in the care of the two Elves and followed Rilen inside.

The room Rilen led them to was at the back of the building. He knocked twice before opening the door, then ushered the group inside. A lone Elf sat behind a mahogany desk, its top covered with stacks of parchment. His jaw dropped in astonishment when Rilen walked into his office, and he leapt to his feet and rushed around his desk to greet Rilen in a great bear hug.

"Rilen! By the hands of Gentra, I didn't expect to see you here."

Rilen turned to his companions, grinning broadly. "Everyone, this is Serano, an old friend of mine. I met him when I was in the service of Prime Minister Lornell. Most of the time, he serves as a Priest of Gentra." Elac recognized the name of the Elven goddess of healing, and when Rilen finished making the introductions, he bowed deeply. Serano poured glasses of wine while Rilen confided in the party that Serano also served in the Intelligence Service, and would therefore have information about what was going on in the East.

Elac sipped his wine while Rilen and Serano began their discussion of current events. Serano returned to his desk, checked a few documents, and sat down heavily.

"What the Unity Council is doing doesn't make any sense. They're allowing an enemy force inside their borders unchallenged. And the Kobold raiders are getting bolder, even going so far as to attack caravans guarded by groups of mercenaries. Although there have been a few battles between the renegades and the regular Kobold army, most of the time the Kobold forces arrive too late to help. Conveniently late, unless I miss my guess. As if what was going on in Unity wasn't bad enough, the Council has to add this idiocy to their list of problems."

"Do you mean the kidnappings?" Elac asked.

"We don't know that they are truly kidnappings, since there have been no ransom demands. There has only been one witness, a young boy, and about all he could tell the officials was that one of the men involved had a tattoo of a dagger encircled by a ring."

Elac started. "Near the Caldan Forest, we were set upon by a group of bandits. One of them had such a tattoo. It looked more like a shackle than a ring, to me."

Serano cocked his head to the side. "There might be a connection, I suppose, but it's probably not an unusual tattoo design among ruffians. The initial disappearances were businessmen, but now the victims are becoming more prominent. Just two days ago, the wife of interim Councilor Falstoff disappeared."

Silvayn set his cup down, cursing under his breath. "That's not good. He was our greatest supporter on the Council. If he is distracted by personal tragedy . . ."

"Actually, from the information I've been receiving, Falstoff is carrying on business as usual. You know these politicians. They can be very single-minded about their careers. How much do you know about him?"

"Falstoff? We know he's a temporary member of the Council. I realize he's overly ambitious, but it's not an unusual trait to find in politicians."

Serano rubbed his eyes, stood, and walked to an oak filing

cabinet. He rifled through numerous packets before he seemed to find what he wanted, and returned to his seat carrying a stack of documents. "Falstoff was born in a small farming village, left home to attend the university at Branig, and began his career in politics immediately after graduation.

"In the year 5106, he was elected mayor of Branig, eventually became an advisor to the Duke of Branig, and married his daughter. In 5116, he was elected the youngest mayor in the history of the Humans' capital city of Palim. He frequently drinks to excess, and he seeks other women's beds. According to rumor, the Duke of Branig is aware of Falstoff's adultery and has been working to expose him. Or, at least, he was before his disappearance."

"That just leaves the question of where we go from here," Adalyn said.

"Calda," Silvayn replied. "We need to get permission from Prime Minister Lornell before we can even get near the Springs of Calda."

"That won't be easy," Serano warned him. "A local businessman was recently arrested for selling water from the Springs, so security is tight."

"We'll have to try to convince her." Silvayn frowned. "And we have to find out who is supposed to join us from Caldala."

Hadwyn stroked his thick beard, lost in thought. "I just can't figure what skills this person could have that we would need. Rilen is the best bowman around, and he, my brother, and I are obviously along for the fighting. Silvayn and Adalyn can handle anything as far as magic is needed, and the quest centers on Elac. What else do we need?"

Elac chuckled. "But don't forget my skills. If we need to buy supplies, I'm your man."

"Don't sell yourself short." Unexpectedly, it was Rilen who came to his defense. "Your skills with a sword and a bow are improving. And besides, your knowledge of politics has already proved useful."

Hadwyn gave a short laugh. "He's not very good with an ale mug yet, but we're working on that."

❁ ⊗ ★ ⊕ ⊗

They spent the night as Serano's guests, and at first light they were riding toward Calda. Within the first hour, the ancient trees of the vast Caldan Forest loomed on the horizon, and they were soon riding in the comfortable shade of the towering oaks. As the dazzling rays of sunset blazed across the land, they passed through the gates of Calda.

The first thing Elac noticed was the structure of their buildings. All were made of wood, harvested from the forest sheltering most of the Elven homeland. Some were firmly embedded on the ground, but many were nestled high in the branches of the trees, accessible only by rope ladders or long, winding wooden stairs.

Rilen led them to the north side of the village, where they encountered a second set of gates. Rising from behind the thick, wooden wall, the palace towered into the sky, surmounting the tips of the oak trees surrounding it. Guards in ceremonial golden-hued armor flanked the gate, while a number of soldiers in the more traditional green and brown woodland garb patrolled from behind the wall's battlements, their longbows in hand.

The palace itself was a glaring contrast to the wooden buildings Elac had seen previously. The walls were made mostly of unpolished granite, and the roof from wooden shingles. The tall, curving doors were at least half again as tall as anyone Elac had ever met, and they swung ponderously open at the group's approach. A servant offered beverages, but Hadwyn frowned sharply upon learning water was the only drink available.

"The Prime Minister finds something morally wrong with drinking ale and wine," Rilen told him. "She refuses to allow anyone in her presence who has been drinking."

"That reminds me," Silvayn said, his own water mug close at hand. "You and the Prime Minister are not on the best of terms. Perhaps it would be best if Elac and I met with her alone."

Hadwyn gave an indignant snort, reaching into a small pack at his waist while his brother laughed. He searched through the pouch briefly, his eyes focused on the ceiling in concentration. Finally, with a smile, he removed a bottle and worked the stopper free. While Gillen looked on with a frown, Hadwyn took a long drink from the bottle.

"Feel better?" Gillen asked, crossing his arms.

"Much, thanks."

There was a disturbance in the hallway beyond the sitting room, and Rilen was on his feet immediately, his hand resting on the hilt of his sword. Elac peered through the doorway where an Elf, dressed in brightly colored finery and with a face red with suppressed rage, was arguing with a young woman. She was wearing a plain, gray tunic, with woolen slacks and leather boots. She appeared to be slightly shorter than Elac, and he realized even that height was probably an illusion created by the size of the heels on her boots. Two guards were rapidly approaching, and Silvayn and Rilen stepped into the hallway.

"Guards! I want this woman arrested! She has stolen from me!"

Surprisingly, Silvayn stepped into the hallway. "What has happened here?"

"This thief stole my signet ring. I used it to seal a few documents for the Agriculture Minister, and a moment later it was gone. She is the only one who could have taken it."

"He's lying," the woman said simply. She brushed her blond hair back from her face, and Elac was surprised to discover she was a Human. He had never considered Human women to be attractive, but the closer he looked, the more he had to revise his opinion. "You can search me if you want. I have no ring."

The two guards rummaged through her pockets, and she stood still without objection, even when their search became more personal than was absolutely necessary. A few minutes later, one of the guards looked to the incensed Elf standing before them and shook his head.

Silvayn cocked his head curiously. "What were you doing here in the palace?"

"I came to petition Prime Minister Lornell for the release of my brother. He has been arrested for a crime he didn't commit, and I would see him set free."

"What is your name?"

She looked at him curiously, eyes narrowing. "I'm Jayrne, and my brother's name is Bollaz. Why?"

"I'm on my way to see the Prime Minister. I'll speak to her on your brother's behalf."

"What do you want in return?"

"I'll explain later."

She gave a short laugh, shaking her head. "Not a chance, old man. You'll find those girls at the riverfront hotels."

Silvayn looked at Rilen in confusion, then laughed. "No, not that. I need a favor."

"Forget it," the nobleman interrupted. "She's going to the dungeon for theft."

"Your Grace," one of the guards said, "she didn't have your ring."

"Arrest her anyway! She must have hidden it somewhere in the palace, and she means to come back for it later." He continued his tirade, and the guards led the protesting woman away.

A half hour later, the servant returned to tell the party the Prime Minister would see them. Silvayn glibly told the servant that only he and Elac would need to talk to the Elven ruler. The man shrugged his acceptance and led Elac and Silvayn from the room.

They followed the Elf through the palace, and Elac tried to ignore the curious stares from other Elves who passed them by. To his surprise, the Elf didn't lead them to some massive throne room, but instead to a rather elaborate outdoor garden situated somewhere in the center of the palace itself. There was a maze of narrow paths, allowing the caretakers to reach the different flower beds for watering, weeding, and feeding the foliage.

Prime Minister Lornell's throne was situated along the rear wall of the garden. Dressed in loose-fitting green robes with gold trim, she sat primly upon her throne, which was carved from the trunk of an enormous, fallen oak tree, and engraved with ornate designs. A crown made of tightly woven leaves from various trees sat gingerly upon her head.

The Elf who led them to the Prime Minister bowed deeply while he made the introductions, then backed out of Lornell's presence without any further pomp. The Prime Minister sat silently for a few moments, studying the two travelers.

"What brings Silvayn, of the school at Aleria, and Elac, merchant of the late village of Lanor, before me?"

"A matter of utmost importance, your Majesty," Silvayn answered. "We have been tasked with a quest by the seers of Divinity, and it leads us across the length and breadth of the continent of Pelacia. We must acquire certain objects and companions through the course of our travels, lest the world fall under a certain, and dire, period of darkness."

"How can I help you, mighty Silvayn? What small thing do you need from the throne of the Elves?"

"A mere pittance, Majesty. One matter involves the companions I spoke of. The seers gave me the ability to recognize these individuals without ever having seen them before. I found one such person in your palace mere moments ago." This time, Elac's shock showed itself, his jaw dropping open wide despite his best efforts. "She is a Human named Jayrne. I need her to accompany me on this quest."

Prime Minister Lornell propped her chin up on one hand. "What authority do I have over a Human to oblige her to go on such a quest?"

"Her brother is a prisoner in your dungeons. I know not what crime he stands accused of, but offering a pardon in exchange for her cooperation would probably be quite compelling."

The Prime Minister considered the proposal gravely for a few moments. "It shall be done. Give their names to the scribe when you leave, and as long as he has not committed a high crime against the crown, he shall be set free upon your return from this quest."

"It's a bit more complicated than that, my Lady. She was just arrested for theft, without evidence, on the order of Minister Charoff."

"That matter will be disposed of, as well."

"Thank you, your Majesty. There is one other matter. We were instructed to acquire a vial of water from the Springs of Calda, and—"

"Absolutely out of the question!" the Prime Minister roared, rising from her throne. "Those waters have been sullied in the past by lowborn worthless scum who wanted to turn a quick profit, and I have vowed never to allow it to happen again!"

"I understand the situation, your Majesty, but could we not—"

"Begone! We shall speak no more of this matter. Give your other request to the scribe, but get out of my sight before I change my mind about helping you at all!"

Chapter 8

"Y ou want me to what?" Jayrne was almost doubled over with laughter. "You'd have a better chance with the other idea I thought you wanted, old man."

"I want you to come with us on a quest," Silvayn told her calmly. "As I explained to you, the seers at Divinity have said you must accompany us, or our task will fail, to the world's doom. We need you."

"You think I care about the rest of the world? Forget it. The world has never cared anything about me, so why should I be concerned if it ends?"

"Because I have arranged for the pardon of both you and your brother, but it will only happen after we return from this quest and I report back to Prime Minister Lornell."

Jayrne bit her lip, a gesture Elac found to be quite alluring. "You've got me, haven't you, old man? What happens if I go along, but you don't make it back? What then? Will my brother still be released?"

Silvayn shrugged calmly. "I don't know. I'd say the

possibility of my demise would give you added incentive to watch after my protection."

"I guess I have no choice. Who else is with us?"

"I'll introduce you to the others shortly. We will be leaving Calda in the morning, so we need to eat and get some rest."

An hour later, the party was assembled in Silvayn's room at the rather plain inn where they were staying. Dinner was still being prepared, and Elac found the aromas wafting up from the kitchen to be very enticing. He sipped at the ale in his mug, watching Hadwyn finish his second tall glass of the bitter drink. As usual, Gillen sat nearby, frowning but saying nothing.

"We still need water from the Springs," Silvayn said. "I'd hoped the Prime Minister would listen to reason, but she seems to be very stubborn."

"Now there's a bit of news," Rilen murmured, swirling the ale in his mug and staring at it indifferently.

"Can't we just get some from the Calda River itself?" Adalyn asked. "It's the same water, since it all comes from the Springs."

Silvayn was already shaking his head. "No, the qualities of the water are too diluted outside the Springs themselves. We must obtain water directly from the main pool at the river's source. We also can't risk trying to obtain some on the black market. We might get lucky and buy the real thing, but we would be just as likely to buy a vial of water from Unity Lake. I'd hate to come to the end of the quest, only to find we've been duped. No, we have to get to the Springs. Rilen, any ideas?"

"Good luck. The Springs are guarded night and day by an entire brigade of Elven archers. They have orders to shoot anyone trying to sneak past them, so I don't advise stealth. The only way anyone gets past the sentry lines is with an order signed by a high-ranking official within the government. I don't think any of them would risk their careers to help us on this one."

"I can forge a document," Jayrne said, her soft voice offering a solution. "I even have the perfect name in mind: Environmental Minister Charoff, the man who accosted me in the hallway. Give me an hour, and the sentries will think we have the blessings of the Prime Minister herself."

"One problem," Gillen countered. "All official documents must have the seal of the issuing dignitary, and the guards are going to know our order is phony without it."

"Oh, so all we need is an official-looking stamp?" Jayrne asked, removing a boot, her brown eyes wide with innocence. She twisted the heel, and it separated from the rest of the shoe. Jayrne dumped something from the heel into her hand, set it on the table, and replaced her boot. "Do you mean a stamp such as you would make with a minister's signet ring?"

❀ ⊗ ★ ⊕ ⊛

They rode out of town later that evening, ostensibly taking the road to Southton on their way to the Humans' capital city of Palim. They traveled at a steady pace, not slowing even when the sun went down, plunging the forest around them into near-absolute darkness. The Elves, ever conscious of the sanctity of life, didn't clear-cut the trees of the Caldan Forest when they had made their system of roads. On the contrary, their roads tended to meander through the trees, following small clearings and disturbing as few trees as possible. As a result, nighttime on an Elven road resulted in an almost complete lack of illumination, especially with the ancient law banning torches on the forest roads for fear of fires.

They stopped before passing the point where the road to Lakeshore broke away and turned southeast. Rilen led the group off the road and into the forest, turning north toward their true destination at the Springs of Calda. Silvayn had decided heading south first was a necessary deception, given the attitude of the Prime Minister. In fact, before they had traveled two blocks from the palace, Jayrne had identified a hooded, cloaked man skulking along behind them and dogging their steps.

If it had been dark on the roadway, then the forest could only be described as impenetrably black. Elac could only see a few feet in front of him, barely able to discern the lithe form of Jayrne in her leather armor riding in front of him. If not for the sounds of the horses passing through the undergrowth, Elac feared the group might become separated.

It took two hours to reach the road from Barton to Calda, and Rilen motioned for the others to remain hidden in the woods while he dismounted and moved ahead. He ghosted closer to the road, then slid back into the surrounding foliage. Elac suspected the Elven hunter had seen someone on the road, a suspicion proven correct moments later when a group of four Humans rolled past in a crude wagon, some unseen goods hidden under a tarp.

The wagon rattled out of sight, and Rilen once again crept closer to the road. He gave a low whistle, and the others came up as swiftly as the trees would allow. They crossed the roadway and returned to the trees on the other side, moving once again in single file.

It was nearing midnight when he heard the sounds of running water somewhere to their front. Silvayn called a welcome halt, and they set up their camp near the banks of the Calda River. While the Dwarves and Rilen gathered for a final planning session, Silvayn and Adalyn worked by candlelight to prepare their forged document for the garrison at the Springs. Jayrne set up her bedroll, obviously planning to turn in rather than join in the discourse.

"Need any help?" Elac asked her.

"I've done this before," she told him, not even bothering to look up.

Elac was somewhat taken aback by her abrasive attitude, but he decided to try once more to draw her into a conversation. "I hope your brother is okay."

She snorted. "My brother is an idiot. I promised our mother I would take care of him, though, so here I am."

Elac knelt beside her as she lay down. "I'm sorry you were forced to come along with us."

"I'll be here for as long as it takes to get my moron brother out of the dungeon, but not a second longer. Now, if you don't mind, I'd like to get some sleep." Without another word, she rolled over and quite deliberately turned her back on him.

Dawn came early, and the group rode north along the riverbank, following the swiftly flowing waters to their source. The trees were thinner there, and they made better time. Shortly after lunch, they rode to a halt in front of a series of low earthen breastworks marking the defensive perimeter for the Elves guarding the Springs of Calda. A group of twenty

Elves galloped forth to meet them. The leader dismounted, and Silvayn indicated his friends should do the same.

"Well met, Sergeant," Silvayn told him grandly. "We have come to fill a small waterskin with the magical waters of the legendary Springs of Calda, to use their divine properties for the betterment of the villagers under our tutelage. We have the proper documents for your perusal."

Silvayn handed the papers to the perplexed soldier, and Elac found himself wondering if the poor man understood half of what the aged wizard had just told him. The Sergeant carefully studied the wax seal on the sheaf of papers Silvayn handed him before apparently deciding it was indeed the mark of the Environmental Minister. He broke the seal and read through the papers, lips pursed, then motioned the Elves behind him to stand aside.

They left their horses with the sentries, which Elac believed a bit imprudent, considering they might have to leave in a hurry. Following the Elf Sergeant, they walked along a forest path dotted here and there by wildflowers. With the ground turning rockier and the trees thinning out, they reached the Springs of Calda.

Elac felt his spirits soar. He had never seen such beauty in his entire life. Although the waters of the Springs were quite deep, they were crystal clear, and he could see schools of trout swimming around the rocky bottom. In the center, the pool was roiling where water jetted up from far underground to breach the surface and fountain into the air. Even the simple act of breathing around the Springs seemed magical, filling him with a sense of well-being and erasing his aches and pains from the road.

Silvayn stepped forward, waterskin held high above his head in both hands. "Praises be to Gentra, Maya, and Novia, whose divine grace has brought us to this magnificent place. May their hands bless this water and all those who protect it."

He handed the waterskin to Adalyn, who knelt and held it underwater. After a few long moments, she stood and placed the stopper back in the skin, returning it to Silvayn.

"So have we completed our awesome task. Blessed be those who serve here." Silvayn bowed to the pool, turned, and led the way back down the path. They returned to their horses, where Silvayn secured the waterskin deep inside one of his packs. The others remounted, and Silvayn bowed deeply to their escort.

"My thanks, again, Sergeant. You have performed your duties well, and I will mention your help and thoroughness in my report upon our return."

The two shook hands, and Silvayn climbed into his saddle. They followed the river south for a few miles before turning due west. Silvayn explained to them while they rode that he planned for them to return to Barton, where they would take ship to Palim. There was no sense in riding the whole way through the dense forest, he explained, so they set out for the open plains between the Caldan Forest and the Palim Sea.

They stopped along some unnamed stream, where they replenished their supply of water before eating lunch. While Elac was eating a meal of hearty stew, he sneaked a glance at Jayrne, who sat with her back against a large rock near the gently sloping bank. His hand stopped halfway to his mouth when he saw her pull an exquisite jeweled dagger from her belt, which she used to slice a piece of cheese. Since his last approach had ended in rejection, he decided to try conversation from a distance.

"Nice knife."

"It works."

Again with the short answers. "Where did you get it?"

"I stole it."

At least she's talking. "From whom?"

She shrugged, still not looking up from her meal. "The Elf who led us through the woods to the Springs."

Hadwyn choked on his drink. "What if you'd been caught?"

"I've never been caught." Elac spied the slightest hint of a smile, with small dimples appearing in her cheeks.

"What about Minister Charoff?" Adalyn asked, daintily eating a slice of bread.

"He saw what I wanted him to see. I needed to be arrested so I could discover where my brother was being held. They would never have found the ring, and the matter would have been dropped. After my release, I would have been able to free my brother."

"Clever," Elac admired. "Just how good are you?"

Jayrne looked up finally, turning the full force of her smile loose on Elac, who immediately blushed despite his best efforts to hide it. "How many bottles of water from the Springs do you think we'll need? If Silvayn's isn't enough, I have a few spares in my pack."

"Water and knives aren't all you've stolen," Adalyn told her, glancing slyly at Elac.

"Your talents may just prove useful," Gillen said, brushing crumbs from his beard.

Hadwyn gave a hearty laugh. "They already have! And all this time, we were expecting to add an Elf, since we were in Caldala."

They reached Barton shortly before sunset, and Silvayn wasted no time in booking their passage to Palim. The following morning, the ship sailed out of the harbor with the tide. Silvayn made everyone stay below decks until they were well out of sight of the Elven city, just to be safe. When Elac emerged from the cramped crew quarters, he strolled to the front of the ship, where he found Jayrne sitting alone, staring out to sea. After a moment's hesitation, he found an open ale barrel and drew two mugs. He carried them to where Jayrne sat in silent isolation, and offered her one of the drinks. She looked to the sky, almost as if she was going to refuse his offer, but then accepted the mug and patted the bench next to her. He sat down gratefully, sipping ale to hide his nervousness.

Surprisingly, Jayrne broke the silence first. "Why are you here?"

Elac's mouth opened in stunned shock, and he answered, "I . . . just wanted to talk."

She smiled, looking down at her weathered boots. "Sorry. I mean, why are you on this journey? You know why I'm here. What is it that drags you away from home to spend your nights sleeping on the ground?"

Elac set his mug down, covering his face with his hands. Although he hadn't spoken of it for many days, he still found a deep ache inside when he thought of his home. Jayrne put a supporting hand on his shoulder.

"If you don't want to talk about it . . ."

Elac shook his head. "No, I'm okay. It's just . . . painful." He proceeded to tell her everything that had happened since the tragic day when the Kobolds had attacked his caravan. He left nothing out, even the more incredible parts of the story, involving undead minions and mystic seers. She sat quietly the whole time, letting him tell his story at his own pace. A lone tear ran down his cheek when he spoke of the razing of his village, and she reached out a gentle hand to wipe it away. When he finished, she took his hands in hers.

"I'm sorry. I didn't mean to drag up painful memories for you. I just . . . I feel like I have no control over my life right now."

Elac forced a smile through pursed lips. "Your turn."

She nodded. "I was born in North Hold. My real mother died giving birth to my younger brother. When I was twelve, my father was killed by Kobold raiders in one of the border wars, and we were orphaned.

"I left home the next year, joining a group of merchant Elves who were passing through, and spent the next five years doing odd jobs for them. In return, they fed me, clothed me, and one of them taught me the Elven arts of stealth and archery. I must have been about eighteen the night one of the merchants got drunk and decided to have his way with me. I kept my dagger sharp, which he learned the hard way. I was never charged with his murder, but I was no longer welcome with the group.

"Since then, I've made my way as a thief, drifting from city to city. I check in on my brother now and then, which was how I learned he'd been arrested."

Elac raised his mug in salute, a gesture she returned. They sat quietly for a few minutes before Jayrne broke the silence.

"You speak of ghosts, seers, undead minions, ancient magical artifacts, and other incredible things. How much of it do you really believe?"

"At first," he confided, "not much. Even after the first encounter with thralls, I was still a bit skeptical. I really wanted to believe, but my upbringing just wouldn't allow me to accept such things. I'd always believed if the undead were real, they were confined to Nightwood Forest. Now I'm willing to take everything at face value. There was certainly no denying that the creatures in Nightwood Forest were skeleton warriors. I think we're safest if we suspend our cynicism for now."

They sat talking quietly the rest of the afternoon, and the coast of Caldala slowly slid past. The weather remained clear and warm, and they made good time. The sun turned to a glowing ruddy ball, dipped below the horizon, and seemed to sink into the sea, disappearing from view.

❀ ❁ ★ ❅ ❆

Their ship rounded the breakwater at the mouth of Palim Bay, and Elac noticed the pitching and rolling had dissipated. They cruised to a stop, meeting the wharf with a bump, and the sailors went about their business of tying the ship to the pier. The air had a salty tang about it, mixing unpleasantly with the odor of tar and unwashed bodies.

Once their horses were unloaded, they made their way to the palace. Unlike other cities Elac had visited, where there were central marketplaces, vendors in Palim were everywhere, hawking their wares and competing with their neighbors. The buildings were a strange hodgepodge of stone and wood, and those near the water had been liberally smeared with tar to protect them from the saltwater of the ocean.

The opulence of these houses and shops, however, paled in comparison to the palace. Elac had seen expensive construction before, but the palace went beyond good taste into the realm of gaudiness. The wall around the palace was fully thirty feet high, sheathed in marble, and polished until it glowed. The metal gates had been gilded with gold, and he cringed, thinking of what even the perimeter of the palace grounds alone had cost to construct. Silvayn displayed their order from the Unity Council, and they passed through the gates unchallenged to enter a massive courtyard. Great flagstones covered the ground, and stone-lined gardens were in abundance.

The palace itself was also covered with polished marble, and most of the doors were made of brilliantly shining brass. The guards, both those at the gate to the grounds and at the entrances to the palace, were clad in ceremonial armor. Their helmets were forged into the likeness of fearsome creatures, complete with sharply pointed ears protruding from the sides. The breastplates were massive, burnished in gold and trimmed in silver, and appeared incredibly heavy. They looked impressive, but even Elac's limited combat experience told him the armor would be ineffective in a fight, providing limited vision, protection, and mobility.

The guards at the main entrance opened the towering mahogany doors, and they bowed in unison as the party passed. By the time they entered the palace and were trooping along in the main hall, Hadwyn was openly giggling at the frivolity the Humans displayed. A servant dressed in a fine blue cloak led them to a sitting room. Tapestries hung on the walls, interspersed with war banners from various battles the Humans had fought during their long and bloody history.

The room was decorated as if for a banquet. There were brightly colored buntings hanging from the ceiling, covering the entirety of the interior walls, except for an opening for the one window looking out over Palim Bay. A long, wooden table stood against the far wall, laden with various fruits, cheeses, and bread at one end, while the other had what looked to be an entire haunch of roasted deer resting in a pool of gravy. To Hadwyn's obvious delight, an ale barrel stood in one corner, with a number of mugs conveniently located nearby. The servant told them to make themselves comfortable, and the King's advisor would be along shortly.

Hadwyn wasted no time in filling a plate with steaming food, complimented with a mug of ale. He took his place at the closest table and immediately attacked his plate with a vengeance. Elac shrugged and joined him, albeit in smaller portions. Gillen also followed suit, although he gave his gluttonous brother the usual dark, disapproving look.

The door to their room opened to admit a middle-aged man, who firmly closed the door behind him and approached the group seated around the hall. His dark hair, neatly trimmed at shoulder length, was touched by streaks of gray. He wore a shining suit of chain mail covered by a cloak, deep blue in color and trimmed in silver. On his head, he bore a ringlet of silver leaves, designating him as the Duke of Palim. His cape also bore his family crest, a great silver sailing ship. A broadsword was in plain evidence at his side, and Elac assumed he also had any number of smaller weapons concealed about his person. Human politics always made Elac nervous.

"Welcome!" he bellowed in a voice they probably heard in the wastelands where the village of Lanor had once stood. "I am Adroc, Duke of Palim. I understand you have a declaration directly from the Unity Council."

Silvayn's face was unreadable, and Elac made a mental note never to gamble against the old wizard. "That is correct, your Grace. A matter of utmost importance and greatest secrecy."

Adroc's eyes went flat at the word "secrecy," and his voice dropped to a conspiratorial whisper. "A moment, please, my friends."

He glided to the door, calling for a pair of guards who were standing attentively down the hall and giving them explicit instructions that no one, themselves included, was to come within fifty feet of the door to the meeting room. The soldiers crashed their fists against their armored chests, then marched away to take up their posts.

"What great and momentous mission brings to you our fair city?"

"We are on a quest, your Grace," Silvayn told him, leaning close, "one that has taken us around the continent. In the Kingdom of Palindom, we need to complete two tasks. First, there is someone here who must join us in our travels. Although I know not who this person is, I will recognize their aura if I am close enough.

"The second is a simple matter. We need to acquire a certain artifact, which the minions of the spirit world have told us we must have, lest we fail in our quest. We need the Dagger of Rennex."

Duke Adroc retrieved a knife from a nearby table, which he used to peel an apple. "Obviously, until you identify your new companion, I cannot help you there. But as far as the Dagger goes, I have some bad news for you. It has been stolen from the Temple of Rennex by the minions of the vampire lord, Noran. He has it in his castle, deep in the Paheny Mountains."

Gillen gave a low whistle. "Now what, Silvayn? I don't think the good Duke here will be able to convince the King to mount an expedition to Noran's castle."

"We need to do something," Adalyn snapped, crossing her arms.

"Actually," the Duke said, his eyes distant, "I might be able to help you, at that. Gillen is correct in regard to the King, but there may be another way. If you don't think it will hinder your efforts, I'll speak to the Necromancer ambassador, and see if he could talk to Noran for us."

Hadwyn choked on his ale, slamming his mug on the table and trying to regain his composure. "Ambassador? From the Necromancers? This has to be a joke!"

"It is no joke, most honorable Dwarf. There have already been two catastrophic wars between the Eastern nations and the Necromancers. The only way to prevent another is with open dialogue. In fact, we are looking at potential candidates right now to be our ambassador to the city of Malator."

Silvayn was already shaking his head. "I'm sorry, your Grace, but we need to keep this within the family, so to speak. Besides, the Necromancers can't help you there. Noran has taken a different path. Vampires and ghosts do not fall under the influence of the Necromancers."

A timid knock at the door interrupted the proceedings. Duke Adroc rose swiftly to his feet, his face assuming a haughty expression before he had taken a step. He yanked the door open to find one of the guards standing before him, his face pale and his hands trembling.

"Your . . . your Grace, I'm sorry. I realize you said no visitors were allowed, but . . . but Prince Cassius insisted upon seeing you and our guests."

The guard stepped aside; actually, Elac noticed, he was pushed aside by the man outside the door. He stepped boldly through the doorway, and Duke Adroc admitted him with a bow. Once the Duke's back was turned to the Prince, however, the scowl on the Duke's face spoke volumes about the relationship between the two men.

Prince Cassius was young, perhaps in his mid-twenties. His dark hair was neatly trimmed, and he had a long, thick mustache. He wore no armor, but instead had a bright blue surcoat draped over black hose. His surcoat was emblazoned with the figure of a winged black panther, crouched as if to strike, which Elac assumed was his family crest. The only weapon in evidence was a large dagger hanging from his belt.

"Everyone," the Duke said, all traces of his feelings for the Prince now buried deep inside, "this is my nephew, Prince Cassius, whose father is Crown Prince Diar. My Lord Prince, I'd like to introduce Silvayn, a mage of great power." The two shook hands, and Elac noted a look of great respect on the Prince's arrogant face. "Adalyn, his pupil." The Prince's eyes widened slightly, and he noticed Adalyn for the first time. He knelt before her, took her hand, and kissed it gently.

"My Lady," he said.

"Your Highness," she replied indifferently, brushing a lock of hair behind her ear. The gesture revealed her obviously Elven heritage, and the Prince stood rather quickly. The introductions continued, and Elac noticed the Prince's eyes narrowing into a smugly conceited look when the Dwarves and Elves in the group were introduced.

Silvayn concluded the introductions with Jayrne, although there was no repeat of the performance Cassius had given with Adalyn. Elac suspected it was Jayrne's choice of attire. Where Adalyn wore robes of a soft brown color, Jayrne was wearing her usual leather armor and short sword. After briefing the Prince, Duke Adroc handed an ale glass to Cassius, seated himself, and turned to Silvayn. "You were saying about the undead minions?"

"Vampires and ghosts are different, in that they are the only undead types not created by Necromancers. Therefore, the Necromancers have no direct control over them, as they do the other undead creatures we see, such as skeleton warriors and wraiths.

"In the year 2209, twelve Humans of surpassing evil sought out Malator, that he might make them immortal. Through the hand of the Necromancer, Oralan, Malator cast the incantations required for the transformation. The spell was of such power that over one hundred of Oralan's lesser Necromancers exceeded the limits of their chala, and were destroyed."

Cassius looked askance at the old wizard. "Chala?"

"Chala is the Death Magic equivalent of Kata. If a

147

Necromancer exceeds his limits, his body will shrivel, becoming completely desiccated in an excruciatingly painful manner. Their soul is then destroyed, and the body slowly turns to dust.

"So, the twelve Humans became the first vampires. Their power grew over the centuries, until they became what we now refer to as vampire lords. Only a vampire lord can create other vampires; it requires a tremendous amount of power and leaves them in a weakened state. The victim will become a vampire with the following sunset, but can still be saved if the vampire lord who attacked them is killed within one moon cycle."

Duke Adroc pulled the corners of his short, neatly trimmed mustache. "One moon cycle . . . do you mean a month?"

Silvayn held up one hand, palm downward, and rocked it back and forth. "Not necessarily. A moon cycle is close to a month, but there are slight differences. It's not a good area for experimenting. As I was saying, with the death of the vampire lord, any vampires created in the last moon cycle are restored to living status, while all other vampires created by that vampire lord are destroyed. Noran is the sole remaining vampire lord. The others, through one means or another, have all died out over the past three millennia. If he is destroyed, all remaining vampires will be eliminated with him."

Cassius leaned back in his chair and crossed his legs, lacing his fingers behind his head in a grossly arrogant expression. "So, you intend to sneak into the castle of a vampire lord, kill him, and take the Dagger of Rennex back from him? Foolishness. I was under the impression you were here on serious matters. I have no further time to waste on this idiocy."

"Actually," Silvayn told him, "we need you to come with

us." Elac's eyes flew open wide, and he stared at Silvayn in un-disguised shock.

"Impossible." Cassius stood and picked up his flagon of ale. "There are too many important tasks here requiring my atten-tion." He spun on his heel and marched to the door, yanking the door open so hard, it seemed the Prince would rip it from its hinges.

Duke Adroc sat chuckling, appearing to enjoy the looks on the faces of Elac and his friends. "Ah, the son of our Crown Prince. He is quite arrogant, and he seriously believes the king-dom will fall apart if he isn't here to watch after our affairs. He entertains himself and the asses in his retinue by participat-ing in gladiator games against men who have been sentenced to die. His claim to fame is in not having had any of these men ever mark him. Of course, the fact that his opponents are given overly heavy weapons and thin, weak armor is not public knowledge. I take it he is the one remaining person who has yet to join your campaign?"

Silvayn gave a nod, and Hadwyn gave a loud groan of pro-test before picking up his mug of ale and downing the contents in one swallow.

"Duke Adroc," Adalyn said, "if he is indeed the one sup-posed to join us, we absolutely must have him."

"I'll talk to the King," Adroc said, nodding. "He will un-derstand the nature and importance of your quest, and he can order Cassius to join you. Will you journey straightaway to Noran's castle, then?"

"Yes, your Grace," Silvayn said. "We need the Dagger. It is just as important to this as any of us are."

"So, are you planning a direct confrontation, then?" Rilen asked curiously.

"That would be foolish," Jayrne said. "I could be in and out of his castle with the Dagger, and have the vampire lord none the wiser."

"I would prefer Jayrne's idea," Silvayn told them, his face serious. "A vampire lord is an incredibly powerful entity, and he may have any number of servants to help him. Stealth should be our primary plan, with strength at arms only as a fallback position if we are compromised. We won't send her in alone, but if we find out where the Dagger is, we'll give her a chance to show her skills."

"I've fought many creatures and men in my life, Silvayn, but never anything with his power," Rilen said, his eyes bright and intent. "What are his strengths and weaknesses?"

"Vampire lords are exceptionally strong, not as powerful as a Death Knight, but definitely stronger than any of us. They are able to change shape, becoming a wolf, a bat, or even fog. However, they are vulnerable to direct sunlight. A vampire lord can handle the sun briefly, but a lesser vampire would be destroyed. They are weakened by the presence of blessed religious objects, so we'll want to bring something of the sort with us. Since they're not incorporeal, you don't need a blessed weapon or magical object to hit them.

"If it comes down to a fight, we hit him hard and fast. Adalyn and I can provide assistance with magic, but we'll be depending upon the rest of you to handle him."

"What about a stake through the heart?" Elac asked timidly, a slow flush coming over his face. "Is it a legend, or does a stake through the heart really kill a vampire?"

"In a way, yes," Adalyn answered. "It will immobilize the vampire, and unless someone comes along and frees him in the next week or so, he'll die from not feeding."

The Duke looked down at the drink in his hands, his eyes distant. "There is one other matter, Silvayn. As you are probably aware, King Aldaris is not the strongest leader. In fact, with his recent decline in health, the Dukes of many of the individual districts have leeched more and more power for themselves, to the point some have become nearly autonomous. You may experience some difficulties along the way in this regard. Having the Prince along with you may help, but the authority of the crown isn't entirely respected anymore."

The Duke then set down his cup and stood, shaking his head sadly. "It is a poor state of affairs, my friends. Well, I shall leave you to your planning. I realize you are in haste, so I will go immediately to the King and make arrangements for Prince Cassius to join you. I wish you luck in your ventures."

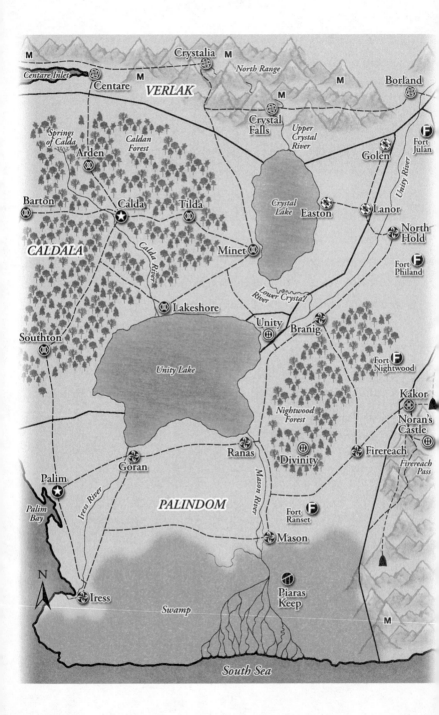

Chapter 9

Blac saw Cassius as an extremely arrogant man. The Prince had stormed into the guest room where the group was eating breakfast and demanded Silvayn rescind the request to have Cassius accompany them. When Silvayn refused, the Prince raged and shouted for several minutes, all to no avail. Cassius, frowning sharply, was dressed in full-plate mail armor, a large broadsword hanging at his side. His blue cape still adorned his shoulders, framing the bright silver armor. His horse, also encased in steel armor, was one of the tallest steeds Elac had ever seen. He assumed such a beast would be needed to carry so much weight. A visored helmet hung from the saddle, and a massive two-handed sword was strapped along the horse's flank. His shield, embossed with the royal family's panther crest, was strapped to his left arm. He carried a long, steel-tipped lance, which bore a blue and silver pennon on its end.

Silvayn pulled himself into his saddle. "If everyone's ready, let's get started."

Cassius snorted, his lip curling in derision. "Where are we going first, mage?"

If Silvayn noticed the look of disdain on the Prince's face, he didn't let it show. "We'll follow a caravan track across country to the Iress River. From there, we'll pick up the road to Mason. It'd be quicker to take the road to Goran, and from there to Ranas, but I plan to give Nightwood Forest a wide berth."

Cassius nodded without speaking, and Rilen led the group away. They left by the city's main gates, picking up the track to the river at an easy canter. Elac chatted with Jayrne while they rode, and he felt their friendship developing nicely. He hoped it could build to something more, but at least it was a start. Although she participated enthusiastically in the conversation, she kept glancing behind the group as if waiting for someone.

They reached the river just before sunset, with trees casting long shadows across the river in the dying light. The clear, cool water gurgled noisily over small stones, and to Elac the sound seemed almost musical. They crossed the ford, and Silvayn told Rilen to find a suitable campsite.

Jayrne bit her lip with a frown, then stopped her horse and waited for Cassius to catch up to her. "Cassius, would your—"

"You will address me as 'your Highness.'"

"Ah. I see. Well, *your Highness*," she said, crossing her arms and emphasizing the words with a tilt of sarcasm in her voice, "would your father, or anyone in your government for that matter, have sent a bodyguard to watch after you?"

"Bodyguard? Me? I need no bodyguard."

Silvayn guided his horse closer. "Why do you ask, Jayrne?"

"I've been catching glimpses of someone all day. He's been

riding about a half mile behind us since we left Palim."

"The last time I checked," Cassius said coldly, "it was no crime to ride about in the King's lands."

Jayrne covered her eyes with her hands. "Silvayn, this man has paced us since this morning. He stops when we stop, and he moves out when we do. Right now, he's hiding in a copse of trees on the other side of the river. I'll bet he comes over to our side by morning."

"We could set up an ambush," Hadwyn said, his eyes bright.

"Let's not be hasty," Silvayn replied. "We'll post a two-man watch all night, for now. We can't go assaulting everyone who rides behind us. I want to see what he does."

A few minutes later, they topped a small rise to find Rilen waiting for them. He led them off the road and into the woods, where a murmuring stream ran through a small clearing. Elac tethered his horse to a convenient tree, and had his tent set up before he realized Jayrne was missing. Alarmed, he hurried to find Silvayn.

"Where's Jayrne?" he asked breathlessly.

"She went to check on our friend who has been following us," Silvayn said with a smile. "I'm sure she'd be touched by your concern, though."

"I don't know that we need to tell her about it," Elac said, his eyes darting about wildly.

"Silvayn is just teasing you," said Adalyn, tugging at the straps supporting her tent. She blew a lock of hair out of her eyes, and a sudden grin spread across her face. "It is cute, though."

"What's cute?" Jayrne's voice cut suddenly out of the darkness, and Elac jumped in surprise. The lithe thief emerged from the shadows and began to unpack her gear.

"Just something I heard," Adalyn said evasively. "Did you find him?"

"Yes. He's camped about a half mile west of here. He's a Human mercenary, and he has descriptions of all of us, including our newest addition."

Cassius scowled and looked up at the night sky. "And just how can you know all of this? Did you ask him?"

"His equipment is a bit rusty," Jayrne said, crossing her arms. "Mercenaries are notoriously unconcerned about inspections by superior officers. He wasn't wearing a helmet, so I could make a reasonable guess at his race. And I read the papers he has on all of us. Would you like to know what they said about you?"

Gillen looked up from working on his axe, still trying to grind out the nicks received from the statue in the Dwarven mine. "Just how close did you get?"

"Close enough. By the way, Elac, I noticed you have no shield, so I borrowed his for you." She handed Elac a plain-looking steel shield, splotched with rust, but with the leather straps still intact. "You might want to clean it up some."

Cassius stepped closer, his hands on his hips. "What are you, some kind of thief?"

"Not just 'some kind' of thief. I'm a good thief. A very good thief, actually."

"Silvayn, this is outrageous. It's bad enough I have to share this quest with Elves and Dwarves, but this . . . thief! This is unacceptable."

Hadwyn rose to his feet menacingly, but his brother pushed him back down. Rilen, however, was not so easily cowed. His hands balled into fists, he stormed across the clearing to stand directly in front of the armored form of the Prince.

"Let's get one thing straight, Cassius. I don't care what you think of Elves or Dwarves. But we're on the same side here, and if this quest is going to succeed, we need to work together. You are no better than anyone else here, Prince or not." He jabbed his finger at the startled Prince's face. "Your attitude had better change, and soon."

"This whole quest is a waste of time. While I'm out here galloping across the countryside, the Duke of Palim is busy usurping my grandfather's throne out from under him. And the rest of you should be addressing problems at home, too, rather than running around following some half-baked plan. You Dwarves . . . you said your uncle is concluding dangerous deals with the Kobolds. Are you trying to curtail further damage? No. You're out here, chasing eons-old artifacts. Silvayn, you should be trying to talk some sense into the Unity Council. And Rilen, despite what you say, I'm sure you have some influence left with Prime Minister Lornell, at least enough to convince her the Kobolds are a threat to us all." He threw the cup he was holding and stalked off into the night.

❁ ❂ ★ ❀ ❁

They rode out again at first light. Cassius rode some distance ahead of the others, ostensibly to check the road before them. Although a man in full armor tended to make for a poor scout, no one saw fit to argue with him; indeed, they seemed to welcome the chance to spend some time without his harsh comments and infuriatingly superior attitude.

Elac casually brought his horse closer to Jayrne's. "With all the fun we were having last night, I forgot to ask if, while you were spying on our friend back there, you might have seen any names that would point to his employer."

"No," she said, shaking her head. "Nothing like that. I would definitely recognize the handwriting if I saw it again. There were oddities in the way the writer made certain letters."

"That's something, anyway."

"But it's not all. He had a certain tattoo on his shoulder. A tattoo you might recognize. It had a dagger thrust through a shackle."

Rilen's eyes went flat. "Twice is a coincidence. Three times is not."

Hadwyn shifted his massive hammer to a more comfortable position. "Maybe a few of us should go have a talk with him. Even if he didn't have any names written down, I'll wager a cold flagon of ale I could convince him to name someone. We could at least persuade him to explain the significance behind the tattoo."

Elac laughed, squinting into the morning sun. Although there were no clouds overhead, great banks of thunderheads were gathered upon the western horizon, bringing with them the threat of rain. Elac brought his new shield up in front of him, using oil and a cloth to rub out the rust stains. When he was satisfied, he strapped it to his arm as Rilen had shown him, to get used to the feeling of the added weight. He brought the shield around to a guarded position, and grinned in spite of himself.

Without warning, an arrow shattered against his shield. Instantly, the veteran warriors around him reacted, shields and weapons at the ready as they looked for the source of the shot. From a deep draw to their left, a dozen armed men charged the group, bellowing their bloodlust. Rilen spurred his horse, sword raised, and rode directly at his attackers. Elac called to Cassius while the others joined the battle.

Hadwyn met the first man with a hammer blow to the head. His foe collapsed with a grunt, blood gushing from the gash in his skull. Without slowing, the battle-hardened Dwarf reversed his hammer, and the sharply pointed 'crow's beak' took another attacker full in the chest, penetrating his chain mail and knocking the man from his feet. Rilen drove his horse directly into the center of the mass of bandits, his short sword weaving with amazing speed. He cut his way through their ranks, leaving a trail of dead and dying men behind him. Gillen attacked the left flank, and his newly sharpened axe drew a bright red gush of blood from a man who was too slow in bringing his shield to bear. Elac, still lacking confidence in his ability to handle a sword, positioned himself between the melee and Silvayn, with Adalyn and Jayrne at his side.

The raiders tried to meet the onslaught of the men they had sought to ambush, but they made one fatal mistake: they forgot to watch for the return of the armored form who was leading the group. Cassius charged into their midst, lance lowered and visor down, wreaking havoc. His lance pierced the closest opponent through the chest, and he staggered, gurgling, to the ground. Cassius discarded the lance and drew his broadsword, swinging wildly to the left and right.

Elac's personal feelings about Cassius aside, he had to admit the charge had a devastating effect on their enemies. They were looking all around, stepping backward and searching for a place to run. But their leader rallied them into a circle where they could protect each other's backs. They stood in the center of the road and prepared for their final stand, weapons ready. Elac's companions dismounted, and they implacably stalked their prey.

Gillen had discarded his axe in favor of the flail, and the spiked ball whistled demonically, whirling in circles over his head. His nearest foe seemed entranced by it, and never saw Hadwyn's hammer descending point-first in a deathblow aimed at his chest. The crow's beak pierced his steel breastplate, and the impact knocked his lifeless body into the man next to him. Rilen and Cassius darted in, blades swinging. In moments, the fight was over.

Silvayn and Adalyn rushed forward to check on their fighters, but there were no major injuries. Rilen knelt to check the pouches of the various dead men. Elac watched with fascination while the Elf ignored the blood and gore coating the bodies, going about his gruesome task as if was an everyday occurrence.

"What in the name of Vantra are you doing?" Cassius asked, sputtering with outrage. "Have you no decency?"

"This wasn't some random highway robbery. These men picked us out specifically for this attack. I want to know who hired them."

Cassius, despite his stated respect for the dead, wiped his

bloodied weapons on the cloak of one of the fallen men. "And you think they're going to conveniently provide a name?"

Rilen held up a bloodied scrap of parchment. "Elac, see if you can clean this up enough to read what's on it."

His skin crawling, Elac lightly pinched the paper between thumb and forefinger, holding it in front of himself as if it was a live snake. Jayrne laughed, taking the paper from him. Together, they used water and a cloth from their packs to clean it up. Elac took the sodden paper to the roadside and sat down, trying in vain to find any writing on it. On a whim, he held it up to the sunlight, revealing a series of runes, which he couldn't comprehend.

"Do you have something?" Silvayn asked.

"Just runes of some kind. I don't recognize them."

"Let me try." Elac handed the paper to the old Elf mage. He studied it for several minutes, occasionally shaking his head in frustration. The others took their turn attempting to decipher the message, but to no avail. Elac looked up and noticed Jayrne was missing again.

"Where's Jayrne?" he asked. "She was standing here not two minutes ago."

"She went slinking off into the woods as soon as you two finished cleaning up this piece of bloody garbage, which I can't seem to read," Hadwyn told him, storming away in frustration. Almost as an afterthought, he smashed a hollow log with the mallet of his hammer, accenting the blow with an angry oath. The outburst seemed to mollify the angry Dwarf, and he stalked away.

The others were ready to remount their horses when Jayrne

returned about fifteen minutes later. Although she was moving with haste, she still made no sound in her approach. When she drew near, Elac could see her eyes were open wide, fear etched into her face.

"I found our friend from last night," she said in a trembling voice. "I overheard him talking to someone."

"Did he chase you?" Cassius asked, his sneer belying the concern he struggled to display.

She shook her head, looked down at her feet, and held up her hand as she caught her breath and tried to calm her shaking hands. "He hired the men to attack us. He told them we had gold in our saddlebags, and if they killed us, he would split it with them. He was with a man cloaked all in black. There was something about that man that absolutely terrified me. I've not been afraid of anyone since I was fifteen, but it was all I could do not to turn and run."

Elac didn't miss the long look Silvayn exchanged with Adalyn. "We'd better be moving along," Silvayn announced. "We can worry about what was on the parchment later."

Everyone turned to their horses except Elac, who treaded lightly to where his favorite thief was securing her saddle harness. "Are you okay?"

She nodded, taking a deep breath. "That was the most terrifying thing I've ever experienced. I can't explain it." She shook her head, almost seeming with that simple gesture to throw off the cloak of fear. "Did you find something?"

"Just some runes. We can't decipher them." He handed the scrap of paper to her, and she studied it briefly. Her eyes lit up, and Elac knew she welcomed anything to take her mind off the experience she'd just had.

"These are thieves' runes. Part of the message is missing, but I'll be able to decode what we have. Just give me a few minutes."

The group gathered around while Jayrne studied the ornate writing. A feeling of uneasiness crept over Elac, and he shuddered involuntarily. Jayrne tapped one of the letters a few times, looking skyward, her mind deep in concentration. She cocked her head slightly to the side, the familiar lopsided smile coming to the fore.

"This is part of an order from the assassin's guild in the town of Goran," she said. "I would guess the man who has been following us is a hired thug."

Cassius placed his hand on the hilt of his broadsword. "Can you identify the assassin in Goran?"

"Yes."

"Then what are we waiting for?"

"I agree," Silvayn said. "We need to know who this assassin is, and put a stop to this before one of us gets hurt. We go to Goran."

Jayrne folded the scrap of paper, placing it into a pouch. "There's one part of the note I still need to work on. I can only make out a single word, because the rest of the sentence has been blotted out. I'll try to decipher it as we go."

Elac reached for his horse, but he stopped, feeling the hairs on the back of his neck standing on end. His entire body seemed chilled to the bone by a sudden, frigid wind, but the trees around him were unbending, as if there was no wind at all. He looked down just in time to see the bodies of the men who had died in the fight stir to life, slowly climbing to their feet like puppets on strings. They groped for their weapons, and faced the party menacingly. Although they didn't have the characteristic odor, Elac knew there was only one explanation.

"Rilen!" he shouted, drawing his sword with a trembling hand.

The others turned to see the source of Elac's fear. Rilen immediately leapt to the attack, while Cassius and the Dwarves stood momentarily dumbfounded. Rilen's short sword hissed through the air, neatly decapitating the first thrall. The body collapsed soundlessly to the ground, but the others continued shambling forward, weapons at the ready.

"Go for their heads!" Rilen called to the others as he parried a sword stroke.

Hadwyn was the first to recover his wits, and he rushed to Rilen's side. His hammer shattered the skull of a thrall that had moved within reach. Elac heard the deadly whistling that could only mean Gillen still had his flail in hand. Cassius joined the fray, the unbelievably large two-handed sword in his hands. Elac heard the snap of Jayrne's short bow, and an arrow buried itself in a thrall's head. It stumbled and fell, one hand clawing at the piercing shaft. Adalyn's sword cleared its sheath with a steely ring, and she also joined the fray. Led by Rilen, the group deftly finished the battle.

"Quickly now," Silvayn told them in a tense voice, his eyes on the woods surrounding the road. "There must be a Necromancer nearby. We have to get out of here!"

A solitary man on horseback emerged from the same draw where their earlier foes had been hidden. He was dressed all in black, the cowl of his cloak completely hiding his face. His horse, wearing black leather armor, snorted defiantly at the group. The horse's breath was steaming, despite the midday heat. The rider reached up and pulled back his hood to reveal a hideous black helmet, embossed with a demonic face. He drew his sword, and the horse stalked implacably closer.

"Keep him busy," Cassius said through clenched teeth. He retrieved his lance, wrenching it free of a corpse. Elac's fear reached a level where he could only stand immobile, watching the scene play out before him. The rider moved closer and brought a shimmering black shield around in front of him, his impossibly large sword held in one hand. With a deadly certainty, Elac knew this to be the figure Jayrne had seen earlier.

Rilen was the first to engage their new foe. He swung a low blow, meant to disable the black figure's horse, but the rider easily blocked it. The return blow came faster than Elac's eye could follow. Rilen managed to raise his shield, but the impact knocked him a dozen feet away, where he landed on his back, stunned. Hadwyn swung an overhand strike from the other side, taking the man full in the thigh. He grunted in pain, but followed Hadwyn's attack with a thrust from his shield, knocking the valiant Dwarf into a nearby tree.

"Death Knight!" Adalyn screamed, sheathing her sword. "We have to get out of here!"

Elac, breaking free of the paralyzing fear, rushed to Rilen's side. Rilen waved him off and staggered to his feet. "Help Hadwyn," he said, his shield arm hanging limp. "He may have been knocked out."

While Gillen danced around the Death Knight, looking for an opening, Jayrne kept him off balance by firing arrows into the armored form. Adalyn had grabbed Rilen's bow from his horse, and she launched shot after ineffective shot. Elac dodged around the fighters, coming quickly to Hadwyn's side. He grabbed the limp Dwarf by one arm and dragged him to the horses.

Then there was the sound of another horse in the fray. Cassius, crouched behind his lance, prodded his mount forward in a reckless charge against the enemy. The lance caught the Death Knight by surprise, knocking him from his saddle and shattering the shaft of Cassius's weapon. His horse crashed into the mount ridden by the Death Knight with a stunning impact, knocking the black-clad beast to the ground and shattering one of its front legs.

"Let's go!" Rilen called out, running for his horse. Elac laid the stunned Dwarf across his saddle, and with Jayrne's help strapped him down. He swung into his own saddle, and brought his horse around in preparation for flight. The others all re-mounted, and they were off in a frenzied dash to the north.

They rode hard for the next two hours, trying to put as much distance between themselves and the Death Knight as possible. Once, while they galloped along next to the waist-high prairie grasses, a covey of quail burst from hiding. Elac sheepishly looked at the sword that seemed somehow to have leapt into his hand of its own volition, almost feeling embarrassed until he realized that he wasn't only one with a drawn weapon.

It was late afternoon when they entered the town of Goran. The only lodging they could find was in a filthy inn near the wharfs, its dingy windows looking out over the swift waters of the Iress River. They gathered in Silvayn's room to plan their strategy.

Adalyn helped Rilen out of his armor, his face contorting with pain every time she moved his left arm. Concern was mirrored in her eyes, and she meticulously examined his injuries. Once his tunic was off, it was obvious even to Elac that Rilen's left shoulder was dislocated. Gillen offered to help, and the Priest of Gentra attempted to put the arm back where it belonged. Hadwyn offered the only help he could, a bottle of potent Dwarf wine, which Rilen accepted gratefully. While Adalyn braced the battered Elf's body, Gillen held the damaged arm, gritting his teeth and setting his grip. He gave a sudden, stout pull, and Rilen grunted in pain when the arm popped back into place.

Gillen used his magic to help with the healing process; in the meantime, Cassius gave voice to the unasked question in everyone's minds. "That was impossible! My lance should have run him through. At the very least, he shouldn't have been able to get out of bed for a week. How can it be?"

"A Death Knight is a very powerful foe," Silvayn explained. "They are evil men who, while they lack magical abilities, still desire immortality. Their strength is many times what it was while they lived. Had you not disabled his mount, I fear he would've been too much for us."

"You know," Adalyn said, looking up from where she was bandaging Rilen's arm, "we're seeing an interesting puzzle developing right in front of us. We're fairly certain the Kobold raiders were specifically hunting for Elac. Now, with the intervention of a Necromancer and a Death Knight, it seems undead forces are also deliberately coming after him, or at least trying to stop what we're doing."

"Is it possible the Kobolds and the undead are working together on this?" Hadwyn asked.

"They couldn't be," Silvayn explained. "The undead would attack the living on sight, including Kobolds. I'm not sure what the answer is."

"Dalos," Jayrne said excitedly, her eyes bright.

Silvayn looked at the young thief, one eyebrow raised in confusion. "What was that?"

"Dalos. That's the other word on this parchment. I've been working on this all afternoon. A large portion of the writing of thieves depends upon the syntax, and with no other legible words around, it was difficult to translate."

Elac leaned forward, peering at the parchment in Jayrne's slender hands. "Who or what is Dalos?"

"I really don't know. It's not the name of the assassin we're looking for, though. No one would dare write down a name in their business."

Cassius stroked his long, dark mustache. "Then Dalos is likely a place, not a person." He looked down at his armored feet and drew a deep breath. "I want to apologize to everyone. I'm afraid we got off on the wrong foot. There is much going on here in my country, and it's all I can do to keep that foul Duke from taking over. When I found out he'd convinced my father to send me on this journey, I was very angry, and I'm afraid I took it out on you. The fight on the way here seems to have cleared my head some."

They nodded in acceptance, and Hadwyn gave him a hearty pat on the back. The Dwarf adjusted the bandage on his head, wincing with pain when he touched the swollen lump, a result of being knocked into a tree by the Death Knight. "So what do we do now?"

"We need to find the assassin and convince him to tell us who hired him. Maybe we can find out if there are any other surprises waiting for us."

"I can find the assassin," Jayrne said confidently. "Convincing him to talk to you will be your job."

Silvayn rubbed his bearded jaw, staring at the far wall, considering his options. "Okay, Jayrne. Take Cassius and Gillen with you. Find out what you can, but don't bring him back here. We don't want anyone to know where we are."

"I can go, too," Rilen said, trying to rise.

Adalyn pushed him back into his chair. "You can stay right where you are. You, too, Hadwyn. Neither one of you is going anywhere, so have another drink."

Hadwyn looked at her, his eyes serious, a tankard of ale already in his hand. "Doctor's orders?"

Gillen stood next to Cassius, leaning against a building while keeping an eye on Jayrne. For the last three hours, she had spoken to at least a dozen unsavory characters, each sending her off in another direction. At one point, he and Cassius had drawn their weapons, thinking to come to her rescue when a pair of ruffians had grabbed her arms. It proved to be unnecessary, however; Jayrne had easily overcome the two footpads. Gillen came away with a new respect for the agile thief.

He glanced over at his companion, and grudgingly

admitted he had a bit more respect for the Prince, also. At first, Cassius had been easy to dislike. His arrogant attitude struck a raw nerve with Gillen, and he thought of Cassius as another spoiled, pampered member of Human royalty. But the timely charge against the Death Knight had quite possibly saved Hadwyn's life. Cassius's apology required a different kind of courage, but was no less respectable than the prowess he had shown on the battlefield.

Five minutes later, Jayrne returned. She called Gillen and Cassius over, and in a whisper, told them what she had found. "Okay, we're looking for a man named Wraist. He's the Guildmaster for the local assassins in Goran. Any assignment for a hit in this area would have to come through him. His guild is this way."

She led them along the filthy lakefront streets of the city, casually stepping around piles of trash and debris. A number of the buildings had fallen into disrepair, with oddly shaped scraps of wood nailed over holes in the failing walls. The streets were unpaved, and the frequency of potholes in the road gave mute testimony to the lack of maintenance. Gillen had left his flail behind, but his axe was strapped across his back, and he was ready to draw it at a moment's notice. Cassius had agreed to cover his family crest, in order to protect his identity, but his broadsword hung menacingly outside his cloak.

They turned onto a dead-end street, and Gillen knew they had arrived. He didn't need to see the metal door set in a brick wall to tell him the building housed the Assassins' Guild. The archers standing indolently on the surrounding roofs were more than adequate proof there was something inside to be protected.

Jayrne strode boldly up to the steel door, seeming to ignore the armed men standing above her.

Jayrne pounded on the door with three slow, measured strokes. She repeated the signal once, twice, then stepped back. A narrow slot in the door slid open, and a man's face appeared in the opening. He eyed the group suspiciously before he spoke in a deep, gravelly voice.

"What do you want?"

"We're here to see Wraist," Jayrne told him.

"Never heard of him."

"Jaran sent us."

The man's eyes seemed to frown. Without another word, he slammed the opening shut, leaving the group standing there. Gillen again looked nervously at the archers, his hand constantly twitching toward his axe, but knowing the weapon wouldn't help him against a barrage of arrows.

After a brief but nervous pause, the door rattled with the sound of chains and sliding bars. With a great metallic boom, the door released and slowly creaked open. The hallway beyond was sparsely lit by torches, and a smoky haze hung in the air. The ambient light was too low for Gillen to see clearly, and he assumed the assassins had that effect in mind when they designed their guild hall. The man who had opened the door for them stood, arms folded across his leather armor, waiting for them to enter. They passed through the doorway, and the portal behind them closed with a hollow echo reverberating through the building.

Chapter 10

I wouldn't make any sudden moves, if I were you," Jayrne warned them as they entered the hall. "There are hidden archers all over the inside of the building, not to mention at least fifty men-at-arms. They deal harshly with people who upset them."

"How nice," Gillen said.

They followed a pair of black-robed men, who led them wordlessly through the guild. They entered a large audience hall, somewhat bigger than the taverns frequented by Gillen's brother. A scattering of tables was interspersed with an occasional ale barrel, and several guild members were lounging near the center of the room, far gone with drink. At one end, sprawled on a pile of furs, was a thin, outlandishly dressed man, his silky clothes a mismatch of clashing colors. Gillen knew he had to be the Guildmaster. He had long, dark hair and a shaggy beard, and a short sword was strapped about his waist. Two scantily clad women were standing nearby, holding trays of food. The Guildmaster seemed to be sampling his servers as much as he was the food they carried.

One of the men who had led them to the audience chamber stepped forward and bowed low. "Your Excellency, these three wished to speak with you. This one," he said, pointing to Jayrne, "has requested Thieves' Truce."

The Guildmaster laughed raucously, setting a piece of baked chicken back on his tray. The serving girl closest to him held out a cloth, which he used to wipe his hands. "I am Wraist, the Guildmaster. Speak."

Jayrne, apparently either following the lead of their guide or through some etiquette she already knew, bowed to Wraist. "An assassin in your employ recently hired a group of mercenaries to attack certain travelers from Palim." Wraist sat unmoving, no hint of emotion showing on his face. "Those men failed in their attempt, and the entire lot of them were slaughtered."

"Twice," Gillen murmured.

Wraist looked at them, shaking his head. "What has this to do with me?"

"One of the men in the party was Prince Cassius, son of the Crown Prince and grandson of the King himself."

"Impossible," Wraist said, pulling a serving girl onto his lap, where she received the full attention of his lustful gaze. "Everyone in my guild knows the royal family is off limits. We're given a certain unofficial autonomy by the government because they never know when they'll have need of my special services. But if we were to kill a Prince, King Ervik would bring the entire Goran garrison down upon me."

"I assure you, your Excellency, it is true."

"Even so, what would lead you to my doorstep? There are

many freelancers and highway robbers out there. Just because a man hires some thugs to attack someone doesn't mean I was involved."

"We found a note on one of the dead. Runes on the note, written in the language of the thieves, directed us to Goran. No assassin in Goran would dare operate without your approval.

Wraist chewed his lip thoughtfully. "And how do I know what you say is true?"

Cassius had apparently had enough. He stepped forward boldly, throwing back his cloak and removing the cover from his armor to reveal the royal family crest. "Because I, Prince Cassius, say it is true."

Several men, who had been sitting quietly off to one side, rose to their feet, their weapons in hand. Wraist held up a fist, motioning them back to their seats. "I would doubt such a claim, but I recognize you now, your Highness."

He clapped his hands sharply together, and a woman emerged from the shadows. She wore tightly fitting black leather armor, and she moved with a feminine grace that set Gillen's ears aflame. He chuckled to himself, picturing his philandering brother's reaction. While keeping a cautious eye on the three before him, Wraist conducted a whispered conversation with the woman in black.

The Guildmaster's face turned dark, and his lips curled into a sneer. He knocked the tray from a serving girl's hands. "Out!" he bellowed. "I want this hall emptied! I will speak to these visitors alone!"

The men who were gathered about the hall cast suspicious glances at Gillen and his friends, but nonetheless did as they were told. In moments, the hall was empty, save for Wraist and the three companions.

Wraist placed his palms together in front of his face, almost as if he was praying. "What we discuss here is just between us. Your Highness, I would appreciate it if you could be discreet, as well."

Cassius nodded somberly. "So be it."

Wraist drew in a deep breath and let it out slowly. "We were approached yesterday morning by a man from Ranas named Johl. He paid twice our usual fee in order to make the deaths of a certain group of people appear to be the work of highwaymen. We were hoping one or two of the ruffians would be killed in the fight, which would make the story we were building seem more plausible. I can assure you, he never said anything about any members of the Palindom royal family being involved, or I would've turned him down."

"Prince Cassius was not the only member of a royal family in our party," Jayrne told him. "There are also two nephews of the King of the Dwarves traveling with us."

Wraist looked more closely at Gillen, then rolled his eyes with a groan as he sat back, his head banging against the wall behind him. "I'll give you all the information I have about the man who hired us. I do have to warn you, however, that as of this moment his life is forfeit. I'll be sending a message to my associates in Ranas, and they'll be out in force looking for him. His deception would have upset the balance we've worked so hard to maintain."

Gillen nodded in agreement. "Not to mention the political ramifications of having my brother and me murdered here in

Palindom."

"Exactly," Wraist said. He stood, straightened his tunic, and walked to a desk in the corner of the room, where he drew a rough map of several city blocks. "This is an area in Ranas where you can reach my contact who initially talked to Johl and set up the whole deal."

"What's his name?" Cassius asked.

"*Her* name," Wraist said with a humorless smile, "is Serana. She can lead you to our client. I'll write up something with my seal on it to convince her you're there on my behalf."

"Do you know the name of the client?" Gillen asked.

"No. All I can tell you is that one of my employees . . . borrowed the man's coin purse. There was something in it referring to a group called Dalos."

Gillen looked at his companions. "At least we know we're on the right track."

Wraist leaned forward and rested his elbows on his knees. "There is one other bit of assistance I can offer you. When you begin your search for Dalos, watch for the emblem of a dagger encircled by a manacle. They use it as a recognition symbol of some kind."

❀ ◍ ★ ✤ ❁

Elac studied the map Jayrne had brought back with her. "This is in the waterfront district." He looked up at Jayrne, his brow furrowed in puzzlement. "Why do thieves always gather at the waterfront?"

She shrugged. "Easy access to transportation. You can

stow away on board a ship, if you need to leave town quietly. Also, the less time you have stolen merchandise in your possession, the better. Besides, we like the view."

Adalyn chuckled, continuing to massage Rilen's injured shoulder. "What do you think, Silvayn? Do we stop in Ranas and deal with the situation, or do we stay with our quest?"

Silvayn ran his fingers through his white hair. "As long as it isn't taking us out of our way, I'd like to make certain this person loses interest in us. If things change, and he moves someplace off our path, we'll let Wraist's people handle him."

Rilen winced under the pressure of Adalyn's fingers. "I'd certainly like to pay my respects to this person face-to-face."

"Here, here!" Hadwyn laughed, draining his tankard. "Well, I'm glad that's settled. I'm heading to the taproom. Who's going to join me?"

"I will," Rilen announced, standing up. "I need more medicine for my shoulder."

"Me, too," Elac said.

Gillen was already shaking his head. "I'd prefer not to give my brother the chance to embarrass me publicly."

Elac glanced over where Jayrne stood waiting, almost afraid to ask her. She smiled knowingly. "I'll go."

Hadwyn was already striding energetically to the door. "Anyone else?"

The four of them marched down the stairs and into the noisy taproom. They spent the evening drinking ale and swapping stories, the troubles of their journey left behind. Hadwyn finished a rather bawdy joke, leaving the four of them roaring with laughter.

"So, what do you do back home, Hadwyn?" Jayrne asked him. "When you're not busy being a Prince, that is."

"Drink," he said simply, burying his bearded face in his mug. He slammed the empty tankard on the table and motioned for the barmaid to refill it. He laughed. "Actually, I'm a Captain in the army. As you can probably tell, I'm an independent sort of fellow. That's why I chose to carry a hammer, instead of the more traditional axe. I also refused any special treatment from the military. Damned fools wanted to make me a general. I told them I would earn my rank, like everyone else. My soldiers wouldn't respect me if it was any other way." He looked around the bar, spying an Elven woman seated at the next table with two Human ladies. "Women wouldn't respect me, either, for that matter," he said, grinning. He stood and motioned to the table next to them. "Rilen, you with me?"

"I'd better pass," he said with a laugh. "Adalyn and I aren't exactly together, but I think she would be upset with me."

Hadwyn grunted and moved to the Elven woman's table. He seemed to be well-received.

"How's the shoulder?" Elac asked Rilen.

"A little stiff," Rilen said, rotating the arm tenderly. "Gillen's magic seems to be fairly potent. I should be fine in a day or so."

"Lucky you," Jayrne told him.

"Rilen, there's something I've been meaning to ask," Elac said, setting his mug on the table. "Adalyn once told me that mages like Silvayn can sense when magic is being used around them, be it Life Magic or Death Magic. Yet neither he nor Adalyn was able to sense the spell cast by the Necromancer who reanimated the thralls yesterday."

"The way I understand it," Rilen said, swirling his ale and staring into the tankard, "Necromancers are something of an enigma. Even though they are, technically speaking, users of Death Magic spells, they are also something in the line of Priests. They worship Malator, and they're exceedingly evil, but they're Priests nonetheless. The incantation they use to raise the dead is something more along the lines of a prayer than a spell, similar to what Gillen used on my shoulder. That's why Silvayn and Adalyn couldn't sense the Necromancer's magic. It wasn't, strictly speaking, a spell."

"How did they manage to keep us from feeling fear when they were that close?" Jayrne asked. "As strong as the Necromancer and his Death Knight were, we should have been able to feel their presence long before they attacked."

"I asked Silvayn the same question. He said the more powerful undead types can control their fear aura, turning it on and off at will. You could go to services at the Temple of Gentra, sit between a Death Knight and a vampire, and never know the difference."

"They can enter holy places?" Elac asked, his mouth dropping open wide.

"Yes, unless they are confronted by a Priest."

They sat silently for a few minutes, and Elac passed the time by listening to the outrageous flattery Hadwyn was delivering at the next table, much to the delight of the ladies he had joined. Elac finally broached one more topic that had been bothering him.

"Rilen, when those men were reanimated out there, did the

fear affect you as much as it did before? I don't mean to sound flippant, but I didn't feel as afraid this time."

"I was wondering if you noticed. Silvayn says the fear affects you less and less with repeated exposures to it. Maybe eventually they'll be afraid of us."

Elac chuckled, taking another drink. The night slipped away while they enjoyed each other's company. Elac welcomed the change in Rilen, because the battle-hardened Elf was once again becoming talkative and outgoing. Eventually, Hadwyn and his new friends joined them at their table. When the night was over, Elac staggered up the stairs to his room, where he lay in bed watching the ceiling spinning endlessly overhead.

A few hours after daybreak, they set out for Ranas. Elac found the sun to be offensively bright, and he pulled his hood about his head to try to block some of the light. He was comforted by seeing similar signs of suffering in Rilen and Jayrne. He almost laughed out loud, however, when he saw Hadwyn. The normally sturdy Dwarf was almost doubled over in his saddle, holding his head in one hand and a waterskin in the other. Just as he had been when Elac met him, Hadwyn's hair was unkempt, his beard knotted, and his eyes were bloodshot. His brother, of course, rode beside him, browbeating him endlessly.

"How are you feeling this morning, Hadwyn?" Gillen asked with a wicked grin.

"Oh, I feel like dancing," Hadwyn growled. "And how are you?"

"Me? I'm enjoying the morning. And how was your night? Which one of those little bar flowers did you take to your room last night?"

"One?" Hadwyn asked, somehow managing an impudent grin despite his obviously miserable disposition. Gillen muttered something unintelligible and rode ahead, leaving his brother to suffer in silence.

It was twenty-five leagues from Goran to Ranas, but Silvayn had said at the outset he had no intention of spending the night on the road. They drove their mounts at a steady pace, conserving their energy in case of emergencies, but still making good time. Elac found the scenery to be breathtaking. Although the road itself was over a league from Unity Lake, it sat on a ridge high enough to allow a panoramic view of the waters below. Fishing boats drifted lazily across the blue expanse, nets trailing along in their wake. Larger merchant vessels also sailed the lake, albeit moving at a much faster pace than their smaller counterparts.

The sun had long sought its bed when the group finally reached the city of Ranas. Elac found it to be like any other Human city, with a widespread marketplace, military barracks near the gates, and housing areas ranging from the well-kept mansions of the wealthy to the slovenly hovels in a surprisingly litter-free slum. Jayrne led them to a nondescript inn near the center of town, close enough to their target to allow her to scout the area without risk of discovery.

Cassius, his family crest once more hidden beneath a battered cloak, rented two large rooms, which were connected by an adjoining door. They retired to their rooms to change

clothes and plan their next strategy. Jayrne, however, immediately slipped back into the rainy night, saying since she was
already wet, she wanted to locate the assassins' guild in Ranas.
Elac offered to go with her, but she turned him down.

An hour later, Jayrne returned. She accepted the gracious
offer of using the bath in one of the rooms they were sharing,
emerging a short time later dressed only in a robe. Elac found
his attention, and his eyes, wandering while the group discussed
her findings.

"The guild is about six blocks from here," Jayrne told
them. "They have their guards disguised as beggars, stationed
all around the building. I think this time we should all go.
With an audience guaranteed by Wraist, we'd be safer with all
of us there."

"Speaking of feeling safer, Elac, I have something for you."
Rilen handed him a bulky sack. Elac peered inside and saw a
sparkling mesh of metal reflecting the candlelight back at him.
"While I was guarding the baths, a friend of mine who I met
at the War College came by. I talked her into borrowing this
from the local garrison. It's a suit of chain mail. It was made
by Elven blacksmiths, so you'll find it to be just a bit lighter than
the suits made here in Palindom."

Elac accepted the gift gratefully, pulling it from the sack
and trying it on, hardly listening while the conversation continued. The armor was cold, but it fit well, just loose enough
to allow him freedom of movement. He found the armor to be
heavier than Rilen's description led him to believe, but still significantly lighter than typical steel armor.

They decided to contact the guild right after breakfast,

which would allow them enough time to act on any information they might obtain. At Rilen's further suggestion, they left the door between the two rooms ajar, and posted a continuous watch throughout the night.

The skies were still overcast the next morning, although the rain had stopped. They left their horses stabled at the inn and proceeded to the guild on foot. The cobblestone streets of Ranas were much cleaner than the other port cities Elac had visited, with none of the piles of litter he had come to expect from such places. Even the buildings looked as if they were washed on a regular basis, something Jayrne confirmed before he had even finished the thought.

"The Duke of Ranas is obsessed with tidiness. A first offense for littering carries a heavy fine, and repeat offenders find themselves in the dungeon or on the whipping post. There are even penalties for allowing dirt to accumulate on the sides of a house or place of business."

She guided them down a narrow alleyway, inhabited by a number of men who sat on their knees, small cups held out imploringly as the group strolled past. Elac, remembering Jayrne's warning the night before, kept a close eye on them. He shrugged his shoulders once more, still trying to get used to the weight of the armor he wore under his tunic.

Jayrne approached a wooden door and knocked twice. She then made an obscure sign with her hands, and handed the parchment from Wraist to the closest "beggar." He examined it briefly, handed it back to her, and waved to one of his companions to open the door. The man pulled a large brass key from his pocket, placed it in the lock, and turned it with an audible *click.* The door creaked open, and the group followed the guard through the open portal.

The air inside the guild was smoky, giving the building a dark, dingy atmosphere. It wasn't a very inviting place, which was probably what the assassins had in mind when they chose it. The interior walls were made of rough stone blocks, with peeling paint and cracked mortar. The floor was also made of stone, and it wasn't much smoother than the walls. Torches lined the walls, spaced a bit too far apart for Elac's comfort. Blackened marks ran up the walls and onto the ceiling where the flames from the torches had scarred the stone.

They followed their new guide down a long passage to the guild audience hall. The room was much smaller than Wraist's hall back at Goran, and it appeared to lack the same level of formality. A keg of ale stood in one corner, and a group of four men stood around it with tankards in hand. One man sat at a desk in a corner, and a tall, lithe woman was looking over his shoulder, pointing to something on a map. The two looked up when the party arrived.

"Greetings, your Excellency," Silvayn said with a florid bow.

The man behind the desk gave a cold, cheerless smile, almost as if such an expression was foreign to his scarred face. "You can dispense with the highborn greetings. We know who you are. Word has reached us from Wraist concerning the situation. Serana will provide you with whatever information you need."

The woman beside him rose to her feet. She had blond hair descending to her waist, caught behind her head in a black band. She wore a simple white robe, tied with a frayed piece of rope. "You seek Dalos." She said it as a matter of fact, rather than a question.

"Yes," Silvayn said simply.

"Then you must first find Johl. He is an Elf." She paused, regarding the group coolly. "Does that surprise you?"

"Should it?" Silvayn asked.

Serana crossed her arms. "Johl is the only member of Dalos whom we have spoken to. It was he who initially spoke to us about the attack on your party, but since the attempt was to take place near Goran, we referred him to Wraist. He owns a shop just outside of town, where they make wagons. It's likely a front for their group, so you may find the answers you seek there."

"We appreciate any help you can provide, of course," Silvayn said cautiously.

"Let's get one thing straight," Serana said suddenly, leveling a finger at the old mage. "I'm totally opposed to helping you out at all. I think we're making a big mistake, and we'll all hang for it later. But I have to obey our code. Just remember, if it was up to me, we would deal with this ourselves and send you on your way."

She turned back to the desk, rummaged through a few drawers, and finally produced a map showing the immediate area surrounding Ranas. She made a couple of notations indicating an area about a league south of the city before handing it to Silvayn. Rilen stepped lightly to Silvayn's side, and the two glanced over the map. Rilen took it wordlessly, folded it, and placed it in a pouch at his waist.

The man behind the desk stood. "Our debt is paid, and we will help you no more."

He motioned to the door, and a pair of men dressed in the

rags of common beggars seemed almost to materialize from the dark recesses of the room. One motioned to the party, indicating for them to follow, and the two disguised assassins led the way back out to the street. The door slammed shut behind them, and Elac heard the locks and bolts slide into place with a grinding noise, securing the door behind them.

They returned to the inn to discuss their next step. "Obviously," Jayrne said, "we need to stay here until dark. I'd like to get a look at the target before we get too close, though."

Gillen nodded, studying the map and stroking his red beard. "We should be able to find a place to hide while you ride ahead. Do you plan to go alone?"

"I'll go with her," Rilen said. When Jayrne raised her eyebrows in question, he shrugged and told her, "We're probably going to have to find a way to sneak into the building, and two pairs of eyes are better than one. I can move without being seen when I need to."

"What if you are seen?" Cassius asked Jayrne. "What will you do then?"

"I won't be seen." Jayrne said it as a matter of fact, and it plainly wasn't an idle boast.

Cassius scowled, a hint of the arrogant man Elac had met in Palim coming to the surface. "I guess you're a better thief than I thought," he said, turning his back.

❦ ❦ ❦ ❦ ❦

There was no moon, and the cloud cover blocked out even the light of the stars, but their resourceful thief was able to find shelter as if it was the brightest daylight. They tied the horses to a group of low bushes, and Gillen and Hadwyn volunteered to serve as lookouts. Jayrne and Rilen took a few moments to rub dirt on their faces in preparation for their reconnoiter. On impulse, Elac also darkened his face. Jayrne opened her mouth to protest, but Rilen cut her short with a raised hand. He studied Elac for several moments.

"Let him come," he said simply. "I think he's ready."

Elac felt a secret thrill at the veteran warrior's proclamation, and he went about his preparations with an extra spring in his step. He carefully covered his chain mail, and while he left his shield behind with his horse, he was careful to bring his bow. Rilen spoke briefly to Silvayn, telling them how far they would travel and how long they would be gone.

They marched quickly for several minutes, and the soft ground of the grasslands muffled all sound of their footsteps. In the distance, Elac could barely make out a stand of trees, and Rilen told him the building they sought was located in the grove. They edged closer, staying low to minimize their silhouettes and soon Elac saw the building slowly appear out of the darkness. It was larger than he expected, much larger than a simple wagon maker's facility would have required.

They approached as closely as they dared, knowing there could be sentries posted somewhere along the perimeter. Rilen motioned with his hand, and they all knelt to the ground and crawled inside a row of thorny bushes, where they studied their target for several long minutes. Although Elac himself could see nothing of use, he knew Rilen would be finalizing the tactics the group would use to raid the building.

The sound of voices drawing nearer reached Elac and he felt his pulse quicken. Rilen eased his sword from its sheath, concealing the telltale glint of metal by covering it with his cloak. Elac followed suit, trying to stay as low to the ground as he could. The voices became louder, and he knew the unseen figures were walking directly to the spot where Elac and his friends were hiding. He found himself holding his breath, waiting for the explosion of violence from Rilen, and he could feel his pulse pounding in his neck. The seconds ticked away, and three armed men appeared to the group's right.

A voice called out from the building in the distance, and one of the three men answered with a shout. They stood in place briefly, hands on their hips and grumbling under their breath, then returned to the wagon facility. Elac carefully let out the breath he had been holding, sliding his sword back into his scabbard. They waited for a few more minutes to be certain the danger had passed, then backed out of the bushes and made their way back to the others.

A low whistle from Hadwyn guided the group in. Rilen rubbed a bare place in the dirt, and he used a stick to draw a crude map of the building.

"The facility is enormous," Rilen said with a low voice. "I'm not sure what's going on in there, but they aren't just making wagons." He looked up at Jayrne with pursed lips. "Could the assassins have given us bad information?"

"No," she said immediately, shaking her head. "It'd be against their code to lie to us, and they knew too much about Dalos to have been wrong."

Cassius stroked his mustache, regarding Jayrne carefully.

"So now we have to trust murderers, as well as thieves?" He gave a short laugh, shaking his head. "As I said, this venture was doomed from the start."

"I've had enough of your insinuations," Jayrne hissed, coming to her feet, hands on her hips. "You think you are better than the rest of us, Highborn, but your rank and title mean nothing. You are nothing but a spoiled, overly pampered noble."

Cassius sputtered in outrage, and Silvayn stepped between them, his voice a whisper. "That's enough! We have bigger things to deal with than the merits of thievery and the benefits of royal birth. You two don't have to be friends, but you will cooperate. I need you, but more importantly, Elac needs you. This quest won't succeed if we don't cooperate."

Cassius pulled the broadsword from the packs on his horse. "I've told you, Silvayn, I believe this quest will fail, regardless. However, it shall be as you say."

They located another draw, one close enough to satisfy Rilen, and they left their horses there and proceeded on foot. Jayrne suddenly held up one hand, motioning for the group to stop. She glided forward, her nimble body making no more sound than a whispering breeze blowing across the rolling plains. Elac waited tensely in the dark for her return, worried something might have happened to her. She emerged from the darkness, and Elac noticed a bloody dagger in her hand.

"What have you done?" Cassius hissed, his eyes wide.

"Slavers!" she told them in a harsh whisper. "Dalos is a group of slavers!"

Chapter 11

Jayrne had spotted two men near the building's perimeter, and she crept close enough to hear their conversation. Dalos was a group dealing primarily in slaves. From what the men had said, she believed the details of the operation were to be found inside. When the two men separated, one had strayed close to where she lay hidden, and he had felt the bite of her blade. The dead man had the telltale dagger and manacle tattoo on his upper back.

Now, as they approached, Jayrne called the group to a halt once more, and she motioned for Rilen to join her. She gestured ahead, pointing to three different locations. She and Rilen whispered briefly, then Rilen eased back to Elac's hiding spot.

"We're going to need your help," he whispered. "There are three stationary one-man guard positions up ahead. We can take them out with bows, but they all have to be dealt with at the same time. Jayrne will take one, and I another. We need you to get the third." He paused, looking Elac in the eyes. "Can you do it?"

Elac regarded him silently for a few moments, licked his lips nervously, then nodded slowly. Rilen gripped Elac's shoulder reassuringly in a show of support. They crawled back to where Jayrne lay hidden, lying down beside her. Elac set his shield on the ground and gripped his bow. Jayrne squeezed his hand with a wink, and she pointed to a spot some thirty yards distant, where a man was rummaging through his pack, oblivious to the little group in front of him. She pointed to her face and neck, and then to the sentry, which Elac understood would be his target area. He sat looking at the man he was about to kill, and he found himself wondering if he could do it.

Rilen tapped Elac's foot to get his attention. The Elf drew his bow, and Jayrne and Elac did likewise. Elac sighted along the shaft of his arrow, concentrating on putting the shot on target, and trying unsuccessfully to force the hesitation from his mind. He considered what he was about to do. He was to shoot a man, an armed man, but an ambush no matter what face Elac tried to put on it. Technically, this man had done him no wrong. Elac shook his head, dispatching the line of thought. The man was a slaver, and in all the lands of Pelacia, there was no crime regarded as more abhorrent than slavery, save Necromancy. He drew a deep, steadying breath. The man had to die.

Next to him, he heard Rilen give a slow, quiet count. "One. Two. Three." Three bowstrings snapped, almost in unison. Time seemed to pause as Elac watched the arrow fly from his bow, streak through the night air, and embed itself in his target's throat. The man's hands immediately grabbed the piercing shaft, and he slowly collapsed to his knees. Without a word of protest, he fell to his back, his hands dropping away from the arrow.

Rilen glanced out to Elac's target. He nodded and shook Elac's hand, an unexpectedly fierce look of pride in his eyes, and Jayrne hugged him impulsively. Momentarily disappearing into the night, Rilen brought up the rest of the group. They slipped forward, meeting no more resistance. They neared the massive structure, but no sounds came from within. It was constructed mainly of logs, packed together with some type of mud and secured at the ends by leather thongs. Windows were sparse, giving the appearance that the occupants valued their privacy. Emblazoned on the side of the building was an enormous dagger encircled by a shackle. Jayrne led them along the edge of the building to a window, and within moments she had pried it open.

They climbed through one at a time, gathering once more inside a small room. It was well-furnished, with cabinets, a desk, and several chairs. From under the heavy oak door, Elac could see the dancing glow of torchlight. The floor echoed hollowly under their feet, which Elac took to mean there was at least one story underground. Jayrne started forward, but Silvayn held her back. Adalyn was already moving, a newly lighted torch in hand, rummaging through the files in a corner cabinet. Elac kept a nervous eye on the door while they waited.

"This is interesting," Adalyn told them finally. "Slaves are brought here, to be kept in pens until there are enough to make a trip worthwhile. They're taken by caravan to a secluded cove near Piaras Keep, where they're loaded onto ships." She paused, her jaw dropping open wide in disbelief. "They are taken by ship to the Bay of Malator, where they are sold to the Necromancers."

"This cannot be!" Cassius raged, his anger evident in the reddening of his face and the veins bulging in his neck, yet somehow he managed to keep his voice down.

"It will be stopped," Hadwyn said in a voice that carried the whisper of death. "They will all pay for this outrage with their lives!"

"Where do the slavers go from Malator?" Silvayn asked, stepping closer to Adalyn.

"According to these papers, they receive weapons in exchange for the slaves. Swords, spears, bows and arrows, even armor. They take these to the port at Hrcac, where they sell them to the Kobolds for gold. Then they return here and gather another group of slaves to be taken south."

"It ends tonight," Rilen assured them.

Adalyn stuffed a stack of papers into her pack. "We should take this information before the Unity Council."

"Forget those fools!" Rilen said through clenched teeth. "They will do nothing to stop the evil. It falls to us." Elac nodded his agreement, drawing his sword and setting his shield.

"We'll still need this as proof," Adalyn told him pointedly. "The Kobold ambassador is likely to file an official protest if we cut off this supply of weapons, so we need to be prepared."

"She's right," Cassius said with a sigh. He set the point of his broadsword on the wooden floor and leaned against the pommel. "Politics at its best."

"All right," Silvayn decided. "But we can only spare a few more minutes. Gather what you can, and then we'll cleanse this place."

"Yes!" Hadwyn said. Elac found the Dwarf's enthusiasm chilling, especially when he took out a whetstone and honed the point on the crow's beak of his hammer.

Elac kept a nervous eye on the door while Adalyn finished her work, but after several minutes, no one had discovered them and she had collected what she needed. Jayrne placed her ear against the door and listened intently for several seconds, one hand held up for silence. Satisfied, she gently opened the door and stepped through. The rest of the group followed, and Elac found himself in a darkened hallway. Sputtering, smoky torches spaced at irregular distances provided barely adequate lighting. Jayrne and Rilen led the way deeper into the slavers' hideout. Rilen cracked open each door they passed, peered inside, and eased it shut once more. At a door at the far end of the hall, Rilen waved the others closer. He pulled the door open wide to reveal a set of stone stairs spiraling down into darkness.

They entered the stairwell. From far below, Elac saw a faint, dancing glow, and he assumed there were more torches on the next level. The unsteady light grew brighter the farther they descended, and when they reached the bottom, Elac realized the light was coming from a series of broad fire pits. They emerged from the stairwell and found themselves in a broad, underground room. The walls were lined with cages, cells blocked away by black iron bars pitted with rust. The floor was made from loosely fitted stones held together by crumbling mortar. Most of the cells contained several disheveled-looking occupants, a wide assortment of people including members of all three races.

A hoarse shout sounded from the far end of the room. A dozen guards, bare-chested men wearing black leather masks and carrying an assortment of weapons, jumped up from their tables. Most had the dagger symbol tattooed on their chest or arm. One ran out of the room through a side passage, while the others closed on Elac and his friends. Elac bit his lip, setting his resolve for the fight.

Rilen met the charge, a short sword in one hand and the familiar black and gold shield in the other. The first guard to reach them was armed with a long sword, and with a roar of berserker rage he swung a two-handed blow at Rilen's head. The Elf easily blocked the blow, then used his shield as a ram, battering the man back against the wall and pinning the sword against its owner. Rilen delivered several lightning jabs with his shorter weapon, and his foe slid limply to the floor, leaving a smeared trail of sticky blood on the wall.

Elac's foe carried a heavy mace, the lead-encased end whistling menacingly at his approach. He tried several sweeping strokes, but the guard easily dodged his blows. A strike from the mace pummeled Elac's shield with a resounding *clang*, knocking Elac a step backward. The man raised his club once more, but a dagger whistled through the air and embedded itself in his upper arm. He glanced reflexively at the blade protruding from his arm, and Elac's sword swept up, slicing the unarmored man from hip to shoulder. He dropped to one knee with a cry, trying desperately to keep his entrails from spilling onto the blood-soaked ground.

Jayrne darted past and retrieved her dagger. "Relax your shield arm," she told him over the din. "Don't fight force with force." Then she was up and running, slipping in and out of the melee.

Elac spun to find another foe and saw Hadwyn bury his crow's beak in the chest of a guard. The Dwarf wrenched it free with an oath, and the man crumpled against the wall, then fell to the ground to die in a bloody heap. Off to Elac's left, Rilen had engaged two enemies at the same time, and his short jabs were taking their toll. Both of his foes were bleeding from several wounds, trying desperately to penetrate the Elf's defenses. Elac dashed to his friend's side, and the nearest guard turned to face him.

His left arm still ached from the blow against his shield moments before, but he raised his shield defiantly. This time, when his foe attacked, Elac tried to let his arm give just a bit, absorbing the blow rather than trying to stop it. His own strike was more successful, drawing a red streak down the guard's leg. But Elac's attack left him off balance, and his opponent's next slash bounced off Elac's shield to bite into his leg. He staggered back, trying to shift more of his weight to his right leg. The guard struck again, but this time Elac was waiting. He deflected the blade with his shield, and followed it immediately with a powerful thrust. He put all of his strength behind his sword, and drove it home. The guard stared downward at the metal handle protruding from his chest, coughed up blood, then toppled over backward, Elac's sword still embedded in his inert body. His eyes wide, Elac looked around the room but found the last foe had fallen.

Rilen stepped lightly to the inert form lying on the floor and wrenched Elac's sword free. He wiped the blade on the guard's leather trousers, then handed it to Elac, hilt first. "Remember, use lighter, shorter thrusts. You overextend yourself when you put all your strength behind a single blow like that, leaving you open to a counterattack. Besides, if you bury your blade in a man's chest, it tends to get stuck in bone. Very hard to remove."

Jayrne used a set of keys she recovered from a table to unlock the nearest cage. "Hey, Rilen, I thought he did just fine."

Rilen gave her a long look. "He survived."

"You did alright," Gillen told him. "Let me look at your leg while they open the rest of those cages."

Elac felt a sense of elation rush through his body. He hardly noticed Gillen's prayer of healing, scarcely felt the relief when the stinging in his leg subsided. The nausea and revulsion he felt the first time he had killed a man were gone, replaced with a strange sense of security and power. By the time Gillen finished his healing magic, the cages were all open, and the slaves were gathered in a tight group in the center of the room. Their dirty faces were tinged with mingled fear and hope, dreams of freedom playing out before them.

At a signal from Silvayn, Rilen led the group up the steps at the far end, away from where they had entered. He eased up the steps and tried the door, but found it locked. Jayrne immediately took charge. She pulled a pair of thin metal rods from the top of her right boot, and she went to work on the lock. The door opened, and Rilen once again led the group forward, the newly freed slaves trailing behind. Some of them had grabbed weapons from the fallen guards, while still others had picked up improvised weapons, mostly implements of torture.

In the hall beyond the stairs, a room with plain wooden

walls and a dirty wooden floor, they were met by another rush of guards, this one larger than before. Rilen forced his way deeper into the room, an act Elac saw as reckless until he realized the Elf was trying to allow the rest of the company to enter the fray. Elac had to put Rilen's harsh advice to work immediately when he found himself hard-pressed by a man with a pair of long daggers. He used his shield as Rilen had, blocking the attack and using it to batter past his foe's defenses. With a pair of short, rapid thrusts of his short sword, Elac put his man down.

All about the hall, the battle raged. Cassius called out his family's ancient battle cry and swung his broadsword about him, the cold steel finding a home in more than one guard. Hadwyn reversed his deadly hammer, and used the mallet to crush the life out of two men who ventured too close. Gillen's axe was at least as deadly, and at one point Elac caught sight of the Dwarf's axe cleaving a hastily raised shield in two. The weapon struck the shield's owner squarely in the chest, and spilled his blood on the floor. Rilen was a blur, dancing through the crush of guards and leaving behind the dead and dying. Jayrne positioned herself atop a table, bow in hand, and she rained deadly fire into the enemy ranks. Adalyn, who had placed herself squarely between Silvayn and the onrushing forces, felled two men who rushed her position.

At last, the remaining handful of guards turned and ran, to the cheers of the escaping slaves. Elac surveyed the carnage before him, and was dismayed to see four of the slaves had perished in the fight, with a few more seriously wounded. Undernourished and mistreated, they had been in no condition to fight, but with a taste of freedom, they had battled fiercely.

He made eye contact with Rilen, and the veteran Elf nodded his silent approval of Elac's performance in the battle. A thrill rushed through Elac's body, and he felt almost like a young boy whose childhood hero had just shaken his hand. But then the smell of smoke brought the entire entourage up short.

"Wait here," Rilen ordered. He dashed through the doorway, forsaking silence for speed. Without hesitating, Elac followed him. He knew the Elf would disapprove of what he was doing, but he was tired of staying behind while the others risked their lives for him. He caught up to Rilen when the other slowed to peer around a corner.

The burning odor was stronger there, and Elac had to cover his mouth to suppress a cough. He could hear the crackle of the flames and see the orange light dancing on the walls ahead, which he knew could mean only one thing.

They retreated to where the others waited, and Rilen broke the news to them. "They've set the building on fire in several places. We can't get out this way."

There were several panicked shouts from the group of slaves, but Cassius raised his voice to silence them. "Hold, my people! All is not lost! Follow us now, quickly, and we will yet escape!"

His brief oration seemed to calm the worst of their fears, even though not all the slaves were Human. The panic assailing them dissipated somewhat, and Elac and his friends were able to slip back through the thirty remaining slaves and take the lead once more.

They reentered the slave pens, and once again the repugnant odors assailed Elac's senses. He quickened his pace a bit, trying to be free of the vulgar place. He climbed the steps behind Rilen and Jayrne, and he sensed their escape was close at hand. Once again, the group and its charges ascended the stairs toward freedom.

And again they were thwarted. The fire was worse at that end, and they were forced to immediately retreat to the pens. The air became hazy, and the smoke pushed its way into their sanctuary. The dirty cloud billowed down the stairs at both ends of the room, and Elac could sense the panic rising in the slaves once more. Some screamed in terror; others dropped their weapons and ran from place to place in a futile effort to find a way out.

"Over here," Jayrne called to the group from an especially dark corner of the pens. She ran her fingers lightly over a section of the wall as if searching for something. She stopped, leaning closer and concentrating on one point. With a noise of stone grating on stone, the section of wall slid open to reveal a darkened passage beyond. Elac raced to grab a nearby torch, and he thrust it into what he hoped was their new escape route. The passage was empty, and while the air smelled stale, it was infinitely better than the choking air he would leave behind.

With Rilen and Jayrne once again in the lead, they entered the secret underground walkway, weapons ready. It was clearly a little-used passage, built for some long-forgotten purpose. They followed the winding tunnel for several minutes, and Rilen slowed the pace once he sensed they had left the fire behind.

At last, the path curved around a bend to end in the open countryside. It was still dark, but Rilen extinguished his torch immediately to avoid giving away their location. Although most of the guards were dead, and the rest were likely scattered, he would take no chances. With uncharacteristic empathy, Cassius climbed onto a nearby rock and called the slaves over to him.

"You are free, for now," he told them. "The slavers are defeated, and their stronghold is destroyed. Although it nearly claimed us, we have escaped, as I knew we would with such a righteous cause.

"But do not become complacent. The slavers may regroup and attempt to minimize their losses by recapturing some of you. We cannot help you, as we have our own task to complete, and have no more time to spare. Most of you have weapons, and you are capable of defending yourselves. The city of Ranas is just north of here, and if you start now, you will reach it by sunrise. Go to the local army garrison there and tell them your story. They will take care of you and see to it the remaining slavers are dealt with severely."

The crowd of former slaves milled about as they muttered softly to themselves. Finally, two men emerged as leaders of the group, and they led the way into the night. Jayrne sat beside Elac, smiling warmly.

"You showed great courage this evening, Elac."

"Thank you," he said awkwardly, not knowing what else to say. Like a young schoolboy with his first crush, he found himself nervously short on words.

"How's the leg?" she asked, taking a seat beside him.

"Better, but sore."

She sighed. "Look. Rilen was harsh, but he was right about your technique. You have to be careful not to overextend yourself. I don't want anything to happen to you."

With those words, Elac's heart pounded so hard he could

feel it thudding in his chest. His face flushed red, and he wanted to look away to hide his embarrassment, but he found himself spellbound by her eyes. Time seemed to freeze, and he was seized by the uncontrollable urge to kiss her.

"Let's go," Silvayn announced. "We need to be well away from this place before the sun comes up."

Jayrne gave Elac a sympathetic smile, patted his cheek, then stood and joined the others. Rilen knelt and scraped a clear spot on the ground.

"This is Ranas," he told them, indicating one of the marks he had made in the dirt. "This is the Mason River, and over here is Nightwood Forest. Farther south is the city of Mason, and off to the east is Fort Ranset. I think we should head due south for a few hours until we find a place to ford the river. We can bypass Mason and make for Fort Ranset."

"Why not go directly to the city?" Adalyn asked.

"Politics," Rilen answered without smiling. "The military will help Cassius, no questions asked. But if we go to Mason, we have to deal with Duke Ters. With the internal power struggle among the Humans right now, I would just as soon avoid the situation."

"He's right," Cassius added. "Most of the Dukes covet my position. They seek to take away what is rightfully mine." Elac didn't miss the irony of the statement: Cassius was far removed from the crown, but just as ambitious as the others.

"At Fort Ranset," Rilen continued, rubbing his eyes wearily, "we can replenish our supplies and turn toward Noran's castle. After we recover the Dagger, we can head directly for Piaras Keep and find out what the spirits there have in mind for us."

"Then we have a plan," Silvayn said as he rose to his feet. "Lead on."

It took almost an hour to locate their mounts. They had exited through the long, winding tunnel, and they were unsure how far away the horses were. Jayrne, ahead of the group as usual, stumbled upon the hidden draw and whistled softly to the others.

It was well after midnight when Elac heard the gurgling sound of shallow water rushing over rocks, and he knew they had found the ford. They crossed the river without incident and turned east. Rilen led them through the darkness for another hour before he called a halt. Elac slowly dismounted, his body a ball of agony after what he had been through in the past several hours.

The sun was peeking over the edge of the horizon, the sky was a ruddy haze when Gillen gently shook him awake for his turn at the watch. He stood and leaned against the oak tree, not daring to sit for fear of falling asleep. He stared into the darkness, his mind wandering back to his last conversation with Jayrne. Was she interested in him as more than a traveling companion? Shrugging, he contented himself with watching her blanket rise and fall with her breathing, and stood unmoving until the time came to awaken Cassius.

Rilen allowed the group to sleep a few hours past sunrise, giving them the chance to recuperate after the long night. They ate a late breakfast, loaded their gear, and rode east once more. While the Paheny Mountains were still over twenty leagues away, their reach was felt even here. The land was covered with rolling hills and crisscrossed by streams of water that had begun their long trek as snow melting from the distant peaks. The grasses weren't as tall, and the wildlife was a bit more widespread.

Shortly after noon, Rilen had led them to a paved road, which would take them to Fort Ranset. Silvayn allowed them to move off the road and rest while they ate lunch. Jayrne built a cooking fire, and Elac enjoyed his first hot meal in days.

Late that afternoon, Elac found himself daydreaming about home. He was snapped from his reverie by a crack of thunder; the storm that had built all but unnoticed all day suddenly turned loose its full fury upon the unsuspecting travelers. The wind rushed out from the center of the deluge, blowing the rain sideways and whipping Elac's cloak behind him. Ignoring their discomfort, the party resumed their journey.

After an hour, the downpour slackened to a light but steady rain, and travel was less miserable. Elac looked upon his sodden clothing, covered with blood, sweat, and soot, and decided he was in need of a hot bath.

Elac noticed Jayrne was studying some of the papers Adalyn had taken from the slavers' stronghold. He nudged his horse over beside hers.

"Finding anything?"

"I can't make any sense of it," she admitted with a shake of her head. "Business transactions are a bit over my head sometimes. Usually, if I want something, I take it."

"Do you mind if I give it a try?"

She handed the papers over with her crooked half-smile. "Be my guest."

Near the bottom of the stack, the topics covered varying

aspects of the arrangement with the Kobolds. Weapons, armor, and shields were assigned specific monetary values. He glanced down the page of one such order. At the bottom, a small symbol caught his eye. A cold lump formed in the pit of his stomach.

"Rilen!" he said anxiously, kicking at his horse's flanks. He pulled alongside the veteran Elf and reined in. Rilen looked at him quizzically, one eyebrow raised, until Elac held up the document in question. At the bottom was inscribed a picture of a coiled black serpent, preparing to strike.

"I found this in the papers Adalyn picked up from the slavers."

"What is it?" Silvayn asked, guiding his horse closer as Rilen stopped and dismounted.

Rilen's nostrils flared as he read the paper. "This is a list of weapons purchased by the Kobolds, supplied by Dalos. This symbol at the bottom represents the Drablok clan, a supposed renegade faction whose professed desire is to cleanse Pelacia of all non-Kobolds."

Adalyn shrugged. "If the slavers are providing weapons to the main Kobold forces, it only makes sense they would also try to sell to the renegades."

"True," Rilen acknowledged, one finger raised, "but to do so, they would need to go overland to the Northern Plains to make contact with the Drablok clan. This order was delivered a month ago to the Kobold port city of Hrcac."

"Zantar preserve us!" Gillen exclaimed, his eyes wide in shock. "If they are getting their weapons in Hrcac, it would prove an undeniable link between them and the Kobold government!"

"Let's ride," Silvayn told them suddenly. "We have to get

this information to the leaders of the three nations immediately. Those regular Kobold units patrolling the eastern half of Pelacia are poised to strike at the heart of our defenses. The existence of this arrangement erases all doubt about the intentions of the Kobolds!"

They rode off at a gallop, fatigue and discomfort forgotten in their rush to reach Fort Ranset. They had only covered a league before they encountered a patrol of Human soldiers, at least one hundred strong, approaching them from the east. They slowed their horses to a walk, then stopped and sat waiting. His banner waving proudly from the tip of his lance, Cassius nudged his horse forward. Most of the soldiers were on foot, but a group of two dozen men were on horseback. They rode out to meet him, and one man, presumably the leader, dismounted. Cassius did likewise, and as the two met, the other dropped to one knee. Elac and the others joined them as the Prince acknowledged the soldier's obeisance.

"This is Captain Legat. He has agreed to provide us with an escort to Fort Ranset."

"It is my pleasure, your Highness," the man said, rising. "Prince Cassius tells me you have urgent news. We will make haste. My mounted soldiers will ride with us, while the others will find the rest of my detachment and join us later. If you are ready . . ." He gestured to the east with a courtly bow. Cassius leapt into his saddle, brought his horse about with a flourish, and fell in line behind the soldiers. Although Elac thought it was unnecessary, Rilen rode ahead of the patrol.

The sun was a dim, red orb just beginning to dip below the horizon when Fort Ranset came into view. To Elac, it appeared to be just what the name implied: a fortress, impregnable, erected to secure the eastern reaches of the Kingdom of Palindom. It was reinforced by multiple defenses. The land around it had been cleared of trees and tall grasses for several hundred yards, preventing an enemy from being able to make a stealthy approach. A curtain wall surrounded the main citadel, providing an initial defensive position from which the defenders could retreat if necessary. If an enemy penetrated the first wall, the soldiers inside could fall back to the main fortress using walkways, specially rigged to collapse and prevent the enemy from following. There was only one gate in each wall, reinforced by a barbican, a massive gatehouse that provided reinforcement for the gate. Soldiers stationed inside could fire arrows and dump burning pitch upon the hapless enemies below who were trying to breach the gates.

Elac heard a low whistle, looked to his right, and saw Rilen waving emphatically from the cover of a nearby gulley.

"Silvayn," Elac announced, pointing to where the Elf awaited them. "Rilen."

Captain Legat called his soldiers to a halt, waiting while Elac, Silvayn, and Cassius met with Rilen. He had left his horse tied to a tree, and he ran to them breathlessly.

"Get those men out of sight!" he half-shouted. "I think we're in trouble!"

Cassius paused to assess the Elf's demeanor, then returned to the column. While the Prince led the contingent of soldiers into a place of cover, Rilen, Elac, and Silvayn slipped forward on foot. They topped a low rise, where they could see Fort Ranset, not a half mile distant. Soldiers manned the walls, and the banner of

Palindom flew proudly from atop the ceremonial watchtower in the center of town. Everything seemed to be in order.

"What is it?" Silvayn asked.

"The flag," Rilen answered, never taking his eyes off the base. "Humans stand on ceremony. Without fail, they are required to lower the flag before the sun touches the horizon. It's considered an act of disrespect to allow the flag to fly in darkness."

"What does it mean?" Elac asked, his palms turned up in confusion.

"It means something is wrong. I used a scrying spell Adalyn taught me." Elac saw Silvayn roll his eyes in disgust, obviously still distraught over Adalyn's lessons. "Those soldiers manning the walls aren't Humans. You can't tell from this distance, because they're wearing helmets."

"Then what are they?" Elac asked, half-rising for a better look.

"Kobolds."

Chapter 12

Impossible," Captain Legat said, shaking his head pointedly as he rose to his feet. "There is no way the Kobolds could have taken the fort so quickly. There are over one thousand men inside those walls. With Ranset's defenses, half their number could hold out against any force for a month. I've only been gone for two days."

Rilen folded his hands in his lap. "Did you have a detachment of Kobold soldiers assigned to Fort Ranset?"

"Yes, but we outnumbered them better than two-to-one."

"But there were other Kobold forces patrolling between Fort Ranset and the Paheny Mountains, correct?"

"Certainly, but I don't see what—"

"Then one or more mounted Kobold units could've ridden right through the gates. With Kobolds already inside, your men wouldn't have thought twice about letting them in."

"But how could they have overpowered an entire legion so quickly?"

Hadwyn snorted. "Bah! It would be a matter of great

simplicity. At night, how many of your men are actually awake? Half? A third? Less?" Captain Legat's eyes opened wide with horror at the possibility.

"He's right," Cassius said. "Most of your men were probably butchered in their sleep."

Captain Legat slowly shook his head. "Then we let them position their forces to take our eastern bases all at once and almost without a fight. You are certain of this, your Highness?"

"I am."

"Captain," Rilen asked, "did you say you had another detachment of men?"

"Yes, but by now they should be . . . on their way here! They'll be slaughtered!"

"Okay," Rilen said, rubbing his chin, "our first order of business is to catch up to that patrol. We need all the men we can get, and we don't want them walking right into an ambush. Obviously, we can't retake the fort with what we have, but we can certainly try to hurt them." He pulled a map of the region from his pack, his fingers tracing the lands between Nightwood Forest and the Paheny Mountains.

"Wait a minute, Rilen," Adalyn said, stepping up beside him. "We can't get involved in this. We have an appointment to keep, if you remember."

Rilen looked up from the map with a sarcastic smile. "And just how far do you think we'll get with mounted Kobold patrols coming out of Fort Ranset? We wouldn't make it halfway to the mountains. What we need to do is lure their cavalry into an ambush."

"Oh, really?" Cassius said, folding his arms across his chest.

"And how do you propose doing that? Do you realize most of their mounted troops are heavy cavalry? All we have are mounted scouts. Javelins against knights wouldn't be an ideal tactical situation."

"Then we'll change the tactical situation," Rilen told him pointedly. "Obviously, we aren't going to charge out and meet them head-on. We'll have to bring them to us. Let's go find the rest of your detachment."

Midnight found Elac and his friends united with the rest of Captain Legat's unit. There were over three hundred soldiers, a number that appeared sizeable to Elac but that he knew wouldn't be nearly enough to retake Fort Ranset. They had retreated about two leagues northwest of the fort toward Nightwood Forest, hoping to avoid random Kobold patrols. They made no fires, and no one was allowed to set up a tent. The men flitted about like ghosts in the darkness, setting up their defenses while Rilen and the others planned the next move.

"Here's the situation," Captain Legat announced. "We have fifty cavalry scouts, armed with bows and javelins. We have sixty archers, armed with longbows. They aren't as effective as the longbows of the Elves, but they'll do in a pinch." He managed a weak smile. "The remaining two hundred soldiers are all infantry, armed with short swords, shields, and chain mail.

"Also, the detachment we just located had a lieutenant returning from Unity. Since he spoke with the Council, he may be able to brief us on the situation there."

Captain Legat gestured, and a young man in a crisp uniform stepped forward. "Lieutenant Georay reporting as ordered, sir," he said with a smart salute.

"Lieutenant, please be so good as to tell my friends here what is happening at Unity."

He shook his head. "Madness. The Council just completed a deal with the Kobold ambassador giving them greater access to our forts, our lands, and our military secrets. Dralana is pressuring the others to go along with the insane suggestions. Not that the other Councilors need much encouragement. The vote was unanimous."

Elac's jaw dropped open in surprise. "Even Falstoff?"

The lieutenant shook his head sadly. "Falstoff is no longer on the Council. He has been appointed as the Council's ambassador to the Necromancers."

Hadwyn swung a mighty blow with his hammer, shattering a large rock. "The Unity Council has opened communications with the Necromancers? This is unconscionable! How could Falstoff lend himself to this idiocy?"

"We can't do anything about it now," Rilen said, turning back to the map. "But we can do something about limiting the mobility of the Kobold forces around Fort Ranset. Captain Legat, if we were to eliminate the Kobold heavy cavalry, could your army keep the fort loosely under siege? Not completely locked down, but enough to stop messengers from leaving?"

"Certainly, and in fact, we can probably spare a few men on fast horses to pass word of this along to our commanders farther west."

"And the Unity Council," Gillen added, "before they give away anything else."

"Just how do you plan to eliminate their heavy cavalry?" Cassius sneered, his arms folded across his armored chest.

"Very carefully," Rilen answered with a smile.

⊕ ⊗ ✪ ⊕ ⊗

It was a few hours after dawn, and Elac sat astride his horse, watching Rilen intently. His eyes squeezed tightly shut in concentration, the Elf cast his spell of scrying in an attempt to locate the enemy. He suddenly snapped out of his reverie and urged his horse forward, leading the group of mounted soldiers closer to Fort Ranset. Rilen had wanted to put as many bodies into his patrol as possible, and he led sixty soldiers on a rendezvous with the enemy.

They emerged from the low gulley they had been following, and Fort Ranset came into view, startlingly close considering it was occupied by Kobolds. Rilen led the body of horsemen directly toward the hostile fortress, seemingly heedless of the danger. They were almost within bowshot of the walls when Rilen suddenly pulled up short, gesturing to the towering walls and the fur-covered soldiers defending them.

"Kobolds!" he yelled at the top of his lungs. He turned and spurred his horse away from Fort Ranset, pounding across the road and riding away north, the others behind him. In answer, the gates to Fort Ranset's outer wall swung majestically open, and the Kobold heavy cavalry charged out in pursuit. Elac glanced over his shoulder, a strong sense of déjà vu coming to him as he watched the Kobold forces dashing after them. He thought back those many weeks before when he had been all alone, pursued by Kobolds, and had been saved by Rilen.

"I make it about four hundred horses!" Cassius shouted over

the rattle of equipment.

"Perfect!" Rilen responded. Elac was inclined to disagree. Sure, the Kobolds were unlikely to catch them, since their cavalry soldiers were too heavily armored for their horses to run at top speed for long, but anything could happen.

"My Lord!" a soldier behind Elac shouted. "They're turning back!

Elac looked back and saw the soldier was right. The Kobolds had stopped the chase, and were returning to Fort Ranset at a slow trot. Rilen raised his javelin and pointed it to the right. As one, the column slowed to a walk, turning around and heading back to the Kobolds. They trotted along at an easy pace, fast enough to close the gap between the two groups but slow enough to conserve their horses' energy. After several minutes of the slow chase, the Kobolds stopped and turned to face them. Rilen nudged his horse into a light canter, and the others followed suit.

The distance between them and the Kobolds dwindled considerably. With a roar, the Kobolds charged, lances lowered and shields held ready. Rilen held his javelin high, and the column spread out into a single line. They picked up speed, galloping to meet their foes.

Rilen led the entire group sharply left, exposing their flank to the Kobold charge. When the heavy cavalry drew close enough, Rilen reared back and threw his javelin at the encroaching force. The others also threw their javelins, and dozens of Kobold bodies tumbled from their saddles. Rilen led his forces back to the north, the enraged Kobolds in hot pursuit.

The chase wore on. Twice more, the Kobolds realized they

couldn't catch the fleet horses under Rilen's command, and turned back toward Fort Ranset. Both times, Rilen repeated his trick with the javelins, and both times the Kobolds rejoined the chase. After the third assault, their javelins were spent, so they couldn't turn and attack again, but the outer reaches of Nightwood Forest were visible ahead. Rilen continued to lead them at a gallop, which was about all the Kobolds' exhausted horses could manage. They gap between the two groups was about three hundred yards; too close for Elac's comfort, but apparently just right to Rilen.

They were almost within the protective confines of the forest. Rilen reined in his sweating mount, bringing it about to face the approaching enemy. He dismounted and retrieved his bow before sending his horse into the trees, and the others did likewise. Rilen allowed the Kobolds to continue to close the distance, standing stoically and watching the approach. Elac found himself wondering when the veteran Elf would spring the next phase of the trap.

Rilen gave a shrill whistle, and Captain Legat's archers emerged from hiding to stand defiantly before the Kobolds, arrows nocked. Elac watched their progress nervously, his pulse racing, and he fingered the fletching on his arrow.

Rilen's bow broke the silence with an audible *snap*, a signal immediately answered by the archers under his command. The first volley of arrows arced across the sky to fall like a deadly rain upon the charging Kobolds. Most bounced harmlessly off the well-armored bodies, but a few found a home in gaps in their armor, eliciting howls of pain and sending several spinning to the ground. Others caught vulnerable areas of the horses, which collapsed with a squeal and sent their riders flying. But still the rush came on, with no signs of slowing.

The archers fired as rapidly as they could, but it was obvious arrows alone wouldn't stop the charge. First one, then a handful of archers broke and ran into the woods, and it quickly became a rout. Elac followed suit, dashing between the trees as quickly as he dared, knowing Rilen was right behind him. They discarded their bows during the reckless sprint through the trees, knowing they couldn't possibly outrun mounted troops. Howling with bloodlust, the Kobolds plunged into the forest after their quarry.

Rilen stopped and drew his sword, shouted a command, and the rout became an ambush. The archers drew swords and formed up ranks to face their pursuers. From hidden positions all around the Kobolds, the remainder of the Human forces arose to face the encircled cavalry. The Kobolds paused in surprise, but their leader spurred them to the attack. With a clash of steel on steel, the battle was joined.

Elac dodged through the forest, keeping a tree between him and his nearest foe, a lesson Rilen had taught him. The Kobold heavy cavalry, which would have slaughtered the infantry in the open, found itself at a severe disadvantage among the heavy foliage. The fleet-footed soldiers of the Human army danced between the boughs, striking at the Kobolds who had their backs turned, then slipping away before another enemy could rush in to meet their attack. Elac artfully drove his sword into the gap between a Kobold's breastplate and the back of his helmet, and the Kobold fell from the saddle without a sound.

All around him, his friends carried the battle to the demoralized enemy. Cassius gleefully peeled away one Kobold's armor before running his broadsword through the hairy chest. A fountain of blood erupted, and the Kobold slid limply off the Prince's sword. Gillen delivered a massive two-handed blow with his axe, splitting through a Kobold's armor and knocking him bodily from the saddle. Hadwyn used the mallet of his hammer and smashed another full in the chest. The Kobold rolled off his horse and landed on his back, gasping for air until another hammer blow finished the fight. Rilen was like death incarnate, leaping back and forth through the thickest part of the fighting, his short sword flicking out in rapid blows, nearly every swing drawing blood. The last few Kobolds tried to turn and flee, but there were too many Humans all around them. Though they fought to the last man, none escaped.

Captain Legat and his junior officers surveyed the carnage while those with medical training saw to the wounded. Gillen helped out as best he could, offering healing prayers to Zantar. In all, almost fifty Human soldiers had been killed, but the entire Kobold heavy cavalry unit had been destroyed. Elac felt guilty when he realized he took comfort in the fact that, although so many Humans had died, none of his companions had received a serious injury.

"You men!" Captain Legat bellowed. "Bring water for the wounded. And I want a burial detail for the fallen to be ready by nightfall."

"Captain," Rilen said cautiously, "you might want to belay that order."

"Which one?"

"Burial. This close to Nightwood Forest, I highly recommend cremation."

Captain Legat's face turned red with anger. "Those men have fallen on the field of battle! By our ancient rites and traditions, they will be buried on the ground where they fell, as a tribute to their sacrifice."

"You bury them, and you'll be fighting them by tomorrow morning."

"What are you talking about?"

"There is at least one Necromancer in the area, and he could turn your dead into thralls."

Legat became so enraged, he was actually shaking. "You come to me with these fairy tales, expecting me to insult the honor of my fallen men by—"

"It's your call, Captain. I just wanted to give you fair warning."

The Captain stormed off, sputtering in outrage, his voice soon lost among the moans of the wounded. Nonplussed, Rilen left the woods on horseback, riding across the rolling hills toward Fort Ranset.

Hadwyn had finally set his plate aside, after his third helping, when Rilen came back. His horse looked as if it had been ridden hard, and he made certain the animal was fed and given water before he joined the group. He accepted a wineskin gratefully, and took a long drink before speaking.

"There is a unit of Kobold foot soldiers heading our way. There are only about a hundred of them, so they shouldn't be difficult to eliminate. But they are heading north from Fort Ranset. I'm curious as to what they are about. It doesn't appear to be a routine patrol. Based upon their movements, they have a definite destination in mind. Their departure might explain why the heavy cavalry responded to our presence so quickly. This could be important."

"You want to take them out." Hadwyn said it almost as a statement.

"Yes. I think we might find something interesting if we do."

They managed to mollify Captain Legat enough to gain his cooperation. Planning for the attack was completed in relatively short order. Despite his anger about Rilen's suggestion for the disposal of his fallen soldiers, Elac saw the Captain had a great respect for the skills of the Elven warrior. His battle plan against the Kobold cavalry had been nothing short of masterful, because by all rights, the infantry should have had no chance against their mounted and heavily armored foes. Elac smiled, thinking the Captain would probably follow Rilen if he announced he had a plan to attack the city of Malaton itself.

Within the hour, those troops not injured in the earlier battle were on the move, heading west to their next conflict. A rear guard was left behind to take care of the wounded. Men on horseback, outfitted once again with javelins, rode in front of the column, followed by the archers, and finally the infantry. Elac and his friends rode directly behind the mounted soldiers, accompanied by Captain Legat and a scattering of his junior officers. Rilen and Jayrne had ridden south to locate the Kobolds and confirm they were still on the same route.

Rilen's best guess for the Kobolds' path placed them within a few hundred yards of Nightwood Forest at one point. The battle plan was at once brilliant and simple. A phalanx of infantry would hide in the tall grasses, blocking the Kobolds' path. At a prearranged signal, they would rise from their places of concealment to confront the enemy. When the Kobolds stopped to meet the challenge, the archers would emerge from their places of hiding and open fire. When the Kobolds attempted to confront the new attack, a different threat would emerge . . .

The waiting began.

Elac tried to pass the time by inspecting his bow, then using a whetstone on his sword, but he couldn't take his mind off what was coming. And then there was the nagging feeling that kept him looking over his shoulder. Somewhere deep in the forest, he knew, bands of undead roamed and thirsted for blood.

Another brilliant facet of Rilen's plan soon became apparent, even to Elac, with his limited military knowledge and experience. The afternoon had passed, and evening was coming on. The sun sank slowly to the horizon, and the advancing Kobolds would be looking directly into its glaring brightness.

Rilen and Jayrne came back at a gallop. Jayrne went directly to the infantry positions, while Rilen came to Elac's hiding place. He brought news that the Kobolds were, indeed, still coming their way, and they would probably be there within a half hour. Without waiting for a response, the Elf was off again, carrying the news to the archers who would be under his command.

The Kobolds appeared in the distance, a tight formation marching steadily north. There was a sudden bustle of activity around Elac when the enemy was spotted, and runners were sent to the other positions to put them on the alert. Eventually, Elac could see their standard waving in the breeze.

With Hadwyn and Gillen in the center of their lines, the infantry rose from the prairie grasses to stand defiantly in front of a Kobold detachment, which was at least their equal in number. The Kobolds broke formation briefly, apparently startled by the appearance of this force directly in their path. The Human infantry soldiers locked their shields together and thrust their swords into an attack position. The Kobold leader barked a few orders, and the marching configuration smoothly morphed into a wedge-shaped attack formation. They drew their swords and charged.

From their carefully hidden positions, Rilen's archers rose and opened fire on the unsuspecting Kobolds. Unlike their more heavily armored counterparts in the heavy cavalry, these Kobolds proved a much easier prey for the archers' arrows. The screams of the dying filled the air, and the charge faltered. Hadwyn raised his hammer high in the air and called to his troops.

But instead of the phalanx line, it was a second command of infantry, led by Captain Legat, that arose and charged from the Kobolds' left flank when the archers stopped firing. The charge devastated the Kobold column, catching them completely unprepared. The Kobolds turned to meet the newcomers, but the original line under the Dwarves' command also joined the fray. The Kobold leader shouted and rallied his troops, trying to regain control.

"Charge!" The bellowed roar came from Elac's left. Cassius spurred his warhorse forward, and Elac followed, accompanied by fifty light horsemen. They brandished their javelins as the charge began, some clashing their weapons against their shields. They crossed the open ground and threw themselves into the battle. While most of the horsemen circled the Kobolds and threw their javelins into their midst, Cassius never slowed. Lance leveled, he blasted into the rear of the Kobold column, scattering bodies across the grassy plain. He discarded the lance, which was embedded in the body of the Kobold leader, and drew his broadsword. The three groups of Human forces converged on the hapless Kobolds, and the battle was over in minutes.

Elac carefully wiped the blood from his sword before he sheathed it. Off to his right, Rilen checked the body of the fallen Kobold leader, casually discarding Cassius's broken lance in the process. He rummaged through various pouches tied about the Kobold's waist, but apparently didn't find anything of importance. Elac joined him in the search, checking the over-sized pack carried by another Kobold, who appeared to have been armed only with a dagger.

The first thing he noticed was the large pouch of gold, which seemed out of place in a group of soldiers. He dug deeper into the pack, removing a number of personal items before he found a bundle of papers. He pulled them from the pack into the dying light, trying to decipher the writing, but he realized they were written in the Kobold tongue.

"Rilen," he said. "This might be important." He handed the papers to Rilen, who muttered a choice oath about the darkness before casting a light spell. He stared at the first page for several long moments, comprehension chasing anger across his face. He turned and kicked the nearest Kobold body, cursing once more.

"Come on," he said coldly.

Elac followed Rilen to the edge of the forest, where Captain Legat had set up a makeshift headquarters. When they drew near, Elac heard the Captain discussing the number of dead and wounded from the battle, as well as the logistics of moving the entire contingent to the nearest secure fort. The opinion seemed to be that anything east of Nightwood Forest was considered to be in Kobold hands; the remaining force would probably have to limp its way to Unity Lake and the town of Ranas.

"We've got trouble," Rilen announced angrily, hands on his hips. "Elac found some papers on a dead Kobold courier. According to these documents, Dralana, the head of the Unity Council, is taking bribes from the Kobolds. She was to continue to recommend the Council allow greater freedoms to the Kobold troops, including unlimited access to our eastern forts near the Paheny Mountains." He held the papers out for the others to see.

"How can you tell?" Cassius asked. "I see nothing but a bunch of Kobold gibberish."

"I speak Kobold gibberish," Rilen said through clenched teeth. "When you live under their constant threat, as I have, it becomes necessary. I can translate the entire stack of papers if you want, but it will just be more of the same."

"We must go directly to the Council and confront her!" Captain Legat announced forcefully.

"On what grounds?" Rilen asked. "She would deny it, and with this as our only evidence, they would dismiss it out of hand. Remember, the whole Council is corrupt. They are all taking bribes from one person or another, so they won't be too quick to come down on one of their own."

"Then what do you recommend?" Cassius asked, arms spread wide. "Let her get away with it?"

"No. Take it to the leader of one of the nations. Probably

the Dwarves, since Dralana is a Dwarf. Give them the evidence, and let them deal with it. If the accusation comes from King Ervik, it will have a bit more substance."

"I'll do it," Captain Legat said. "Once I have reassembled my patrol, we'll be making for Unity Lake anyhow. I'll send a detachment of men with the package to the Dwarf consulate. They can take it from there."

They were interrupted by a piercing shriek from deep in the woods. Their swords seemed to leap into their hands, and they stared into the darkness to find the source of the scream. Silvayn cast his light spell and released it into the trees. Elac was taken aback by how much more powerful Silvayn's spell was than Rilen's; the trees were illuminated for quite some distance. At the farthest reaches of the light, something moved.

Elac flinched when the stench of rotting flesh reached his nose. Dark, shambling forms edged into the light, becoming the figures of the undead. All around him, Elac heard mutterings of fear from the Human soldiers, but the fear didn't rise up in him as sharply as it had before. The soldiers stood awkwardly, looking to each other for reassurance, but Elac and his friends stepped forward to join the battle. Many of the thralls wore the uniform of the Human army. Farther back into the trees, Elac saw a scattering of skeleton warriors pressing forward. He brought up his sword and set his feet.

"To me!" Rilen shouted encouragingly, trying to bolster the army at his back, which seemed on the verge of routing. "Go for their heads! They're strong, but slow. We can do this!"

Captain Legat was the first to regain his wits, and he rallied a large group of soldiers just as Rilen engaged the first undead.

Several soldiers surged forward to join the battle, and when the remaining soldiers saw their fellows charge, they followed suit. Elac danced through the melee, keeping his feet moving as Rilen had shown him. He alternated blocking the slow, clumsy attacks with delivering swift blows at the heads of his enemies. Beside him, Rilen's short sword whistled through the air and connected with a dull *thud*, splitting a thrall's head down the middle. Hadwyn's hammer shattered the skull of another, and the creature collapsed on itself. Cassius, roaring with righteous fury, swung his sword left and right.

While the thralls were slow and nearly ineffective, the skeleton warriors were different. Their greater speed allowed them to dart past the clumsy swings of the tiring soldiers, and a number of men were slain. Silvayn stepped to the fore and chanted in the language of magic, gesturing toward the skeletons. A blue-white bolt of energy leapt from his fingers, shattering a half dozen skeletons in its path. The soldiers' lines, which had begun to crumble under the onslaught of the skeletons, surged forward under the leadership of Captain Legat.

Then a new apparition appeared. Its translucence made it difficult to see clearly, even by the light of Silvayn's spell. Its countenance was a mask of sheer horror, with sharp, piercing fangs, pointed ears, and a gaunt, cadaverous face. Scattered locks of hair dangled from the otherwise bare scalp, and the eyes were drawn up at the corners. Filmy robes draped the body, and the arms protruding from the end of the robes ended in clawed fingers. It came forward, more drifting than walking, and a low moan came from the mouth, a voice of unspeakable horror.

Several men threw down their weapons and ran, screaming

in terror. Captain Legat and a few other soldiers held their ground, however, and prepared to meet the new challenge even while the last of the other undead were destroyed. The Captain attacked first, and his sword thrust passed right through the creature's body without effect. With a sweep of its arm, it knocked the Captain sprawling, blood flowing freely from a gash across his face. The remaining soldiers rushed to his defense.

"Ghoul!" Silvayn shouted. "Stay back! You can't hurt it!"

Heedless of his warning, two men rushed to their fallen leader's aid. The ghoul grabbed the first by the throat, lifting him clear of the ground. He dangled from that clawed appendage, choking and gasping for breath, and the other soldier vainly swung his sword at the cloaked apparition before them. Silvayn swore at the men to get out of the way, shouting to them that he couldn't use his magic until they were clear, for fear of hurting them.

Then Gillen was there. He swung his axe in a mighty, two-handed blow. The ghoul gave a shriek of agony when the blade passed through its robes, and it dropped the soldier and attacked its new opponent. Too late, it saw Gillen's axe descending once again. This time, the axe struck the ghoul with a burst of light. The ghoul's filmy body swirled into mist and vanished.

Gillen rushed forward to Captain Legat's side and checked for signs of life. He placed his hand over the fallen soldier's eyes and muttered a prayer to Zantar. The Captain twitched a few times before lying still once more, but his breathing became less labored. Gillen moved on to the soldier who had been caught in the ghoul's deadly grip, but it was too late for him.

Once more, the grisly business of checking for life among the wounded began. Elac wandered through the carnage, at times having difficulty distinguishing between fallen soldiers and men who had fought against them as undead. For the next hour, the wounded were brought to a central location to be tended to, while the dead were gathered and burned. A number of make-shift litters were hastily constructed; the soldiers had no intention of staying near the accursed woods. They were to begin their long trek west as soon as their wounded were loaded.

Silvayn gathered everyone about once their horses were packed and saddled. "We need to be away from here as quickly as possible," he told them quietly. "We'll head southeast first, to put some distance between us and Nightwood, then turn west to the mountains."

"Why did Gillen's axe affect the ghoul, when no one else could touch it?" Jayrne asked in a trembling voice.

"As a Priest of Zantar, my weapon is blessed," Gillen explained, holding his axe before him. "As we ride, I can work on blessing all your weapons, as well. Ghouls are incorporeal, and as such can only be hurt by blessed or magical weapons."

"The night is getting on," Silvayn told them, reaching for his horse. "We need to be going."

They rode southeast, away from the woods but staying north of Fort Ranset. Shortly after midnight, Rilen reined in his horse. There was a narrow defile ahead, and they decided to spend the rest of the night hiding inside. Rilen and Adalyn stretched a canvas tarp overhead to keep the weather out if it should rain, and Jayrne added a touch of camouflage by sprinkling dirt and foliage on top. They set a watch, and Elac was quickly asleep.

The next morning they ate breakfast in the saddle while their horses trotted along the gently sloping ground. Gradually, as the morning passed, the slope became steeper, the foliage thinned out, and they found themselves in the Paheny Mountains. The turf, which had been comprised mostly of clay, slowly changed to sand and rock. Higher up, Elac could see traces of the winter's snows stubbornly clinging to shaded outcroppings of boulders. Overhead, a pair of hawks circled lazily overhead, their wings unmoving, searching for prey.

They slowed their mounts, conserving their strength in the thinner air. At a leisurely walk, they turned northwest in what Silvayn believed to be the direction of Noran's castle. Elac found himself having trouble breathing, and he remembered the Paheny Mountains were considerably higher than those of the North Range. More than once, he caught himself gasping for air. He forced himself to remain calm, keeping his breathing smooth and even. They rested the horses while they stopped beside a mountain stream, where they ate lunch and refilled their bottles. By nightfall, they were within sight of Noran's dark castle.

Chapter 13

They left their horses behind and proceeded on foot. While Rilen secured their mounts on long tethers, giving them access to adequate food and a nearby mountain stream, Elac drew his sword and examined the blade. It didn't look any different. During the night, Gillen had performed his holy rite, blessing Elac's weapon in the name of Zantar. By theory, it should enable him to strike incorporeal creatures. He hoped he wouldn't have to put it to the test.

Rilen chose a circuitous route, trying to keep as much elevated terrain between them and the castle as he could. They gathered behind a concealing mound of stone to peer cautiously at their destination. Noran's castle was a tall, forbidding structure. The outside walls were constructed of squared-off basalt blocks held tightly together by mortar. Vines had crept up along the sides, clinging tenaciously to the stone. The citadel was surmounted by battlements, and each wall junction bore siege engines capable of inflicting significant casualties on any army foolish enough to attempt an assault. Four spires rose from behind the outer walls, with a taller tower in their center marking the highest point in the castle.

The ancient keep itself was surrounded by a gaping abyss, dropping away into darkness below them. The only access to the castle was by a narrow stone walkway leading directly to the castle gates from the west. The near edge of the walkway was flanked by towering gargoyles made of black shimmering stone. Their faces were twisted into hideous grins, baring rows of sharp teeth. The long, obsidian arms were tipped with claws, and a set of wings curled out from their backs.

Rilen went first, sword in hand as he crossed the path bridging the chasm. He pressed his hands against the man-sized portal directly off the path, and it swung silently open at his touch. Hadwyn was next, his hammer held tightly in his fists, glancing continually at the long drop-off to either side of the path. Once he was across, he waited for his brother, who seemed to share Hadwyn's nervousness about the depth of the abyss. The two Dwarves entered the castle.

Elac went next. His weapon hung in its scabbard, and his shield was strapped to his back, leaving both hands free. He stepped carefully, deliberately, trying to stay in the middle of the walkway. The winds tore at him, threatening to tear him from the safety of the stone path and deposit him in the chasm. The castle loomed nearer, and its shadow blocked out the sun. With a heavy sigh of relief, Elac stepped from the walkway and into the castle beyond.

After several minutes, the entire group stood assembled within Noran's castle. Silvayn invoked his magic light, revealing a vast hall before them. The floor was covered with narrow wooden slats, stained a dark oak color and polished until they glowed. The gray stone walls were hung with elaborate tapestries, interspersed with various weapons and shields. No windows interrupted the unyielding stone, which Elac found odd until he realized a vampire lord would have no desire to see the sun. There were several doors leading into the hall, some standing ajar while others appeared securely fastened. In one corner, a spiral staircase was visible through an open doorway. Rilen looked to Silvayn for guidance.

The old mage paused, his eyes distant. "We aren't here to fight Noran. He's a vampire lord, and in all likelihood that puts him beyond our power. We need to concentrate on finding the Dagger of Rennex. Noran's sleeping chamber should be in the castle's lowest levels, but the Dagger won't necessarily be with him. I suggest we start with the upper levels and work our way down. If we haven't found the Dagger by late afternoon, we may have to alter the plan. We definitely don't want to spend the night here."

"Agreed," Rilen said. He drew his short sword and, without another word, led the group to the staircase in the room's center. On a whim, Elac nocked an arrow and readied his bow.

The staircase wound upward into the dim reaches of the castle's tall central spire. They emerged from the stairs into a musky chamber, the air stale and the walls and floor covered in a layer of dust. Footprints carpeted the room, showing signs of recent passage. Rotted furniture stood along the walls, some of it collapsed upon itself. What caught Elac's immediate attention, however, was the grim collection of skeletons lying in neat rows along the far wall. Elac raised his bow nervously, but none of the skeletons moved.

"It's alright," Adalyn assured him, gently pushing his bow down. "Remember, the vampires are a separate entity, completely independent of Necromancers. They cannot reanimate the dead."

By unspoken agreement, Jayrne carefully examined the room while the others stood watch. Despite Adalyn's assurances, Elac kept a close eye on the bones, while the others divided their attention between the stairs and the room's only other exit, a closed and barred door. After the nimble thief had declared the room free of traps and hidden compartments, they edged across the room to the door. Hadwyn stepped forward, hammer held at the ready.

The door was secured by a long wooden bar, locked in place by metal chains and a padlock. Hadwyn delivered a crushing blow to the center of the bar, and it splintered with a loud report. Another blow from his deadly hammer, and the bar split apart, falling to the floor in a pile of wooden shards. He slipped the remaining pieces out of the latches, released the latch, and opened the door.

A lean, dark creature rushed forth, bowled Hadwyn over, and threw itself at Cassius. He shouted an oath and latched onto the beast with his gauntleted hands, throwing it aside. It crashed through a solitary table and whipped around to face the group. It was lean, almost emaciated, with bones protruding nearly through its skin in places. The dark gray skin was covered with slime, and a long, forked tongue flicked into view between the fanged jaws. It stood hunched over, almost as if there was something wrong with its spine. It snarled, spraying green spittle from its mouth, and lunged at Rilen.

The Elf deflected the claws swiping toward his throat and retaliated with a light, whip-like stroke from his sword, drawing a flow of blood resembling black slime. It howled with pain and spun to attack once more. From behind Elac, a bowstring snapped, and their attacker suddenly found an arrow protruding from its chest. Around the room, the rest of the warriors encircled the beast. While the others lunged and feinted, drawing it off balance, Hadwyn snuck up behind and delivered a blow with his hammer. The weapon caught the creature in the middle of the back, eliciting the sound of breaking bones, and it dropped to one knee. Gillen finished the battle with a two-handed blow to the neck, severing its head. The body fell against the wall and slid to the floor, twitching briefly before it lay still.

Jayrne gave a shriek of agony, and Elac quickly whirled to see a pale man, dressed in dark robes, standing behind her. Blood trickled down his chin, and Jayrne was slowly dropping to her knees, the puncture marks in her neck plainly visible. *Noran! But how can he be out during the day?* Elac tried to move, but he found his muscles paralyzed with fear.

"Fools!" Noran hissed, licking the blood from his lips. "You will all suffer for this! You shall be made to endure an eternal hell. None of you will leave!" He faded into a mist, which passed through the group before any could react and vanished into the stairwell, leaving behind his maniacal laughter.

Elac dropped his sword and rushed to Jayrne's side, his heart in his throat, and began to examine her injuries. Gillen was there with him, offering up a prayer of healing while Elac held her close. Tears rolled down his cheeks unbidden, and he was shocked to detect the depth of his feelings for her. He turned to Gillen with pleading eyes, but the Dwarf Priest shook his head.

"I can't explain it," Gillen said, taking a closer look at Jayrne's neck. "Zantar will not help this woman."

"The touch of Noran," Adalyn said in answer. "He has bitten her, but the wound was not enough to kill her. She is now undead, or at least partly. With the mark of Malator upon her, none of our gods would consider healing her."

"What about the water from the Springs of Calda? She acquired extra water while we were at the springs. Would that help her?"

Silvayn shook his head sadly. "No, Elac. With the curse of the undead upon her, the water would actually cause her harm."

"We have to do something!" Elac shouted, his frustration bubbling over, veins bulging in his neck. "I won't abandon her to this fate!"

"There is one way," Cassius said solemnly, his hand straying to his dagger.

"No!" Elac reached for his sword, realized it was several steps away, and brought his shield in front of Jayrne's inert form defensively.

"Stay," Silvayn said, stepping between them. He stooped for a closer look, took Jayrne's chin in his hand, and examined her eyes. "The change has already begun. But there is still time. One way exists for us to help her, and it must be done before the moon makes a complete cycle."

"What must we do?" asked Rilen.

"Kill Noran."

"Bah!" Cassius kicked the body of the fallen creature. "This is madness! Kill a vampire lord? Why should we throw our lives away for a thief?"

"Because we need her," Adalyn told him evenly. "She is just as important to this quest as the rest of us. If she dies, we fail, and the West will suffer."

Elac angrily dashed away his tears, rage overcoming his sorrow. "How can Noran have done this? It's not even night outside!"

Silvayn sighed. "Vampires are destroyed by direct sunlight, it's true. But vampire lords gain a certain amount of immunity to their weaknesses over the eons, and Noran is no exception. Make no mistake, if it was nighttime, he would have stayed to finish us off. If we can find him before the sun sets, we have a chance. His conversion of Jayrne will have left him in a weakened state. But we must make haste."

They made an improvised litter out of pieces of wood salvaged from the broken furniture, lashed together with leather thongs, and covered with Elac's cloak. He laid Jayrne carefully on the stretcher, and while the others examined the rest of the floor, he kept a careful watch over her. When they started back down the stairs, Hadwyn picked up the other end, and the two of them carefully brought her back to the main level. Adalyn replaced Hadwyn, who took up his war hammer, and the group continued their hunt for the elusive vampire lord.

They checked two of the lesser towers, finding piles of treasure but nothing else. Noon had come and gone when they mounted the stairs to the third tower. Elac was drenched with sweat by the time they topped the stairs. His arms burned with the effort of carrying his burden, but he refused to yield and let someone else carry Jayrne. The others had more to contribute than he in a fight, he told them, and they needed to conserve their strength.

The room at the top of the stairs was filled with implements of torture. Shackles lined the walls at regular intervals, many of them dark with dried blood. A saw-toothed blade lay on a table, pieces of what appeared to be flesh and bone wedged into its teeth. There was a rack and a stock, both showing signs of heavy, though not recent, use.

Footsteps sounded on the stairs, and a dozen armored forms charged through the door. Each bore a long sword and a shield, and their faces were hidden behind steel masks. Their suits of banded armor were partially covered by black cloaks bearing a depiction of a full moon. They attacked the group, howling as they came. Elac backed Jayrne's stretcher into a corner and stood protectively in front of her, sword in hand. Rilen intercepted the assault, smoothly running his sword through the first attacker while easily blocking a blow from another. Cassius found himself hard-pressed, with two of the masked men attacking him from opposite sides. Silvayn came to stand with Elac while Adalyn joined the fray, trying to even out the numbers. The two Dwarves battled back-to-back, each protecting the other as their foes ringed them in.

Gradually, their foes lost the advantage of numbers. Cassius delivered a crippling blow to one of his assailants, severing one leg and knocking him to the floor. With a backhanded swipe that caught his other opponent off guard, he spilled the man's entrails across the blood-slick floor. Hadwyn struck another in the face with the mallet of his hammer, which stunned him long enough for the sturdy Dwarf to finish him with another blow. Adalyn's blade claimed the life of one of the two menacing Rilen, who easily dispatched the other.

One of the men burst past the others to challenge Elac. Although he had learned much from Rilen, Elac was no match for a skilled fighter. A series of furious blows from his foe left Elac backpedaling, desperately blocking the strikes with his shield and unable to mount an attack of his own. His foot caught the edge of Jayrne's litter and he went down, his sword clattering across the floor. Elac tried to regain his feet, but the man who was trying to kill him toppled forward to land on him. He raised his head, pushed the body to the side, and saw Rilen's dagger protruding from the dead man's back.

Elac scrambled to his feet and regained his sword, but the fight was over. Rilen cleaned his sword, then casually retrieved his dagger.

"Thanks, Rilen. I owe you again."

"Not your fault," the taciturn Elf told him. "These guys were trained warriors, with the skills that implies. They've probably been studying swordplay for most of their adult lives."

Elac turned back to Jayrne, but her condition hadn't improved. If anything, her skin color was worse, having changed from a healthy glow to a gray pallor. Her breathing was more labored, and her heart was racing. Elac held her hand helplessly until the others were ready to move, then he picked up one end of her litter. Someone else, Adalyn, he assumed, picked up the other end, and they descended the stairs.

They returned to the main hall, with one more tower to search before they checked the lower levels. Rilen tried the door to the final tower, but it was locked. He knelt down where he could study the locking mechanism more closely. "This may take a few minutes," he told them.

Cassius snorted. "Just when a thief might have been useful."

Elac's nostrils flared, but Adalyn artfully intervened. "Elac," she said carefully, "let's set her down on that bench over there. We can see if there's anything we can do for her."

His anger not entirely diverted, Elac nodded and started toward the bench . . .

And the floor beneath him dropped away, plummeting him down a steep metal chute. He tried futilely to get a grip on the sides of the trap, but his hands couldn't find a purchase, and his slide continued. Above him, he heard the trapdoor swing shut, then the clicking of latches as the trap secured itself against further opening. After a tumultuous descent, he struck a sandy floor with jarring force. A sharp blow to the head from Jayrne's litter almost knocked him unconscious, and Jayrne exited the slide to land on top of him.

He lay there gasping for several moments, trying to force air back into his lungs. When he regained his senses, he crawled over to Jayrne, but she seemed to have suffered no further injury. Her litter had fractured at one end, probably after striking his head. Memory of that brought his hand to his temple, where blood flowed freely. There was a ringing in his ears, and he shook his head to clear it. For a few moments, he expected his friends to join him in the descent, but then he realized the meaning behind the locking mechanism in the trapdoor. He was on his own.

They had landed in a small room, with bare stone walls and a sand floor. There was an open doorway directly across from him, and it appeared to be the only way in or out. Low, rotted wooden beams crossed the ceiling. The slide itself was sharply inclined; so steep, in fact, as to make climbing it without equipment difficult. To do so bearing Jayrne's litter would be impossible. That left the option of finding a new way out, or leaving her behind.

He rolled Jayrne back onto the litter, then tore several long strips from his tunic. He used two of them to reinforce the damaged litter, and used the others to secure Jayrne to it tightly. With a quick check to make sure everything was ready, he picked up the end by Jayrne's head and walked along the only route available to him, dragging his burden behind him.

❀ ❀ ★ ❀ ❀

While Gillen watched in horror, Adalyn released her hold on Jayrne's litter when the floor fell away beneath them. She spun around as she dropped, catching a desperate handhold on a nearby rug. She slipped deeper into the gaping maw below her, but Gillen was there. He dove forward and caught her hand, arresting her fall. Hadwyn joined him, and they managed to pull her back to safety. Before anyone could act, the trapdoor snapped shut, and Gillen heard the locks seal the portal shut.

Rilen rushed to his side and tried to force the door open once more, but it wouldn't budge. Hadwyn tried his hammer, but his most powerful blow bounced aside ineffectively. Gillen stepped forward with his sharp-bladed axe, drew it back, and swung.

With an explosion of sound and blinding light, Gillen was thrown backward, his arms going numb and the axe bouncing aside. He landed on his back with an oath, rolled over, and stared with disbelief at the undamaged floor. His axe hadn't even scratched it.

"Enchanted," Silvayn said. He stepped closer to the trap, muttered several words in the language of magic, and gestured at the floor. The trapdoor and the floor around it glowed brightly. The old mage stepped back and shook his head, hands on his hips. "The way down is sealed. We cannot follow them."

"Can't you use magic on it?" Gillen asked, coming to his feet groggily.

Silvayn shook his head and ran his fingers through his white hair. "Someone has cast a powerful enchantment upon this. I might be able to break it, but I would be left too weak to be of any further use to you. No, we'll have to descend by the stairs and try to find Elac and Jayrne before Noran does."

"What about the tower?" asked Cassius, his hands spread wide in disbelief.

"I'll check it," Rilen said simply. "It will only take a moment."

Before anyone could object, Rilen vaulted lightly to the stairs and was quickly out of sight. Gillen shrugged and leaned on the handle of his axe. True to his word, the Elf was back in only a few minutes, reappearing wraithlike at the bottom of the stairs.

"There are more warriors up there, but nothing else," he told them.

Cassius's eyes narrowed. "Why did they allow you to leave?"

Rilen shrugged indifferently. "They never saw me." He led the way to the stairs leading down into the castle's lower levels.

🔹 ⬤ ★ ⊕ ⬤

Elac stopped once again and carefully lowered the litter to the floor. His tunic provided several more long bits of cloth, which he wrapped around both ends of Jayrne's litter. At one end, he used the cloth to provide better handholds; at the other, he used several layers to muffle the sound of the wood dragging on the ground. He rested while he shook out his arms, trying to restore some circulation.

From the litter at his feet, Jayrne stirred, briefly thrashing against the bonds holding her to the poles. Elac knelt to her side and felt her brow. Her skin was cold and clammy, and the gray color was more pronounced. Her open eyes stared at him, unfocused. He stroked her hair lightly, helpless tears of frustration forming in his eyes. Suddenly, she seemed to come alert.

"What happened?" she asked weakly.

Elac gave a low cry and hugged her fiercely, a gesture she returned as best she could. "We were fighting in the tower . . . and Noran . . . and you . . ."

"Easy, Tiger." She gave a feeble smile. "Slow down, take a breath, and tell me."

Elac took a shuddering breath before he told her of the fight in the tower, which she vaguely remembered. She knew nothing of Noran's attack on her, and her lower lip quivered when he told her what her fate would be if they couldn't destroy the vampire lord. He finished by describing their predicament.

"Do you think you can stand?"

She shook her head gently. "It's all I can do just to talk to you. This won't work, Elac. You're exhausted, and you don't know where we are. You have to leave me behind."

"Never!" He ended the discussion when he stood, lifted one end of the litter, and stubbornly plodded forward once more. She objected, but to no avail, and Elac refused to even answer. Eventually, her cries fell silent.

❁ ❁ ★ ❁ ❁

Rilen led the way down a spiraling flight of stairs to the castle's next level. Gillen shifted the great battle-axe in his hands, taking comfort from the leather-wrapped handle. He wished the strange warriors would attack once more, so he could vent the rage threatening to consume him. At times, Gillen admired his brother. If something angered Hadwyn, he felt no urge to hold back, and he dealt with the situation accordingly. Gillen maintained a calmer outward appearance with a tighter grip on his emotions.

His chance came at the bottom of the stairs. They emerged into a torch-lit room, apparently a barracks of some kind, judging by the bunks on the walls. A dozen men dressed similarly to the ones they had fought earlier leapt up from the tables where they were eating. Though they had no helmets or shields, all had their weapons strapped about their waists. Without a moment's hesitation, they charged the group, howling with berserker fury. As was his style, Rilen launched himself into the teeth of the enemy, using his shield to batter his foes while he made short, lethal blows with his sword.

One of the men charged Gillen, weaving his blade about in an intricate display of swordsmanship. Gillen looked at him with disgust, reared back, and swung an overhead blow, splitting the man's head nearly in half. He toppled backward with a spray of blood, and Gillen wrenched the axe back and forth to free it. He silently cursed himself for losing control like that; he knew such a blow could cause his weapon to become lodged and leave him defenseless.

Adalyn crossed blades with one man who came too close, but Hadwyn darted up behind him, his heavy hammer striking him solidly in the back. The man fell to the ground, and Adalyn drove her sword home. She gave Hadwyn a look of approval with a curt nod, and he returned to the fight. Cassius's broadsword was a blur as he kept two of the men at bay, looking for an opening. He found the opportunity with the man on his right and drove his blade up to the hilt in the man's chest. He seized his foe's long sword and turned on the other, their blades meeting with a clash of steel and a shower of sparks. Rilen had already felled three, and he was driving two back into a corner. When one of the men stumbled over the other's leg, Rilen's blade passed sharply across the fallen man's throat, and he lay there, grasping his neck while death slowly took him. The other bumped into the wall and had nowhere left to go. He swung a blow at Rilen's head in desperation, but the blow landed on Rilen's shield. The first swipe severed the man's sword arm, the second ended his life.

❀ ❁ ★ ❂ ❀

Elac stopped, his shoulders slumping in defeat. The hallway had seemed promising at first, leading deeper into the castle with no side exits, but had come to a dead end. He shook his head and looked disconnectedly at his feet. He feared to go back, because they had heard voices behind them, but he didn't know what else to do. On her litter, Jayrne stirred once more.

"What's wrong?" she asked in a trembling voice.

"The hallway just ends. There are no doors, nowhere else to go . . ." he trailed off, not knowing what else to say.

"Elac, my friend," she said with a sigh, "people don't make a long passage like this and have it just end. There has to be a way out. There may be a hidden portal in the wall somewhere."

He looked up sharply, his eyes scouring the wall before him. "How do I find it?"

"First of all, you have to put me down. You won't find it with your eyes." Elac gave a short laugh and gently lowered his burden to the ground once more, feeling mingled pain and relief rushing into his hands. "Second, you're looking on the wrong wall. Only an amateur would put the hidden doorway straight ahead. For some reason, most of the architects like to put them in the wall on the right."

Elac turned obediently to the next section of wall and lightly ran his fingers over the stone surface. Before, he hadn't paid much attention to the construction. The walls were made of a brown stone, held loosely together by mortar. He tried to use both his eyes and his hands, carefully checking the entire surface.

"You're trying too hard," she chastised him lightly. "Close your eyes and concentrate on your hands."

He did as he was told, taking long, slow breaths to calm

himself. He checked the wall systematically, working from one side to the other and from top to bottom. He was about half-way done with the wall section, and had found nothing, when the voices sounded in the corridor behind them.

"Elac!" she whispered anxiously.

"I hear them." He never turned, never opened his eyes. He continued working lower on the stones, finding nothing, and the voices continued to grow louder. He was on his knees, and the voices were quite close, when he found what he was looking for; a small area gave just a bit when he pressed on it. He pressed harder, and a section of the wall grinded slowly to the side. Without a word, he dragged Jayrne's litter through the open doorway. The mechanism on the other side for closing the door wasn't hidden, and he latched it as soon as he had her through.

Off to his right, he saw a small alcove where they might hide. He carefully dragged Jayrne's litter into what turned out to be a narrow hallway leading to some sort of shrine. At first glance, it seemed he had wandered into a fight, but he realized the figures before him were statues. Very life-like statues, he corrected himself. Without a closer examination, there was no way to tell these weren't live people, engaged in a life-or-death-struggle.

He eased Jayrne off her stretcher and tossed it to the side. He dragged her limp body into the midst of the battle scene and told her to lie still. From the hallway outside the room, he heard the sound of stone grating on stone as the hidden door opened. Elac drew his sword as quietly as he could, assumed a fierce expression, and placed the tip of his blade against Jayrne's breast.

"Keep looking!" a harsh voice shouted. "The master said two of them fell through the trap in the main hall. One of them has already felt his sting, and she is to be taken alive. Lord Noran wants her for his bride. You may kill the other."

Footsteps sounded in the alcove, but Elac didn't dare look up. At least two men, or so Elac judged by their footfalls, entered the grotto and walked slowly through the room. He hoped they didn't look too closely, because beads of sweat were standing out on his forehead. In his mind, Elac planned how he would react if he were spotted, how he would strike the first blow.

Without another word, they spun and abruptly left the room. Elac was afraid to move, other than to glance down and bask in the adoring look of gratitude from the beautiful woman on the floor. He waited until he had heard no sounds for several minutes before he dared to budge. He held up a solitary finger to Jayrne and stepped lightly to the doorway. He eased his lean form into the hallway, but it was deserted.

A few minutes later, Jayrne was secured to the litter once more, and he was dragging his burden deeper into the depths of Noran's castle. It seemed a bit eerie to be following in the footsteps of those who sought to kill him, but his instincts told him it was right. Besides, those searching for him would likely be looking in the area where he would be able to make his escape, so they were probably leading him where he wanted to go.

Although a number of smaller passages branched off from the main path, he stayed in the primary hallway, moving unerringly forward. A few minutes later, however, he stopped once more. Something about the hallway on his left, he couldn't say what, caught his eye.

"Something wrong?" Jayrne asked, her voice barely a whisper. Elac wasn't sure if she was just trying to avoid detection, or if that was all the volume she could manage.

"I don't know. There's nothing solid to go on, but I seem to have this . . ." He frowned. "This urge to take this side hallway. I can't explain it."

"Do it," she said immediately. "Trust your instincts, and don't second-guess yourself."

He bit his lip and turned left, dragging her forward once more. He followed the hall only briefly before it ended in a small antechamber. There was a black wooden door in a corner of the far wall, as well as a series of slitted viewers looking out onto whatever lay beyond. He sat Jayrne's litter down carefully and trotted over to the wall. Placing his face against one of the slits, he looked out on the chamber on the other side.

A massive room lay sprawled out before him, lit on all sides by brightly burning fire pits. The stone walls were hung with paintings and busts of people who likely were long dead. Dozens of coffins lay in orderly rows around the perimeter of the room, although they seemed to have fallen into a state of disrepair. The coffin on a raised dais against the far wall, however, was different. Trimmed with gold, it appeared to be made of a dark hardwood, possibly mahogany. Even the hinges were made of gold, as was the representation of a full moon emblazoned upon its top. The wood had a dull, worn surface, however, showing long years of use. Another coffin was positioned next to it, the new wood shining brightly. A high-backed throne sat against the wall at the back of the platform.

A door near the dais opened, and several figures entered. All but one wore the black cloaks and steel helmets of the men who had attacked Elac and his friends in the tower. The other, however, Elac recognized immediately. Noran, the vampire lord, the ultimate finale of the quest, stomped angrily onto the platform. Surprisingly, Elac found he could hear the powerful figure from his vantage point.

"I want them found! All of them! Bring her to me alive, and kill the others."

"We are trying, my Lord," one of the men answered in a solemn tone. "We have had a few encounters with them, but their battle prowess is considerable."

"There is one among them who has substantial power. I must wait until the sun goes down before I can confront him." He gestured contemptuously. "Now, leave me. Find the intruders and kill them."

Chapter 14

Blac whirled about and rushed to Jayrne's side. "Jayrne! It's Noran! He's in the next room! I . . ." He stopped, realizing she had slipped back into unconsciousness. He pried open one eyelid and was shocked by what he saw. Her eye color had changed from a brilliant blue-gray hue to a bright orange, and the pupil was shaped like that of a cat.

The transformation begins.

On an impulse, he peeled back her lips, revealing the sharpened eyeteeth that had elongated, slowly growing into fangs. He knew she hadn't much time before she would fall wholly under the sway of Noran. The process would still be reversible for some time, but she would soon be uncontrollable.

Shouts of alarm from the next room brought Elac around, senses alert. He dashed back to the peephole and peered out breathlessly. One of the armored warriors rushed back into the room.

"My Lord! They're here, and we can't stand against them! They're coming!"

Noran gave the cringing warrior a contemptuous slap, knocking him sprawling against the nearby wall. The vampire lord strode deliberately to his side, knelt, and sank his teeth into the man's neck.

"Your sacrifice is not in vain, my loyal servant. Your blood has made me strong, which our enemies will soon learn." The sounds of battle grew louder in the hallway beyond, and Noran crossed his arms. He slowly faded into a faint mist, and several more warriors burst into the room in a wild panic, Elac's friends in close pursuit. The battle continued to rage in the huge chamber while Elac tried to force open the door, which was locked with a key. He returned to the holes in the wall and called to his friends.

"Rilen! That mist around you! It's Noran!"

The Elf jumped in response to his name, glancing around at the mist surrounding the group. Gillen called out the name of his deity and delivered a wide, sweeping blow with his axe, cutting through the hazy vapor. The blessed weapon bit Noran deeply, and the evil figure gave a cry of pain and dismay despite his seemingly invincible shape. The mist swirled into a maelstrom atop the dais, and the vampire lord stood before them.

Elac darted back to Jayrne's side, desperately trying to rouse her. He shook her, patted the sides of her face, and frantically called her name. Finally, her eyelids fluttered, and she stared at him blankly.

"Jayrne! Can you hear me?"

She tried unsuccessfully to speak, and decided to nod instead.

"I can't open this door because they've locked it. How do I open the lock?"

She beckoned him to lean closer, her voice barely a whisper. "In my left boot . . . lockpick set." He slid his hand gently into the side of her boot and withdrew a small leather pouch containing metal rods and probes. She motioned for him to lean closer once more, and she described, as best she could, how to go about unlocking the door. He kissed her cheek before returning to the lock.

He pulled two instruments from her kit and inserted them in the keyhole. Beyond the heavy wooden door he could hear the din of fighting, steel pounding against steel mingled with screams of agony. He thought he had it once, but the lock clicked stubbornly back into place, and he had to start over. He paused for a quick glance back at Jayrne, but she had slipped into unconsciousness once more. The sounds of battle abated just as the lock came free with an audible click.

He shoved the lockpick set into one of his pouches and pushed the door slightly ajar. He was about to pick up Jayrne's litter and drag her into the next room, where he could try to keep her safe, when he saw the box. It was an ornate wooden chest, stained a light brown color, with intricately carved trim and the familiar full moon emblem carved into the front. The top was held fast by a large black padlock. On a hunch, Elac decided he had to know what the box contained.

He pulled out the lockpick set once more, selected the rods he needed, and studied the keyhole to try to decide how to proceed. He was about to insert the first probe in the lock when he felt something poke the back of his leg. A quick glance told him Jayrne was awake once more, using Elac's discarded longbow to get his attention. He knelt beside her and leaned close, but she was unable to speak. The best she could manage was to mouth the word "trapped".

Elac's eyes went wide with horror. He turned back to the lock, this time standing well off to one side. He drew his short sword and prodded the lock, but nothing happened. He tried once again, more firmly this time. With a high-pitched metallic ring, a long needle shot from the lock, protruding several inches from the box. Elac shuddered, staring at what was likely a poisoned needle.

Staying to the side, he delivered a blow to the box with every ounce of strength he had left. The sword bit deeply, splitting the wood forming the front face and dropping the lock to the floor. He stayed where he was, and pried the box open with his sword. There were no further traps, however, and the lid broke open rather easily.

He tentatively peered inside, half-expecting some other devious trap to activate and claim his life, but nothing happened. Inside, he found a single blade, a beautiful silver dagger with a leather-bound, jewel-encrusted hilt. He lifted it reverently from the chest, wondering how long such an invaluable item had lain hidden in the vampire lord's castle. As soon as he finished the thought, however, he knew. The knife had not been there long; Noran had concealed it in this locked box after acquiring it from that temple in Palindom. He tucked the Dagger of Rennex within his belt, picked up one end of Jayrne's litter, and pushed his way into the chamber beyond.

He set Jayrne down just inside the door, far enough into the room to allow him to watch her, but not close enough to endanger her. He looked out across the vast chamber and saw his friends encircle the vampire lord. Noran roared with rage and finally entered the fray. Hadwyn immediately swung his heavy hammer at the vampire lord's unprotected back, but the vampire dodged the blow with a speed that amazed Elac. Noran delivered a stunning backhanded blow to Hadwyn, knocking him off the dais onto a coffin and shattering the rotten wood.

Rilen and Cassius darted in simultaneously, both swords descending in apparently lethal blows. This time, Noran wasn't quick enough, and although he kicked Cassius in the chest, Rilen's blade bit home, drawing a bright red gash down his right side. Cassius crashed to the ground, stunned despite his armor, and he lay unmoving. Rilen jumped back out of range, and Gillen moved in from the vampire's left.

Silvayn had been murmuring in a low chant, and when his voice reached a crescendo he raised his right hand. He gestured to Noran, and a sizzling bolt of red energy burst forth from his hands and streaked across the room. But the vampire lord showed his amazing dexterity once more, dodging the attack. The blast from Silvayn's spell struck the wall beyond the dais, where it heavily fractured the stone with an earsplitting thunderclap. Noran snarled, his lip curled in defiance, and he started toward Silvayn.

"Keep him off me!" Silvayn shouted. "I need time!"

The old mage chanted once more, and Adalyn stepped forward to meet the vampire lord's rush. Elac reached her side, while Rilen and Gillen pressed him from the flanks. Cassius was on his hands and knees, still trying to regain his feet. Hadwyn hadn't moved, and he lay sprawled not far from where Silvayn's magic had ruptured the wall. Elac brought his sword up, facing the evil figure bearing down on him.

Gillen struck with his axe, but Noran caught the weapon by the blade and thrust the attack aside contemptuously. Rilen took advantage of the distraction and buried his sword in Noran's back, up to the hilt. Noran gave a cry of rage, his bloodied fangs giving him a nightmarish look. With incredible agility and strength, he leapt to the back of the dais, where he turned into mist once more. Rilen's blade fell to the floor with a steely clatter. Noran reformed once again, picked up the weapon, and snapped it in half as easily as Elac might break a small twig. Rilen cast about for another sword; undaunted, Noran stalked the group once more.

Elac suddenly remembered the holy dagger tucked inside his belt. "Rilen!"

He held the Dagger of Rennex out for Rilen. The two Elves came together and Rilen whirled to face Noran, dagger in hand, while the vampire closed with him once more. Rilen danced aside, looking for an opening, so Elac waved his blade in small circles. He made several feints, drawing a smile from the vampire lord who stepped within range of Elac's weapon, almost daring him to attack. Elac tried a light thrust, but Noran sidestepped, grabbed Elac's sword arm, and threw him across the room. He crashed into the wall, and for a few moments everything went black.

He sat up, leaning back on one arm while he waited for the room to stop spinning. The battle continued, but Cassius had sluggishly come to his feet and rejoined the melee. The three veteran warriors, Cassius, Rilen, and Gillen, tried to keep the vampire lord from reaching Silvayn, who gestured once more.

The bolt of energy came closer this time, leaving a large, smoking hole in Noran's cloak.

Elac tried to stand but fell supine. His eyes were drawn to the damaged wall looming above him, where Silvayn's first bolt of energy had struck. Closer inspection showed a bit of light coming through. Yellow light . . . daylight! A desperate hope arose in his heart. He rolled over on his stomach, ignoring the waves of nausea and dizziness rippling through his body.

He dragged himself the short distance to where Hadwyn lay crumpled on his side. He firmly grasped the fallen Dwarf's massive hammer and struggled to his feet. Using the hammer as a crutch, he limped to the crumbling stone wall. With a brief pause to summon the last of his strength, he hefted the hammer and swung.

The hammer struck the wall with a deep *thud*, displacing several stones and opening the gap to the outside a bit further. Elac risked a glimpse back and saw only Rilen and Adalyn still on their feet, the last barrier between Noran and Silvayn. He called out the mage's name and swung once more, and this time a bright beam of light came through. Somehow, from a deep inner reserve of willpower, Elac summoned the strength to swing the hammer yet again. The third impact knocked several stones loose, and they tumbled away into the chasm surrounding the castle. The sun, sinking low in the sky but visible through a gap in the surrounding peaks, poured through the hole like a waterfall. The light caught Noran with its full force, and he shrieked insanely, falling to his knees. He staggered back to his feet, trying to escape the deadly rays, but Adalyn thrust at him with her shield and sent him sprawling across an ancient coffin.

The sun sank lower, and Noran found himself out of the burning orb's direct rays.

The vampire lord appeared to have aged a hundred years almost instantly, and smoke wafted from his exposed skin. His clawed hands came up, reaching venomously for Adalyn. Rilen lunged forward and plunged the Dagger of Rennex into Noran's chest. The blade pierced the frail body and drove him backward, where it pinned him to the coffin. Noran struggled vainly, trying to remove the blade holding him transfixed. Adalyn raised her sword to strike another crippling blow.

But Silvayn gestured a final time. The bolt of fiery red energy flashed across the room to strike the damaged wall. With a deafening explosion, an entire section erupted in fire and disappeared, taking part of the roof with it. The sun blazed into the room in all its glory, engulfing Noran's body in a halo of power. He screamed his hatred once more, clawing at Rilen in defiance. The Elf slapped Noran's hand away and used his shield like a hammer, driving the Dagger of Rennex through the stricken vampire lord and deeper into the coffin.

Noran's body began to glow, and the others backed away cautiously. Elac struggled to stay on his feet, wanting to watch the vampire lord in his final death throes. Noran's fingers stiffened, reaching to the safety of his coffin in a final act of supplication. His writhing form flared brightly, and Elac had to avert his eyes. When he looked back, the vampire lord was gone. In his place was a pile of ashes, already scattering before the gentle breeze coming through the opening in the wall, and carrying with it the odor of burnt flesh.

A violent shudder rippled through the castle. "Quickly!"

Silvayn said tensely, gesturing for the still-standing members of the party to come closer. "The castle is collapsing. We must gather the injured and leave this place before it falls on top of us!"

Somehow, Hadwyn managed to rise to one knee. The dazed look on his face told Elac the Dwarf wasn't aware of what was going on around him. Gillen slipped under one arm and helped him to stand. Rilen, having picked up a short sword from one of the fallen warriors of Noran, grabbed Hadwyn's hammer. Elac paused long enough to retrieve the Dagger of Rennex before he was back at Jayrne's side. Her skin had turned a healthier color, the sun-darkened skin of her beautiful face no longer bearing the pallor of death. He scooped up her limp form, abandoning the litter. Somehow, he found the strength to hold both her weight and his own, and he staggered across the chamber to where the others waited. He refused Adalyn's offer of assistance and insisted on carrying Jayrne himself.

They left following the route the others had used to reach Noran's chambers. The castle continued to tremble sporadically, and with each quake Elac feared it would collapse upon them or slide into the surrounding abyss. Another violent wave ripped through the Keep, this time driving Elac to his knees. Blood flowed freely where he had struck the paving stones, but he was back on his feet in an instant.

They burst through a door and into the main entry hall just as the tallest of the towers collapsed, crashing through the roof and filling the air with a choking dust. Elac staggered out the open doorway, the portal that had once closed it hanging wildly from one hinge. He somehow lurched across the narrow walkway bridging the chasm and collapsed on the other side. Gillen lowered his brother to a sitting position before he checked on Jayrne.

"Don't worry, Elac," Gillen told the obviously worried Elf. "I can help her now. The curse is broken." Elac managed a weak smile of gratitude, refusing to release Jayrne's hand even for a moment while Gillen recited his prayers.

"She should wake up soon," Gillen said. "Make sure she drinks some water. I have to check on the others, but let me know if anything changes."

They spent an hour trying to recover from the battle with Noran. Within minutes of their exit, the vampire lord's ancient fortress slid off its perch, disappearing forever into the mists of time. With its passing, the last of the vampires was destroyed.

Jayrne opened her eyes, and Elac's own filled with tears. She smiled, placing a gentle, trembling hand against his cheek.

"How are you feeling?" he asked her quietly.

"Weak," she replied shortly. "Where are we?"

He explained what had befallen the group since Noran's initial attack in one of the lesser towers. She admitted that much of what followed the vampire lord's bite was a blur, and she could only clearly recall bits and pieces of events. He helped her to a sitting position and offered her his waterskin.

"With Noran destroyed, am . . . am I . . ."

Elac managed a genuine smile. "You're fine. You'll regain your strength soon. Rilen and Adalyn are retrieving our horses, and once they return we'll be on our way."

Moments later, there was a great clattering of hooves and the two Elves led the group's horses back to the clearing. On a sudden impulse, Elac eased Jayrne back to the ground. He rummaged through the packs on Jayrne's horse until he found one of the extra flasks of water from the Springs of Calda. He brought it to her side and offered it to her. She looked unsure of the idea, her brow crinkled with doubt, but a reassuring look from Elac convinced her to drink it.

The change in her was almost immediate. She was able to sit unaided, and the sagging of her fatigued muscles eased noticeably. Elac lifted Jayrne once more, and with Rilen's help he strapped her into the saddle.

"You showed great courage and strength of character today, Elac," Rilen said, looking Elac in the eyes. "You made me proud to call you my friend."

By the next morning, only Jayrne and Hadwyn still showed major effects of the battle. Hadwyn had a ringing in his ears that wouldn't subside, and he had difficulty maintaining his balance. Jayrne continued to be severely weakened by her experience. Her eyes were swollen and red, and she sat slumped against a hollow log after breakfast. Concerned, Elac went in search of Gillen, finding him sharpening his axe.

"Gillen, can I talk to you about Jayrne?"

"Certainly." He patted a spot on the ground next to him, and Elac seated himself. "How's she doing this morning?"

"No better," Elac said, shaking his head sadly. "She's trying not to let me see it, but I think it's all she can do just to hold her head up."

Gillen nodded, stroking his long, red beard. "It may be some time before she fully recovers. Make sure she eats, and force her to drink plenty of water. And, like my brother here," he said, emphasizing his point by kicking Hadwyn, who was reaching for a wineskin, "keep her away from ale and wine for a while."

They rode southeast through the mountains for the rest of the day, avoiding the more heavily traveled trails. They kept their pace slow, and it was all they could do to keep Jayrne in her saddle. Cassius frequently chafed about their lack of progress, and Elac finally took action. He climbed up behind Jayrne and held his arms about her waist. With his own horse's reins secured to the back of Jayrne's saddle, Elac was able to keep both horses moving without fear of Jayrne suffering a fall. She leaned back against his chest gratefully, and was quickly asleep.

By early evening, they had reached the western edge of the peaks. To Elac's astonishment, Silvayn told Rilen to turn south, staying within the mountains. By keeping off the plains, Silvayn explained, they could more readily avoid detection, since the Kobolds were likely in control of everything between the Paheny Mountains and the Mason River.

Rilen located a large cave, one with an opening barely wide enough to bring the horses through, but which widened once inside, providing more than enough space to provide accommodations for the entire retinue. A steady flow of water trickled down the back of a niche near the far side of the cave, collecting in a pool roughly five feet across and three feet deep. They replenished their water supply and enjoyed a much-needed hot meal.

The next morning, they continued their southward trek. Although Jayrne seemed stronger, she suggested Elac ride with her for yet another day, and he didn't argue. Jayrne stretched, watching a herd of deer dart away at their approach, their tails held high in panic. She glanced back, catching Elac with her subtle half-smile. "Can I ask you something?"

He smiled. "Of course."

"I vaguely remember the trap you and I fell through. I was on the litter, and you and Adalyn were carrying me. I wasn't lucid most of the time, so there are gaps in my memory."

"I'm surprised you can remember any of it."

"You and I were cut off from the others, and we knew the enemy was looking for us. You would've escaped much more readily by yourself. In fact, you may have even been able to climb up the slide."

"It was locked."

"But you might have been able to unlock it. So instead of safely finding your way out on your own, you chose to exhaust yourself by dragging me through the castle, increasing your chances of being caught. Why?"

"You're my friend. I would have done the same for anyone in the group. Except maybe for Cassius . . ." he trailed off with a short laugh.

"I heard that!" the Prince called back to him.

"Kidding!" Elac replied.

"Seriously, though, Elac. Even after we'd been discovered, you protected me. When we were trapped on the other side of the secret door, you could've hidden among the statues and left me where I would've been found. And when the battle with Noran started, you dragged me inside the room instead of leaving me there."

Elac pulled her close. "I won't let anything happen to you," he told her plainly. He saw the question forming in her eyes, and he pressed a finger to her lips, answering before she could give voice to the matter. "Because I care for you."

She was silent for some time, and there was only the sound of the clatter of the horses' hooves against the stones of the mountainside. Finally, she looked back to him once more. "No one has ever cared about me before. I mean, my mother, sure, but I think it was more out of a sense of obligation than any sense of closeness."

He kissed her cheek. "Get used to it. I'm not going away." He reached into a pouch and pulled out her lockpick set. "I almost forgot I had this."

She turned the full, devastating force of her smile on him, and he felt his knees tremble. He was glad he wasn't standing. "Keep it," she told him. "I have two more."

When the group stopped for the night, Silvayn announced they would be leaving the mountains the next morning. In the evening's blushing haze, Elac could make out the vast expanse of the Piaras Swamp in the distance. It was late spring, and the heat and humidity in the immeasurable swamp would be matched in discomfort by the swarms of mosquitoes seeking their blood.

They rose early and packed away their heavier cloaks. The group spent the morning descending the outermost slopes of the Paheny Mountains, and by lunchtime they were trotting along through the wetlands marking the edge of the swamp. While most of the swamp was impassable for their horses, Silvayn knew of a little-used route leading from the mountains to a point within a few leagues of Piaras Keep.

Trees near the path somehow managed to grow, despite being embedded in four feet of water, which reeked of rotting vegetation. The narrow trail they followed appeared no different from the rest of the swamp, at least at first glance. A closer inspection revealed the water's depth at only a foot, allowing easy passage for the horses. The bottom was also more solid there, due to its original use as a roadway. Anyone trying to cut directly across the swamp would have found the opposite to be true; the muck at the bottom was deep enough to hold onto a boot in some places, deep enough to pull a person under in others.

A few hours after they entered the swamp, Elac spotted what he believed was a pair of logs drifting along in the gently pulling current. Rilen noticed them, too, and he called to Silvayn. The old mage took the situation in with a glance, and he immediately chanted in the language of magic. When he released this spell with a wave of his hand, there was an earsplitting explosion of sound. The waters of the swamp actually recoiled in response, pushing away from Silvayn in a semicircle. The two log-shapes reared up from the water, their mouths gaping wide to show row upon row of sharp teeth. With a roar of their own, they turned and disappeared into the swamp.

"What in the name of Gentra was that?" Elac asked, his eyes wide with shock.

"Crocodiles," Rilen answered, watching the animals' retreat with satisfaction. "I think they were looking for dinner."

Elac stared at the retreating monstrosities. "They could bite a man in half with those teeth."

"Not really," Silvayn corrected him with an impish grin. "They prefer to bite, hold on, and take you to the bottom until you drown. Then they can eat you at their leisure."

Hadwyn gave the mage a sarcastic smile. "Thanks for the reassurance."

The members of the little group spent the night in the wide, sweeping branches of the trees, trying to stay dry enough to sleep. They found a small hillock, which was mostly out of the water, and they secured their horses to the sparse trees near the summit. Elac slept poorly that night, and he awoke feeling sandy-eyed and tired.

Late in the afternoon, they arrived at another area of high ground, considerably larger than the last. Silvayn told them they would have to leave their horses there and proceed afoot. There was some grumbling about this, especially from Cassius, who was reluctant to leave his prized warhorse unattended.

"How do you know the animals won't simply wander off?" he asked Silvayn, his face red and his nostrils flaring.

"Where would they go?" Silvayn asked.

"And what about those crocodiles? Won't they attack the horses?"

"I doubt it. If they were extremely hungry, maybe, but they tend to like their prey a bit smaller. These crocodiles don't grow very large. Down by the shores of the South Sea, however, is another matter. The crocs down there get to be fifteen to twenty feet long. They wouldn't hesitate to attack something the size of a horse."

"Can't we leave someone behind to watch over them?"

Silvayn shook his head. "We were told all of us needed to be there when we meet with the ghosts. We've come this far. Let's not tempt fate by changing things now."

Cassius stood there for several moments, hands on hips, then stormed off to gather gear from his warhorse, gesturing wildly to himself as he went. Elac stared after him for a bit, then looked at the mage who stood there smiling at the Prince's back.

"Silvayn?" he asked quietly. "You told Cassius the crocodiles wouldn't attack our horses. Weren't they about to do just that a little earlier?"

Silvayn met his gaze, his face unreadable for several moments before a smile began to play at the corner of his lips. He chuckled finally, then made his way to his horse to finish his own preparations.

They continued their journey to Piaras Keep, this time on foot. At first, Elac didn't mind wading. It was a hot day, for one, and the cool waters were refreshing. Besides, whatever part of him was underwater, the mosquitoes couldn't bite. But after a time, he felt blisters forming on his feet.

Through a massive tangle of interwoven tree branches, the ancient, vine-covered walls of Piaras Keep came into view. They pressed forward eagerly, anxious to reach the high ground around the castle and change out of their wet clothes. Once that was accomplished, they circled the Keep, looking for the way in. They found it on the fortress's north face, the towering double doors forming the main gate hanging half-rotted from rusty hinges. Clawed footprints in the soft ground gave ample evidence that the swamp's natural residents had explored the castle.

Rilen led the way through the outer wall, an immense barrier surrounding the bailey and providing a redoubt for the defenders inside the Keep. Small shrubs mingled with trees in the courtyard. They passed a well near the entrance, and the stones forming the rim were crumbling into dust. Through the screening trees, Elac caught an occasional glimpse of doors leading into the castle, most of them in as poor condition as the gates. Rilen brought the group before one of the doors, and at first, it seemed to Elac to be no different from any of the others. A closer look, however, revealed a set of runes above the doorway, barely visible, the writing having faded in the elements. With the rest of the group gathered tightly around, Rilen pushed on the wooden portal. The decayed hinges gave way, and the door fell into the darkness beyond. Silvayn brought his magic to bear once more, and the illumination he provided revealed a set of stairs leading down into the unknown reaches of Piaras Keep.

Chapter 15

The steps seemed to go on forever. Elac followed Rilen and Hadwyn during their descent, his longbow ready with an arrow nocked. They reached the bottom and found themselves in a small room, with jagged clay walls and hard-packed dirt floors. There was only one passage leading away from the stairs, and Rilen took it without hesitation. The loose dirt muffled the sound of their footfalls while they explored the cellar passages, searching for the Crypt of the Seven Knights. The passage connected with another, which formed a square, likely following the edges of the castle above them. Several minutes later, they returned to their starting point, having found nothing to show them where the knights' crypt would be. Cassius mumbled something under his breath having to do with the group's lack of organization.

"Are you certain this was the correct stairway?" Rilen asked. "After all, there were a number of doors up there."

"Absolutely," Silvayn replied, pulling a small scroll from a pouch at his belt. He browsed the brittle document for a few moments. "Those markings above the door mark the entrance to the crypt. We're missing something."

Jayrne stepped forward, her face bathed in sweat and her skin still looking slightly pale. "Are there any other indications of what to look for?"

Silvayn gave an irritated sigh, rolled his eyes, and raised the scroll once more. "Here's what we have. First, there's a rather straightforward description of the road we followed from the mountains to get here. Then there is mention of how to find the door, and a description of the runes above it." He scratched his head, exhaling slowly. "From there, it gets a bit cryptic. 'And once thou hast gained the lower levels, shall it be left to thee to find the labyrinth. And once thou hast defeated the sentinel, then shall the way be clear, and the crypt revealed.' I hadn't anticipated the entrance to the labyrinth being concealed."

"Can I see the scroll?" Jayrne asked.

Silvayn unrolled the scroll and handed it to her. The others wandered aimlessly about, and Elac scoured the walls around them for another of the secret doors. He knew the odds of randomly finding such a door were abysmal, because the area was simply too large.

"'Left to thee to find . . .' 'Left to . . .' 'Left two?'" Jayrne said, her eyes wide with excitement.

"What are you babbling about?" Cassius asked without looking up.

"Just doing something constructive," Jayrne answered smoothly. "What are you doing?"

"What have you found?" Adalyn asked, heading off further argument.

"Sometimes, the best place to hide something is right out in the open. Usually, people who conceal something within a message use words with a double meaning. The message says the task of finding the entrance to the crypt has been left to us. The part that catches my attention is 'left to.' The word 'left' might also refer to a direction, as in turning left when we first reached the square. If I'm right, we need to return to the entrance and turn left. The trick will be in finding out if we need to go two steps, two feet, or something else."

"That's really helpful," Cassius said with a snort.

Elac turned, anger flashing in his eyes. "Then what would you have us do? Wander around in here until we grow old?"

"How about go home and give up this folly? In case you haven't noticed, my people are at war! Yours, too, unless I miss my guess. We should be helping with the fighting!"

"And that is exactly what we're trying to do," Rilen interrupted. "How much help do you think you could be? You are only one man, and in the greater view of the things, one man will not win or lose the war. But maybe what we do here will make a difference."

Cassius didn't answer; he threw his hands in the air and walked away. Elac returned to the entrance, turned left into the square, and began a methodical search. For the next half hour, they scoured the area two feet into the square, then two steps, then two yards, even two fathoms, and found nothing. Rilen and Adalyn were conducting their own random search. Hadwyn and Gillen were arguing loudly about where they should look, and Silvayn was stroking his beard, lost in his musings. Cassius simply leaned against the wall, grinning at their futile efforts.

"Jayrne," Elac whispered, "we can't let this thing beat us. Not with Cassius and his 'mightier than thou' attitude. What else could the message mean?"

Jayrne rubbed her eyes wearily. "What other units of measurement are there? Leagues and miles are too big, obviously. We may be interpreting this part too literally."

"Do you mean the entire 'left two' idea may be wrong?"

"No. I'm certain we're on the right track. But maybe we're being too rigid in our thinking. We need to change our frame of reference. Without using standard units of measurement, what else could be used to determine a distance down here?"

Elac glanced around the hall. "The walls are seamless, as is the floor, so we can't go with two sections." He looked up suddenly, eyes wide with discovery. "Two corners?"

Jayrne's head snapped up, mouth agape. "Let's go!"

They raced around the first corner, breathlessly arriving at the second. Once again, they conducted their hands-and-knees, meticulous search of the walls and floor. It was Jayrne who found what they were looking for, just a small, circular depression in the floor. Elac called to the others excitedly, and Jayrne inspected the depression more closely. Jayrne performed a painstaking inspection of the depression, but she found nothing that would turn, push, or move in any way. Cassius chuckled and said nothing.

Elac was certain they had found the entrance, and opening it was just one more enigma they needed to resolve. They had brought certain artifacts on the quest. Were the items supposed to be used to gain entrance to the crypt? Obviously, the water from the Springs of Calda wouldn't help here, and there was nothing to be cut or pierced with the Dagger of Rennex. *The Orion Stone.*

Wordlessly, the hope springing up in his chest causing his hands to tremble with excitement, he pulled the Orion Stone free from the pouch at his belt. Jayrne looked at him quizzically when he placed the stone in the depression and sat back. At first, nothing happened. Then the maelstrom of colors on the Orion Stone suddenly swirled more quickly. With a soundless flash of light, a five-foot section of the outer wall of the corridor vanished, revealing another passageway beyond. Curious, Elac retrieved the stone, but the opening remained.

Gillen clasped his hand on Elac's shoulder. "Excellent!" The others moved forward excitedly, and Jayrne threw her arms about Elac in an exuberant hug.

Rilen was the first to step into the labyrinth. The darkness beyond Silvayn's spell seemed so complete as to be almost palpable. The dust of the ages coated the floor, stirring into the air with their passage. At a suggestion from Silvayn, Adalyn brought forth a second magical light, but she projected hers farther into the distance, lighting more of the maze and giving them advanced warning should trouble arise.

They had gone but a short distance when they reached the first intersection. Tunnels branched in four different directions, and there was no indication as to which was the correct path. After a brief discussion, Rilen used the tip of a dagger to mark where they had come from. With the return path safely recorded, they started forward once more.

An hour later, they still hadn't found the entrance to the

crypt, and tempers were short. Cassius and Rilen were bickering openly, and Hadwyn's waspish temper had also surfaced. It was Gillen who arrived at their next plan. With skills all but unique to the Dwarves, he paced off distances and kept track of changes in direction. In a few hours, a crude but effective map of the maze was created. Elac would have sworn they had checked almost every passage in the labyrinth, but the map showed otherwise. Aided by this invaluable tool, they backtracked and inspected the parts of the warren they had missed.

"Silvayn, can we talk to you?" Gillen motioned to the mage without looking up from his map, and Hadwyn was just as intent. Silvayn joined them, and Hadwyn pointed a weary finger to the center of the map.

"If you will notice, there seems to be a small gap in the center of our chart of the tunnels. We think this should be our next destination."

Rilen joined them, running the fingers of one hand through his short hair. "It's worth a try. At least we won't be wandering around aimlessly."

They shouldered their packs and set out once more. Aided by the Dwarves' map, Rilen brought the group to what appeared to be the center of the network of passageways. When they reached uncharted territory, he prudently returned the map to Gillen before they entered. Elac noticed a difference almost immediately. There seemed to be a faint, naturally occurring light, some type of phosphorescence giving off a weak glow. He fingered the fletchings of his arrow, his nervousness about to boil over. Somehow, instinctively, he knew their destination was near.

They followed a sharp turn in the corridor and came upon a wooden altar, set against the end of the tunnel. Despite the dampness in the air, the wood was preserved. Intricate carvings lined the fringes of the lightly stained wood, and seven busts were engraved in the panel rising up starkly from the top. The knights from the legend of the Keep, Elac realized.

An apparition rose from the altar, soundless in its threatening approach. The ephemeral hands raised, and one finger leveled at Rilen. A burst of white energy shot forth, knocking the Elf across the room and into the wall. He was on his feet immediately, but Elac's bow was already singing. The arrow passed harmlessly through the figure before them to shatter against the wall. He discarded his bow and drew his short sword, and the others closed in about the incorporeal creature before them.

"Specter!" Silvayn shouted. "Be careful!" He chanted in the language of magic to bring his powers to bear.

Cassius was the first to strike. His broadsword passed through the filmy body, and while it did no visible damage, the apparition did seem to flinch. Elac hesitated, filled with chagrin when he saw the minimal effect Cassius's weapon had. Their blades had all been blessed by Gillen for just such a contingency, but they seemed almost useless.

A swipe from the specter sent Cassius sprawling, and the Dwarves answered by challenging their foe from both sides. Gillen's axe had a much greater effect, likely due to the emblem of Gentra engraved on the face. The specter actually took a step back from the Dwarf Priest, allowing his brother to strike with his hammer. With a contemptuous swipe, the apparition knocked Hadwyn aside and came for Gillen.

Silvayn's magic burst forth, and a blast of red fire streaked across the intervening space to strike the specter full in the chest. For an instant, it disappeared in the ensuing fireball, and Elac hoped it was destroyed. But the specter reappeared, seemingly unharmed, and pointed at the old mage. Its own magic flared to life, but Adalyn was able to bring forth a shield of magical energy to protect Silvayn.

Elac brought his sword to the ready position, but he paused. The Orion Stone had bought them entry. Could this be the purpose for the Dagger of Rennex? He brought forth the ancient weapon, and it glinted coldly in the magical light of the tunnel.

With that, he had the creature's full attention. Ignoring the blows raining down upon it from the others, the specter stalked Elac, reaching out with a finger to summon the magic once more. The white light burst forth yet again, too quickly for Elac to dodge. But when the bolt of energy reached him, it simply dissipated into the Orion Stone.

The Dagger of Rennex flashed when he brought it down upon the specter. The blade seemed to strike something solid when he made contact, and an inhuman shriek erupted in his ears. Abruptly, a powerful vortex of wind exploded around the altar, and everyone was blasted to the ground. The specter slowly disappeared, fading into nothingness, and the wind gradually subsided.

"How did you know to do that?" Jayrne asked, panting with exertion.

"Lucky guess," Elac told her with a smile. "The Orion Stone got us in here, and our weapons weren't getting the job done."

"That leaves only the flask of water," Silvayn said, studiously looking over the altar. They watched as Silvayn brushed the dirt and debris from the busts. The mage stepped back and shook his head, hands on hips as he contemplated what they hoped was the final puzzle. His frustration got the better of him, and he yanked the stopper from the flask containing the special water. He stepped to the altar and liberally sprinkled the contents across the surface. When he finished, he stepped back, waiting for something to happen.

He didn't have long to wait. Moments later, the altar wavered as if made of smoke, then vanished, revealing another chamber behind it. They stepped through the opening, and Elac found himself in a high, circular chamber, filled with several sarcophagi.

Seven, to be exact.

Each burial casket was topped with gold and inlaid with jewels. Many of the knights' worldly possessions were gathered about the tomb, and the battle standards of each were painted on the walls in an unending frieze. On the lid of each sarcophagus was the likeness of the knight interred within.

A low moaning filled the room, and weapons came up guardedly. Elac drew the Dagger of Rennex once more, and he awaited the next guardian. In an instant's time, the wispy figures of seven knights stood before them.

One raised his hand in a gesture of serenity. *Be at peace.* Elac found the voice to be less a sound than a thought projected into his mind. *I am Sir Draygen. You have come before us and subdued the barriers, as the prophecies have foretold. Upon your shoulders rests the future of all of Pelacia.*

"What must we do?" Silvayn asked in a solemn voice.

All in good time. First, we must provide you with the tools by which the world shall be saved. He gestured to another of the figures. *This is Sir Aleron. He was the greatest archer of all time. He was given a special longbow and quiver, blessed by the gods. Rilen, this is yours.*

The ghost of Sir Aleron stepped forward, the translucent form of the bow and quiver shimmering in his hand. When he passed it off to Rilen, it was as substantial as Elac's armor. Elac wondered how the spirits knew Rilen's name.

The bow is the best ever made, and the quiver will never run out of arrows. Use them to good fortune.

Rilen nodded, not taking his eyes off the gifts. The ghost of Sir Aleron retreated to his crypt once more.

This is Sir Salenas. Adalyn, his sword will now pass to you. The ghostly knight stepped forward and offered the blade, hilt first, across his forearm. Adalyn accepted the weapon with a respectful bow, and as Rilen had found, the sword turned solid at her touch.

Sir Salenas's sword was endowed by the gods with the ability to cut through virtually anything. Use it well against your foes.

Sir Flemane, he said, gesturing to a third knight. *His father, Limor, was a powerful mage, and his abilities helped us mightily in our struggles against the undead. When he was murdered by Volnor's spies, Sir Flemane carried his father's spellbook into battle. Silvayn, you must use the spells contained therein to complete your quest.*

"And what would you require of me?" Silvayn asked, reverently taking the spellbook.

Patience, Silvayn. Sir Omonis. Yet another ghostly knight stepped forth from the shadows, this time to stand beside Cassius. *Sir Omonis was grievously wounded during an attack by skel-*

eton archers. *For the rest of his days, he bore a shield imbued with special protection against arrows. Carry it with honor, Lord Cassius, and it will protect those around you, as well as yourself.*

Cassius accepted the gift, his lip curled with outrage.

Lord Gillen, you wield an axe in battle. For you, Sir Penosan's axe. The enchantment cast upon it rendered the weapon weightless to him. That property now extends to you.

Gillen took the axe, his mouth agape with wonder when he hefted it, obviously amazed at the lack of weight. He was still marveling over the axe when Sir Draygen spoke once more.

For your brother, Lord Hadwyn, we give the war hammer of Sir Thalitt. Draygen glanced at the weapon in Hadwyn's hand. *You will find it carries the same properties as Sir Penosan's axe.*

He regarded Jayrne for several moments before he gestured to the next apparition. *You are a thief by nature.* It was more a statement than a question, and Jayrne nodded. *You shall have my boots and cloak. The boots shall cover all sound of your passage, and the cloak will enable you to walk unseen when you wish. Use them wisely.*

Sir Draygen turned to face Elac, who stood unmoving before him. The ghostly knight drew his sword and saluted Elac. *Upon your shoulders will fall the greatest burden, and therefore you shall have the mightiest weapon.* He handed his sword, hilt-first, across his ghostly forearm. *It was forged by the greatest mages and Priests in all of Pelacia, solely for the purpose of destroying the undead. All but the most powerful of those foul creatures will be instantly destroyed by its touch.*

You have come far. But the most dangerous part of your journey lies ahead. You must use the tools we have given you to destroy the forces of Malator, for all eternity.

"Malator?" Cassius said, so angry he was almost choking

on his words. "The Kobolds are the threat here! They have invaded the West, and I have done nothing but chase shadows with this pack of fools."

DO NOT SEEK TO RISE ABOVE YOURSELF! Draygen's shade grew darker, and the voice thundered in Elac's mind. *You see only what is in the moment. Even those of us beyond the grave cannot see to the end of all things, but the threat of Malator dwarfs anything presented by those insignificant creatures. Ignore my warning at your peril!*

Silvayn, it falls to you to lead this group into the mountains once more, to the valley where Tracker's Peak once stood. Using the spells contained in Limor's spellbook, you will retrieve the Temira from the Plane of Mist.

"I was told the Temira was lost, when Tracker's Peak disappeared during the First Necromancer War," Silvayn said.

So the world believes. When the Necromancers cast the spell to destroy the fortress, the mages fighting from within Tracker's Peak used the Temira to deflect the spell. But their efforts had the unexpected reaction of sending the castle, along with everyone inside, into the Plane of Mist, carried on the currents of the displaced magical power. You will enter Tracker's Peak, recover the Temira, then return to this world.

In the presence of the Temira, Elac must use my sword and destroy the accursed Necromancer for all time.

Cassius, undaunted by the earlier tirade, crossed his arms. "And I suppose they will fail if I leave."

You must all be present at Tracker's Peak to gain the Temira. Once you have the talisman, all that matters are the Temira and my sword.

"Why did the sword fall to Elac?" Cassius asked. "He is incompetent with a weapon."

The blade can only be used by a direct descendant of my lineage. While Elac is an Elf, at one point an ancestor of his married a Human of my descent. This is why he is being hunted. He is the last of my line. Only he can bear my sword. Only Elac. This is his legacy and his alone.

With that, the seven figures faded into nothingness. There was silence in the room while the eight travelers contemplated the shade's words. Cassius broke the stillness with an oath, hurling the shield across the room. It struck the wall with a clatter, bounced off a sarcophagus, and came to rest on the floor.

"Let's get this over with," he muttered, and marched from the room with clenched fists. Elac stood immobile, the Sword of Draygen clutched in his hands, staring in wide-eyed disbelief at the Prince. The others filed wordlessly from the room, but Elac looked back to where the Shield of Omonis lay. He briefly considered retrieving the ancient artifact, but discarded the idea. If Cassius had rejected the shield when it was the gift of the ghost of a long-dead knight, he would have spurned it just as quickly coming from an Elf.

Elac paused at the entrance to the "square" and gazed at the depression where he had placed the Orion Stone. The open space behind him remained there for the span of several heartbeats, then began to shimmer. The wall returned, as solid as ever. Elac pressed on the wall experimentally, and it didn't budge.

Elac drew forth the Sword of Draygen and admired the blade, his jaw slightly open in stunned amazement. The blade itself was made of steel, polished to mirror brightness, and engraved along the entire length with runes from a language Elac couldn't understand. It had the length of a long sword, but weighed less than a dagger, and he was confident he could wield it successfully with one hand. The hilt was wrapped in a fine, soft leather, and the pommel was a green gemstone, possibly jade. The cross guard was made of steel, but gold in color and inlaid with more of the green gemstones. In the exact center of the cross guard, on both sides, was engraved the likeness of Sir Draygen's standard, an eagle in flight with the setting sun in the background.

"Do you mind if I look at the Sword?" Adalyn asked. Elac shrugged and handed her the weapon after placing it back in the scabbard. She examined it closely, looking suitably impressed by the skill that went into its making.

Rilen took the Sword of Draygen from Adalyn, brought it up to the ready position, and swung it around a few times. "It's an excellent weapon, Elac," Rilen told him. "Use it well."

They emerged from the bowels of Piaras Keep into the darkness of the approaching evening. A small sliver of the sun was visible over the horizon, and night was falling rapidly. Silvayn announced they would spend the night in the castle's courtyard; it was too dangerous to wade through the swamp at night. They built a fire for a hot meal, and after dinner, Adalyn located the baths. A few of the tubs were still sufficiently intact to hold water, and she and Jayrne insisted upon everyone bathing before they went to sleep.

Rilen, Elac, and Hadwyn sat up late, warming themselves by the fire in the cool evening air and sharing a waterskin the Dwarf had thoughtfully filled with ale. Surprisingly, Cassius came over and joined them, gazing silently into the flames. Rilen offered ale to the Prince but, rather predictably, he refused. Rilen shrugged, took a long drink, and passed it to Elac.

Finally, Cassius stirred. "Elac, I would like to see the Sword of Draygen, if you please."

Elac hesitated, suspicions racing through his mind for the

briefest of moments. But he shook off the doubts plaguing him and drew forth the Sword, handing it to Cassius.

"What did you do with your old sword?" he asked in a quiet voice, his eyes fixed on the Sword.

"It's tied onto my pack. I figured I should get used to wearing this one, since it's a bit longer than my old short sword."

"It is an excellent weapon." He returned the Sword to Elac. "I only hope the shades didn't make a mistake."

"How do you mean?"

"I'm not trying to offend you, but you're no warrior. They expect you to go after the most powerful Necromancer who ever lived, with the most powerful blade ever forged. I think it would serve our cause better in the hands of a warrior."

"The Sword is useless in your hands," Hadwyn growled, wiping ale foam from his beard. "Only the heir of Draygen can wield it."

"So they gave me a shield instead. I'm sure I'll put it to good use."

Elac looked at him sharply. "You left it in the crypt," he accused.

"And in the crypt is where it shall stay." He stood and returned to his blanket.

Elac shook his head and reverently eased the Sword into its sheath. From across their camp, Cassius launched into a tirade of oaths, standing with the Shield of Omonis in his hands.

"It was on my bedroll. Who put it there?" He stormed across the courtyard, opened the door to the labyrinth, and hurled the Shield into the void. Even from where he sat, Elac heard the Shield bouncing down the stone stairs. He sat, too stunned to speak, watching the sputtering Prince return to his blankets. Hadwyn shrugged, rolled his eyes, and took another drink.

They were up with the sun, and in fairly short order they were wading through the fetid waters of the swamp once more. Elac donned the clothes he wore on the way in, thereby only soiling the one pair of pants and tunic. His skin initially cringed away from the chilly dampness of the muddy fabric, but in time he became accustomed to them. After a few hours of battling the waist-deep waters, fallen trees, and knee-deep sludge, they located their horses.

"This has gone far enough!" Once again, it was Prince Cassius who protested. His face was red, his brow furrowed with rage, and the veins in his neck were bulging ominously. "Whoever keeps bringing this shield to me, I'm not amused."

Elac stepped out where he could see the Prince and his war-horse. Lying atop the animal's pile of armor and saddle was the Shield of Omonis. Elac's jaw dropped open wide; he had been fairly certain no one had gone after the artifact, and they had all arrived at the horses together, leaving no chance for anyone to sneak ahead and leave it. Although Prince Cassius was quite verbose in his rambling criticism of whoever had brought the Shield, he nonetheless kept it attached to his saddlebow while he strapped various pieces of armor onto his horse. He swung up into his saddle, a scowl firmly embedded on his face.

"Everyone ride ahead. I'll catch up shortly." Cassius grasped the Shield negligently in one hand while the others rode ahead, and the Prince became lost to their sight through the tree trunks and the mist. When he reappeared several minutes later, the Shield of Omonis was gone.

"This time, I buried it deep in the sludge. Even I couldn't locate it now."

Silvayn smiled and said nothing. They maintained their pace, still riding west and hoping to clear the swamp early the next day. They made camp that night on a hillock similar to the one where they had left their horses the night before. After dinner, Elac went to bed early. He found a decrepit old tree, not very tall but with broad, sweeping branches. Part of the tree had actually fallen away, revealing a wide shelf partway up the trunk. He wrapped up in his blanket and fell asleep.

He may have been asleep for a few hours, or only a few minutes, but he awoke with a start and felt the warmth of someone sitting next to him. He opened his sleep-heavy eyes and saw Jayrne, wrapped in her own blankets, sharing the shelf with him. On a whim, he pulled her close, and she snuggled up against him. Content, he fell asleep.

He was awakened by laughter from the two Dwarves. He was facing the wrong way to see what was so humorous, so he gently removed his arm from the slumbering form beside him and climbed to the other side of the tree. His eyes were immediately drawn to the spotless Shield of Omonis hanging from a branch near Cassius, who sat staring wordlessly at the gift he had refused so many times before. This time, however, his shoulders were slumped in defeat. It appeared the Prince had finally accepted his gift from the dead.

Chapter 16

Late that afternoon, they rode clear of Piaras Swamp and returned to the foothills of the Paheny Mountains. Rilen led the group north for several more hours, through rolling, rocky terrain covered in pine trees. Elac's spirits soared once he found himself clear of the putrid odors and omnipresent stagnant waters of the swamp. He was startled to see a cougar perched in the branches of a nearby tree, its tail snapping with curiosity, watching the party but making no move to follow them.

They stopped for supper, and although they didn't feel safe lighting a fire, Elac found even the danger of discovery by Kobolds couldn't dampen his mood. Jayrne sat nearby, and the two laughed and chatted while they ate. Silvayn sat silently, reading page after page in Limor's spellbook, seeming fairly perturbed. Finally, Elac could stand it no longer.

"Silvayn, are you okay?"

"Yeah," Hadwyn chimed in. "You look like you've seen a ghost." His last comment brought a hearty bout of ironic laughter from the group, even the taciturn Cassius.

"I was trying to decide where we should go next. We need to get to Tracker's Peak, but we also promised Falstoff we would keep him abreast of developments. I would hate to cross our closest ally, yet I don't want to give up the extra time of a side trip to Unity.

"But after reading this spellbook, we have nothing to lose by going to Unity first, and everything to gain. We can't actually enter Tracker's Peak for about ten more days."

"Enter?" Hadwyn said, almost choking on his water. Water, or whatever he had in his waterskin. "Who said anything about entering Tracker's Peak? How can we do that?"

"Entry to the lost fortress can only be made within a certain time period each month; specifically, we have to be there within two days of the full moon, giving us a five-day window. Going directly to the valley where the castle once stood would be futile. In fact, we would only be risking discovery by Kobold forces patrolling the nearby mountain pass by arriving so early. Instead, we shall keep our promise to Falstoff and return to Unity."

"You are certain we have no means of recovering the Temira sooner?" a disconsolate Cassius asked, chewing on his lip. "I had hoped to end this as soon as possible so I can return to the defense of my homeland."

"And so we shall. The trip to Unity will cost us nothing, and we have a lot to gain. We maintain our alliance with Falstoff, and we can also get an idea of how the war with the Kobolds is faring."

They left immediately after breakfast, riding northwest out of the foothills and onto the vast, grassy plains covering the lands between Nightwood Forest and Piaras Swamp. Cassius had remained in a foul mood ever since he realized his special item from the seven knights was defensive in nature. Elac knew such a circumstance would rankle the arrogant Prince, because the very nature of the gift relegated him to a secondhand role. Cassius would want to be at the forefront, leading the forces of Palindom against the great evil, Sword of Draygen in hand.

Cassius charged over the hill in front of them, waving for them to stop. Elac reined in his mount as Cassius brought his horse in at a dead run.

"There's a patrol about two leagues ahead," he announced. "I couldn't see if they were Kobolds from this distance."

"Let's not start jumping at shadows," Silvayn said. "Take us where we can see them."

Following Cassius's lead, Elac rode over a series of deeply rolling hills carpeted with deep, green grass and multicolored wildflowers. Cassius dismounted near the top of one of the hills, motioning for the others to do likewise. They kept their bodies low to the ground and crawled to the top of the last mound. In the distance, Elac could see a group of at least fifty figures on horseback.

Silvayn chanted softly, gazing at the tiny figures on the horizon. He gestured with one hand, fingers pointing to the patrol. His eyes closed in concentration.

"Humans!" Silvayn said excitedly. "We must be doing fairly well against the Kobolds to have a patrol this deep in occupied territory."

They mounted once more and set out at a canter in the general direction of the patrol. The riders spread out and surrounded Elac's group. Prince Cassius stepped forth, and he was immediately recognized by the leader of the soldiers.

"Your Highness! We weren't told you would be in the area."

"We require an escort to Unity," he said plainly. "How far can you take us without leaving your patrol zone?"

"I'm Captain Nalos, your Highness. We can ride with you as far as Ranas, but we should be in friendly territory by then." He shouted orders to his men, and the entire retinue trotted along, the soldiers forming a protective ring while Captain Nalos rode next to Cassius, briefing him on events.

"The treachery of the Kobolds cost us dearly, your Highness. Before we even knew what was happening, we had lost Fort Ranset, Fort Nightwood, and Fort Philand. Aside from Fort Ranset, all the soldiers assigned to those bases were killed. The only reason Fort Ranset was any different was due to your party's intervention. The soldiers you saved were able to prevent the other patrols from returning to Fort Ranset and walking into an ambush.

"The eastern Dukes have been stockpiling armies, weapons, and supplies in the event of civil war insurrection. We were able to requisition their troops for the war effort. I just received word this morning that we are laying siege to Fort Ranset and Fort Nightwood. The generals figure we can retake those bases within the week."

Prince Cassius half-turned in his saddle, an incredulous look on his face. "A week to retake Fort Ranset? Surely you jest."

Captain Nalos suddenly looked less sure of himself, his eyes darting wildly. "I . . . your Highness, that's what I was told."

"Those defenses will withstand the best we can throw at

them for months!" Cassius paused, taking several deep breaths to calm himself. "What other news do you have?"

Elac almost felt sorry for the Captain, who sat astride his horse, staring at the ground for several moments, obviously choosing his next words carefully.

"I heard we have eliminated the Kobold invasion forces from Firereach to Piaras Swamp. We own all the ground from the swamp to Nightwood Forest, and from the Mason River to the Paheny Mountains. We have mounted patrols scouring the area to prevent communications between their commanders and the forces inside Fort Ranset. Our next goal is to push our area of control north, beyond Fort Nightwood.

"There are small pockets of resistance, but their actions are few and far between. For the most part, we have them contained. The Dwarves have sent a division of light infantry to strengthen the contingent at Fort Julan. A detachment of Elven archers is already en route to assist the Third Army, which is entrenched along the Unity River north of Nightwood Forest."

Cassius stared impassively at the horizon to their front. "Thank you, Captain. That will be all."

Captain Nalos seemed relieved at the dismissal, and he urged his horse forward in the formation, away from Prince Cassius's rebukes.

It took them a day and a half to reach the city of Ranas. They stayed on the east side of the Mason River, never actually entering the town itself. They encountered only one Kobold patrol during that time, and a contingent of Human horsemen chased them down and eliminated them. When they were in the narrow passage between Unity Lake and Nightwood Forest, their escort left, but urged them to make haste and not stop for the night so close to the dreaded woods. With a shouted word to his soldiers, Captain Nalos turned his men south.

"I tend to agree with the Captain," Silvayn said. "Based upon what the spirits of the knights told us at Piaras Keep, I don't think we can assume the undead aren't going to have a role to play in this. Let's not take any chances."

Following Silvayn's guidance, Cassius galloped away on his warhorse, leading the group north toward Unity. The perilous tracts of Nightwood Forest were faintly visible on the horizon to his right, a dark smudge against the fading colors of the evening sky. Elac found himself relaxing for the first time since they left Piaras Swamp. If the Captain's information was correct, they were back in secure territory, and the war was going well.

The luck he was hoping for betrayed him moments later. With the last of the light fading from view, several Kobold archers seemed to materialize from behind bushes, trees, and even out of the ground. As one, their bows snapped, and a volley of arrows raced toward the party . . .

And curved to meet Cassius's Shield. They bounced harmlessly away, and the astounded Prince swiftly recovered his wits and drew his broadsword. The party turned to meet the attack, and another volley of arrows followed the first, with the same effect. A vicious grin slowly spread across Cassius's countenance, and with a deadly, implacable pace he spurred his horse forward. He charged into their midst, Elac and the others close behind. Cassius swung his sword in a tight arc, and one of the archers fell to the side, pressing his hands against the gaping wound in his abdomen. Another fired a third arrow, but Cassius's Shield seemed to swing about of its own volition to block the deadly missile before it could find a home in its target.

There was no time to ponder the mystery, however, when several swordsmen emerged from their hiding places to join the fray. Rilen drove his horse into a knot of fighters, the great beast scattering the men before it, while Rilen swung his sword from side to side. Hadwyn and Gillen dismounted and stood back-to-back, their deadly new weapons wreaking havoc among their foes. Elac parried a blow, followed with an immediate counterattack, and felt a satisfying crunch when his magic blade bit through his opponent's armor to carve into flesh. Two men charged Adalyn and Jayrne, trying to put an end to Jayrne's longbow. The first fell victim to the very weapon they were trying to silence. Adalyn intercepted the second, blocking his clumsy stroke with her shield. She struck back with Sir Salenas's enchanted Sword, and the blade cleaved the man's shield in half, severing his arm at the elbow. He stood dumbfounded, staring at the stump of his arm, and she drove the point of the sword through his breastplate. He staggered to the ground with a gurgling sigh.

Silvayn came forward with Adalyn and Jayrne, calling the others to him. "Is anyone hurt?" Elac shook his head, the rush of battle still coursing through his veins, and he wiped his blade clean. "Let's ride," the mage told them tensely, eyes on the surrounding terrain. "I don't know who sent them, but there may be more."

"Bring them on," Cassius said coldly, staring in wide-eyed awe of his Shield.

Elac had just grasped his own reins when he felt the fear rise within him. At his hip, he could actually feel the warmth of the Sword of Draygen in its sheath. He spun to face Rilen, who had hesitated in the act of placing his foot in a stirrup.

"I feel it, too," the Elf said quietly. He released his horse and drew his blade once more. They formed a protective circle, Adalyn and Silvayn at its center, and stared out into the darkness. When nothing appeared, Silvayn, almost reluctantly, brought forth his magic and created a halo of light overhead. At first, Elac could see nothing. Then there was a rustle of movement to his right. He felt his blood run cold, and his heart pounded wildly in his chest. From the depths of the evening twilight stepped the Death Knight.

Chapter 17

D o we go for the horses?" It was Adalyn, from over Elac's shoulder, voicing the question.

"There's no time," Rilen answered, his eyes never leaving the heavily armored form advancing on them from out of the darkness. The creature was cloaked in darkness, and the black helmet, black breastplate, and black cloak seemed to exude evil. The helmet left part of the face exposed, and two glowing red eyes peered out at them. A broad shield was strapped to his left arm, and his right hand held a colossal two-handed sword, which he wielded as easily as a child's toy. "Spread out, and try to come at him from all sides."

Elac drifted to his right, but the Death Knight paid no attention to him, his focus riveted on Silvayn. Elac knew the old mage couldn't use his magic on the undead creature with so many of their group gathered around him.

Jayrne seemed to materialize out of thin air behind the Death Knight, and she slashed at his unguarded back. The blow was deflected by his armor, and it bounced away harmlessly.

He swung a vicious slap at Jayrne with his shield, sending her tumbling. Rilen took advantage of the distraction to dart in and slash at the seam between two pieces of armor, and the Death Knight howled with pain. Hadwyn's hammer whistled through the air, descending upon the creature's shoulder with a resounding *crack*. Cassius and Gillen struck simultaneously, and while their blades drew cries of pain, they didn't seem to slow the Death Knight. His sword flashed out, knocking Cassius to the ground, blood flowing freely from a deep gash on the side of his face.

Elac brought the Sword of Draygen down sharply, but the Death Knight's shield was there, and the Sword was deflected in a great shower of sparks. The others continued their assault, but to no avail. Soon, both Dwarves had joined Cassius on the ground, bleeding from many wounds, and the battle continued. Jayrne persisted with her hit-and-run tactics, but the blows were little more than a distraction.

A treacherous foothold betrayed Rilen, and when the small branch rolled away, he lost his balance and fell to one knee. A blow from the Death Knight's shield knocked him supine, and the breath rushed from his lungs. Rilen lay gasping for air, struggling to regain his feet while the Death Knight stood over him, his enormous sword raised for the deathblow. In desperation, Elac raced in close and drove his Sword home, aiming for the exposed, unprotected armpit of the fearsome creature.

With a flash of light, Draygen's blade slid home. The two-handed sword tumbled from the Death Knight's hands, and a piercing shriek emerged from his lips. Elac withdrew the Sword of Draygen and struck again, this time slicing into the opening in the visored helmet. The Death Knight staggered back, hands raised to ward off further blows, but fell to the ground. He weakly climbed to one knee, then fell back once more. He collapsed face-first, and Elac rushed in to thrust the Sword one last time. The Death Knight twitched violently, another scream bursting forth, then the creature lay still.

Rilen came unsteadily to his feet, coughing and struggling to force air back into his lungs. He limped over to where Elac stood entranced, staring at the body of the fallen Death Knight. Elac felt the veteran Elf lean heavily on his shoulder for support.

"The other day," Rilen told him, wheezing slightly, "you mentioned owing me a debt for saving your life." He held out his free hand to Elac. "I think we can consider that debt paid."

Elac took his hand gratefully, not knowing what to say. Adalyn immediately tended to Gillen, and the valiant Dwarf Priest was soon on his feet, offering prayers of healing for the fallen fighters. They spent as much time as they dared recuperating from the battle, then the battered warriors climbed gingerly into their saddles and rode north once more.

✥ ✪ ★ ✤ ✪

In the afternoon of the next day, the disheveled-looking group entered the city of Unity. Silvayn brought them directly to his house, where they could prepare for their meeting with the Unity Council. Jayrne and Adalyn were taken to one part of the estate, while Elac and the others were taken to another. He doffed his filthy, bloodstained clothes, and sank his aching body into the refreshing waters of the hot baths in Silvayn's cellar. Steam rose in white, insubstantial tendrils as he soaked, the water seeming to rinse away more than just the dirt of the road.

Their own clothing was being laundered and repaired, so elaborate sets of finery were brought to them. Although he conceded the need for ceremony and wore a formal set of pants with a bright blue doublet, he insisted on bearing the Sword of Draygen. Having seen what the great weapon could do to the undead, he wasn't about to let the Sword out of his sight.

They met the ladies at the entrance to Silvayn's home, where two carriages waited to take them to the Unity Council. Silvayn informed them that the Councilors were already meeting, and had been briefed about the group's successful return. Elac climbed into the first carriage, joined by Jayrne and the two Dwarves. Gillen scowled at the tankard in his brother's hand, but said nothing. Jayrne sat beside Elac on the cushioned bench, and she gently took his hand.

His eyes met hers, and he found himself speechless. Her long, brown hair was caught behind her head in a silver brooch, and she wore a red dress, tight fitting with a plunging neckline. He found himself taken by her beauty, and was contented simply to hold her hand in silent admiration. With a lurch, the carriage started forward.

Hadwyn chuckled into his ale. "Do you two need a room?"

Embarrassed, his face flushing, Elac smiled uncomfortably and looked away. Jayrne laughed outrageously, setting Elac's face aflame more brightly. He heard her say, "I think not," and then his chin was firmly in her grasp. She pulled his head around and kissed him full on the lips, a deep, lingering kiss that left Elac breathlessly wanting more. He felt a sharp pang of regret when she released him from her grasp. He glanced over to where the Dwarves sat, arched his eyebrows knowingly, and took Hadwyn's tankard from him, enjoying a drink of the bitter ale.

The carriages rolled to a stop, rocking slightly, and several porters held open the doors while they dismounted. They filed into the ornate hall housing the Unity Council, and Elac mentally prepared for the coming confrontation. From what he had learned, he knew there would be some Councilors who would vehemently oppose any action, as a matter of principle.

The Councilors were all seated around the semicircular table, some of them already scowling openly. He looked for Falstoff, finally spotting him standing off to one side, wearing ornamental state robes. Belatedly, Elac remembered Falstoff's promotion to ambassador to the Necromancers. In his place sat a middle-aged woman, one who didn't seem to bear the self-righteous look carried by many of the other members of the Council. Perhaps she would continue the support where Falstoff left off.

A row of eight chairs had been lined up across the open end of the table, and Elac and his friends seated themselves. Dralana, the Dwarf who headed the Council, called the meeting to order. "Silvayn, Elac, and Rilen. Please come forward."

Elac complied, stepping forward and taking his place at the polished wooden rail, Rilen on his right and Silvayn on his left. Jarm, the woman who had replaced Falstoff, rose to her feet.

"If the Council will indulge me, I would like to brief these travelers on the events that transpired in their absence. The

Kobold forces caught us completely off guard. In Palindom, they burned Firereach to the ground. The Kobolds stationed inside Fort Ranset, Fort Nightwood, and Fort Philand waited until the middle of the night, dispatched the sentries, and butchered entire garrisons. An alert soldier at Fort Julan saw what was happening and sounded the alarm. There was a pitched battle inside the fort, but our forces prevailed, and we still hold the fortress.

"In Caldala, the Elven army rallied, and they managed to keep the Kobolds bottled up between Crystal Lake and the Unity River. In Verlak, the Dwarven army marched immediately, and they stopped the invasion east of Crystal Falls.

"Our counterattacks have been coordinated through the generals at the Fort Julan War College. We have the three Human fortresses under siege, and the plains around them have been virtually swept free of Kobolds. Another contingent of Human forces, mostly archers and heavy infantry, have established a picket line along the Unity River near North Hold. The Elves are steadily pushing the Kobolds east, and they will be caught between the two armies."

Silvayn's eyes opened wide. "Have you seen the bodies from any of the cities and fortresses the Kobolds ransacked?"

Jarm looked to the others of the Council, but none had an answer. "If you're asking for a count of the number of dead, I could estimate, but none of the bodies have been recovered. They are either still inside the occupied areas or, more likely, they have been burned."

Dralana cleared her throat. "You needn't concern yourself, Silvayn," she said haughtily. "The dead in our eastern lands have been avenged with the blood of Kobold soldiers. Our ambassadors are already at work on a peace treaty. The matter will be dealt with."

"Peace treaty?" Rilen roared, leaning over the rail and jabbing a finger at the surprised Dwarf. "You would declare peace with a treacherous force that just murdered hundreds, perhaps thousands of our people? People who trusted you to keep them safe?"

"Would you have us see to the deaths of hundreds or thousands more, by continuing this costly fight?" Dralana asked smoothly. She leaned back in her chair. "Your opinion of the Kobolds is well known, Rilen. If this Council believes you are a threat to the peace process, we'll have you arrested. That goes for all of you."

"What about the message we sent?" Rilen asked. "We intercepted a message for a certain member of this Council. There was a hefty sum of gold, accompanied by instructions to thwart any attempts at going to war with the Kobolds."

Several Councilors started nervously, but silence reigned supreme. Cordos, an Elf Councilor, leaned forward in his chair. "To whom was this note addressed?"

Rilen looked at him incredulously. "You didn't receive it?"

Dralana clasped her hands behind her head, a smug smile playing at the corners of her mouth. "The roads are treacherous in time of war. Your messenger must have been waylaid by Kobold forces."

Rilen opened his mouth to speak, his face red with anger, but stopped. He slowly regained his self-control, but his narrowed eyes betrayed the roiling emotions he held inside.

"What of the matter of your mission?" Jarm asked, apparently brushing the matter aside with a casual directness. "What did you find?"

Silvayn sketched in the details of their journey, but Dralana and the others disbelieved the tale. Even showing the artifacts they had been given by the ghosts of the Seven Knights of Piaras Keep didn't sway their incredulity.

"If we can return to the matter at hand," Silvayn said, "we were informed by the spirit of Sir Draygen that we can use the spellbook I was given to recover the Temira, lost all these long centuries. He said that without the Temira, all will be lost."

Several members of the Council chuckled at that point, giving each other looks of smug superiority. "In case you didn't hear the briefing, Silvayn," Councilor Oaklyn said, "we are already winning the war, without you, without your quest or your sacred artifacts."

"Yes, the artifacts," Tanne said. "This brings up an interesting point. All the artifacts they claim to have been given by these phantom knights are, technically, the property of the Human government. I believe we'll want them back." He rose to his feet. "I'd like to make a motion to place an immediate claim on the items."

Ralore, the third Human Councilor, rose to his feet. "I would like to second that motion."

Oaklyn fixed Silvayn with a look of undisguised hatred, her eyes narrowed. "I call for a vote on the matter."

Dralana stood and raised her arms. "All in favor of bestowing these artifacts upon the government of Palindom, raise your hands." With the exception of Jarm and the Elf, Nasontas, the entire Council voted for the action. Dralana smiled beatifically, sinking back into her seat and reaching for the implements to draw up a proclamation.

"Point of procedure!" Jarm called out, stunning the room to silence.

Dralana slumped her shoulders, giving Jarm an annoyed look and rolling her eyes. "State your point."

"As a representative of the Human government, I understand the need to preserve historical artifacts. However, I also respect the rights of personal property ownership. How can we be certain these are, indeed, the items these travelers believe they are? Before the Council takes possession of these items on a whim, I insist we form a committee to investigate further."

Oaklyn leaned back in her chair and crossed her arms. "And what would you have them investigate? Should they travel to the Keep and speak to the ghosts themselves?"

"Don't be ridiculous. They could check historical documents and verify, based upon descriptions in the accounts of battles, whether these are, indeed, the items they claim them to be."

"Your point is well taken," said Todos, pulling his gray beard, "but you need to have someone second such a motion before you can claim point of procedure."

"Second." Nasontas raised her hand, her small eyes displaying fear and determination.

Dralana looked to the ceiling for several long moments. "So be it. Your point of procedure is accepted. These travelers shall retain possession of the items for the time being."

There was a commotion at the doors leading into the audience hall. After a heated but hushed argument, a fatigued messenger, covered with the grime of the road, was ushered forward. He raised his right fist to his chest in salute.

"You may speak," Dralana said haughtily, gesturing with one hand. "What news have you, of such importance to compel you to interrupt these proceedings?"

"Lord High Councilor, I bring news of the war."

"Ah. And have we recovered more territory from the Kobolds?"

"No, your Eminence. A new force of Kobolds has issued forth from hidden tunnels in the Paheny Mountains. They have counterattacked our efforts to recover our fortresses."

There was complete silence in the room. Tanne rose from his seat. "How many?"

"Several legions, from what I was told."

Rilen shook his head, looking at the floor in disgust. "What are our losses?"

The messenger glanced nervously at Rilen, unsure if he should answer the question, since it hadn't come from a Council member. He looked back to Dralana, who nodded curtly.

"Our entire army attacking Fort Nightwood was routed. We are retreating on all fronts."

Oaklyn looked to Dralana, her hands trembling. "What do we do now?"

"I'm sorry, your Eminence, but there's more. We were also attacked by a massive army out of Firereach Pass. I . . ." He stopped, unsure how to proceed.

"Out with it, man!" Dralana ordered angrily, slamming her fist on the table.

"The force coming from Firereach Pass consisted of undead creatures. Thousands of them. The thralls turned north and attacked our recovery effort at the site where the Kobolds burned Firereach. The skeletons turned south and drove us from our siege of Fort Ranset. The Kobolds opened the gates and allowed the Necromancers and Death Knights to enter."

"Nonsense!" Falstoff said, stepping forward, hands on hips. "The Necromancers have had a number of incidents where they engaged in open conflict with the Kobolds!"

"Several weeks ago," Elac said, drawing several surprised stares, "regular Kobold forces were fighting renegade Kobold groups. We know now they were allied all along. Why should this be any different? Everything points to an alliance between the Necromancers and the Kobolds."

"He's right," Jarm said. "The military will have to handle the war, but I have a thought. Let's send these travelers on another mission for us. For all of us. Let them recover the Temira and bring it here to us. Maybe what the spirits told them will be true, and they can save us."

"I guess it wouldn't hurt," Oaklyn said, staring at her empty cup thoughtfully. "At best, they might save us, but at worst, they will perish, and our situation will be no different."

A quick voice vote followed, and Dralana announced the Council's ruling. "It is hereby proclaimed that these eight diverse persons are, now and until their quest is fulfilled, Soldiers of the Council, with all the rights and obligations the title implies. It is furthermore decreed that they shall, with all haste, travel straightaway to the Paheny Mountains, where they shall use all means at their disposal to recover the Temira, and to return said object to the Council chambers."

Elac's elation ended when he saw the consternation in Rilen's frown. "Rilen, what's wrong? They are sending us where we wanted to go."

"Do you know what they just did to us?" Rilen rolled his eyes and exhaled heavily. "Soldiers of the Council. Now we must obey their every decree or face imprisonment. I'm afraid of what they will do to bend this to their benefit."

As if on cue, Elac turned back to the Council table to see Falstoff deep in conversation with Dralana, with both of them casting an occasional glance in the direction of Elac's party. Dralana seemed to be arguing against Falstoff's point of view, but she finally acquiesced. The Dwarf returned to her place at the head of the Council and banged her fist on the table.

"To insure the safety and therefore the success of this mission, Falstoff's personal bodyguard shall accompany them on their quest."

Cassius rose to his feet, his hands spread wide before him in protest. "This is absurd! We have fought our way through countless dangers already. We can protect ourselves."

Dralana leveled her finger at the angry Prince. "You forget your place, your Highness. You may be a Prince in Palindom, but in this room you are a Soldier of the Council, and as such you are subject to our orders. I had intended to send a company of soldiers, but Ambassador Falstoff convinced me we would be better served by sending a single able warrior."

Elac and the others were dismissed after that to tend to their preparations. Falstoff met them in the hall outside the room. "I apologize for the unwanted addition to your group," he told them, "but it was the best I could do on such short notice. Morfal, the guard who will accompany you, is very capable, and he knows the western Paheny Mountains fairly well. He has been with me only a month or so, but he has my fullest confidence."

Falstoff continued, "I assume the implication you made earlier, about a corrupt member of the Council, was about Dralana?"

"Yes," Silvayn told him. "We had proof of her duplicity, showing she has been cooperating with the Kobolds for money, but it appears our messenger didn't make it."

"Yes, and she seemed rather smug about that." Falstoff paused, staring at a painting blankly, hands behind his back. "There may be another way."

Elac looked at him sharply. "What do you mean?"

"If a few of you will take a stroll with me, I can point out an office Dralana uses for dealings she tries to keep secret from the public. All the Councilors have them. If you were to somehow gain access to the information she has stored in there . . ."

Rilen licked his lips. "Silvayn, you and the others go on back to the inn," he said, loud enough to be heard by passersby. "Elac, Jayrne, and I are going to go with Falstoff to meet our new companion. We'll join you for dinner."

Minutes later, Elac peered from the open window of Falstoff's carriage, rolling and bouncing through the streets of Unity. The buildings in the area were all plain and drab, more utilitarian than attractive. The streets were clean, however, and the air was free of the offensive odors lingering in many parts of large towns. There were few alleys, and in fact, most of the buildings were jammed up against the structure next to it.

"Dralana's office is just a few blocks away," Falstoff told them. "We won't want to slow down, which would call attention to us. Take a good look when we ride past."

Two blocks ahead, their target was clearly visible. It stood out from its neighbors, not only because it was the only two-story building in the area, but because of the mahogany doors, stained so dark they were nearly black. Elac understood the significance of the composition of the doors; it would be more difficult to force entry when the wood was so hard.

They met the others in the taproom an hour later. Hadwyn was already deep in his ale cup, talking to an Elf woman who seemed quite taken with him. They took the open seats at the table, and everyone ordered dinner. Elac knew there would be no discussion of plans to visit Dralana's office until they retired to their rooms, but he followed the example of Rilen and Jayrne, and ordered water with his meal.

The discussion began as soon as the door to Rilen's room closed. It was crowded with the eight of them in a room meant for two, but they managed to find a place for everyone to sit. Hadwyn had a full mug of ale at his side and a loaf of bread in his hands.

"What did you find?" Silvayn asked.

"The problem is," Jayrne answered, "the buildings are all jammed together. There are no alleys, so there is only a minimal opportunity to get inside. The only windows are on the first floor, on either side of the front and back doors. They have people openly guarding those entries, so there's no chance of sneaking past them."

"Their guards appear to be professional mercenaries, and well-paid ones at that," Rilen added, rubbing the stubble on his chin. "Their equipment is higher quality and in better shape than the average merc. I'd say they wouldn't be easily distracted."

"What about a bribe?" Hadwyn asked.

Rilen shook his head. "Too risky. There are three guards at each door. If there was just one, he might be inclined to take the offer, but with a group of them they would have the fear of being turned in. We have to try another way."

Elac looked to Jayrne for the next answer. "Is there another way?"

She smiled and bit her lower lip, putting on her best innocent look. "Maybe." She laughed. "The building next door has an alley, and there was a single door with no windows And no guards. My idea is to break into that building, and use the roof to cross over to Dralana's office. I can break in from there with no one the wiser."

Silvayn nodded, rubbing his hands slowly together. "Rilen?"

Rilen was silent only briefly. "I like it. We need one other person to go with us. Jayrne will do her part while I watch the guards at the main entrance, but we need someone else to keep an eye on the vacant building."

"I'll do it," Elac did not hesitate to answer.

"When will you go?" Silvayn asked.

Rilen leaned back in his chair. "Jayrne, how much time do you want?"

"I'd like several hours. Actually . . . wait. I have a better use for Elac. If we can have someone else watch the entry point, I'd like Elac to come in with me. With his background in finance and politics, he might be able to find what we need more quickly."

"Good point," Adalyn said. "Okay, I'll go with you, also.

I can handle the vacant building, if Rilen thinks he can watch the main entrance by himself. Besides, someone needs to keep an eye on Rilen, anyway."

Rilen rewarded her with his best tight-lipped, phony smile. "Okay, Silvayn, I think we have a plan. I'd like to have these two burglars in place before midnight. That would give them several hours in there together, so we should be able to turn up something."

"I'll drink to that," Hadwyn said with a thunderous belch, raising his tankard.

🍀 ⊗ ★ 🌐 🔅

The lock released with an audible click, and Jayrne eased the door open, preventing it from squeaking. "Did you see how I did that?" she whispered. Elac nodded and added the knowledge to the catalogue of talents Jayrne and Rilen had taught him. Even Adalyn had begun educating him in new fields of learning. She had secretly taught him a couple of minor spells, one of them the spell bringing light to dark areas, the other a means of detecting traps.

He put his newfound abilities to use immediately, casting a spell to bring a very dim light into the room. The building appeared to be a series of small, confined rooms, smelling heavily of dust and disuse. There were old pieces of furniture scattered about the office they had entered, most of them with rotten fabric. With the dim lighting from Elac's spell, they followed the hallway deeper into the building without fear of being discovered.

Jayrne found the staircase and followed it to the top floor.

She edged the cover off the opening to the roof, peering carefully about before pushing it farther open. She motioned for Elac to stay low, and the two of them practically crawled across the slate roof to Dralana's office. She scampered up the wall, finding sufficient handholds to reach the higher roof next door. Elac followed suit, although his climbing skills were much clumsier. Jayrne gave his arm an approving squeeze, then crawled to the roof entrance. It was unlocked, and after a brief peek inside she removed the cover and climbed through, with Elac close behind.

They descended a short staircase and came to a locked metal door. Jayrne inserted her lockpicks into the keyhole, but stopped and removed them. "You give it a try."

Elac nodded, trying unsuccessfully to keep the boyish grin from spreading across his face. He went to work on the lock, but was frustrated in short order by a lock that just didn't seem to want to give. Jayrne helped him, her small hands guiding his in their work. He felt his pulse race from her touch, and he barely noticed when the lock snapped open. She gave him a quick kiss before she slipped through the open door.

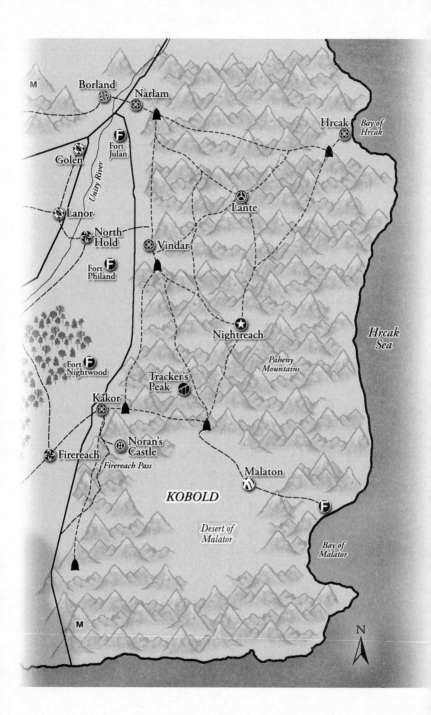

Chapter 18

Elac guessed the time at shortly after midnight, so he knew they had several hours before they needed to leave. There were stacks of papers to be inspected and drawers to look through, but since they were using only Elac's magic, which provided a dim light, they decided to work side-by-side.

Jayrne asked Elac about the significance of several documents she located, and while they showed indisputable corruption on the part of the Councilor, none of them showed any connection to the Kobolds. Elac collected those papers in a parcel they had brought just for that purpose, but they kept looking. Eventually, his ability to keep even a small area illuminated came to an end, and he had to allow the light to dissipate. Jayrne compensated by using a small lamp, covering three sides and allowing a small beam of light to be emitted.

At least four hours had passed by Elac's estimation, and still they had found nothing. This isn't working," Elac said, shaking his head and staring at the floor. "She is leaving less-important documents out where they can be found, because she knows she has nothing to fear. I think the papers we're looking for will be hidden elsewhere."

"Are you sure she'll even have these papers? Keeping incriminating evidence like that seems a bit foolish to me. I certainly never kept a log of houses I had burglarized."

Elac licked his lips, his eyes busily scanning the office. "Absolutely. She has an ongoing deal with the Kobolds, so this is different. Smugglers are the same way. Once their business is established, they keep meticulous records. It makes them much more organized and much more profitable. The documents we need are here somewhere. We just need to find them."

Jayrne sat in silent reflection for several moments, idly playing with the hilt of a dagger, running options through her mind. "So, what you're saying is, if I can find where she might hide something valuable, we could possibly get what we're after?"

"Essentially, yes."

Jayrne turned slowly about and turned her trained eye on the furniture. She pulled several paintings off the wall but found nothing behind them. She returned to the filing cabinet and pulled the drawers completely out, one at a time, reaching a probing hand inside.

She paused near the bottom drawer, the triumphant grin slowly growing, and withdrew her hand. Elac eagerly took the small pouch from her, and opened it to find a sheaf of papers.

"This is it!" he whispered excitedly, throwing one hand around the beautiful thief at his side. "This is the proof we need!"

She threw both arms about his neck and kissed him exuberantly. They lingered in that embrace until, regretfully, it was time to make a strategic withdrawal. Elac removed a few of the more relevant documents from the pouch, and handed it back to Jayrne. She carefully returned it to its former hiding spot, then replaced the drawers. They made a quick check of the office to be certain they had left nothing behind to show the office workers someone had been inside, and they quietly backed out of the office.

When they entered Silvayn's room, Elac saw an enormously muscled Human waiting for them. He wore a plain tunic and pants, and had a long sword strapped to his waist. His head was shaved bald, and his piercing black eyes stared out from under a heavy brow.

"This is Morfal," Silvayn said by way of introduction. "He is the bodyguard Falstoff spoke of, the one who'll be accompanying us to Tracker's Peak." Silvayn completed the introductions. Elac took Morfal's hand in greeting, and he found his hand dwarfed by the other's. At Silvayn's prompting, Rilen sketched in the details of the night's adventure. Falstoff, who was seated rather unobtrusively in one corner, rose to his feet triumphantly.

"Excellent," he said, one hand clenched into a fist in celebration.

"When do we take this before the Council?" Gillen asked, with a pained look at his inebriated brother who sat slouched across a table.

"Let's not be hasty," Falstoff cautioned. "If we take this information public now, Dralana will be dismissed, but another Councilor would be appointed in her place, and will likely be no friendlier to our cause than Dralana is now."

Elac folded his arms across his chest. "Probably even more hostile, considering we would have run a colleague out of office. I think I see where Falstoff is going with this."

Jayrne gave him a playful shove. "You would," she said, laughing.

"It's rather simple," Elac said. "Instead of settling for knocking a corrupt politician from power, we can use this knowledge to make her work for us."

Cassius rose to his feet, hands on his hips in outrage. "That's blackmail!"

Elac looked up to the ceiling, pretending to consider the matter. "You know, I believe he's right."

"Then we would be no better than Dralana," Cassius argued, slamming a fist on a nearby table. "Not to mention, we'd be letting her get away with what she's done."

"On the contrary, I never said anything about letting her get away. When this business is finished, we can handle her then."

With Rilen back at his customary position scouting in front of the group, they rode out of Unity at first light. Morfal, Falstoff's bodyguard, accompanied them. He wore a suit of banded mail, embossed with black enamel and with the likeness of a wolf's head engraved in the center of the chest. His legs were protected by fur-covered greaves, and he wore knee-high brown leather boots. He carried no shield, so Elac assumed Morfal would rely upon his strength and speed with the long sword to compensate.

Each member of the little band wore a special brooch at the neck of their cloaks, indicating their position as Soldiers of the Council. They left the main road and headed east, making for Nightwood Forest. Reports from the war indicated the likelihood that most of the undead forces inside Nightwood were gone, having participated in the invasion. With the reversal of fortune in the war, Silvayn wanted to spend as little time in the open as possible.

Later that day, they reached the borders of Nightwood Forest and plunged inside. There was an ancient, abandoned road leading from Branig to Firereach and passing directly through the dangerous woods. While the trees had long since reclaimed the road, much evidence of it still remained. They used the path as a guide, since it would allow them to know where they were once they had emerged on the forest's eastern border.

They made camp that night deep with the concealing boughs of Nightwood Forest. Rilen established a watch list, making certain two people would be awake at all times. Elac knew the Elf wasn't as sure as Silvayn was about the forest being clear of undead, and he was taking no chances. Elac felt a bit of disappointment when he learned he wouldn't be keeping watch with Jayrne, but he knew it was just as well.

The next day, they kept the pace easy since speed would not be an issue on that leg of the journey. They made it to the eastern edge of the forest by late afternoon, but stopped well back inside the trees. Rilen and Elac slipped forward, finding a concealed spot where they could keep watch. They planned to wait until nightfall to make their rushed trip to the mountains, in order to minimize their odds of being discovered.

"I understand Adalyn is teaching you some rudimental magic skills." It was the first Rilen had spoke since they had taken up their observation post.

"Yeah. Two spells so far, but she said she might teach me more later. Don't worry, I'm not going to let Silvayn find out."

"Good," Rilen said, his eyes distant. "I'm causing Adalyn enough trouble as it is. I'm fairly fond of her, in case you hadn't noticed. I don't want to hurt her chances of completing her field studies." He paused, then gave a great sigh. "Actually, I guess I'm more than 'fond' of her. We were very close once, but our careers took us in different directions. She went to Aleria to study magic, and I was sent to Fort Julan to the War College. We agreed back then to keep our relationship from proceeding further. It made sense then, but now it's not so easy."

Elac nodded knowingly. "You're free to go where you will now."

"Exactly. I'm not sure why I'm telling you this. I guess you are the closest thing to a friend I've got."

"I'd like to think we *are* friends," Elac said with a smile.

Rilen gave a short laugh. "I hate to admit it, but I didn't think much of you when we first met. I thought of you as a pampered, overdressed city merchant who had gotten himself in a fix and who expected the rest of the world to help him out."

Elac rolled his eyes. "You weren't far from the truth."

"You've really changed, do you know that? And I'm not just talking about your skills with a blade, or the magic Adalyn is teaching you, or even the less common abilities you've learned from Jayrne. I'm glad to call you a comrade-at-arms and a friend."

"I've had a good teacher," Elac replied, his face flushed

with embarrassment.

"Just remember, the time may come when I won't be there to help you, or the Dwarves, or even Silvayn. You're ready to stand on your own, but you have to believe it for yourself."

After nightfall, they crossed the plains at a gallop. There had been a debate about the benefits of stealth versus speed, and speed had won out. They were more than halfway across when they encountered the Kobold patrol. The Kobolds moved in from their flank by pure chance, catching both sides off guard. Rilen had been riding with his bow in hand, and he put it to immediate use. The Longbow of Aleron snapped three times in rapid succession, and three Kobolds tumbled from their saddle before Elac could even bring his own bow to bear. Several Kobolds returned fire, but their arrows curved to meet Cassius's Shield and bounced away.

The Dwarves turned their horses and met the charge, the others close behind. Gillen and Hadwyn each knocked a pair of Kobolds from their saddles on the first pass. Morfal charged into the Kobolds' midst, wreaking havoc with his long sword. Cassius set his lance in place and drove it home in the chest of the lead Kobold, discarded it, and drew his broadsword. Elac and Rilen charged in from opposite flanks, and the dispirited Kobolds were cut to pieces. One broke free from the fighting and turned to flee, Cassius in pursuit. Rilen calmly readied Aleron's Bow once more, and he swiftly let an arrow fly. Even from a distance, Elac heard the sound when the arrow struck home in the Kobold's back. Their last foe tumbled from his saddle, and Cassius moved in to finish him off.

"Hurry, everyone," Silvayn admonished them. "Let's get

out of here quickly, in case there are others. Someone may have been close enough to hear the commotion."

It was about an hour after midnight when they rode into the westernmost peaks of the Paheny Mountains. They continued for a time, hoping to be deep enough in the mountains to prevent any Kobolds who found the night's battleground from tracking them to their resting place. Elac sank gratefully to the ground next to Jayrne and slipped into his bedroll. He was worn out from the long day of riding and the brief battle, and sleep came easily.

The next day, they continued their trek at a more leisurely pace, the earlier need for speed having passed. Footholds could be precarious on those mountain passes, and they could ill afford for a horse to come up lame because they had hurried for no particular reason. Once again, Elac was still taken by the sheer beauty of the mountains. Even the sky seemed different, a pale blue-white color near the sun, but the deepest color of sapphire everywhere else. Elac took a deep breath, enjoying the scent of the pine trees and the sounds of the outdoors.

As their first day of mountain travel drew to a close, Elac noticed a heavy mist gradually forming about them. Unlike a typical fog, it seemed unaffected by wind and the radical changes in elevation they found all about them. It hung like a miasma, penetrating everything with a chilly dampness. Elac huddled down into his cloak, but found little warmth or comfort. He heard a light step beside him, and he knew without looking that Jayrne was beside him. He drew her close, and the two wrapped a pair of blankets about them to ward off the coolness they were both feeling.

By morning, the fog hadn't cleared off, and in fact seemed even thicker. Silvayn called everyone in around him.

"We are close to the valley where Tracker's Peak once stood. The fog is a remnant of the exchange of energies and matter when the Keep was carried into the Plane of Mist. While we are in this fog, we are partially in our world and partially in another. We must find the actual spot where Tracker's Peak once stood, and I'll cast the spell to carry us into the Plane of Mist.

"However, the text of Limor's spellbook warns of an imminent danger. Since the area around Tracker's Peak exists both here and in the Plane of Mist, a powerful demon has crossed over to our side and roams the mist. This creature will stalk us when we make our approach. It isn't a question of whether or not it will find us and attack, but a question of when. We're close enough to our destination that we won't have to spend the night in the Mist Demon's realm, but we'll still need to be on our guard."

"Can we kill it?" Rilen asked, eyeing the fog around them.

"I'm not sure. We aren't quite close enough to the interplanar junction for the demon to attack us, but we will be soon. Likely, the beast will study us for some time before it attacks. It may even probe us a few times, hit us, and back off, to see what we are capable of doing. Limor didn't know a whole lot about the demon. Limor did say it was incorporeal, but we have weapons capable of breaching that barrier. And since the Mist Demon isn't of this world, Adalyn and I are free to use any means at our disposal to try to destroy it. But remember, and this is crucial: we won't use any magic until the Mist Demon has committed itself fully to the battle. Magic is most effective as a weapon of surprise."

They gathered their belongings, saddled their horses, and edged into the deepening mist. The gray-white fog swirled around them, agitated by some unknown force; there wasn't even a hint of a breeze.

The first thing Elac noticed was a sensation of being watched. He had a prickly feeling on the back of his neck, and he turned rapidly to the rear to locate the source. He found nothing, but the impression of being watched soon returned. He saw a few of his companions show signs of being jittery, as well, which convinced him it wasn't his imagination. It didn't take him long to deduce the root cause of their feelings of un-ease; indeed, only one being lived in these swirling vapors: the Mist Demon.

"Silvayn," he said quietly.

"Yes, I know. It has been following us for the last fifteen minutes."

"What are we going to do?" Jayrne asked, her eyes darting about wildly.

"For the moment, nothing. Be on your guard, however. There's no need to ride the rest of the way to Tracker's Peak with our weapons drawn, but let's not get careless, either. Stay close to each other and don't get separated, no matter what happens. And try to keep a shooting lane open for Adalyn and me."

"How much farther is it to the castle?" Cassius asked, seemingly unperturbed by the mystical beast stalking their every step.

"It's hard to say, but I would guess about two hours."

The deadened landscape crawled by, and still nothing happened. Elac knew the demon was still there, just out of sight, following them, watching. He felt an almost overpowering urge to turn and fight, to fire arrows into the fog, to shout his defiance if necessary.

The wait didn't last much longer. Elac heard a scuffed footstep off to his right side, then caught a glimpse of something huge, and vaguely humanlike in appearance, seem to materialize out of the mist. A shadowy arm swept toward him, and he barely raised his shield before the arm struck, knocking him from his saddle. He hit the ground with jarring force, rolling over several times before he came back to his feet. His friends all had weapons drawn, but there was no enemy to fight. The demon was gone.

Elac assured the others he was okay, then climbed back into his saddle. He rode for a bit with his sword in hand, keeping an eye on the roiling fog surrounding them. Rilen nudged his horse closer, and Elac knew by the serious look on the Elf's face he was obviously intent on delivering some advice.

"I'd put the Sword away, if I were you. If you'd been carrying your weapon in hand when that creature hit you just now, you probably would have lost your grip on it, and in this mist you would've stood a good chance of never seeing it again. Since the demon doesn't appear to have weapons, I think you're better off with your blade sheathed."

Elac pursed his lips, considering what Rilen had told him, and then he carefully slid the sword back into its sheath. As a further precaution, he tightened the straps binding his shield to his left forearm.

With a clank of armor, Gillen flew from his saddle, but he

bounced up immediately, axe in hand. Hadwyn grasped the reins of his brother's surprised mount to keep it from bolting, while Rilen, Elac, and Cassius dismounted and dashed forward. A heavily muscled figure emerged from the mist, an indistinct silhouette of nightmare proportions. It stood fully a head and shoulders taller than Cassius, and was bulkier than the stoutest Dwarf. Its indistinct silvery body seemed to shimmer and sway like the misty fog around it, stirred by some phantom wind Elac could not feel. The long arms ended in hooked claws, and the oversized feet caused it to amble forward with a shuffling gait. Its mouth, set low in the ape-like face, bore long fangs, and from the toothy maw issued a low rumbling.

Hadwyn struck first, the magic hammer slowing the creature and causing it to howl with pain. Cassius slid in behind the demon, and his first blow landed solidly on its back. With a roar of rage, the Mist Demon swung an arm in a wide arc, catching Cassius solidly on his shield and sending him sprawling. Gillen, having caught his breath, rushed the creature from one side, while Elac charged from the other. Rilen kept it busy with a series of brief feints from its front.

Silvayn finished his incantation, but he had to hold the spell in check, waiting for an opening. Jayrne slipped in low, swiping at the demon's legs. With a savage snarl, it kicked a tree-trunk-sized leg at her, sending the wind whooshing from her lungs and leaving her gasping for air. Elac rushed in, the Sword of Draygen flashing as it fell across the demon's upraised arm. There was a surge of light when the Sword bit into the filmy creature.

Silvayn saw his opening and let his spell fly. The blast took the Mist Demon full in the chest, knocking it backward several feet and leaving a trailer of smoke from the impact point. It climbed slowly to its feet, staggering as if the blast had dazed it. It slowly backed away, keeping the entire group in view, then turned and fled from sight.

Elac sheathed his sword and rushed to Jayrne's side. She was still gasping for air, and a trickle of blood ran from one corner of her mouth. Then Gillen was there, offering up prayers of healing. He frowned, set himself, and tried again. This time, the pained look on her face eased somewhat, and her breathing became less labored.

"It's harder to reach Zantar from here. It must be the mixing of the Plane of Mist with our world." Gillen shook his head, setting his lips. "Silvayn, we need to stay here for a bit. She needs more healing than I can give her before she is moved. I think she has some broken ribs. If we put her on a horse, we could puncture a lung."

Jayrne smiled weakly at Elac. "I guess you'll be carrying me again. This time, try not to be so rough."

Elac somehow managed to laugh, although his heart was in his toes. Then he stiffened, an idea coming to him. "Why didn't I . . . Silvayn! Do we still have some of the water from the Springs of Calda?"

Adalyn rushed to her saddlebags and pulled forth one of the remaining bottles of spring water. She gave it to Elac, who removed the stopper and held the bottle to Jayrne's lips. She drank, slowly at first, then with more strength. At Gillen's suggestion, Elac tore the sleeve from his tunic, soaked it with the healing waters, and applied it as a compress, reaching beneath her leather armor and her plain tunic to apply it directly to her skin where the injury was centered.

"Hey," she said, forcing a weak smile, "watch where you're putting your hands."

Elac laughed louder then, heartened by her words and feeling encouraged by her attempt at humor. When she proclaimed herself ready to stand, Gillen made her wait a bit longer while he tightened the straps on her leather armor. The tension, he told her, would provide some support for her injured ribs.

After another hour of riding, they reached a broad depression, more than a half mile across. The rounded sides and bottom were perfectly smooth, as if somehow the ground had been scooped away. As with the rest of the fog-enshrouded lands, nothing grew in the deep bowl; in sharp contrast to the lands around, however, there were no snags, no cuts, and no protruding rocks. Somehow, though the swirling fog still covered the land, it wasn't as thick near that point, and they were able to see the far side of the crater. Silvayn led them up to the edge of the bowl, where he called a halt.

He removed Limor's spellbook from a saddlebag, thumbing through the pages until he found what he wanted. He cast an incantation, speaking in a low, deep voice using the language of magic, accented with occasional sharp gestures. The fog surrounding the bowl swirled faster, agitated by some unseen maelstrom. Elac heard a cry, as if from a thousand voices crying out in pain, then the world was falling sharply away from him, and he slowly tumbled to the ground.

When he looked up, the mist was there as before. But standing before him was a towering stone wall, with twin wooden doors at least fifty feet high in the center. The tops of the walls were lined with battlements, and the surface was pitted and marked from the impact of countless arrows and siege weapons. He looked at his companions, his head full of wonder. They had found Tracker's Peak!

The gates of the great Keep ground slowly open, parting far enough to allow them to enter. To Elac's great surprise, a Human dressed in ancient battle armor strode forth, with several similarly clad men behind him. He wore a plain helmet with no face guard, and his iron sword was in one hand, a wooden shield in the other. He stopped at the entrance to the castle and planted the tip of his sword in the misty ground.

"Who art thou?" he demanded, his face creased by a deep frown.

"Travelers," Silvayn answered with a fluid bow. "We hadn't expected to find anyone still alive after so many years."

"Time stands still in the Plane of Mist. It is our doom to dwell in this accursed land forever, and not be allowed to die in glorious battle."

"We would speak with your leaders. We have been sent on a quest to recover the Temira, lost these long years along with Piaras Keep."

The man before them regarded them coolly for a few moments. "It may be as thou sayest. My name is Ganor. I judge thee to be a man of honor, so thy friends shalt be allowed to keep their weapons. Come with me."

He led them into the ancient fortress, and the doors closed slowly behind them after they passed. It was soon obvious, even to Elac, what the purpose of the structure was: war, and nothing else. There was an inner wall with a smaller gate, along with accessways allowing defenders on the outer walls to retreat to safety. Several archer towers reinforced those positions, topped with siege equipment capable of taking out the very weapons meant to weaken the fortress's defenses. Soldiers were everywhere, lining the battlements and manning the towers. There appeared to be a mixture of the three races present.

Ganor brought them through the second wall and took them to what appeared to be a castle within the castle. They crossed a drawbridge and found themselves in a short hallway. The ceiling and the walls had small slotted openings, and Elac knew any foe who reached that point would find himself subjected to burning oil pouring from those murderous holes. Ganor took them deep into the building, down stone-floor hallways hung with the banners of the three armies occupying it. He knocked twice on a plain wooden door before entering.

There was a long, ornate wooden table inside, and five men were seated along its far end, two Dwarves on one side, two Humans on the other, and an Elf at the far end. The Elf appeared to be a mage, while the others all had the look of warriors. The Elf rose to greet them, smiling.

"Welcome to Tracker's Peak. My name is Fession. I have been expecting you."

Silvayn voiced the concerns running through Elac's mind. "Expecting us? How?"

"Our mages have the ability to see beyond our prison. While the vision isn't exact, we are able to acquire a vague sense of what the future holds. Through one such vision, we learned of visitors who would come to us out of the old world."

"What do you know of the events since your banishment to the Plane of Mist?"

"Banishment? Yes, a proper term for what has happened. We are aware that a long era has passed since the war, although we have no way of measuring time. In the Plane of Mist, there are no days and no nights, only the perpetual gray sky. We also have no need to eat, drink, or sleep, and we don't age. With no indicators of the passage of time, there has been no way of determining how long we have been here. We still have most of the original twenty thousand soldiers within these walls. Some died during the casting of Volnor's spell, and others have fallen before the demons haunting this land."

"We were sent by the spirits of the Seven Knights of Piaras Keep," Silvayn said. "We were told to retrieve the Temira and use it to defeat Volnor. The Third Necromancer War has engulfed the continent."

"Another war with those foul creatures? How long have we been trapped here?"

Silvayn glanced around the room nervously, rubbing his chin with one hand, then sighed. "It's been about fourteen hundred years."

Fession slowly lowered his eyes to the table. "It's true, then. I had feared it was so. All our families, our wives and children, have long since perished. We are truly alone." He buried his face in his hands. A long, awkward silence covered the room.

"Volnor and his minions must be made to pay dearly. I will ensure the Temira is delivered safely into your hands. Can you use it to return to the outside world?"

"Yes," Silvayn told him. "Using a spell from this book

in conjunction with the Temira, we will be able to leave this place. Unfortunately, since you were all here at the time of the Banishment, you're still tied to this castle and can't leave until the spell is broken."

Fession set his face in a look of grim determination. "I understand." He stood and motioned to the chairs around the room. "Make yourselves comfortable. Silvayn and I will return shortly." With a grand gesture toward the door, Fession led the old mage from the room.

Elac tried to occupy himself in conversation, but without much success. Jayrne was resting; sleep was impossible until they returned to their own world, but she still needed rest. Rilen and Adalyn were sitting rather close together speaking in hushed tones, and Elac prudently decided not to disturb them. He stepped closer to the newest member of their party.

"So, Morfal, how long have you been with Falstoff?"

The cold, glittering eyes turned to stare at him. "A while."

"He has been very helpful to us so far. The regular members of the Unity Council have been obstructionists, but he risked his political career to help us. I'm glad he was able to convince the Council to send you with us."

"Yeah."

The conversation went nowhere after that.

He sat quietly with his favorite little thief, her head nestled snugly in his lap, until Silvayn returned. Elac started to rise, but changed his mind and stayed where he was. He absently stroked Jayrne's hair, enjoying the chance to look after her. The room fell silent, and the others gathered closer to hear what Silvayn had to say.

"They will bring us the Temira. I have given my pledge that if there is a way to free them from this domain, even if it means their deaths, I will do so."

"You would kill these men?" asked Morfal, his eyes wide with incredulity.

"They have been trapped here these last fourteen hundred years. Their only anchor to sanity has been the slim hope of seeing their loved ones again, but they were unaware those people died over a millennia ago. To leave them confined here for all eternity would be a fate worse than death."

"How will you free them?" Gillen asked.

"I'm not certain. I'm hoping I can find something in Limor's spellbook that, coupled with the Temira, might free them. But this is all beside the point. Our first priority, as I explained to Fession, is the defeat of the Necromancers and the destruction of Volnor. Time is of the essence, especially with our not knowing how long we've been here. We'll leave as soon as the Temira is delivered to us."

Chapter 19

The Paheny Mountains reappeared around them, and Silvayn slowly lowered the Temira. The polished, glittering golden circle was inlaid with seven precious metals, each representing another of the gods worshiped by Humans, Elves, and Dwarves. A series of runes around the perimeter spoke of the holy object's connection to the gods, and its power granted by them. The ancient relic, about the size of the palm of Silvayn's hand, fit easily into a deep pocket of the old mage's cloak.

Night came quickly, and still there was no end to the fog. They found a sheltered niche in a cliff wall, which would provide them with both comfort and safety. They posted a double watch at the exposed end of their alcove and settled in for the night. Elac took the first watch with Morfal. They sat silently for the first hour, and Morfal made no attempt to break his reticence. Elac gave some pretense of checking on Jayrne, but she was sleeping comfortably and there was no need to rouse her. He determined to try to draw the big man into a conversation.

"Cold night, isn't it?"

"It's the fog." As far as Elac could remember, it may have been the first answer from Morfal composed of more than one word. He decided to count it as a success. Morfal pulled out a wicked-looking dagger and a sharpening stone. The sound of the two scraping together set Elac's teeth on edge, and for the second time, he gave up any hope of starting a conversation with the towering bodyguard.

At the end of the second hour, Elac awakened the two Dwarves, then laid out his bedroll next to Jayrne. He had no way of knowing how long he slept, but he was awakened by a firm hand on his shoulder. "Wake up, Elac," a stern voice whispered. He opened his eyes to see Hadwyn crouched over him. "Something's out there. We think it's the Mist Demon."

Elac rolled swiftly to his feet and strapped Sir Draygen's enchanted Sword about his waist. He stood immobile, listening to the sound of the wind whispering among the rocks, searching for any sign of their hunter. He glanced back and saw everyone but Jayrne on their feet. Silvayn was murmuring to himself, and Elac assumed the mage was readying another spell in case the demon showed. On an impulse, Elac reached down and covered Jayrne with Sir Aleron's cloak, hoping it would hide her from the demon's searching eyes.

With an earsplitting roar that betrayed an inhuman hunger, the Mist Demon launched from the depths of the cave, storming right past the still-unconscious Jayrne and knocking Elac from his feet. Somehow, it had found a way to get into the niche behind them without being seen. It charged directly for Silvayn, but twin blasts from him and his apprentice knocked the demon back several feet and halted its advance. Rilen took advantage of the momentary respite and positioned himself between the demon and the two mages. The Dwarves spread out, meaning to come at the demon from two sides. Cassius strode forward, his broadsword carried readily in his right hand, and Elac managed to scramble back to his feet.

Morfal surprised them all, including the demon, with a reckless charge, his long sword descending in a vicious blow directed at the demon's head. The creature's speed compensated for its surprise, and it lurched backward, all but avoiding the blow. Undaunted, Morfal pressed forward, swinging a backhand blow that drove the demon to its knees. Morfal closed in for the kill, but the Mist Demon suddenly lurched forward, a single clawed hand raking the side of Morfal's face. He spun away, blood flying from the wound as he fell. The demon reached for the supine form, but Rilen and Cassius delivered such a furious counterattack that it had to step back and leave the fallen man where he lay.

Elac heard Silvayn break off unexpectedly from his incantation. He risked a glance at the old mage, and saw him remove the Temira from its pouch. Silvayn held it high, and despite the almost total lack of light, the relic glittered in the fog. The Mist Demon seemed to sense the Temira's presence, and it whirled to face Silvayn, who stood defiantly with the artifact of the gods raised over his head. The demon bounded forward.

Elac chose that moment to strike. He lunged forward, reaching out with his sword arm and driving the magic blade home. It slid easily through the ghastly body, burying itself up to the hilt. A bizarre wailing noise arose within the fog all around them, and the demon raised its arms as if in supplication to the invisible sky. The Temira flashed its own internal light, and the Sword of Sir Draygen glowed in return. The wail rose to a fever pitch, and everyone dropped their weapons to cover their ears in agony. Everyone, that is, except Elac, who stood immobile as if he was the one transfixed on the magic blade.

The mist seemed to close in more tightly about them, swirling faster and faster where it surrounded the Mist Demon. It voiced its own howl of rage and pain, and its form wavered, becoming opaque. The body of the Mist Demon drew in upon itself, shrinking down to a single ball of glowing, incandescent energy. With an eruption of sound that reverberated through the surrounding mountain peaks, the globe of energy that was the Mist Demon exploded into nothingness.

A moment of stunned silence followed, then Gillen was at Morfal's side. He tried to use his healing magic, but as had been the case when Jayrne was hurt, he wasn't entirely successful. Hadwyn wondered if the death of the Mist Demon might be causing problems, but Gillen shrugged in confusion, shaking his head slowly. Elac suggested the water from the Springs of Calda, but Gillen told him they had used the last of it on Jayrne. Nevertheless, the big man soon opened his eyes and sat up, wiping the blood from his face and looking wildly around as if searching.

"It's okay," Gillen told him, trying to get him to stay seated. "The demon is gone, sent back to where it came from." Morfal visibly relaxed, and some of the stress went out of his eyes. He lay back and allowed Gillen to clean the three nasty scratches on his right cheek, which were still bleeding. Elac knelt at Jayrne's side, holding her hands while she also struggled to sit up.

"What happened to it?" Cassius asked, sheathing his sword.

"The Temira channeled its energy back to the Plane of Mist when Elac's Sword struck it." Silvayn looked upon Elac with sadness in his eyes, and gave a heavy sigh. "The same should happen if Elac strikes Volnor with his Sword, in the presence of the Temira." Silvayn explained.

"We'd better be moving on," Rilen warned. "I know we have some people who are injured, but noise from the fight will have alerted every Kobold within ten leagues of us. The mountains will make it difficult to locate the source of the sound, but they will be swarming these hills by sunrise."

They pushed their horses as much as they dared, given their physical condition and the rough terrain, but it was still nearing dawn when they broke free of the mist. With many hours of travel still ahead, Rilen resignedly cast about for a hiding place. He found one about an hour after sunrise, a hidden cave with a narrow opening, but which widened out inside and provided enough room for them all to sleep comfortably, even with the horses inside. Elac and Gillen took their bottles to a nearby stream and replenished their dwindling water supply. When they returned, everyone seemed to be settling in to sleep. Rilen volunteered to stand watch, so Elac automatically moved to Jayrne's side.

Gillen stepped lightly to stand with Elac, lips pursed, looking down at the injured thief. "I could try my magic again," he suggested softly, stroking his thick red beard. "Now that we're clear of the mist, I might be more successful."

Elac nodded his approval of the idea, and the Dwarf knelt

to pray for Jayrne. Within moments, the pained look left her eyes, and her breathing eased somewhat. Gillen stood, looking down at her speculatively. "Better?"

"Much," she said with a weak smile. "Sure took you long enough."

Elac and Gillen both laughed at her remark, more out of relief than anything else. Gillen stepped over the discarded equipment littering the floor to stand before Morfal, who had doffed his armor and was clad only in a rust-stained tunic and an old pair of pants.

"I could try my healing magic on your face, if you wish. Now that we're clear of the mist, it seems to be—"

"No." Morfal's eyes narrowed dangerously, and he glared at the Dwarf standing before him.

"Are you sure? The bleeding has stopped, but I'm sure it's still painful. Besides, the gouges will leave a nasty scar."

"Warriors bear their scars with pride." With that, Morfal turned away and lay upon his makeshift bed.

They stayed in the cave for several hours before setting out once more. By the time they reached the edge of the Paheny Mountains, night had fallen once again, and they took refuge among the last of the peaks. They set out once more about two hours before dawn. They had wanted to cross the plains under cover of darkness, and with the horses fresh, they were able to traverse the open grasslands at a gallop.

The sun grudgingly rose from its bed the next morning, brightening the skies to a ruddy haze, and the distant boughs of Nightwood Forest gradually came into view. They continued their pace unabated, and the trees moved perceptively closer.

Wildflowers, small shrubs, and shimmering grasses seemed literally to fly past, and they made their final dash for the questionable safety of the forest ahead of them.

They slowed to a walk, cautiously approaching the wall of the forest, and Rilen peered about for a likely place to start their journey to the other side. They trotted through Nightwood Forest, alert for any signs of undead forces that still might be prowling the woods. The journey to Unity lasted two more days. They had to dodge Kobold patrols once they left the concealment of Nightwood Forest, but with Rilen leading the way, they easily avoided any more pitched battles. The hills and plains around Unity were strangely deserted, as if the whole of the land had been swept clean of travelers. The guards at the city walls were hesitant to open the gates for them, until the entire party showed them the brooches identifying them as Soldiers of the Council.

They went first to Silvayn's residence, where they bathed and donned clean clothes. The smells and cares of the road seemed to wash away, and Elac found himself feeling more refreshed than he had in weeks. Jayrne was fully recovered, they had successfully taken possession of the Temira, and his quest was nearing its finale. He tried not to think about his one remaining task, since his chances of success didn't seem very high. Silvayn looked them all over to be sure they were ready, then led the way to the waiting carriages.

They entered the Council chambers, and Elac was surprised to see the Council already assembled. He hadn't known word was sent about their arrival, but then he realized they probably met almost nightly, with the onset of war. Once Elac's entire retinue had entered, Dralana pounded on the table for silence, and the voices slowly quieted down. Falstoff stepped to one end of the Council table, an unmistakably eager look in his eye. Elac saw the ambassador's hands lightly trembling with anticipation.

Dralana stood, gesturing grandly to the new arrivals. "So, the Soldiers of the Council have returned. What news do you bring?"

"Behold," Silvayn announced in a full voice, arms spread before him, "we have done as the Council asked. We journeyed straightaway to Tracker's Peak, a ride of many days and many hardships. We did battle with one of the denizens of the mist surrounding the castle, gained entry to Tracker's Peak, and recovered the Temira. And let all rejoice: those souls believed lost fourteen hundred years ago are found! The brave soldiers, trapped in the castle when foul Volnor's spell was cast, are still alive, held prisoner in the Plane of Mist."

The news of the soldiers of Tracker's Peak seemed to pass right by the Council unnoticed. Dralana looked to the other Councilors before she spoke. "Let us see the Temira."

Silvayn brought forth the ancient talisman, the precious metals reflecting back the light of the torches lighting the Council chambers. At a simple gesture from Dralana, Silvayn carried the relic forward and, almost reluctantly, handed it over. The nine Councilors gathered around, and silence reigned supreme in the room while they admired the Temira.

The Councilors took their seats, and Dralana spoke once more. "One question yet remains. To what use shall we put this mighty weapon?"

"We must do as the spirits of the Seven Knights of Piaras

Keep have instructed us. Using the implements given us by those sad specters, we must make our way to Malaton, and there, Elac will destroy Volnor once and for all."

"Folly!" a Human general shouted, striding forward with angry, stomping steps. "Honorable Councilors, I am General Gorat. I have consulted with the wisest of the Priests at the Temples of Rennex and Vanta, and they all agree. The Temira has many powers besides those Silvayn mentioned.

"The Temira also weakens undead in its vicinity, up to a few leagues away. Thralls and skeletons are more readily destroyed, and even incorporeal creatures such as wraiths can be eliminated with normal weapons. The forces of Volnor have been ransacking villages with bands of ghouls and wraiths, which our soldiers are powerless to fight without blessed weapons. The Temira would enable us to destroy them. To send it with this motley crew into the very teeth of the enemy would be sheer folly."

Several Councilors shouted responses, their words lost in the sudden waterfall of sound. Dralana asserted herself once more. "I would vote to pass the Temira along to the military. I see no way for these brave adventurers to reach Volnor alive, and if they were to try they would only deliver the Temira to him. We would be better served by allowing our soldiers to take advantage of the Temira's powers." Todos and Roktal nodded their agreement.

"The Elves concur," Oaklyn said, half-rising from her chair and gesturing to Cordos and Nasontas. "The Temira should go to the military."

Ralore leaned forward and motioned to Elac's party with

a contemptuous flip of her hand. "Then the Council is unanimous. Tanne, Jarm, and I agree the Temira should—"

"Hold!" It was Jarm who interrupted the leader of the Human Councilors. "How can you tell the Council my thoughts if you haven't even asked me?"

"I was just—"

"You were just usurping my vote! You believed that since I'm new, I would be afraid to speak my mind! I disagree with the idea of turning the Temira over to the military. It exerts its power over the undead for what, ten miles? Fifteen miles? How many miles of front lines do we need to cover? I say we need to trust in our destiny and send this courageous band against Volnor."

"Your objection is noted," Dralana said, her lip curled with contempt. "However, with the other members of the Council in agreement, the Temira will forthwith be given to the leaders of the military, thereby to use it to—"

"That's about enough of this," Silvayn said, striding forward to the center of the room, his cloak billowing behind him. "This Council has thwarted my purpose for the last time."

Dralana's face turned red with anger. "That sounds vaguely like a threat, mage."

"It is." Silvayn's hand dipped into a pouch at his belt, and emerged with the pilfered documents. "Before we left Unity, we acquired certain troubling documents. These documents, in fact." Silvayn deliberately selected Jarm, handing her the papers and continuing his explanation. "The information contained therein proves Dralana has been accepting money from the enemy in exchange for certain policy decisions."

Pandemonium erupted in the Council chambers. The

three Human Councilors examined the papers first, while the Dwarves sat silently in ashen-faced anticipation. Oaklyn and the Elves pushed their way across the floor of the chamber to join their Human counterparts.

Jarm stood finally, and pointed theatrically across the room. "Guards! Arrest Councilor Dralana! Hold her in the prison on charges of high treason!"

Dralana's eyes darted about wildly, and she appeared poised to flee, but Todos and Roktal grabbed her arms, holding her until the sentries arrived and took her into custody. Falstoff climbed atop the table. He raised Dralana's silver mug high in the air, then threw it sharply to the floor. The crash from the mug striking the floor drew everyone's attention.

"Hear me! This Council is in disarray, and we cannot expect a decision to be made until this issue has been properly addressed. Therefore, I respectfully suggest the Temira be locked away for safekeeping for the time being. If the Council agrees, I will take the Temira, under guard, to my safe house. It can be secured there until such time as this debate can be completed."

The Councilors, who moments before had been arrogant and full of confidence, looked skittishly about the room, and more than one cast a fearful eye at the corner of the room where Dralana was being placed in shackles. With surprising insight, Elac realized the entire Council, with the likely exception of Jarm, was in fear of suffering the same fate. There were several nods and shrugged shoulders, and then Falstoff took the Temira from the table where Dralana had left it. After seeing the Temira safely escorted to Falstoff's residence, a rather well-reinforced structure with a high fence and guard towers,

Silvayn brought the group back to his house.

"For one, I am ready to have this whole business finished," Cassius said, scowling darkly at Hadwyn, who was already finishing his second tankard of ale. "My people need me in this war. I feel I need to go to them."

"You're doing them a greater service here," Silvayn reminded him. "If we succeed in what we are attempting, Volnor's forces will be defeated."

"But what of the Kobolds? They still menace my lands, as well."

"The Kobolds are in league with the Necromancers," Rilen said, stretching his bare feet closer to the fireplace. "When the Necromancers are destroyed, the Kobolds will rout."

Gillen sipped at his own mug of ale. "Our first task will be recovering the Temira. Falstoff helped us out by keeping it out of the hands of the military, but I don't think he can simply give it to us."

Jayrne sat playing with one of her lockpicks, turning it back and forth to catch the glint of light off the metal. "There's always a more direct way to get it."

Adalyn chuckled softly. "I think we can keep that as a last resort. It wouldn't hurt to ask for it. I doubt he'd believe we'd actually take it from him."

"I like Jayrne's idea." Hadwyn belched thunderously, peering into his empty tankard.

"We'll talk to Falstoff," Silvayn said. "Tonight, after things have quieted down, we will go see him. But not all of us. It will just be me, Cassius, and Gillen. The rest of you can stay here and get some rest. With any luck, we'll be on the road in the morning."

✤ ⊗ ★ ⊕ ⊛

Hadwyn passed a small coin to the barmaid, who brought more tankards of ale to the table. Elac was feeling light-headed from what he had drunk, but he didn't feel like stopping. He was expected to travel to the Paheny Mountains, somehow cross the vast Desert of Malator, enter the city of Malaton, and engage in combat with the most powerful Necromancer in history. He had options, of course. He could refuse to go. He could hide and hope it all went away. But he knew avoiding his destiny would do no one any good, least of all himself. If he didn't try to defeat Volnor, the combined forces of the undead and the Kobolds would, in all likelihood, overrun the armies of the West, and they would all be killed or enslaved.

The enemy forces outnumbered the Elves, Humans, and Dwarves, and the situation grew worse every day. Reports were coming in from all fronts, telling of Necromancers enchanting the bodies of fallen soldiers, turning them into undead warriors, who would in turn fight against their former comrades. The cycle would repeat itself until the army of the Necromancers was victorious, or Volnor himself was defeated. Elac could see no other alternative.

He caught Jayrne's concerned look, and he realized she had discovered him staring blankly at the dusty floor of the tavern. He forced himself to smile.

"Sorry. I'm just thinking about what lies ahead."

"Forget about tomorrow." She fixed him with a devastating smile. "I think you had better worry about what lies ahead tonight." She set her mug down firmly on the table, took Elac by the hand, and led him from the taproom. After a quick stop with the bartender, they mounted the stairs of the inn, and Jayrne unlocked the door to a vacant room. She turned to face him, wrapped her arms around his neck, and kissed him deeply. Elac managed to open the door and usher her inside without breaking off the lingering kiss. He felt a passion rising inside, like nothing he had felt in years. Or had ever felt, he realized. His hand slid lightly down her back.

A light step behind him brought him up short. He half-turned, just in time to catch a cudgel across the temple, and everything went black.

❦ ❀ ✪ ❦ ❀

Hadwyn wiped ale foam from his beard, laughing raucously at the joke Rilen had just told. He couldn't remember the Elf ever talking so much. Then again, he couldn't remember Rilen ever drinking so much. He leaned over to put his arm around the young Dwarf sitting next to him, and she giggled drunkenly in response. Adalyn and Rilen were actually holding hands, Hadwyn noticed, which he hadn't seen them openly do before.

The benefits of the drink.

A hand slammed firmly onto his shoulder, and he turned to see Prince Cassius standing behind him. "Where is Elac?" the Prince demanded.

Hadwyn frowned. "He and Jayrne left an hour ago. The way she dragged him out of here, I'd say they were headed to a room."

"What's going on?" Rilen asked, rising to his feet.

"We went to Falstoff's house, but it was dark and empty. Silvayn was worried about him, so we forced the door open. There were signs of a hasty packing job, but Falstoff and the Temira are gone. Silvayn and Gillen are checking the house further for any clues about what happened. I came back here to find you five."

Rilen's eyes flew wide open. "Elac!"

He pushed past the others, knocking a table over in the process. Hadwyn was right behind him, his extended fling with an ale barrel and his female companion forgotten. The startled barkeep told them where to find their companions, and they charged up the stairs. The door to the room was closed, but Rilen was through it without stopping, knocking the portal from its hinges. Hadwyn rushed into the room behind him and found Rilen standing motionless in the center of the floor. Furniture was in disarray; chairs were upended, a table lay on its side, and there was a small amount of blood on the floor. There was no sign of either Elac or Jayrne. With a roar of rage, Hadwyn lifted a chair high over his head and smashed it to the floor.

🔆 🔆 ★ 🔆 🔆

Elac's eyes fluttered open, and with an effort he brought the world into focus. Judging by the way he was being bounced around, he seemed to be in an enclosed carriage. His head throbbed with pain, and he suddenly remembered the attack in their room. His mouth was parched, and he realized a wad of cloth was held firmly in his mouth by a tight gag. He tried to lift his hands to remove the gag and check his wound, but he found his hands bound securely behind his back. Directly across from him, Jayrne sat in stoic silence, eyes closed, her jaw muscles clenching and unclenching in restrained fury. He reached out and nudged her with his foot, and her eyes opened wide.

"Elac! You're alive! You . . . I was worried. They hit you, and . . ." She trailed off, biting back tears of frustration. "They've gagged you. They knew you have been instructed in magic, I'd bet, and that was why they rendered you unable to speak. They searched me, rather enthusiastically, I might add, and took my lockpick sets. They also have the Sword of Draygen, along with my cloak and boots.

"As far as what happened, all I can tell you is we were ambushed. I would guess they are working for Dralana."

Both he and Jayrne were secured to iron rings set in the floor, so they couldn't move any closer together in an effort to free themselves. Elac sat with his head against the wall, eyes closed, contemplating ways to escape, but finding nothing feasible.

An hour later, the carriage jolted to a stop. Elac heard the rattling of chains when several locking bars slid free, and the door to their tiny chamber creaked open. A torch provided illumination, but Elac could see no one. There were several different voices barely audible through the open door, but he couldn't quite understand what they were saying. At last, a set of footsteps approached, and Falstoff's sneering face appeared in the doorway.

Wordlessly, Silvayn, Cassius, and Gillen entered Rilen's room. Gillen hefted his axe, swung it over his head, and smashed a table into splinters. He kicked the pieces aside and stormed across the floor to a chair. Under normal circumstances, he kept his temper in check, but the evening's events had been too much. Silvayn rubbed his chin, then looked up, pursed lips betraying the frustration he felt. Hadwyn crossed his arms and waited for the worst.

"Falstoff has deceived us," Silvayn told them. "I fear he has taken the Temira to Malaton, and with it our hopes of ending this war."

"Malaton?" Hadwyn asked incredulously. "How can you be certain?"

"We found evidence at his house, hidden behind a false wall. It appears he had been consulting with agents of Volnor for some time. Volnor promised him power in exchange for his assistance. Falstoff convinced the Duke of Palim, and through him the King of Palindom, to appoint him as the ambassador to the Necromancers. It was on his first trip there that the deal was sealed. Sealed with the blood of Falstoff's wife and her father, who were kidnapped by Dalos and taken to Malaton. There, at the gates to the city, Falstoff performed the hideous rites of torture and murder to gain the acceptance of Malator.

"Falstoff helped us along the way only because our interests coincided with his. In this case, war between us and the Kobolds. The deaths among our soldiers served to weaken our forces, but in many cases also boosted the numbers in the undead armies. Once it became apparent what our objective was, the recovery of the Temira, Volnor instructed Falstoff to assist us, then take it from us if we were successful. It appears we obliged him quite nicely."

"Why would Volnor want us to find the one thing that would kill him?" Adalyn asked.

"Because he feared we would go after it anyway, with or without Council approval. This way, he could control it, and eventually gain possession of it. And now, Cassius tells me Elac and Jayrne are missing. I can only assume they were taken by Falstoff's people."

"What do we do now?" Rilen asked, rubbing his eyes.

Before Silvayn could answer, there was a commotion in the hall. Swords rang clear of their sheaths, and Hadwyn cautiously opened the door. He saw the way was clear, so he stepped out of the room. A panic-stricken Elf dashed toward him, and Hadwyn grabbed him before he could slip past.

"Calm yourself!" he ordered harshly. "What in the name of Zantar is going on?"

"Haven't you heard?" the man said, gibbering with fear. "The city is under siege! An army of Kobolds and undead has surrounded the city, and they are preparing to attack!"

Chapter 20

Daybreak revealed the extent of the enemy forces surrounding Unity. Row upon orderly row of Kobold infantry covered the plains, interspersed by wandering bands of undead. Siege engines were massed near the rear of the formations. Hadwyn surveyed the enemy ranks coolly, appraising the situation with the eye of a veteran soldier. Although vastly outnumbered, the defenders still carried the advantage. Assaulting even poorly prepared defenses would cost an attacker dearly, and the walls of Unity had been designed specifically for the purpose of repelling invaders. The gates would be the key, Hadwyn knew.

Next to him, Rilen stirred restlessly. He was leaning out over the edge of the wall, trying to get a better view of the forces aligned against the city.

"What is it, Rilen?" Hadwyn asked.

"This doesn't make sense. The undead attack the living on sight. It has always been their weakness in every battle account I've read: they immediately close with enemy forces, making them easy to bait into ambushes. Yet here they are, wandering around between Kobold formations, and they haven't had a single scuffle."

Silvayn stood stoically, eyes closed, seemingly at peace. At length, he opened his eyes. "Necromancers. Somewhere in the enemy ranks, they have hidden Necromancers. They're exerting direct control over the undead."

Rilen eyed the field before them speculatively, one eyebrow raised. "What would happen if a Necromancer was to die unexpectedly?"

"The undead he was controlling would be loosed upon the Kobolds, or whoever was nearest. If they were engaged in hand-to-hand combat with our soldiers, not much would change, but if they were still at a distance, it could be interesting."

They waited in silence for a time, contemplating the possibilities of Silvayn's revelation. The only difficulty, in Hadwyn's opinion, lay in identifying the Necromancers. They were all out of range of bowshot for the time being, but when the undead closed with the city, the Necromancers would have to follow suit in order to maintain their control.

⊕⊛★⊕⊗

The carriage slowed to a stop once more, and Elac tried to relax his battered and bruised body. His head continued to throb, and he assumed his wound was serious, based on the amount of blood on his shirt. His mouth burned from the heavy gag, and his throat was raw. How long had it been since he'd had anything to drink? A day? Two days? The door to the carriage opened to spill gleaming sunlight onto the two prisoners.

Morfal climbed on board and removed the ties securing Elac to the wall. He seized the Elf by one foot and dragged him from the carriage, and Elac fell to the ground to land with a painful jolt. He rolled onto his left side, curling into a fetal position, pain and thirst racking his body. Another thump and a cry of pain told him Jayrne had been similarly treated, but he was unable to roll over and see how she was doing.

"Stand them up." Elac recognized Falstoff's voice, even through the haze of pain and fatigue he was feeling. He was lifted roughly from behind and shoved against the carriage. Jayrne was placed next to him, and she gave him a barely perceptible nod to show him she was alright. Elac shifted his swollen eyes back to the form of their captor.

"Elac, I am about to have my associates remove your gag, and you will both be fed. Morfal will be right by your side the entire time. If you attempt to use magic, he will cut your throat where you stand. In fact, we will kill the little thief, as well. Do we understand each other?" Elac nodded weakly, and Morfal stepped forward to remove the gag. Elac licked his dry, cracked lips, but there was no relief to be found. They were both given water, and Elac drank greedily.

"Why?" he managed finally.

"Why else? Power. Power, and nothing else."

Two nameless henchmen brought them a meal consisting of bread, cheese, and water, and Elac and Jayrne ate greedily while Falstoff told his story. "When I became Palim's mayor, there was nowhere left for me to go. Marrying into the royal family wouldn't legitimize me as a candidate for a higher position, and a coup d'etat had no chance of succeeding.

"Your encounters with the undead from Nightwood Forest actually gave me the idea to try opening negotiations with Volnor. I consulted the records in the library of Unity. It seems the foolish scholars there faithfully committed to paper everything they knew about necromancy, including the means by which someone could become a Necromancer.

"I prayed to Malator for guidance, and Morfal appeared only days later. He told me the means by which I might gain the power I so desired: bring my greatest love and greatest enemy to the gates of Malaton, there to torture and murder them in front of the Gatekeepers. Morfal suggested I contact a slaver group located south of Unity Lake, and coordinate their disappearances through them. The leaders of Dalos and I came up with the idea of the string of kidnappings in an effort to disguise the true targets: my wife, and the Duke of Branig."

Falstoff took a deep breath, sighing in ecstasy. "Ah, you should have been there. The deaths of those two ranked among the most brutal, heinous rituals the Necromancers had ever seen. I think even the Gatekeepers were shocked. I gained admittance to the city, and my exceptionally vicious show won me a personal meeting with Volnor himself.

"Everything has gone exactly as we planned. Once we were clear of the city, I gave the signal and a combined army of Kobolds and undead marched on Unity. If you harbored any hope about your friends rescuing you, I don't think they'll be leaving Unity anytime soon.

Falstoff marched several steps away from his prisoners, gazing over the empty miles before them. "Eat while you can," he told them. "Your ride to Malaton will be here soon."

✤ ⊗ ✪ ⊕ ⊛

"The meeting of the Unity Council will come to order!" Todos bellowed, his voice shaking despite his efforts to hide it. "The matter before us is of the utmost urgency. Unity is threatened by the army outside our walls. Indeed, even as we speak, word has reached me that the forces without are about to launch their offensive. The Council has already met in secret, and we have decided unanimously to turn command of the city defenses over to our Soldiers of the Council."

There was an outcry of protests from the assembled military commanders, and it took some time to restore order. With the disturbance quelled, Todos was able to deliver the rest of his speech. "The reason for the decision is simple. None of the commanders stationed here has ever seen combat. The Soldiers of the Council, on the other hand, have seen years of fighting against the roving bands of Kobold raiders."

Hadwyn and the others were ushered out of the meeting and brought to the city walls. Even before they arrived, Hadwyn heard the slow pounding that could mean only one thing: Kobold catapults were firing, and the assault on the city had begun. The actual attack on the walls wouldn't come right away. It could be weeks away. The Kobolds wouldn't risk harming their own soldiers by trying to scale the walls or breach the gates while still firing the siege engines. The delay would give the defenders time to assess the full tactical situation.

He already knew the gates were the weak point. It was true

in any walled city, but especially in Unity. The designers, while making the city defenses appear impressive, wanted to keep the weight of the massive portals to a minimum in order to provide for easy opening and closing. As a result, the wooden gates were only minimally reinforced, a weakness that could come back to haunt them. He had instructed the city engineers to begin work on the gates as soon as possible, but he wasn't confident in their ability to shore up the defenses in time to make a difference.

As far as numbers went, the enemy held the advantage by about ten-to-one. It would have been worse, but the timing of the assault worked to the defenders' advantage. A combined arms training exercise had been planned for that week, so battalions of soldiers from the armies of the Elves, Dwarves, and Humans had already gathered in Unity, bolstering the defensive forces tremendously. The increased numbers should be able to hold the city against any assault, provided the gates held. Hadwyn sighed. It all came down to the gates.

Under his brother's direction, the engineers were tearing down houses and buildings near the gates, using the materials to shore up the reinforcing material backing the wooden portals. Occasionally, the gates would tremble violently, telling Hadwyn one of the projectiles from the Kobold catapults found its mark. The engineers paled visibly at each impact, but they maintained their efforts.

Hadwyn entered the new military office, a large, one-story brick building with an audience chamber at its center. The facility had been more ceremonial than functional, and changes were underway. At Cassius's insistence, one wall had been painted with a map of the surrounding lands out to about ten leagues, and an entire quarter of the room was covered with a scale model of the same area, including the terrain features. Rilen was in his element, instructing the military leaders on the tactics to be used for the coming battle.

"Here, then, is the essence of our strategy against the Kobolds. Whenever they mass at a point along our wall, or even outside the gates, we'll line the area immediately inside the walls with heavy infantry. The front ranks will each throw their spears before closing with the enemy, and then the ranks behind them will throw over the closest combatants and strike the Kobolds farther back. Archers upon the walls will harass the enemy. The cavalry will be held in reserve in case a force of Kobolds breaks through the walls.

"The undead are a different matter. The greatest difficulty in fighting the lesser forms of undead lies in their fear aura. Some of our veterans have fought undead before; these soldiers will be dispersed throughout the ranks of our army. Repeated exposure to the fear aura produces a certain level of immunity.

"Also remember, there are bound to be incorporeal undead confronting us at some point. Only magic or blessed weapons can harm them. We have Priests blessing weapons as fast as they can, but it isn't an easy process. Tell your soldiers who have no special weapons not to confront wraiths and ghouls, because they'll be throwing their lives away."

Rilen continued his dissertation, and Hadwyn glided to the corner of the room holding the scale terrain model. The locations of the various enemy forces had been noted using colored wooden blocks, with larger blocks denoting the location of the siege engines. He hoped their preparations would be enough.

⊕ ⊗ ★ ⊕ ⊛

Falstoff continued to stalk anxiously about the clearing, pausing occasionally to gaze eastward. Elac watched him apprehensively, his throat burning once more from the tightly bound gag. His wrists were almost numb, but he could still feel the warm, sticky blood dripping down his hands. His head ached from his latest injury, a gift from Falstoff when Elac had refused to acknowledge the former ambassador's self-proclaimed brilliance.

"The Kobolds will be here soon. The beasts pulling their wagon are like nothing you have ever seen. They are Volnor's personal pets. They run at speeds you never dreamed of. You will reach the mountains before daybreak, and when the sun rises tomorrow, you will behold the awesome power of Malaton."

Falstoff's lip curled in a sneer of discontent, an expression that seemed to frequently find a home on his haughty face. He struck Elac a stunning blow to the side of the head, knocking him sprawling. Jayrne screamed in protest, which only bought her a stinging slap of her own. Falstoff returned to Elac, seized him by the front of his tunic, and hauled him to his feet.

"Ah, the Kobolds. The ultimate irony! Not only were they allied with Volnor from the beginning, but Volnor and his cohorts actually created them! Well, I suppose 'created' is too strong of a word. 'Altered' is more like it. They were an advanced species of predator, living in the northeastern Paheny Mountains, when Volnor found them. It took hundreds of years, but he finally perfected a new killing machine. The Necromancers remained isolated in the Desert of Malatora, while the Kobolds intervened in your affairs of state, opening the door for the invasion."

With a streak of red light, a substantial-sized wagon raced to a stop, pulled by four creatures out of Elac's worst nightmare. They had the shape of horses, with black, hairless skin and long, pointed snouts. Tendrils of smoke poured from their noses, and gleaming white fangs protruded from their mouths. Their well-muscled legs ended in long, sharp claws. One of the beasts looked at Elac with undisguised hunger.

He and Jayrne were loaded into the wagon and secured in separate compartments where they could neither see nor hear each other. Not that it mattered if she could hear him, he conceded, since he couldn't speak through the confining gag. He sat in silence for several minutes before Falstoff stepped in front of him, glowering down with fiery red eyes.

"You should keep your insolence to a minimum, worm. Your little friend doesn't fit into Volnor's plans at all. If I get bored during the ride to Malaton, I might just start on her early." Elac struggled vainly against his binding cords, ignoring the blow to his face. "In fact, there are other ways to torture someone besides the infliction of pain. She's an attractive woman, isn't she? Why don't you spend the rest of this journey wondering what I'm doing?"

●◉★⊕◉

The sound began with a crackle, but in a grand crescendo built to a roar, and one section of Unity's wall crumbled into rubble. Dust rushed outward in an expanding cloud, and pieces of the wall bounced and rolled away. The night gradually died into silence, punctuated by shouted commands from the soldiers manning the walls. The reactionary force sprinted through the deserted streets, racing against time to be in position near the breach. Hadwyn and Gillen were with them, leading several companies of Dwarf infantry, most dressed in glimmering chain mail and bearing oversized battle-axes.

They arrived at the north side of town, and Gillen slowed them to a walk. The gaping hole in their defensive wall came into view. Archers were already in place atop the still-intact portions of the wall and were providing information about enemy troop movements. Hadwyn took in the entire scene in the span of a few heartbeats, and he established a defensive line just beyond the main body of rubble. At his order, several Dwarves moved about the formation, throwing the smaller pieces of the wall back into the mound of broken rocks in front of them. With any luck, the uneven footing the debris would provide could give his fighters an advantage, since whatever foe they faced would be fighting from a treacherous landscape.

"Kobolds, sir!" the shout came from above. "Looks like a full brigade or more!"

Hadwyn signaled his acknowledgment. He and his brother paced back and forth behind his force, shouting words of encouragement. From outside the walls, he heard the booted feet of the approaching Kobolds.

Hadwyn heard the snapping of bowstrings. "Here they come!" he shouted. Cries of pain came as the answering call, and the Kobolds rushed into view. Several staggered and fell under the onslaught from the archers above, but still they came.

They climbed across the peak of the rubble and charged the Dwarf lines. Steel rang on steel, and the dust of the rubble soon ran red with blood. Hadwyn's strategy proved out, and the unstable rocks rolled away beneath the Kobolds' feet, often causing their sword strokes to miss their targets. The Dwarves, however, had no such problems, and the sturdy, axe-wielding warriors wreaked havoc among the raiders. The archers atop the walls found easy targets in the Kobolds milling about behind the battle lines, and within minutes, the survivors retreated howling through the gap. A combined force of mages and engineers emerged from hiding to repair the breached wall, and the relief force arrived to secure the area. Hadwyn and Gillen lead their exhausted but jubilant soldiers from the battlefield.

They returned to the headquarters building, where Rilen was scrutinizing the terrain model. The Elf looked up at their approach.

"Did it go as well as the reports are saying?"

"I haven't heard the reports," Gillen said with a smile, removing his helmet, "but we did defeat them soundly."

"Why don't you two get some rest? The catapults have picked up the pace once more, so we probably won't see any more action until dawn."

✤ ⊗ ★ ⊕ ⊛

The wagon rolled to a stop yet again, and Elac heard the rattle and creak of the gates of Malaton. Falstoff opened the cover of Elac's confined prison, and the black, tar-smeared gates loomed ominously over him. The newest servant of Malator pulled Elac from the wagon and tied a rope around his feet, connecting the other end to the wagon. The strange beasts started forward once more, albeit at a much slower pace, and Elac was dragged along the cobblestone streets to the enormous enjoyment of the crowds of black-robed onlookers. Most jeered loudly, and some spat on him as he bounced past.

Elac was battered and bleeding from several places by the time they stopped for the final time. A muscle-bound Human, dressed in black leather and wearing a mask, tossed him over one shoulder and carried him inside a stout, stone-walled building. A hunchbacked Dwarf led the way deep into what appeared to be a prison, and he produced a large key from a pocket in his filthy cloak. With an echoing *snap*, the jailer opened an iron-bound door and gestured within. The thug carrying Elac allowed him to slide off his shoulder, sending him crashing painfully to the floor. The jailer shuffled into the cell and untied Elac's hands. The ropes were replaced with manacles and shackles, and the two figures retreated from the room, leaving Elac alone with his ruminations.

He tested the strength of the chains binding his arms and legs, and found them to be formidable. The door might or might not be penetrable, but until he unlocked the bindings holding him in the corner, he was going nowhere. He couldn't even remove the suffocating gag from his mouth, because the cunningly placed chains held his hands too low to reach his face. He could reach his feet, but nothing above his chest.

My feet! The realization came to him in a flash. Jayrne had given him an extra lockpick set, and she even helped him design a special flap of leather to conceal it within his boot. He slid his thumb and forefinger inside his right boot. After he probed about for a few heart-stopping moments, he found the familiar slender rods of metal. Beads of sweat appearing on his forehead, he worked the tools free.

His heart nearly stopped beating with every sound, fearing he would be discovered, but no one intruded upon his desperate efforts. It took him several minutes to disengage the locks holding the manacles on his wrists. He took a few moments to remove the gag, and he massaged his aching jaw, licking his lips and trying to restore feeling to his face. His efforts with the chains on his legs were successful, and he tiptoed to his cell door. He flattened himself against the wooden portal and carefully peered out through the small opening, but he could see no one. In moments, the door stood unlocked.

Elac edged into the hallway and looked about. He couldn't remember the way he had come in, but then that wasn't surprising, considering the way he had been brought to his cell. The young Elf turned to his right and crept along the corridor. Torchlight flickered from around the corner ahead, and he slowed to see what awaited him.

Swords lined the walls, and several shields hung from pegs on the far side of the room. In one corner, several shirts of chain mail had been dumped into a chaotic pile. A short Human in a patched tunic sat at a table, tankard of ale at hand, with his back to Elac. The Elf glanced about the room and selected a wicked-looking dagger, then skulked up behind his victim.

He yanked the unsuspecting but intoxicated fellow's head back and pressed the knife firmly against the exposed throat. Fear leaped into the drunken eyes, and he spilled his drink.

He tried to speak, but Elac silenced him by pressing the knife harder against the fragile flesh.

"Don't yell," Elac told him in a voice as still as death. "Where are my weapons, and what have they done with Jayrne?" Seeing the blank, uncomprehending look and the weak shake of the head, Elac glared down at him. "The thief who was brought in with me. What have they done with her?"

"Don't kill me! They took her to the Temple of Malator!"

"The Temple? Why? Where is it?"

"It's through the back of the prison." He trembled violently. "They took the thief to the Temple because she is to be sacrificed, with your Sword, upon Malator's altar!"

❀ ❀ ★ ❀ ❀

With an eerie silence, the near-constant rain of stones against the gates of Unity fell into a hushed stillness. The defenders fingered their weapons and shifted their feet nervously, awaiting their enemy's next move. Cassius stood upon the catwalk above the heavily damaged gate, his hair flying in the early morning breeze. Hadwyn and Gillen paced impatiently on the streets behind the gates, and Hadwyn found himself wanting the Necromancers and their Kobold allies to get on with the battle.

Rilen arrived with another company of archers, and he immediately set about placing them in defensive locations. The reserve bowmen were placed where Hadwyn hadn't thought to put them, but then nothing Rilen came up with surprised him anymore. The latest group of archers wouldn't be able to fire upon the enemy outside the walls. Their task was to provide assistance to the fighters behind the gates, should the enemy force a breach and get inside.

Silvayn and Adalyn had been placed in charge of the mages defending the city. Silvayn stood among one such group atop the city walls, where they could try to counter any magic by the Necromancers. The Necromancers had been strangely silent thus far, and Hadwyn was not certain why they were waiting. But the evil wizards were Silvayn's concern, and Hadwyn was content to allow the Elf to deal with them.

"Hadwyn!" It was Cassius, shouting down from his perch above the gates. "Battering rams, being brought up the road to the front gates. We need the oil!"

Hadwyn waved in response and called a runner to his side. He gave a few hurried instructions, and the fleet-footed Elf was off, sprinting the few short blocks to the house where the oil was stored. Minutes later, when Hadwyn could hear the rumbling approach of the battering rams, several Human soldiers appeared upon the wall, rolling wheeled containers closer to the gates. Hadwyn could stand the wait no longer, so he climbed the steep ladder and gained the top of the wall. The rams were rolling along in single file, with about fifty yards between them, and the nearest was already within bowshot. The archers opened fire, but the Kobolds manning the rams were protected by metal plates protruding from its sides.

Silvayn shouted something to his mages, but his words were lost in the wind, and Hadwyn wasn't sure what to expect. Three of the mages stepped to the catwalk over the gates and chanted their incantations. A rain of energy bolts shot from their outstretched hands, aimed not at the battering rams, but at the roadway in front of them. Dozens of paving stones erupted with explosive detonations, leaving gaping holes in what had once been a smooth avenue. The pace of the rams slowed considerably when the wheels dropped into the breaks in the pavement.

Despite the efforts of the defenders, the first ram reached the gates, striking the barrier with a thunderous crash that echoed off the nearby buildings. At a signal from Rilen, cauldrons of boiling oil were dumped over the side, splattering across the ram and scalding the Kobolds manning it. Screams of agony filled the morning, and the Kobolds fell writhing to the ground, in the open, where the archers made short work of them. The second ram rumbled closer, striking the gates with a resounding rumble. More oil poured from the battlements, with the same results.

The third and fourth ram came in simultaneously, spreading out on opposite sides of the road. Rilen ordered the oil dropped before the Kobolds reached the gates. Hadwyn knew what that meant. Just as he expected, once the Kobolds reached the oil-slicked stones, the archers on the wall fired a barrage of flaming arrows, and the four rams were all consumed in the sudden conflagration. The screams of the dying revealed the savagery of the inferno, which was concealed by the thick pall of black smoke.

A runner charged along the wall to speak breathlessly to Rilen. The Elf nodded several times in acknowledgment, then sent the runner on his way. He motioned for Hadwyn.

"Undead forces have launched an attack on the damaged section of the wall. Adalyn has a detachment of mages, and they are doing what they can to stop them. We've got archers and some infantry there to repel them, but they could use some leadership. I need to stay here, and I'd like you with me. Where's your brother?"

Hadwyn shifted his hammer to his other hand. "He's down below with our reserves. I'll tell him to leave them where they are and grab a few hundred men from the reactionary force."

✤ ✪ ★ ✤ ✤

Adalyn sent a cone of flames lancing into the undead below her, and dozens of the shambling forms fell burning to the ground. Beside her, a dozen other mages worked to weaken the foe deployed before them. To her other side, a hundred archers fired their arrows, but for the most part they were ineffective. The skeletons were almost impossible to hit, and the thralls seemed to shrug them off. Below, Gillen waited for the fight they all knew was coming. The undead slowly climbed the pile of rubble from the wall that had once again fractured under a relentless pounding from the Necromancers' catapults.

At last, they could back the storm no longer, and several hundred skeletons led the way into the breach. Gillen stood firmly at the center of his lines, calling out to his men to stand and fight. From where she stood, Adalyn could see the fear in Gillen's soldiers' eyes. They turned to each other, almost seeking reassurance, and more than one of them took an unsteady step backward. Gillen must have noticed, because he stepped forward to meet the rush alone.

His axe was a blur as it cut the first two skeletons in half, sending piles of bones flying. Several Dwarves near him seemed to take heart from their leader's bravery, and they, too, joined the fray. A rallying cry went up, and the whole of the Dwarven line charged forward, encircling the raiders and blocking their progress. Adalyn and the other mages continued their work, carefully choosing targets well away from their Dwarf allies to prevent any risk of accidentally hurting one of their own. The skeletons were slowly pushed back through the breach.

Adalyn was panting with exhaustion, her head spinning in lazy circles, so she took a few moments to catch her breath. It had been long since she had used so much magic. She checked on the other mages and found only two were still actively casting, the others collapsed in various states of fatigue.

She stood straight once more, regaining her composure, and looked over the battlefield to check their situation. The skeletons had been pushed back to the edge of the wall, and the Dwarves were steadily chopping away at their numbers. It appeared that in a few short minutes, the city would be secured once more. Then she peered out over the wall, and she thought her heart would stop when she saw what lay beyond.

"Gillen!" she shouted over the din. "There are at least a thousand thralls approaching the breach!"

Chapter 21

The hallways of the prison were a uniformly depressing color of gray, hard stone set firmly in place by an equally gray mortar. The floors were made of dirt, and little clouds of dust arose beneath Elac's feet where he walked. He shrugged his shoulders to settle his new set of chain mail into place, relieving a bit of the pinching pressure behind his neck. His shield, strapped lightly to his back, weighted him down even more, and his muscles ached as much from the beatings he had endured as from the armor and weapons he carried. He was following the instructions the guard had given him, and he could only hope the man hadn't lied. Elac gave a heavy sigh of regret, momentarily unable to look any higher than the leather tops of his boots.

He hadn't wanted to kill his prisoner. Rilen would have advised him to, but Elac wasn't the trained killer Rilen was. But when Elac had turned his back on him to find a length of rope, the man had reached for a knife, and Elac had buried his dagger into the guard's heart.

Just as the guard had told him, Elac reached a winding hallway, which was not lit by torches. He closed his eyes in concentration for several long moments, then cast the spell that would bring light to the dark corridor. Although he had cast the spell before, he breathed a sharp sigh of relief when he opened his eyes and saw the glowing orb floating before him.

A short time later, a faint light appeared in the distant hall, and he allowed his magic light to dissipate before he progressed any farther. A single door stood open on his right, and he heard the low murmur of chanting voices inside. He slinked closer to the door, step by step, until he was able to peer inside.

Three men in the black robes of Necromancers stood gathered around a center table. They were focused upon an item lying on the table before them, and they seemed to be performing some type of ritual. Elac stepped boldly through the doorway, his self-doubt and indecision about taking the lives of the fiends no longer troubling him. The first Necromancer looked up before Elac plunged a dagger through his back, piercing his heart. He cried out as he fell, and the other two backed away, their eyes wide with fear. Elac didn't allow himself to think about what he was doing, afraid he might hesitate and put his own life in danger. He careened into another of the black Priests, his sword falling sharply and spilling the man's entrails across the floor. The third drew his knife, holding it before him in a trembling hand. Elac slapped the blade aside contemptuously and roared with rage, his blade thrusting forward a final time. The last Necromancer cried out sharply, and he slid slowly, limply, from Elac's bloodied sword.

His attention was immediately focused on the item on the

table. He stepped closer, his mouth agape in stunned disbelief. His borrowed weapon slipped unnoticed from his fingers, landing on the floor with a loud clatter. His hands reached out tentatively to another Sword, one familiar to his grasp. The Sword of Draygen was his once more.

On a whim, he decided to check the bodies of the fallen Priests for anything useful. The first two had small quantities of gold and silver in an inside pocket of their ebony robes. The third had only a small key. Elac held it up to the light, shrugged, and reached to put it in his pocket when he saw the chest under the table. Caution stayed his hand, and he meticulously examined the chest for traps. Finding none, he inserted the key and turned it, releasing the lock. He lifted the lid, and it creaked slowly open.

Jayrne's cloak and boots lay folded inside, along with her daggers and her short sword. One blade in particular caught his eye, and he laughed out loud, wondering when Jayrne had taken possession of the Dagger of Rennex. He laid the cloak on the floor, placed the other items on it, and rolled them into a ball. Elac used a length of rope to secure the bundle, leaving a small lead at one end for ease of carrying. A final check of the chest revealed the Orion Stone, still secured to the stout line that served as a necklace. He slipped the cord around his neck, leaving the Stone dangling outside his armor, and resumed his search for Jayrne.

Almost immediately, the narrow, plain stone halls turned to wider, well-lit passages. The floors were carpeted, and black silk rugs hung along the walls. An evil, sneering face dominated the artwork on the rugs, and Elac could only assume the face was Volnor's. There was an enduring evil in his countenance, the coldness of the features displaying a total lack of dignity, mercy, or human kindness.

A heavily armored form appeared, a two-handed sword carried easily in one hand. Elac dropped Jayrne's bundle and hefted his shield, then drew Sir Draygen's Sword. A low-pitched, humorless laugh burst forth from the figure, and it stepped closer, throwing back its hood to reveal the face of Morfal. He was dressed in the familiar armor of a Death Knight, and he looked down upon the Elf before him with an undisguised eagerness. Elac lifted the Sword of Draygen to his forehead in the warrior's salute and prepared to do battle.

✤ ⊗ ★ ⊕ ⊛

Elven archers rushed to the defense of the breached wall, and the Dwarves battled valiantly against the shambling figures before them. Dozens of thralls fell along the battle lines, but an occasional Dwarf was pulled screaming to his death. Even while the thralls were destroyed under the murderous streams of crackling energy from Adalyn's force of mages, more undead poured into the city to fill the gaps. Gillen paused to survey his defensive lines, and he did not like what he saw. The center of the line was holding firm, and the left side also showed no signs of weakening. But the right flank was buckling, and the Dwarves on that end were giving ground. He raised his arms, waving wildly to a commander posted on a nearby building.

The right flank crumpled further, and several of the undead broke through. Gillen left his position in the center and rushed to the aid of his soldiers. He charged headlong into the fray, his enchanted axe swinging wildly, and the undead fell around him. His reckless assault lent courage to the Dwarves around him, and a rallying cry went up. From behind, he heard the booted feet of the reserves, charging into the battle to help reinforce the endangered right flank. At length, the line was rebuilt, and the Dwarves held their ground. Outside the walls of Unity, the hundreds of fallen undead were replaced by a thousand more.

❀ ⦀ ★ ⊕ ⊛

The smoke from the burning oil billowed relentlessly in front of the gates of Unity, and Hadwyn swore under his breath, kicking a bench in frustration. There had been no choice but to burn the oil, since the two encroaching rams would surely have breached the gates. But with the flames still broiling on the roadway, the defenders had difficulty seeing any distance.

The gates gave a sudden jolt, as if struck by a massive hammer. There was a whirlwind of activity on the walls, the archers vainly trying to peer through the smoke to find the source of the new assault. The gates shuddered hard once more, and this time the wood splintered. Rilen ordered his archers into firing positions, and they unleashed a barrage into the thick, black smokescreen. Hadwyn rallied the ranks of Human heavy infantry into their carefully planned formations, putting them into place for the breakthrough that now seemed imminent.

Another crash, and then another, and the gates split asunder. One of the battering rams rolled into the courtyard, and the two wraiths pushing the ram rushed forth to attack the soldiers standing before them. Hadwyn pushed his way through the lines to confront the incorporeal threat. The first wraith lunged at him, and he swung his hammer in response. It passed cleanly through the filmy body, but the wraith lurched back as if in pain.

Rilen leaped from the wall to a supporting pillar, sliding smoothly to the ground. He ripped his sword from its sheath, and the blessing within it coursed to life when he plunged it smoothly into a wraith's unsuspecting back. Its ethereal arms flew wide, and Hadwyn darted in with a mighty blow to the chest. It shrieked insanely, disappearing in a flash of light. The other charged recklessly, trying to catch Hadwyn off guard. He dropped to one knee, swiping behind him with the Hammer of Sir Thalitt. Rilen raced to his aid, his blessed sword biting into the wraith once, twice. The third blow sent the wraith the way of the first.

One of the archers yelled frantically, waving his arms. "Kobolds! Three brigades of Kobolds are approaching! Undead are on their flanks!"

Hadwyn slowly regained his feet. "Go ahead, Rilen. I'll hold things down here."

While the Elf regained his perch upon the wall, Hadwyn reorganized his forces. The Humans had backed away at the approach of the wraiths, and he hurriedly reformed the lines. The fires had burned out, and through the gaps in the smoke he could see the approaching enemy.

Morfal strode confidently forward, and his great sword whistled through the air, aiming for Elac's head. He raised his Sword to block, and the two blades came together in a shower of sparks. Elac was knocked to the ground, and he rolled across the carpet to strike the wall painfully, his Sword bouncing away. He smoothly came to his feet, shaking his head to clear it. Morfal hissed, starting forward once more. Elac feinted left, in the direction of his Sword, then slipped to the right. Morfal swung his sword once more, and Elac dove to avoid the deadly stroke. He crawled on all fours as quickly as he could, and reclaimed his Sword. From some corner of his mind, he seemed to hear Jayrne's words: *Don't fight strength with strength.*

He raised his Sword once more. Morfal gave a short thrust, and Elac danced away. Before the Death Knight could recover from the attack, Elac slashed the Sword of Draygen across the armored forearm of his foe. The supernatural power of the Sword bit through the armor, and Morfal howled with rage.

Another swipe of Morfal's sword swished dangerously close to Elac's chest. His retaliatory blow struck his opponent's wrist, and again the magic flared in Draygen's Sword. Elac cast his shield aside, and it clattered hollowly against the wall. He knew the shield would not deflect a powerful blow from the foul creature, and its weight was slowing him down.

Morfal's next strike caught the side of Elac's chain mail, sending the air whooshing from his lungs and knocking him staggering against the wall. He slid helplessly to the floor, unable to draw a breath. He fell forward to his hands and knees, wheezing and coughing. He heard the booted feet of the Death

Knight approaching.

"Now," Morfal said in a voice ringing with malicious power, "you will die."

Elac lunged forward, thrusting Draygen's Sword upward with all his remaining strength. The blade passed smoothly through the armored chest, as if the layer of steel wasn't even there. Morfal's sword clattered to the ground, and his hands wrapped around the impaling weapon. No blood rushed forth, but instead a broiling black mist billowed upward. Morfal crashed to his knees, a look of undying hatred in his eyes. His lip curled in a snarl, he reached out to Elac, but the Elf slapped his hands aside and pulled the blade free.

"You will not escape. Your death is inevitable."

Elac's answer was a wide swing of Sir Draygen's Sword, sending Morfal's head tumbling from the falling body.

❁ ❀ ★ ☯ ✾

Rilen sighted along an arrow, Sir Aleron's Longbow held solidly in his hands. The bowstring snapped, and Hadwyn watched the arrow arc impossibly far across the battlefield to strike a black-robed form. The Necromancer collapsed, his body lost in the swarm of undead around him. The effect on the thralls he had been controlling was immediate. Those closest to the fallen dark Priest turned on him, rending his flesh from his bones. The others turned on the closest living creatures around them: the Kobolds. Hadwyn smiled grimly while the enemy did battle within its own ranks before the gates. It took several minutes to bring another Necromancer forth, and bring the raging undead under control.

But the ranks of the enemy reformed once more, and they rejoined their march on the city. The Kobolds arrived first, and their front ranks lowered their spears with their shields held erect. The front rank of Hadwyn's detachment of Human infantry threw their pilums, the heavy spears ripping into the Kobolds' vanguard. Most of the lead-shafted spears pierced Kobold shields and bent under their own weight, rendering the shields more of a burden than a boon.

Hadwyn shouted a command, and the Humans' front line marched forth to meet the enemy, shields locked tightly together. The assault crumbled, and quickly became a rout. The Kobolds went into a full retreat, some of them casting their weapons aside and running for safety. Hadwyn held his soldiers back, not wanting to pursue a beaten foe only to place his own soldiers in danger. Under his direction, the lines reformed, and new spears were passed to the front. The archers atop the walls continued firing their deadly rain of arrows at the backs of the retreating kobolds.

From somewhere nearby, Hadwyn heard a brassy horn sound its challenging note, followed by the sound of rolling thunder. A body of armored horsemen burst into view, with Prince Cassius at the head. They pounded past Hadwyn's carefully drawn formations, ignoring Rilen's shouted protests. The knights crashed into their retreating foe, decimating their numbers. The screams of the dead and dying filled the air, and Cassius's horsemen rushed about the dwindling Kobolds with reckless abandon, slaughtering them by the dozens.

Hadwyn's heart seemed to drop to his toes when he realized

they had forgotten the undead forces that had been a part of the assault. Slower than the Kobolds, they hadn't reached the city when the fighting started, but suddenly they collapsed on Cassius's fighters from every direction. The evil creatures fell in heaps, the heavy blades of the knights wreaking havoc among their undead foes, but still they came on. In the end, the knights were forced to give ground. The size of Cassius's force dwindled, and he tried to rally them together, massing for a final charge back to the safety of the city walls.

Hadwyn looked hopefully up to Rilen, knowing the answer to his question without even giving it voice. With other undead units closing in, no relief could be sent to aid the Prince; the risk was simply too great. Hadwyn sadly took in the scene before him once more. Cassius gestured with his bloody sword, and the twenty remaining knights spurred their mounts forward.

Half their number went down before they forced an opening in the mob of skeleton warriors arranged before them. Cassius stayed at the trail of the formation, gallantly holding the rear guard for his knights who were trying to escape the deadly trap. Five of the knights broke free and dashed for the gates, flailing madly at their horses. Cassius put his boots to his own steed, trying to reach the gap before it closed. Just when his horse gained the open field, a spear flew from the mob behind him, piercing his shoulder and knocking him from his horse. The thralls were on him in seconds.

Elac hefted his bundle once more and moved deeper into the Temple of Malator. He had briefly entertained the idea of donning Jayrne's cloak and boots, but he turned the thought aside. Their incompatible size notwithstanding, he wasn't even certain the magic in them would work for anyone but her.

He came to an open antechamber. The directions the guard provided had brought him this far, but he was uncertain what to do next. Four doors lined the far walls of the room, and there was no clue as to which one he should take. He crossed the room to the door farthest to his left and put his ear against it. He heard nothing, so he moved to the next. In this manner, he checked all four doors, but he learned nothing of consequence.

His decision was postponed when the first door he had checked swung open, and a red-faced Falstoff stepped through. Both he and Falstoff froze momentarily, shocked at the sudden encounter. Elac recovered his wits first and closed the distance between them.

"You shall go no farther, Elf!" Falstoff raised his arms and gestured, and an incandescent streak of light sizzled across the room—

And disappeared. Elac stood dumbfounded, looking down in front of his chest where the bolt had stopped inches from his body. *The Orion Stone!* Its ability to absorb magic, all magic, within a certain distance, had saved him. He wondered why Sir Draygen's Sword still contained its magic, even while he was wearing the Stone, but he had no time for such ruminations.

Elac ran right at the new Necromancer, and another bolt sizzled forth, this time aimed not at Elac, but rather at the roof above him. The ceiling erupted in a dazzling explosion, and great chunks of stone cascaded through the air. He raised his shield over his head, holding firm while the ceiling pounded down upon him. When the dust cleared, he leapt over the debris pile and found himself face-to-face with Falstoff.

Without time to prepare another spell, Falstoff pulled a ceremonial dagger from his belt. Elac swung his Sword sharply downward, severing the Necromancer's hand at the wrist. The dagger skittered away, and Elac placed the edge of his blade against Falstoff's throat.

"Where is she?" he demanded, his face mere inches from Falstoff's.

"The thief?" Falstoff actually laughed. "There's a war going on, Volnor is about to hand this world to Malator, and you are worried about a girl? She will be sacrificed to Malator, in the presence of the Temira, and in so doing Volnor will open the gates of the Land of the Dead. Our armies will march across the world, and all will be in our power!"

Elac cut him off, pressing the sword against his throat so firmly, a trickle of blood ran down Falstoff's neck. "Spare me your political innuendos. If you value your life, you'll tell me where she is."

"You're threatening only my life. Malator holds my soul."

Elac almost reached for the rope binding Jayrne's possessions together, thinking to tie the foul Necromancer's arms, but he passed that idea up immediately. *Never leave a live enemy behind you.* Rilen's words echoed in his ears, and he knew what he had to do. The man was responsible for the abductions of dozens of people from Unity, including Jayrne and Elac. He had handed the most powerful magic item in the West over to Volnor, and in so doing had virtually guaranteed the fall of Unity and the rest of the Western lands.

Elac leaned closer to his captive. "I'll see you in hell." He pulled his Sword sharply across the Necromancer's throat.

❁ ❁ ★ ❁ ❁

Gillen fought like a man possessed, every swing of his axe sending another undead creature spinning to the ground. All around him, the forces of the Dwarven army battled heroically against impossible odds, refusing to give ground. The archers had expended their supply of arrows, and had resorted to throwing chunks of the stone walls into the horde below them. It had been an hour since Gillen had called for the remainder of the Dwarves held in reserve, and yet he was no closer to repulsing the enemy from inside the city walls.

A sharp cry of warning went up from his left, and he chanced a look to the source. A group of wraiths had worked their way to the front of the mass, and his Dwarves were being decimated. Not many of them had blessed weapons, and without such help they had no way to harm the incorporeal enemy. Gillen broke free from the fighting and rushed to their aid.

He took the wraiths from behind, and two of them were down before they even knew he was there. A skeleton struck him from behind, and while his armor deflected the worst of the blow, he was still knocked to his knees. A sergeant shouted his rally cry, and brought several Dwarves to Gillen's aid. While he staggered back to his feet, the group of Dwarves launched themselves into the press of undead menacing Gillen. He gave a fleeting look to ensure the skeleton warriors were engaged, but it was all he could spare. The remaining wraiths came at him, and his axe came up in defense. His weapon was a blur, swinging in short arcs, keeping the wraiths at bay. One ventured too close, and he lashed out, catching the spectral figure with a solid blow to the waist and dispersing it in a flash of light.

Four more Dwarves rushed to his aid, the red armbands indicating they possessed blessed weapons. They encircled the three wraiths, keeping them from reaching the more vulnerable Dwarves around them. One by one, the wraiths were destroyed.

But the damage had been done. While the Dwarven forces on the left flank had shifted around the seething wraiths, a company of Kobolds had made their way in through the breach and gained the top of the walls of the city. The archers fled, routed by an enemy they had no way to fight. Gillen immediately saw the situation was hopeless. He signaled for the Dwarves to try to fall back to their first rally point. It was a tricky maneuver. They couldn't simply turn and run, or they would all be cut down from behind.

The horn of the Human cavalry sounded, and it was followed by the awesome charge of the armored knights. They had been held in reserve all morning for this eventuality, and the time had come. Their lances lowered and their visors down, they charged into the convenient openings in the Dwarven lines to crash into the undead with overwhelming power. The Dwarves pulled back, regrouping a short distance away and moving off at a brisk trot. The cavalry turned, galloped away, then pressed in once more for another charge. The effect on their enemy was devastating. The Kobolds who hadn't gained the top of the wall fled in a panic, and the skeletons and thralls milled about uncertainly while their Necromancers wondered what to do next.

Gillen's Dwarves gained the next defensive perimeter, a redoubt made by pulling down several houses and piling the debris across the street. A fresh supply of weapons waited for them, as well as several Priests who helped with the wounded and blessed as many weapons as they could. As planned, an archer fired a flaming arrow high into the air, angling it in the direction of the gates. He could only hope his brother or Rilen had seen the signal, and would realize the Dwarves had been pushed back.

✿ ⊗ ★ ⊕ ⊗

Hadwyn smashed his hammer to the ground, sending a shower of stone fragments flying in all directions. They needed those cavalry soldiers, and Cassius had just lost an entire company. It had cost him his life in the process, but what it might cost the defenders remained to be seen. Another formation of Kobolds was on the move, over a thousand strong, and they were approaching the city gates. Above him, on the city walls, shouts echoed back and forth, the archers calling for more arrows, and spotters bellowing their observations to those below.

With an earsplitting roar, the Kobolds charged the shattered gates, heedless of the hailstorm of arrows tearing into their ranks. Dozens fell, bleeding from arrow wounds and trampled beneath the feet of their comrades, but still they came on. The front ranks of the defenders threw their spears, with the same deadly results as before, but the Kobolds didn't falter. The two lines came together with a resounding crash, and the battle was joined once more. The tactics of Hadwyn's infantry seemed to baffle the Kobolds, who were all but unable to get past the Human shield wall. The infantry's short swords, however, had no such trouble, and the street was soon slippery with Kobold blood.

But where brute strength failed the Kobolds, the domination of their superior numbers eventually overwhelmed the defenders. Small breaches appeared in the lines, and squads of reserve soldiers dashed in to fill the gaps and eliminate those Kobolds who broke through. Hadwyn saw his number of reserves dwindling rapidly, and he knew the gates were lost.

He sprinted to the rear of the formation and waved a red flag, notifying those on the wall about his decision. As he did so, a flaming arrow arced across the sky, and Hadwyn momentarily despaired. The defense at the breach in the city wall had also been unsuccessful, and they had been forced to retreat, as well. He moved back to the battle line to assist his men in disengaging from the enemy, hearing the cavalry charge behind him, the mounted unit rushing to his detachment's rescue.

✤ ⊗ ★ ⊕ ⊛

The farther Elac penetrated into the Temple of Malator, the warmer the foul-smelling air became. With nothing else to guide him, he had chosen the passage Falstoff had just left, hoping the traitorous Necromancer had come from where Jayrne was being held. He gripped the Sword of Draygen tightly in his hands, his knuckles white with the pressure.

Another heavy wooden door loomed before him, this one partially ajar. He set his lips firmly and pushed, a gentle pressure that moved the door almost imperceptibly. He pushed a little harder, and the door creaked in protest. He froze, holding his breath and waiting for sounds indicating he had been heard. When no one approached, and there were no outcries of discovery, he pushed against the door yet again.

An immense hall stretched away before him, disappearing into the darkness beyond the light of several torches planted in what appeared to be the center of the room. The ceiling was covered with beaten gold, much of it molded into friezes of hideous creatures and dark rituals involving human sacrifice. Five bloodstained altars dominated the room, each set at one of the points of a pentagram inscribed in the floor. The floor itself was covered by onyx tiles, and the lines of the pentagram were made of some type of white crystal. Indecipherable runes were carved into the extremes of the pentagram, and Elac assumed they were used for the unspeakable rites performed in this chamber.

A door on the left side of the room opened, and three Necromancers dragged a violently struggling Jayrne into the room. She was forcibly laid across an altar, on her back, and her hands and feet were secured by chains. Elac rapidly surveyed the room, looking for guards who might prevent a rescue attempt. To Elac's dismay, one of the Priests removed a curved dagger from his belt and cut Jayrne's robe away, leaving only a brief loincloth behind. The other two Necromancers worked on painting symbols upon her chest and face.

Elac slipped into the room and hid behind a low wall. He crawled along the length of the concealing partition until he judged he was as close as he could get. Slipping from his hiding place as silent as smoke, he found himself thirty feet from his prey. With a mighty heave, the Elf threw Jayrne's bundle far to his right, where it landed with a crash. The Necromancers' attention was immediately drawn away from their work, and before they realized their mistake, one of them was falling to the floor, his head severed by Elac's blade. His Sword was red with blood when the second man fell away, ripped open from his throat to his hip, his screams of agony lost in the flow of blood filling his lungs. The final Priest threw down his dagger and turned to run, but Elac plunged his Sword into the black-clad back. He twisted the handle while the stricken man grabbed the blade, its razor-sharp edges cutting into his hands. The Necromancer exhaled his dying breath, sliding off the end of the impaling weapon.

Elac hurried back to Jayrne's side, hugging her tightly, sobs racking their bodies. He pulled away with a sense of regret, his senses returning to him and reminding him of the danger they still faced. He brushed the dark locks of hair away from her face.

"I suppose you'll want your cloak back?"

She managed a weak laugh while he retrieved her bundle, untied the rope, and covered her with her cloak. Reaching into his boot, he pulled out his lockpick set and set about unlocking the chains holding her hands. He surprised himself with how quickly he managed to defeat the lock.

"You're a good student," Jayrne told him in a voice husky

with dehydration. Elac moved to the chains on her feet, but he hadn't even begun to work on the lock when the door opened once more. A tall, cadaverous Human entered, and by the malevolent evil emanating from the glowing red eyes, he knew it to be Volnor. The black robes were emblazoned with numerous runes, and the Temira hung about his neck by a golden chain. A black broadsword hung from his waist, and his head was covered by a black-enameled helmet, bat-like wings protruding from its sides. Elac knew there was nowhere to run, so he handed the lockpick to Jayrne and drew forth his sword once more.

❀ ◈ ★ 🏵 ❁

Gillen swung his axe left and right, battling for his life, the press of undead and Kobolds growing tighter. His secondary defensive position had been overrun more quickly than he had expected, and he had no reserves left to commit. The cavalry stood ready, but he was reluctant to send them into the battle. Their greatest strength was the impact of their fearsome charge, and if Gillen was to commit them to filling holes in his lines, the advantage would be lost. Besides, he needed the cavalry charge to help his troops fall back to their final defensive lines.

To his right, an entire section of his lines was crumbling, and several thralls broke through. Gillen grabbed the Dwarves to his immediate left and right and led them to the breach. They hit the unsuspecting undead from behind, slaughtering them where they stood. A shout of victory went up, and the Dwarf axemen rallied. The lines solidified, and in several places Gillen's forces completely cleared their makeshift barrier of enemy forces.

But once again, the size of the enemy's army proved to be the deciding factor. The Dwarves simply couldn't kill them fast enough, and within minutes, the line was crumbling once more. Gillen called for the retreat, pulling his soldiers back one squad at a time. The cavalry made their irresistible charge, and the bodies of the enemy were trampled under the thundering hooves. Most of the Kobolds retreated over the barrier, but the undead, immune to fear, mindlessly came on. The cavalry charged back and forth, occupying the thralls and skeletons while the Dwarves retreated to safety.

❁ ❀ ★ ❦ ❂

Rilen and Hadwyn stood side-by-side, battling the Kobolds who threatened to overrun them. Rilen fought like a man possessed, and Hadwyn noticed the Kobolds tended to avoid him, allowing the undead forces to fall under his blade. Hadwyn was only slightly less deadly, his nearly weightless hammer shattering the skulls of Kobolds and thralls with equal ease. The carefully drawn defensive lines had been abandoned, with the Kobolds using their numerical superiority to force breaches in the line. The whole battle was reduced to brutal street fighting.

Archers placed on nearby rooftops fired into the crowd, carefully selecting their shots to avoid hitting friendly targets. At Rilen's instruction, three archers weren't firing randomly, but were instead scanning the mob for signs of the Necromancers who controlled the undead pressing against them. The enemy didn't seem to think about concealing or disguising their valuable, black-robed assets, for which Hadwyn was grateful.

Hadwyn saw the number of enemy soldiers who had pierced their lines grow steadily larger. Rilen seemed to notice also, and he shouted orders between sword strokes, repositioning his troops in an effort to pull them together. They fought desperately, and while whole squads of the enemy were decimated, the number of Human casualties climbed at an alarming rate.

With a shout of triumph, a company of Kobolds forced their way through the lines, and Hadwyn and Rilen's forces found themselves surrounded. The whole detachment was on the verge of being annihilated.

Hadwyn heard a shout from above, somehow piercing the din of the battle. "Necromancer!" He risked a look to the rooftop behind him, and he saw a lone archer, an arrow drawn to his cheek. Just as he released the bowstring, a dagger thrown from below pierced his neck, and he tumbled from the roof. The arrow raced across the battlefield to strike true.

The enemy attack faltered, and the undead turned once more to rend their former allies. Rilen recognized their chance, and he signaled for the cavalry charge. The armored horsemen crashed into the Kobolds threatening the defenders from behind, slaughtering them to the last man. With their foes distracted, Hadwyn called for the retreat. They slipped away, the dispirited group falling back to their makeshift military headquarters, where they would join with the remnants of Gillen's force for a last stand.

Volnor drew his sword from its sheath, the metal sliding free with a steely hiss. The entire length of the blade was painted the color of midnight, and one edge was covered with cruel hook points. His face twisted into a sneer, and his eyes bored into the Elf striding toward him. His voice seemed distorted, a strange double-echo superimposed over his hissing monotone.

"You have defiled the Temple of Malator. You have slain my servants. You shall pay the ultimate price for your crimes. Your death will make men tremble for a thousand years!"

Volnor gestured sharply, and a bolt of black fire erupted from his fingers. Despite the magnitude of the force inherent in the blast, the Orion Stone absorbed the spell. Volnor roared with fury, his eyes focusing on the talisman at Elac's throat. He changed tactics, pointing a skeletal finger at a stone bench off to one side. With a contemptuous flick of his wrist, he sent the bench flying at Elac. The Elf rolled away, the stone projectile narrowly missing its target. He regained his feet, but had to throw himself to the floor once more to avoid a wooden table that tumbled past.

Elac's luck ran out, and another stone projectile struck him a glancing blow to the temple. He staggered to his knees, his shield arm lowering and his sword point dropping to the ground to catch his balance. Blood flowed from his head once more, and the room seemed to spin chaotically around him. From somewhere behind him, he heard Jayrne's scream, and he looked up to see the dark form of Volnor approaching, sword swinging eagerly in low, tight arcs.

❀ ❁ ★ ❋ ❅

An eerie silence filled the air, and the defenders eyed the empty streets nervously. Both detachments of soldiers, those under Gillen's command and those with Rilen, had retreated to their headquarters, where they would make their final stand. The rest of the city stood behind them, safe for the moment behind hastily constructed barricades, but if the army retreated farther, the civilians would be in danger. They would stand where they were, and they would win or die. An occasional scream filled the air, evidence that another of the city's residents who had tried to hide had been discovered by the marauding enemy. One Kobold dragged his intended victim by her hair into full view of the defenders, planning to victimize her right in front of them. A well-placed bowshot from Rilen's unerringly accurate enchanted Longbow had transfixed the leering Kobold's skull, and the victim escaped.

The calm was broken by the uneven tramp and shuffle of booted feet, and the outer barricade shuddered under a massive blow. It collapsed into a pile of rubble, and shadowy figures emerged from the cloud of dust. Hadwyn stared in horror at the threat before them, realizing what their enemy had done. The fallen Dwarves, Elves, and Humans had been reanimated as thralls, and they shambled forward to attack. Silvayn and Adalyn were the first to recover their wits, and they sent lances of fire into the ranks of the former soldiers.

In the center of the press of undead came a familiar figure. Hadwyn silently mouthed a protest as Cassius's body staggered toward them, sword in hand. He raised his hammer, uncertain if he could bring himself to fight the disheveled figure before him. He was spared that ultimate decision when another bolt of fire from Silvayn's mages tore into the former Prince, knocking him from his feet and leaving a gaping hole in his chest.

The Kobolds charged howling into view, scampering over the fallen barricade and rushing into the battle. They crashed into the ranks of the defenders, heedless of the number of their own who were slain. Hundreds fell in the first few minutes of the melee, but they kept coming. After several minutes of intense fighting, the Kobolds pulled back to regroup, giving Hadwyn and the others a brief respite. He was breathing hard, and rivulets of sweat ran in tiny rivers through the grime and blood caking his face.

He wondered what their chances were, afraid to voice the question for fear of receiving an answer. Rilen stood motionless at his side, and Hadwyn looked to see if the veteran Elf was alright. What he saw in Rilen's eyes told him everything he didn't want to know about the likely outcome of the battle. Rilen extended his hand.

"Hadwyn, whatever happens here, I want you to know it's been a great honor to fight at your side."

Hadwyn shook his calloused hand with a firm grip, his lips pressed together solemnly. "You, too, Rilen." He faced once more the road where the charge would come. "Bring them on."

Moments later, Hadwyn got his wish.

Chapter 22

Blac somehow managed to roll aside, and Volnor's dark blade crashed to the floor, shattering several tiles and sending shards of marble flying in all directions. Regaining his feet, Elac faced his opponent once more. He expected more of the same strategy from Volnor, but his hurried glimpse around the room showed no incoming projectiles. He took a few steps closer to the evil figure before him, his Sword held firmly in front of him. Volnor stood unmoving, and Elac knew the Necromancer's next plan was probably already in motion.

A shuffling sound came from the area of the altars. Volnor had reanimated the three men whom Elac had slain only moments before. They shambled in his direction, weapons ready. They seemed faster than most thralls he had seen before, and even the one with the severed head was on the move. They spread out to come at Elac from different directions.

Once again, Rilen's lessons came to mind. *Don't let your foes surround you, and never let them move on your flank.* Elac didn't wait for the three undead Priests to make the first move; instead he charged the nearest, Sir Draygen's Sword weaving lightly. He slapped the creature's dagger aside and brought his Sword down sharply, severing the extended arm. The power of the Sword flared to life, and the thrall fell to the floor. Elac whirled and raised his shield, just in time to deflect a dagger thrust from the next thrall Priest. A thrust of his own drove his blade into the Necromancer's chest. Elac kicked the limp body from his Sword and turned on the last Priest. He ran at the black-clad figure, howling, and battered him back with his shield before he slashed the Priest down his right side, ending the fight.

His chest heaving, he faced Volnor once more. Elac took advantage of the lull to think the situation through. Why hadn't Volnor, possibly the most powerful figure to ever walk the earth, simply destroyed him already? The answer was his fortune in finding the Orion Stone. Why hadn't Volnor destroyed him? Because Volnor feared him! He feared the power of Draygen's enchanted blade, and what the weapon could do in the presence of the Temira.

With an inexorable, steady pace, Elac closed the distance between him and Volnor. When they were a mere ten feet apart, he stopped and began to speak.

"Volnor, you are a coward. Your magic has failed you, so you resort to having others do your work for you. You fear facing me in single combat. I hereby declare you to be a craven, impotent weakling." He spat at the ancient Necromancer's feet.

Volnor's pale, cadaverous face flushed red with anger, and he roared with a rage that shook the entire chamber. The flames of the torches flickered in response, and trailers of dust fell from the ceiling. As Elac had hoped, his taunting had unhinged the dark ruler's control.

Volnor raised his sword and stormed forward. Elac took a defensive stance and dropped into a crouch, prepared to meet the attack. Volnor's sword swung sharply down, and Elac blocked it with his shield, giving a bit of ground to absorb the blow. Despite his caution, the attack cut through his shield and bit deeply into his shield arm, causing Elac to cry out in pain. He shook his shield loose and stepped back, cradling his injured arm.

The next stroke from Volnor was a thrust, but Elac was able to turn it aside with Sir Draygen's Sword. His arm throbbed, and he was losing blood rapidly. Already, he felt weaker, and he knew if he didn't win this fight soon, his life would be forfeit. Desperately, he launched a series of retaliatory blows, forcing Volnor back step-by-step, but none of them struck home. He launched a final swing at Volnor's head, but the Necromancer turned the blow aside, catching Elac's sword arm. With a foul grin, Volnor swung his own blade once more. Elac tried to dodge the attack, but the tip of the blade caught him on his left shoulder. The sword bit through his chain mail to rip into his flesh. He tore loose from Volnor, but fell to the ground, unable to rise. His Sword clattered on the marble tiles beside him, and he reached out weakly to take the weapon back into his grip. Laughing softly, Volnor moved inexorably closer.

The remaining companions who had made the journey with Elac gathered together in a tight knot. Gillen and Hadwyn fought back-to-back on one side, their lightweight, enchanted weapons wreaking havoc among the enemy. Adalyn had quit casting spells, and she fought alongside Rilen. Silvayn stood high upon a nearby building, watching for signs of the Necromancers who were keeping the undead under control. Every dark Priest he located became the target of a sizzling bolt of lightning, and each time the surrounding thralls and skeletons would suddenly go berserk, attacking friend and foe alike.

The carefully drawn defensive lines had long since disintegrated, and the chaotic battle raged all across the open courtyards around the headquarters facility. Dwarves and Humans mingled with Elves and Kobolds, and the undead were everywhere. After mounting their devastating charge, the cavalry found itself awash in the sea of enemy soldiers, and they, too, were forced to fight in the center of a maelstrom of violence.

There was a stirring at the rear of the building, and Silvayn's voice shouted down to those below. "The Human army is here! Hang on! Help is on the way!"

Hadwyn's arms, which only moments before had felt leaden, were suddenly rejuvenated. He laughed out loud, his hammer slamming into foe after foe, dispatching undead and Kobold alike. His brother was no less deadly, and the Kobolds had to give way before them.

A hearty war cry went up, and the light infantry of the Human army poured from gaps between the surrounding buildings. The battle, which had seemed a certain defeat for the defenders, turned like an ocean tide. The defensive lines slowly, agonizingly, reformed, and the enemy was pushed back. The ground in front of the defenders was littered with the fallen of both sides, and they had to step over countless bodies to carry the battle to their foes. Hadwyn's jubilation soared at Silvayn's next announcement: a force of combined Elves and Dwarves was within an hour of reaching the city. Perhaps the battle could be won, yet!

❀ ❀ ★ ❀ ❀

"You pathetic worm!" Volnor held his sword in both hands, tip downward, hovering over Elac's throbbing chest. "You impertinent fool! You shall pay for your transgressions with a hundred deaths. Nay, a thousand, each worse than the one before! You—aarrgh!"

Volnor whirled about, the Dagger of Rennex protruding from his back. The weapon couldn't possibly kill the undead Necromancer, but it certainly caused him considerable pain. With the back of his hand, he delivered a crushing swipe to Jayrne, who had just sneaked up behind him to deliver an assassin's blow.

Elac seized Sir Draygen's mighty Sword and thrust it with all his strength, burying the blade up to its hilt in Volnor's exposed back. The ancient Necromancer gave a howl of anguish such as Elac had never heard. The ceiling cracked and popped, and several large pieces of stone came crashing to the ground. The Sword of Draygen pulsed with a white light, which spread out to encompass the whole of Volnor's being. The Temira burned bright red, the emanating glow almost as bright as the sun. Volnor raised his arms above his head, his fingers crooked into tortured claws.

Elac retrieved his shield and staggered over to where Jayrne lay on the floor, her eyes unfocused. He covered the two of them with his shield as best he could, protecting them from the larger fragments dropping from the ceiling.

Volnor's trembling hands slid down to the Sword protruding from his chest, trying vainly to force the blade from his body. Abruptly, a mysterious wind sprang up in the chamber, whirling around Volnor's stricken form faster and faster. The vortex picked up dust and debris, forming a brown haze of racing flotsam around him. The roof exploded, exposing the chamber to the late afternoon sun. Volnor himself was caught in the gyre, and his body joined the debris in the spinning vortex. His form seemed to blur, and with a final cry of protest, Volnor, the leader of the Necromancers, vanished in a blinding flash of light. The Temira and the Sword of Draygen crashed hollowly to the floor, and all was still.

✿ ✪ ★ ✤ ✾

Hadwyn felt his jubilation fade as another wave of undead entered his field of view. Even with the added numbers from the Human infantry, it would be no easy battle. He and Gillen both gave pause to catch their breath, and Hadwyn wondered what difference the arrival of the Elf and Dwarf forces could make, and if they would even arrive in time.

The sky overhead, which moments before had been sunny, became unnaturally dark. Great racing clouds appeared out of nowhere, and a frigid wind sprang up. The undead stopped their assault and stood motionless. One by one, then in greater numbers, the thralls and skeletons simply collapsed, weapons dropping with a clatter at their sides. Living warriors on both sides stood in blinking incomprehension as tens of thousands of undead warriors ceased to exist.

There was a momentary lull, when fighters from both sides stood in shock, trying to understand what had happened. Then the Kobolds slowly backed away, a sluggish retreat that soon became a rout. The defenders pursued them to the city gates, but Hadwyn and his friends reined their soldiers in, not wishing to take any chances. The Kobolds retreated east, heading in the direction of Nightwood Forest.

The companions gathered over dinner that evening. Silvayn explained to them that the only explanation for the day's events was the death of Volnor, and there was only one way such an event could have come about: somehow, Elac had escaped his captors, made his way to Malaton, and destroyed Malator's most powerful servant. Hadwyn was surprised at the emotional output from Rilen, who hugged Adalyn passionately at the news, tears of joy streaming openly down his face. The celebration lasted well into the evening.

Hadwyn slept better than he had expected he would, and he awoke refreshed. The army assembled after breakfast, and set forth on a mission to exterminate the Kobolds. Spirits were high, and they marched with a newfound energy. The Human cavalry took the vanguard position, followed closely by Human light and heavy infantry. Immediately behind them came rank upon rank of Elven archers, flanked on each side by endless numbers of Dwarf axemen. Silvayn and his force of mages rode at the rear of the formation, along with Hadwyn and the other remaining companions.

They marched all day, setting up camp in the cover of Nightwood Forest near the great tract's eastern borders. By daybreak, when they emerged from the trees, tendrils of smoke from the remains of Fort Nightwood were visible ahead of them and slightly to their left. Within the hour, the remaining Kobolds came into view. They were formed up as a mob, any sense of military discipline long since lost. The army of the West was gaining on them, and Hadwyn harbored a hope of catching them before they reached the concealing passes of the Paheny Mountains.

Rilen straightened in his saddle. "Silvayn, what is that ahead of the Kobolds? There's something coming out of the passes leading down to the plains."

Hadwyn strained his eyes, trying to determine what they were seeing. "It looks like another army."

"By the grace of Zantar!" Gillen exclaimed, nearly pulling his beard out. "There must be thirty or forty legions! If those are Kobolds, we're finished!"

Silvayn sat with his eyes closed, chanting softly. His shoulders drooped wearily, but he grinned with unrestrained enthusiasm.

"Those are our soldiers out there. Or at least, they were ours, about fourteen hundred years ago. Those men were taken from this land during the Banishment! The death of Volnor seems to have released the spell holding them in the Plane of Mist."

Hadwyn looked back and forth between the old mage and the approaching army. While the soldiers from Unity continued their pursuit of the fleeing Kobolds, the army from Tracker's Peak spilled out onto the plains. The Kobolds milled about uncertainly, not comprehending who was in front of them. Their indecision was removed for them moments later by the charge of tens of thousands of soldiers, their war cries audible even from Hadwyn's position over a mile away. The warriors from Tracker's Peak had vastly inferior weapons and armor, but their insurmountable advantage in numbers more than made up the difference. The Kobolds tried to fall back, but they were caught from behind by the pursuing army. Within a few hours, the entire Kobold army had been annihilated.

✦ ✦ ★ ✦ ✦

Jayrne used cloth torn from the robes of the slain Necromancers' robes to bind Elac's wounds. The gash in his arm, in particular, had bled profusely, and left him in a dizzy, weakened state. His body ached from the severe beating he had taken over the past day or so, but he knew they needed to leave immediately. Powerful tremors rocked the Temple, and it seemed ready to collapse at any moment. He climbed wearily to his feet, leaning heavily on Jayrne for support. They passed through the wide, double doors at the far end of the room, and into an antechamber. The ceiling was supported by pillars, but the supporting columns had stress lines running through them, and two of them had crumbled to the ground, taking parts of the ceiling with them. A Necromancer was lying on the floor in a fetal position, moaning softly.

Jayrne grabbed him roughly by the shoulder, pulling him around to face them. "What is the quickest way out of the city?"

He stared blankly back at them, not seeming to comprehend that they didn't belong there. "Malator's wrath is upon us!

Why? What have we done?"

Elac was thinking quickly. "We must get Volnor to safety, but we're not sure of the way out. You have to help us!"

"Yes, of course." The Necromancer grabbed his stomach, writhing in momentary agony, then turned haunted eyes back to the pair standing over him. "The tunnel. Take the tunnel back to the mountains."

"Where do we find the tunnel?" Jayrne asked, frowning.

He pointed to a staircase in the corner of the pillared room. "Those stairs will lead you to the cellar. There should still be horses and supplies down there. Follow the north hallway."

"Thanks," Jayrne replied, and she delivered a blow with her knee to the Necromancer's chin, knocking him back to the floor, unconscious.

She pulled Elac's good arm about her shoulders once more, and together they limped down the stairs. Several horses were tied up to a long, wooden beam. The floor was covered with straw, and the room smelled of raw sewage. Leather skins of water hung from the walls, but there was no food to be found. While Elac leaned against the wall for support, Jayrne hurriedly saddled two horses.

"Who are you?" A large man in a leather smock and an eye patch entered the room, and in his weakened condition, Elac hadn't even noticed. Worse, Jayrne was nowhere to be seen.

"I . . ." Elac couldn't form a coherent thought to even begin to answer. The stable keeper hefted a wooden rod menacingly.

"You aren't supposed to be—"

He froze in place, staring in wide-eyed astonishment, blood gushing from his mouth. Incoherent noises escaped his lips, becoming softer until he fell silent. Then Jayrne stepped from behind him, allowing him to fall like a limp doll.

"Draygen's cloak and boots come in handy now and then," she said softly, wiping blood from her dagger before returning it to its sheath. She helped him into a saddle, using some extra leather straps to hold him firmly in place should he lose consciousness. She grabbed several waterskins, and then they were off, dashing away from the stables. From behind them, Elac heard the sounds of the entire roof of the cellar collapsing. His world rushed by him in a blur of dark tunnel walls and supporting beams, and then everything went black.

✿ ✾ ★ ✾ ✿

Elac opened his eyes to find himself riding in a comfortable wagon. Jayrne's lovely face, her features contorted with worry, hovered over him. Upon seeing him awake, she gave a cry of joy and hugged him close. Eventually, he managed to separate himself, and he took in his surroundings. Gillen and Hadwyn sat on a bench next to him, grinning broadly.

"What happened?" was all he could manage.

It was Hadwyn who delivered the explanation. "Your girlfriend here saved your hide, that's what happened. You were passed out and near death when she led your horse out of that tunnel. It led from the city of Malaton all the way to the Paheny Mountains. She made the trip in only two days."

"Two days? How did the horses manage?"

Jayrne shrugged modestly, blushing. "I ran most of the time, once you lost consciousness. I kept moving you from one

403

horse to the other to rest them. It was blind luck that the tunnel opened on the plateau where the rear detachment of the army was waiting."

Hadwyn went on to describe all the events surrounding the Battle of Unity, the arrival of the Human army, and the subsequent destruction of the undead. "You really saved us, my friend," Hadwyn told him, pausing to take a long pull from his ale tankard. "Saved the whole world actually, because if Volnor hadn't been destroyed, he would've easily defeated everyone."

The forces of the West had left behind a rear guard to watch for Kobold stragglers and to burn the dead, and the two Dwarf brothers had remained with them to oversee the operation. It was Gillen who had first seen Jayrne leading the two horses down from the mountains, and he'd performed his healing arts to save Elac's life. The wounds would leave scars, but at least he would live. At that proclamation, Jayrne hugged him close once more.

❀ ❁ ✪ ❀ ❁

There was a joyful reunion in Unity a few days later. Elac had recovered enough to be up and around on his own, but Jayrne never let him leave her sight, and she hovered over him like a mother would her child. He knew his fate with her was sealed, but he found the knowledge to be comforting, to say the least. Eventually, Silvayn presented Elac and Jayrne to the new, re-formed Unity Council. The old ruling body had been dissolved due to corruption, then reformed under greater oversight by the three member nations, with Jarm at its head.

The Humans granted Elac a duchy in Palindom, while the Elves awarded him the title of Baron in their home of Caldala (even though the rank was an honorary one, since technically there were no baronetcies in the country). The Dwarves gave him an estate in Verlak, near the southern tip of the Centare Inlet. He accepted the gifts with many thanks, but what he really wanted was to find a nice, quiet house somewhere and disappear into obscurity. He laughed at himself, at that point. All his life, he had wanted the chance to be the hero, and now that he had reached that pinnacle, he wanted it all to go away.

He and Jayrne managed to have a quiet dinner alone in a remote part of Silvayn's sprawling mansion. They ate in silence mostly, enjoying each other's company. Jayrne sipped from her wineglass, then cleared her throat.

"So, where will you go now?"

"Rilen said his village is rebuilding. He and Adalyn are building a cabin where his house used to be. I figured I'd do the same." He took a deep, trembling breath. "I was hoping you would come with me." Dinner was forgotten, and they reveled in the passion of their embrace.

Several days later, with the celebrations finally behind them and life returning to normal, Silvayn said good-bye to the companions. He had to return to Aleria to make a report on their travels, and the Dwarves were heading home to see to the refitting of the Dwarf army. Early in the afternoon, Rilen and Adalyn rode through the gates of Unity, Elac and Jayrne with them.

They rode in easy stages, arriving at the village on the evening of the second day. Although the entire settlement had been burned to the ground, most of the residents had returned and were in the process of rebuilding. Rilen had declined the opportunity to become a general in the Elven army, instead returning to his position within the militia, to which he had been reinstated. Elac was relieved to learn that the rest of the militia, which had formed his escort when the whole odyssey began, had survived their ordeals, and were serving under Rilen once more. Adalyn was enlisted as his assistant, continuing her field studies on her own. To Jayrne's delight, she discovered that Silvayn had arranged the release of her brother, Bollaz, from his prison cell weeks earlier.

Within a few months, the village was once again a thriving community of cottages and bustling commerce. Elac used his influence in Unity to arrange for Golen to be a major crossroad for Western commerce, and wagon trains were constantly coming and going.

One evening that autumn, while he and Jayrne were cleaning up from dinner, there was a knock at the door. He opened it to find Rilen and Adalyn standing on his porch, grinning broadly in undisguised mirth. They stepped aside to reveal Hadwyn and Gillen hiding behind them. Hadwyn rushed forward to embrace Elac in a fierce bear hug, and Gillen gave Jayrne a more chaste greeting. She kissed his cheek noisily, then turned to greet Hadwyn. They all went back inside, gathering around the fire to share tankards of ale and relive old stories.

There was another knock at the door, and this time it was Silvayn. The old wizard smiled his greeting, removing his travel cloak. "You didn't expect to have a reunion without me, did you?"

Rilen stood, tankard in hand. "I think we need to take this occasion to look back on the events of the last year. We've all been changed in some way, most of it for the better." He gave an appraising look to Hadwyn, who was sprawled in a chair, a tankard of ale in each hand. "Well, most of us have changed, anyway. We're all older, perhaps a bit wiser, and we've come a long way. We all lost some friends along the way, and I'd like to take this time to remember those who have fallen." He raised his tankard. "To the fallen. And especially, to Cassius."

"To Cassius," they echoed. The fire burned on, and the night deepened with the gathering of old friends.

Original cover art for *The Piaras Legacy* by Dave Dorman.

About the cover artist:

Dave Dorman

For the past 25 years, Chicagoland artist Dave Dorman has remained one of the contemporary art world's most prolific illustrators. His traditional oil paintings can be found everywhere—from book and magazine covers to comic book covers, trading cards and licensed packaging artwork. Licensed properties for which Dorman's art is known include Star Wars, Indiana Jones, Batman, Spiderman, Harry Potter, Alien v. Predator, Alien, Predator, G.I. Joe, World of Warcraft, and Magic: The Gathering. For more information on Dorman, please visit www.DaveDorman.com.

For more information
about other great titles from
Medallion Press, visit
www.medallionpress.com